# *The Dream Breakers*

But he believed her. Francesca Gaetini would be a difficult person not to believe. His eyes studied her with open admiration, awed still by the avid beauty, the wide wicked mouth and fiercely alert eyes — the sort of face that occurred rarely, the sort of face that could only ever be involved and hungry for something, something like power. He wondered if either Henry or Vic realized exactly the person or visionary, that had been brought unwittingly into their midst. Suddenly he wanted to laugh aloud; by the time they did realize, it would be too late, far too late and for some inexplicable reason he found it incredibly amusing . . .

# THE DREAM BREAKERS

*Louise Pennington*

ROWAN

A ROWAN BOOK

Published by Arrow Books Limited
20 Vauxhall Bridge Road, London SW1V 2SA

An imprint of Random Century Group

London Melbourne Sydney Auckland
Johannesburg and agencies throughout
the world

First published in Great Britain in 1989
by Century
Rowan edition 1990

Printed and bound in Great Britain by
Courier International Ltd, Tiptree, Essex

ISBN 0 09 963480 5

*For Marc*

*Advertising is like a magician, a genie – weaving pretty potent dreams and with the power to make, or break them . . . .*

# 1

He loved the musky smell of her sex, loved her body's astonishingly perfect curves and valleys as he traced one languid finger over her skin. In the semi-shadows of the room Frankie might only have been sixteen instead of a grown woman, could have been sleeping off a day at the office instead of an amazing bout of love-making. Aidan drew an impatient breath and wondered how she could slide into sleep so easily, leaving him dazed, almost weak. Sometimes he wondered why it had to be like a tournament, a rape, because this was the only way he would ever be first with her. On top. He smiled wryly at his crude metaphor and rolled over on his back, wanting more of her but waiting until she awoke. Soon. Because she would want it too, they had that much in common.

'You hate it when I sleep, don't you . . .' It was a statement rather than a question, and she turned slowly towards him. '. . . hurts your damned male pride – as if I'd sucked you dry and then spat you out.' But she had not slept at all; he was restless, unable to leave her in peace, so he had kept her awake with his sulking fingers.

'You always put things so well.' His hand reached impatiently for the half-crushed packet of cigarettes on the side table and pulled out a black sobranie. 'You're so bloody cold about it – like the ice-queen or something.' A lighter snapped open and shut as he lit the end and took a long, calming drag.

'Don't start, Aidan . . . .' she sighed and took the cigarette from his fingers. 'In any event, if I pawed all over you begging for more you'd treat me like those other poor bitches – the novelty does you good.' She blinked, letting smoke in perfect rings slip from her mouth. He wanted it all, but he'd never get it from her. Aidan was like a demi-god in the agency, the best art director they had and

1

arrogantly good-looking. God had been over-kind to sweet Aidan, that was for sure, and he loved screwing her for the best and the worst of reasons, but she was his boss and pulled every string, and he had behaved up to now. She felt his warm, asking breath touch the curve of her shoulder.

'How was Michael?' he said casually, his tongue sliding skilfully down her arm.

She closed her eyes and saw again her beautiful brother sitting so calmly, so perfectly, as if he had been carved into her office chair. He had surprised her with the visit, he had surprised her with his offer of his shares in the company as if he had known what she planned. She hadn't seen him for over a year. Once he had graduated, Livia safely installed him in her antiques business and he operated from the summer place in Menton, travelling the world, often with her, often by himself, collecting the uncollectable. So much beauty under one roof. She felt a thickness gather in her throat. But they had lost whatever real closeness they had had over the years and yet there was still something, and when she had first approached him about selling his shares he had refused her very politely, and her anger had been unreasonable, ungovernable. Like her father. Now she wondered if he had kept them because he needed to feel there was still a tie that would keep him in her life. For the first time she had felt a trace of pity for the brother she had envied, had idolized for longer than she cared to remember; there had been loneliness for him as well. Livia was formidable, obsessive, coveting him like a precious jewel. Francesca wondered whether there had ever been any women for him, or whether his virginity was something to be coveted too; she could not envisage her father's son being gay, but neither could she see Livia allowing competition. But Michael had sold her the shares, all but five per cent, and she had allowed him that. He had smiled ultimately, and the smile had startled her as it broke the flawless, ivory face. When she was a child she had thought him pure, almost sacred – like Jesus and the angels. No wonder her mother only saw darkness and mediocrity in her daughter. Sometimes she almost understood her.

'Well – will you take up Samuels' offer?' Aidan's voice persisted. And his lips grazed the side of her breast.

'I already have.' Let him be the first to know, it hardly mattered now.

'Christ – you really take the bloody biscuit!' He took the stub of cigarette angrily from her fingers and pulled himself into a sitting position.

'Am I supposed to consult you every time I make a decision?' She wanted to laugh, but instead leaned her head back against the bed-head in a gesture of weary impatience. The package had been too good to resist, but she had goaded them – Henry – first of all, sure that they would back down. But they hadn't. £200 thousand a year, plus a substantial shareholding, plus a Ferrari, plus a ten per cent performance bonus, plus, plus, plus. They had even allowed her to keep Gaetini & Kemp to herself. Almost. It was now an associate company of Samuels, but she still held seventy per cent not including Michael's five per cent. It would be an autonomous entity of Samuels ensuring that there would be no conflicts, no real rivalry between them. It was a good deal for both of them.

'You might have told me, hinted even. . . .' He could kid himself that he was close to her, and everyone almost believed him, but she was about as close as the damned moon. She drove him crazy, but he always had to know that he could have her, and he had up to now. He turned to watch her, so bloody calm, so bloody desirable and his hand reached automatically to the mound of her breast draped provocatively by white cotton. Aidan moved his fingers slowly so that, like magic, the nipple became erect, and he pulled the sheet away and brought his mouth down to the large circle of pink-brown flesh. Her lips parted immediately and he was rewarded with a small familiar gasp of pleasure, felt her move beneath him, felt her hands come up to bury themselves in his hair.

'What about me?' His voice was coaxing now.

'You're a big boy, Aidan, you can take care of yourself . . . .' she arched her back, moaning softly as his fingers moved stealthily across her skin; down, down.

'Take me with you, Frankie. . . .'

She would tell him later – not now – now she wanted him. There was no place for him in her new scheme of things. She had given him a prime slot at Gaetini's, and that had to be enough for the time being; moving to Samuels was not part of the plan. He would stay at GK; there was enough power for him, and if it wasn't enough he would be poached by some other agency with a better offer. Aidan would survive, he was the stuff survivors were made of. But she pushed the thought from her mind and concentrated on the thing that mattered to her most, twisting her body sideways and rolling hungrily across him so that he lay beneath her. Her mouth ran down his neck to the broad chest, down to the line of thick, darkening hair and stiff jutting flesh. Her lips opened and closed around the swollen rosy tip, playing with him for a few tantalizing moments, making him groan deep in his chest. But then she moved upwards, above him, moving her thighs apart, taking his penis in her hand to guide him inside her. . . .

'When?!' Brunning demanded.

'Henry said only yesterday. . . .' Buchanan lowered his eyes, beaten down by Vic's outraged gaze.

'The bastard – fat, Jewish bastard!' He kneaded his hands together in an agony of frustration. 'Not one word, not one bloody word. . . .'

'Oh, come on, Vic, if we'd been in the running, we'd have known weeks ago – you knew there was something in the wind even before I did.'

'But why *her*, for God's sake? Some jumped-up Eyetie just out of nappies from a half-baked agency?!' Vic Brunning almost spat every word. Christ, *he* had wanted the job, he'd thought of practically nothing else for weeks. Joe had retired and the chairmanship should have come to him. Hadn't he always been Samuels' front-boy? Henry's charismatic lap-dog? Wasn't he the one who consistently faced the press because his lord and master hated the publicity, constantly capitalizing on his constitutional

4

shyness like bloody Howard Hughes? Christ! Henry owed him something!

'In case you hadn't noticed, Gaetini & Kemp have jumped from number thirty-eight in the tables to nineteen since she took over.' Geoff's voice claimed his attention again. 'Not only has she revamped the whole staff in the space of a year, but she actually managed to steal one of our accounts.'

'What are you? Her guru, for God's sake?' he responded furiously. 'In any case, you're only talking about one bloody fruit drink. . . .'

'Miami Citrus was worth £1 million, Vic, and if you hadn't been so busy licking Kim Hasam's black ass you might have noticed.'

Vic closed his eyes in exasperation as if the action might blot out the vision of the Arab's sardonic smile, his 'I've got the west by the balls' smile. Hasam had kept him on hold for months with promises and more promises. They had given him the works, from top-class call-girls to the 'loan' of the company yacht in Monaco, and all they had to show for it was an opening in Egypt which they hadn't either the facilities or personnel to deal with properly – and he knew it. But the UK was the big one, a fat chain of magnificently exclusive hotels and country clubs opening in the spring of next year. Time was running out and only yesterday he'd heard that Hasam had been seen having dinner with Matt Summers of J Walter Thompson, one of their biggest rivals. He turned angrily to the window.

'When does she start?' he said finally.

'Officially at the beginning of the month, but obviously she's already spent some time with Henry and the rest of the board, and we're lined up to meet her on Monday, over lunch.'

'Shit.'

'Look, Vic, I don't like this any more than you, but we're going to have to grin and bear it – and, after all, there's no reason why we have to make it easy for her – without being too obvious, of course.' Geoff watched his colleague and sometime friend carefully. Vic had a big

5

ugly mouth, but they had climbed the ladder of the agency together until the board had been unable to choose between them and made them Joint Managing Directors. Somehow they had made it work; somehow, and sometimes against all his instincts, but now the board had decided against them. Presumably Joint Chairmen was something the board were not yet prepared to accept and besides it was obvious to him, if not to Vic, that they had become complacent, or 'fat cats' as Liz had remarked before she had handed in her resignation. He would miss her acid cockney mouth, he thought absently.

'We should have been number one this year,' Vic said reluctantly.

'Henry said as much . . . ,' Geoff replied, remembering Samuels' dry comment. But there had been an edge to his words when he had talked of Frankie Gaetini's starting date, a certain casualness as if he did not expect her reign to last, as if perhaps she was their bait . . . ? He smiled to himself. Henry wouldn't take being dictated to by a woman either.

'Has there been a press release yet?'

'Monday,' Geoff said quietly.

'Have you got a copy?'

'Here –' He unfolded the white sheet of paper and handed it to Brunning.

'"Samuels names top job,"' he read aloud. '"Gaetini to add feminine touch to lead agency – Samuels calls Brunning, Buchanan, Gaetini mixture explosive". . . .' Vic smiled thinly; Henry might find his little concoction just a bit more explosive than he had bargained for.

'Did you know that we've definitely been shortlisted for that Messiah weirdo, Matthias?' Geoff said, in an effort at changing the subject; there was an agency to run and he was getting bored wet-nursing Vic's bruised ego.

'Yeah . . . ,' Vic responded, screwing the press release into a ball and dropping it with great deliberation into the wastepaper bin, '. . . yes, I did.' He turned back to Brunning. 'If we get it, then that would really put us in the number one slot – as well as on the front pages of the national dailies.'

'Gareth is working on it, but I haven't seen anything yet.'

'Get him up here; I want to be in on this one every step of the way.'

'Fine, because I've got lunch with the king of the hamburgers and his boyfriend.' Buchanan grimaced and moved towards the door.

'At least you're sitting pretty . . . ,' Brunning added.

'Yeah, but I'm not sure he is. . . .'

Vic smiled the expected response and shifted his gaze back to the window as the door opened and then closed behind him. The Matthias account could be the prize of the year, rock star turned evangelist/saviour of the world. He had been into everything from Zen Buddhism to heroin, and up until four years ago had won every record award going as well as numerous gold discs, but then nothing – until he had been 'touched by God', or Mohammed, or something. Brunning laughed silently and wondered if the lack of a hit record had had anything to do with his sudden turn to religion. The publicity had been incredible and all because of one clever, masterly trip to Nicaragua and then on to the bloody chaos of Beirut. Christ! He had even managed to wangle an interview with Reagan. 'Peace, man,' – that was his message more or less. It was like the sixties all over again except this time there were no flowers. Vic shook his head slowly. Matthias had literally left a blazing trail behind him and had been christened 'The Golden God' by his adoring fans – becoming almost a household word in the process. But now that the heat was beginning to die down it seemed that he wanted to create some sort of niche for himself within the establishment – something respectable. It was crazy; Matthias didn't even *look* respectable, but nevertheless he needed an agency, a good agency to handle his new profile; there were still a lot of rough edges, still the ghosts of his unappetizing past to lay. Teenagers were one thing, the older generation another. He reached for the door of his drinks cabinet, aware that his mood was changing, enjoying again that rare feeling of adrenaline seeping into his veins. This would be his baby and he would make sure that he got the credit for it – not Geoff, not Henry, and definitely not Francesca Gaetini. He poured himself a large scotch and let it slip down, feeling it spread slowly, warmly through his limbs. He shifted his eyes to his desk and the phone; in a moment he was through to his secretary, Zoë.

'Get me a meeting with Matthias.'

'*The* Matthias, Vic?' Her timidity irritated him.

'Where's your brain, Zoë – who else?' He slammed the phone down and poured himself another scotch.

Several minutes elapsed before Zoë came back with a response.

'The first available date is next month, the 17th . . . ,' she said hesitantly.

'Well, confirm it,' he snapped.

'But you're seeing Mr Hasam on that day – he'll just be back from the States.'

'Tell him to go fuck himself. . . .'

She heard him call her as her finger went agonizingly through her new tights. Sian cursed softly and hobbled to the bed pulling the offending tights from her legs. Sighing with resignation she padded into the adjoining bedroom to Peter who stood uncertainly grasping the bars of his cot.

'Oh, Petie, I wanted you to sleep just a bit longer today,' she said wearily, but unable to keep a smile from sliding across her mouth. She lifted him up into her arms and kissed him, loving the sweet baby smell that clung to him like heady perfume. 'I'll warm you some milk and then leave you to Nana, because Mummy has to go somewhere very special and can't stay to play.' Sian thought of the coming interview, of Samuels' daunting reputation. She had not worked for over a year and hoped that that would not put her entirely out of the running. Her speeds were still good, and she'd even managed to fit in a word-processing course which had cost her more than she could afford. 'Please God,' she murmured, raising her eyes skywards.

\*

The reception area was very long and very white, the polished starkness broken by the occasional work of art, potted palms and ads – glorious, searing ads blazing out from the walls. Every product was a household word, every company big or famous, or both. She tried to memorize them so that she could tell her mother every detail when she got home. But it was not just the glitter of the alluring surroundings; Samuels hummed – phones never stopped ringing, despatch riders seemed to arrive every minute and a constant stream of people ran in and out of the building. Sian felt her nerves tingling with something called excitement. God, it had been so long! Peter had inevitably changed the course of her life, and her decision not to have an abortion had stretched her to the limits of despair. Oh yes, she had loved Adam, but he was married with children of his own, as she had known from the first – and she had 'got involved', of course, as she had also known she would from the first, and of course she had had to leave The Village, his beloved PR company and a job she had relished. She closed her eyes briefly, forcing the memories away. Maybe she could start afresh here, her boss would be a woman, apparently, so she could hardly remind her of the man she had left behind. Sian sighed heavily, realizing quite suddenly that she wanted this job very much.

'You have a child, I understand?' the woman said inevitably.

'Yes, but he'll be taken care of by his grandparents whilst I work,' Sian replied carefully, feeling the nerves in her stomach begin to dance.

'What about working late?' Rachel Gold persisted.

'I have a good idea what the job will entail and I don't doubt that includes working late – it won't be a problem.' She sighed inwardly, biting back the irritability hovering just behind her words.

'Francesca Gaetini will be one of this agency's most powerful figures; she will be new, demanding and very probably a pain in the ass, at least to begin with. I intended

9

choosing someone internally, but don't want any divided loyalties – changes as big as this one inevitably provoke envy and political game-playing. Do you think you could cope with all that?'

'I want this job very much. I've given it a great deal of thought and nothing you have said – yet – has put me off.' She smiled then, trying to take the intensity out of her words. Maybe it would be better if she knew now that she wasn't going to be in the running; maybe. . . .

'Well, there's certainly nothing wrong with your qualifications and you've had plenty of the right experience. . . .' Rachel studied the girl for a moment, assured by her maturity and the conviction in her voice; besides, Adam Gilmore had given her a glowing recommendation. 'You realize, of course, that I do have other people to interview, but I'll be making up the shortlist at the end of this week, so you should have my decision by early next week.' She stood up, offering her hand. 'Thanks for coming.'

'Thanks for seeing me,' Sian said evenly. Was this the big brushoff, or was she supposed to be kept simmering? She closed the door softly behind her, suddenly aware that her year off seemed more like ten and that she felt like an amateur all over again. Her thoughts turned inevitably to Adam. She had seen him only six times in the eight months since Peter had been born and each time seemed more acutely embarrassing than the last. He had been angry when she'd decided to have the baby, almost begged her to change her mind – presumably it was too risky having a bastard son hanging around in the background ready to spoil the career he'd carved out so neatly for himself. A soft, weary sigh escaped her lips; their affair had been wonderful, dazzling, like nothing she had ever experienced. She closed her eyes briefly in exasperation as the memories which she tried to keep at bay forced her relentlessly back and his face, unbidden, slipped effortlessly into her mind. It was hard not to remember how each time she saw him, or heard his voice, it had left her breathless and wanting only more of him after he had gone. And he always *had* gone. But their meetings would inevitably grow fewer and fewer now, until there would be only phone calls, and then they would fade too. But there was Peter, and he was beautiful. Sian smiled wryly to herself as she neared the lifts; no doubt it was her pious Catholic upbringing that had betrayed her into motherhood, had stopped her from breaking its most sacred of rules. Yet she hadn't been to confession or communion in years, had rejected it all long ago, or so she had thought, until Petie. There had been little choice.

A lift opened and she stepped into stale air suffused with garlic and drink. Geoff Buchanan squeezed sideways as she moved beside him, hoping that his client would not be too irked by playing sardines for the space of two floors.

'Glad you liked that spoof . . . even now some people fail to appreciate its – "unsubtlety" – shall we say.' He peered sideways, suddenly aware of a sweet heady scent and for a moment let his glance wander to her hair and its blondeness.

'Well, I thought it *most* amusing, Bobby. . . .'

Bobby, or Bob Kornberg, didn't reply, and Geoff was sure that the pinched white nostrils and tight mouth denoted anything but amusement. He never could understand why Kornberg insisted on bringing along his 'assistant', Danny, when it was quite obvious that he irritated him to the point of distraction.

'Two gigantic hamburgers in lustful pursuit . . . ,' he continued giggling softly, 'and such a good line – "No, no, not without a cucumber.". . .'

Buchanan felt a smile begin to tip the edges of his mouth – the line was designed deliberately to be one of the worst of all time – and his gaze returned to the girl standing by his side who was trying to suppress her own smile. But suddenly the lift drew to a halt, the doors opened and she walked away from them. His eyes rested on her for a brief moment and then returned to the thing that mattered to him most, his client, and his client's happiness. Maybe it was time Bobby got himself a new boyfriend.

*

11

Nick stared into space, suddenly tired and bored. He had to come up with something by the end of the week and his brain seemed to have stopped working. He shifted his gaze back to his desk top and the tinted cellophane packet containing the now stale crumpets. It had been nappies last month and a new line in deodorant before that, but he had come up with the goods and everyone seemed pleased except him. He stood up and moved across his chaotic office to the window and the half can of Fosters that was going warm on the sill. It tasted foul and he wondered why he was drinking it. His gaze was drawn inevitably back to the offending crumpets and he closed his eyes, seeing a private vision of his own – hot, steaming, dripping with butter (the cholesterol factor was a distinct minus point for the waning popularity of crumpets . . .). He saw an old, distinguished man (could be a woman – maybe a Penelope Keith type), sitting in front of a roaring fire surrounded by the comforting luxury of Constables, antique furniture, silver, and smothered in a wave of classical music – perhaps *Swan Lake* to add some humour? Nick opened his eyes, breathed a sigh of relief and sat down at his desk. It wouldn't be the most original of ads, but with a name like Baronets he could hardly be expected to invent a scenario centred around the local punks. . . . He smiled finally, 'Baronets – the aristocratic crumpet. . . .' Not bad. With the right actor, maybe even a big name, and a few of his little finishing touches, it could be okay. The client was an old, traditional family firm, and this was the first time they'd used Samuels. Baronets was a new line and they hoped to follow it up with several other products under the same name – marmalade, kedgeree, even kippers, apparently. If the crumpets went down well he would have plenty of work for the rest of the year. He put his pen down for a moment and took a sharp, exasperated breath. He had been at Samuels for nearly six months now and there had been nothing really 'gutsy' to get his teeth into. The Italian Arts campaign had gone to Keith Todd, 'US Fashion in Britain' to Penny Farish, and now Gareth Jones had got the Matthias pitch. All faithful old soldiers of Samuels. . . . A small tap at his door snapped him out of his thoughts.

'I hope I'm not disturbing your creative reverie.'

'And I bet you really mean that, Caroline, because it means I'm doing exactly what you want me to do.'

His eyes fastened on her face; he never could quite get over the colour of her eyes – a cross between grey and violet – and the way her mouth pouted guilelessly up if he wasn't working to schedule. Like a child's. But he never worked to schedule. Sometimes he did it just to annoy her. She was such an easy target with her Hooray Henry uniform, the turned-up collar and pearls, and the way she tried so hard to be witty without quite making it. Everything had to be safe with Caroline, everything probably had always been safe with Caroline. Nick wondered absently if she'd ever done anything vaguely outrageous in her life, wondered if she'd ever been down the East End, or stood on a corner eating some eels or a bag of cockles. He wondered if she were a virgin.

'I just wondered whether you and Tony had come up with anything yet. . . . I'm not hassling you . . . well, not exactly.' Her voice trailed off weakly and she sighed inwardly. Sometimes she hated coming down to 'creative', and especially Nick, he always made her visits so uncomfortable. He had a way of making her feel that she wanted the ground to swallow her. It wasn't so much *what* he said, but the *way* that he said it. As if he were laughing at her.

'Like hell you aren't.' He continued staring for a moment, enjoying her unease. 'What busy little bees you account execs are – running around after us difficult and temperamental creatives. Christ, Caroline, sometimes I wish you'd just come out and say what you bloody mean!' He saw her face crumple for a second and immediately regretted his harshness. Somehow she had an amazing ability to provoke him. 'It'll be okay by Friday,' he added more gently, 'so you don't need to panic.' His words produced the desired effect and she gave him a brief smile of relief, but there was still that soft wounded look in her eyes and a blotch of sudden redness on each cheek like a bruise; he turned impatiently back to his desk in a gesture of dismissal. 'I'll give you a call when we've done the first mock-up.'

'Fine . . . fine . . . ,' she replied hesitantly, and he knew she was still hovering in the doorway as if she were trying to say something more, but then he heard her move and her steps take her away from his room. For a moment he listened to the sound of her feet until the hum of the agency swallowed her, and then lifted his eyes to the frame of the doorway where she had stood and where her shyness somehow still lingered, reproaching him.

She had smiled in the end because it had broken the tension between them, but Nick's sharp eyes had flicked over her making her cringe inside herself. Nothing she ever said to him seemed to be the right thing, or even said in the right way. He made her feel clumsy, useless, boring. Caroline sighed and with an effort pushed any more thoughts of Nick Keogh aside; she could worry about him tomorrow, and at least he'd started the damned ad. She turned her mind to the evening lying ahead of her, and Guy. Everyone expected an engagement announcement soon; after all, they'd been going out together for nearly four years and it seemed the most natural thing to do. She tried to envisage waking up with Guy beside her each and every day, year after year until, she supposed, they grew old. They had slept together, of course, but never spent a whole night on their own; her parents were very strict in that respect, as were Guy's. Sex with him was really a weekend thing, after a party, or when his parents went to the country and they had the whole afternoon and evening together. But mostly it was a quick, furtive affair, as if they were committing some great sin which they would soon be found guilty of, and Guy seemed to get it over with as quickly as possible. He was, Caroline supposed, very enthusiastic, but he never really *touched* her, never really kissed her the way she imagined it should be. There seemed to be no attempt at control, no gentle caresses, only his thick, rather wet lips, and big clumsy hands dutifully squeezing her breasts, and then the familiar prod of his knee as he prised her legs apart. She wondered sometimes if it would make any difference if she were one of those blow-up dolls she'd heard about (some of them even had real pubic hair, apparently . . .). It hadn't really bothered her until the other evening when Guy had rolled over and dozed off, and she was left alone in the semi-darkness letting his white stickiness run down between her thighs to leave a stain on the dark blue of her crumpled skirt. Somehow her hand had found its way to the fur of her pubic hair, and found the warm secret place between her legs. Her furtive fingers had touched and then slowly quickened as sweet moistness melted within, and she had arched her back automatically, her legs stiffening in response. There was a seeping of pleasure as if from a very far-off place, but then it came in a wave, a heady sensation which began to send vast widening rings through her body, and she realized that she was about to climax for the first time. She was surprised at the simplicity of it all, surprised at the exquisite discovery that her body could give her so much pleasure, surprised and shocked that her mind had made the giver of her climax Nick Keogh. But then there had been only emptiness and guilt, her stained skirt, and Guy snoring fitfully beside her.

A room had been booked at the White Tower so that 'they could have enough privacy'. Francesca climbed the stairs to an upper floor slowly. Vic Brunning and Geoff Buchanan were old hands at shrinking people down to size and she didn't suppose for a minute that this was going to be the most amiable meeting of the year. It didn't take a genius to work out that both of them would be feeling decidedly pissed-off at her being made Chairman of Samuels, and this lunch meeting was simply a not very subtle way of breaking the ice. Frankie laughed silently, sure that the ice would stay as frozen as the polar ice-caps. But she had met their challenge without a second thought and deliberately dressed to kill. She had always looked good in leather and the designer at Cibi had made a superb creation in black, pleating and gathering the suit as if the material were soft cotton. She smiled softly as a waiter came up to her and proceeded to guide her into the chosen room as both men rose to greet her. They had never met, but she had seen plenty of photographs in the ad press and could recognize them immediately. Vic was tall and good-looking in a rough–diamond sort of way and she suddenly recalled his notorious reputation with women. The mouth said it all, really, large and sensuous, but he usually only went for safe prey, the young raw ones who didn't know any better. Her gaze shifted to Geoff Buchanan, a shortish man, dark with good eyes, and she thought absently that his returning smile could almost have been genuine.

'We meet at last,' he said and offered her a drink from the private bar.

'I feel I've met you a hundred times before . . . *Campaign* being the ad man's *Tatler*,' she replied lightly.

'Your picture hasn't exactly been missing amongst its pages either – particularly of late,' Vic interjected. He was almost tempted to add that none of them had done her justice, but didn't want to give her any more points than she had already. She wasn't just very attractive, she was sexy, beautiful, even cute, all rolled into one. But she had teeth, very sharp teeth. In any event, it was often like this with him when he first met a woman he fancied; then he would lay them and the novelty would be gone. His eyes travelled over her again as she turned to Geoff, but there would be no laying Francesca Gaetini, she was too clever for that – and he loathed intelligent women, they always made everything so bloody complicated – almost like pouring cold water over his cock. He took a sip of his scotch as Geoff gave her some more spiel and wondered what pearls of wisdom she intended to drop, no doubt acidly, into their future working relationship.

Francesca waited until the first drink had warmed her through before broaching some of the subjects she wanted at least to touch on, waited until Vic got over his initial shock and his eyes ceased drilling through her clothes to the body beautiful beneath. She laughed soundlessly and wondered whether he was aware how easy he made it for her to read his mind, but she brushed the thought aside and switched to the topics that mattered most to her. This was not going to be just an introductory meeting as far as she was concerned, there was a lot to cover and they had to know to some extent what she had in mind for the agency.

'Samuels has grown pretty well over the last five years.'

'We think so,' Vic responded too quickly.

'What do you think is holding you back from the number one spot?' she asked deliberately, her eyes scanning his face.

'Well, it's been a tough year one way and another, as you know,' he said defensively, 'and our international growth has not happened as fast as we'd hoped, but it's only a matter of time before it takes off. After all we're considered to have the best creative standards, you only have to look at the awards. . . .'

'Of course, I'm aware of that,' she replied softly, 'it's just a pity that you've missed opportunities which you wouldn't have done if your international spearhead had been better organized – from the very beginning.' She paused carefully for a moment before continuing. 'Take Kim Hasam, for example, now in the process of giving the Mogul hotel chain account to J W T – if only Samuels had been better prepared, even in the short term, you could have swung it.' She waited a moment as his face drained of colour, knowing her words had struck home, and then added finally, 'Samuels' international coverage is perceived as weak and is naturally exploited by our competitors accordingly. We need to address this perception fundamentally, but, until I have some real time to tackle it, perhaps you could concentrate on a little cosmetic surgery which can help us to be perceived as – at minimum – comparable.' It had been easy to find out in which areas Vic was most vulnerable and, indeed, what he was up to; he was an upfront guy who rarely covered his ass. She half-wondered why he should be so surprised at her

17

remarks, or perhaps he really did think he operated on a different, celestial plain from the rest of the advertising world.

'How did you know about Hasam?' he said slowly.

'You know how small the ad world is, Vic, it wasn't too difficult to find out how things were going.' A ghost of a smile seemed to settle on her mouth and then, switching targets, she turned to Geoff.

'How are the investigations going with regard to the US merger? Henry tells me you now have a short-list of three.'

'There's still a lot of paperwork to be got through and more research on any possible conflicts that might be involved,' he replied smoothly. 'For instance, Ferrario & Bloom have Shuffreys, who have a line in cosmetics and painkillers in the UK – this in turn could mess up our pharmaceutical line with Paynes. I want to avoid losing £3 million worth of business if I can.' Geoff watched her face, matching her studied gaze, suddenly aware that his palms were moist with sweat. Christ, he felt as if he were under interrogation. He thought of Vic beside him, of the cheap conversation they had had before she arrived and wondered if he regretted his cool indifference; but that wasn't like Vic, his only thought now would be the best way of getting his own back.

'But, on the other hand,' her voice persisted, 'Ferrario are worth almost £1 million here and probably nearer 12 million in the US – and I don't mean dollars. They also have a west coast operation and an extensive, if stale, European network.'

'So has Dunmar-Rock,' he responded quickly, casting any further thoughts of Vic aside to think of later.

'True.' She smiled inwardly, filing the information away; Mr Buchanan had done his homework.

'It's my strongest preference actually – there are no major conflicts as there might be with Ferrario.'

'Okay – then perhaps you could send me a copy of the file with a synopsis of the company and the latest annual report. I'd also like a detailed profile on all of the key people, their past and potential for the future, with particular emphasis on their weaknesses and strengths.'

Geoff sighed inwardly with relief; the probing had ceased for the time being and he relaxed visibly as they returned to 'real' business.

'I've already got that underway, so I could probably get it to you by the end of the week,' he said evenly, realizing that he had scored a point in his favour.

'Good.' She smiled again and shifted her gaze back to Vic. 'How's the Matthias pitch going?'

'We're getting a presentation together and I'm seeing him next month.' His reply came almost too quickly as if he had anticipated her question, like shots out of a gun. If she knew about Hasam she would know practically all there was to know about anything else that really mattered. Bitch.

'The 17th, isn't it? I'd like to be there,' she responded. And he was caught off-guard by her soft smile again, a smile that made him uneasy.

'That won't be necessary, everything's going smoothly and I don't need any assistance at this stage.' He made an effort to return the smile, but felt his lips stiffen in muted rage. How the hell did she know when, unless she'd looked in his bloody diary? Zoë. She never could learn to keep her mouth shut.

'I wasn't doubting your abilities, Vic, but I'd nevertheless still like to come with you – as an outside observer if you like.' Francesca met his hostile stare evenly, knowing that he had no choice.

'I'll keep you posted, then,' he said finally, hard put to keep the sullen frown from his face. Foiled again.

'Fine,' she replied and added, 'I'd like copies of the work done so far, but there's no real hurry at the moment. I'll call your office as soon as I'm ready.'

I bet you bloody will.

She smiled then and he thought he saw triumph in her eyes, but then her hand reached for the waiting glass of wine and the conversation was abruptly steered to other, less sensitive areas. It was a deliberate move; she had made her point and was sure that the pebbles she had just thrown in the pool would send ever-widening ripples outwards and onwards. She had given them enough to chew on, enough to make them, and Henry Samuels, realize that she had every intention of leaving her mark on the agency – just as she had done with GK. They all needed to get off their fat complacent asses, which was just what her father would have said.

Francesca rose from her seat and left them brooding over their cognacs and walked slowly back to the agency. Rachel Gold had made a short-list of the candidates for her PA and the second one was lined up for 3 p.m. Initially she had toyed with the idea of bringing Jane with her from GK, but then had finally decided against it. She was, at thirty-six, surprisingly set in her ways and in any event already saw Samuels as some prey-hungry vulture, and Francesca had neither the time nor the patience to convince her otherwise. But Jane was right, of course – the trick was to know the vulture better than he knew himself. . . .

Sian felt her mouth go dry. She had not known quite what to expect, but naturally a sophisticated woman, even an attractive one. Francesca Gaetini was much more than that. Her beauty was obvious – it was the power and the sense of purpose, as if the sleek loveliness of the outer skin hid a core of solid glittering steel, which were so striking.

'You must be Sian?' It was a statement rather than a question and Sian stood up to shake the proffered hand, surprised and then not surprised at the strength she felt in its grip.

Coffee was ordered and brought whilst quiet questions were put to her, most of them relating to her life, her past and her hopes for the future, but not once did Samuels' new chairman mention Petie. When she realized the interview must be drawing to a close, Sian felt a stab of panic, sure that somehow Rachel Gold had failed to tell her.

'You know I have a son?' The words spilled out, disjointed and a little afraid.

'Of course.'

'. . . I thought – as you hadn't mentioned it . . . ,' her voice trailed off and she suddenly felt foolish.

'I imagined that Rachel had grilled you enough on that subject already. It seemed pointless to cover old ground as I assumed you wouldn't be here if you couldn't handle the job as well as your personal commitments.' She paused for a moment, studying the girl before her, and then continued, 'Did I assume wrong, then?'

'Oh, no, not at all – it's just that sometimes I get a little. . . .'

'. . . oversensitive about it?' Francesca finished for her. 'Please don't. If we end up working together I want as little unnecessary strain and tension as possible. We all have problems and responsibilities, Sian, but we also have our own lives and our own wishes and expectations. Don't make obstacles where none need exist.' She smiled then and added lightly, 'Sermon over!' As her nerves relaxed Sian saw another Francesca Gaetini behind the slick, polished exterior. She felt the edges of her own mouth tilt and then smile in response, but behind the smile she wondered what possible problems someone like Samuels' formidable new chairman could ever have had.

Francesca stood up and watched the girl leave. Her references were excellent and she was obviously intelligent, but her confidence was all but gone. She picked up the personnel folder lying on the desk. Adam Gilmore of The Village had been her last employer and he had given Sian a reference that was almost too good. She had been his PA on joining the company and then progressed to junior executive and was doing extremely well until the pregnancy. Francesca had met Gilmore only once; typically PR, typically sleek media businessman intent on making his mark, with the added virtues of being not only charming, but very good-looking. It was just a guess, a gut feeling, and Francesca shook her head slowly – Sian Hart hadn't stood a chance.

*

'Bring your notebook and come into my office *now*, Zoë.' Vic did not even glance at the girl as he passed, knowing that her young face would be creased in puzzlement, afraid of the hostility in his voice.

He stood by the window looking out across the grey jagged roof tops. London *was* grey. He did not turn around until he heard the door close softly behind him.

'Have you had any calls regarding my meeting with Matthias?' The tone was deceptively soft, deceptively calm.

Zoë stared numbly at his tall figure outlined against the white city sky. She had done something wrong, again, and could feel the familiar sensation of her nerves dancing wildly in her stomach. Now all she wanted to do was to open the office door and run, but then she was surprised by the sound of her own voice, which seemed to come from another mouth and answer him automatically, just as he knew it would.

'Henry Samuels wanted to know if you'd lined anything up –'

'You told him?' Vic said slowly.

'Yes,' she replied, panic beginning to seep into her soul.

'Anyone else?'

It was useless to lie because he would find out; he always found out.

'Francesca Gaetini's office. . . .' Instinctively she knew this was the error, but she *was* chairman now, wasn't she? Wasn't she?!!

'You silly little bitch!' His words tore at the deceptive silence, scalding her nerves. 'You don't tell anyone, *anyone*, my movements without first discussing it with me!' His face was contorted with rage as he turned towards her. 'Christ! Haven't you learned *anything*?! I can't afford to have a secretary around who doesn't even know that her first loyalty is to her boss!'

Her face was white, the large blue eyes now brimming with tears. He watched her for a moment as her features crumpled and then sighed inwardly; she was, after all, not much more than a college-leaver, but he was still meanly

22

fascinated by the effect he always had on her. Well, he had said his piece and it had had the desired effect.

'Come here, Zoë.' His face was expressionless as she walked slowly, hesitantly towards him.

Zoë had full, rather babyish lips, round and just a little plump. He brought his mouth down to the moist pinkness and was immediately rewarded by her eager response. He needed her now, it was always like this after he had had a long lunch – a pressing, but languid need for sex, and he remembered all at once her interview. There had been little competition really, she had been the prettiest by far with the most tantalizing tits he had seen in a long time, very round, very firm. He laughed silently as his hand reached up to knead them greedily, recalling Henry's favourite expression, 'sheep dog bra – rounds them up and points them in the right direction. . . .' But he cast Henry and all other thoughts aside to switch to what mattered to him most at that moment. With one long outstretched arm he pressed a button marked 'Do not disturb', with the other he turned the compliant Zoë around. She had a tantalizing ass as well.

The creative work and the final ad had come together easily once he had got his idea down on paper, and the pitch had apparently gone beautifully, so Nick had been told – the old guy from Baronets trilling happily on its future appeal. They had liked his slick garbage, so the account was theirs. Another feather in Samuels' cap, he supposed. Nick stared into his glass and watched the bubbles of champagne rise enthusiastically ever upwards. It meant more money, and it also meant that he had gained some real credibility within the agency, even Henry Samuels would recognize that the whole Baronets account, kippers and all, could hardly be sniffed at; it was worth over £2 million. Nick looked across the rim of his glass to the Baronets account director, Ben Langley. It was quite obvious to the world at large, if not to Ben, that he was very pleased, almost smug, and for a moment Nick envied him; life would be a real breeze if he could be as easily satisfied as dear old boomerang Ben.

'Aren't you pleased?'

He turned sharply, jarred out of his thoughts. Caroline.

'Hysterical, doesn't it show?' His sarcasm was automatic and he saw the flush of crimson rise from her neck like a flood at his rebuff.

'I only came to say congratulations and to fill up your glass,' she said, wounded, suddenly feeling stupid; she had been so pleased, pleased for him, when she learned they had won the account, but then she attempted a tentative smile as if it cost her an effort.

'It's only another account, Caroline – hardly the launching of the *Titanic*.' The pause that followed was uneasy, almost weighted, and he felt her eyes.

'The *Titanic* sank.'

'What's that supposed to mean?' he snapped impatiently.

She looked hard into his face, suddenly aware of a rising and unfamiliar tide of anger and resentment.

'It would be nice, just once, if you weren't always so bloody rude, Nick.' She put the champagne bottle down on the desk next to him and moved sharply away, unable now to look into his eyes because all her sudden anger had evaporated as quickly as it had come and she was no longer brave.

He watched her go and for a fleeting second was tempted to go after her, but his hand moved mechanically to the champagne bottle; what would be the point? But she had been angry, really angry, which had surprised him, and then he was left with only a creeping tinge of guilt. He swallowed a mouthful of the champagne, letting it spread hazy warmth slowly through his body, pressing any more thoughts of her down to think of later, tomorrow, or the day after. . . .

'You seem deep in thought.'

Nick did not look up, recognizing the American twang as Ben Langley's.

'I haven't a decent thought in my head, Ben – you should know that by now.'

'As long as you keep up the good work I couldn't give a shit what you think.'

24

'You know, Ben, you certainly have a way with words. I've often wondered why you've never used your undoubted talents in the creative field.' Nick felt a smile of pure sarcasm spread across his face.

'You shouldn't waste your valuable time worrying about me, Nick, although I must say I'm touched by your concern.' He replied smoothly, but there was an edge to his words, and then his tone changed as if the barbed insult were of no further interest to him. 'Big Vic wants a word with you.'

'Not more congratulations . . . ?' Nick asked with barely concealed disinterest.

'Who knows? I'm not a bloody clairvoyant. I should just get up there and find out like a good boy.' Still smiling he lifted his glass and walked away. Nick watched him for a moment, suddenly amused, remembering how Alan Boyd, the uncrowned king of advertising, had described Ben as 'having his brains in his dick' – he hadn't been far wrong.

'I don't need to tell you that you did well on the Baronets account, hit the right note exactly.' Brunning stood behind his long teak desk, pouring a large scotch into one of two gleaming glasses. 'Like one?' Nick shook his head. 'Pissed already?' Vic grinned and flashed white teeth with obvious expertise. 'Well, you've earned it.' He seemed to pause for a moment, his eyes flicking carefully over Nick.

'How would you like to work on the Matthias pitch?' He spoke and pointed at him at the same time, hardly interrupting the dazzling adman smile.

Nick felt his throat tighten.

'What about Gareth, I thought it was his?' He tried to sound removed, cool about his interest.

'You might say that golden boy Gareth has gone in for "snorting" in a big way, so we've decided to give him a long holiday until, if and when, he gets his bloody act together again.' Vic took a gulp of scotch, instinctively aware that Nick was not going to turn the offer down. 'Forget about him – we've got to get this presentation together otherwise we're in deep shit. And there's just one thing you should remember, Nick, one very important factor above all else – we're going to win this pitch. Okay?' He paused with great deliberation to ensure that his words would penetrate. '. . . Not Saatchi's, not JWT, not Young & Rubicam – *us*.' The smile had gone now and Nick found his gaze dragged inexorably to those of his MD. The pale eyes were lighter, more empty, more expressionless, as if they had iced up momentarily. 'You could say that your reputation in this agency depended on it.'

Nick felt a soft, knowing smile hover just behind his lips – oh, and yours, Mr Brunning, and yours. . . .

It was a small mews cottage and the study on the first floor at the back of the house overlooked a tiny walled garden. Francesca opened a window to let in the now cooling summer air. She would go through some of the draft papers which Buchanan had forwarded to her on Dunmar-Rock and the profile she already had on Matthias. There were also the files on her prospective PA to go through again. Her smooth forehead crinkled into several familiar lines of concentration; she had not decided who to choose yet. But the telephone rang, shattering the quiet, and she was snapped irritably out of her thoughts.

'Hello, Francesca. Is Michael with you?'

Her mother's voice, remote, distant.

'No. Should he be?' She tried to sound removed, untouched by the familiar coldness, but her mind hurled her automatically back to her childhood and she could feel that surge of hopelessness.

'He said he would be in London over the weekend.' The words were controlled, deliberately expressionless.

'I saw him on Friday, he didn't mention anything about the weekend,' she replied evenly, hating the game.

'Perhaps you could tell him I called if he should contact you again.' She paused then, and Francesca felt the void like a weight, but the voice came back – 'Thank you.' There was a click and she was gone.

For a moment she held the phone motionless, still surprised at the unaccustomed sound of her mother's voice, still surprised at Livia's indifference to the pain which she had always so effortlessly inflicted and which her daughter had suppressed for longer than she cared to remember. It had been nearly two years now since the last time they had spoken and nothing had changed. Francesca shrugged in an attempt at casualness. There was, after all, no logical reason why it should. She turned her thoughts to her older brother; it was easier to think of Michael than allow the memories which she kept at bay to drag her relentlessly back through the years. He would know that Livia would be anxious, yet he had not phoned her, otherwise her mother would never have taken the unprecedented step of contacting the daughter she hardly cared to acknowledge. Perhaps he was really growing up at last – at the age of thirty-three, he should be – and severing the smothering ties that his mother had bound him with. But Livia was formidable, obsessive. Francesca thought of another Livia, the Livia of the history books who had been an Emperor's wife – mentor, brilliant administrator, wit and malevolent manipulator of people. She smiled softly, humourlessly; her mother was not so different.

Her peaceful mood was gone now, broken by the oppressive memories her mother's call had resurrected. She padded softly, inevitably, to the small Victorian cabinet which neatly housed a selection of drinks. The brandy was warm, sliding effortlessly across her tongue and down into her belly. She closed her eyes for a fleeting moment letting the alcohol spread through her tiredness. Her eyes switched to the desk and the waiting files; there was her work – safe, logical work keeping her sane, shutting off the ghosts and the pain, not allowing her to think.

Dunmar-Rock seemed as good a deal as Samuels could get, just as Buchanan had indicated. She hadn't got the profiles on the key people yet, but Philippe Sanchez, the MD, was interesting even on the limited knowledge she

27

had at hand. However, she would wait until the back-up material arrived before coming to any definite conclusions.

Matthias. She stared down at the photograph which lay like a bribe in the front of the folder. White-blond, blue-eyed, beautiful Matthias. Francesca thought of her brother again, unable to resist comparing his beauty with that of the famous, or infamous, star's. But Michael's was a soft, gentle beauty, like a Greek God, chiselled with great care out of the finest stone. Matthias' beauty was another thing altogether. The cheekbones were high, the eyes palely brilliant, the lips curved with a smile that was somehow worldly, all-knowing. She recalled the expression 'come hither' and imagined Matthias playing a flute, playing an irresistible tune that drew one like a magnet. '"Come into my parlour, said the spider to the fly . . . ,"' she murmured softly, and then laughed aloud, surprised at her flight of imagination. So unlike her. He was a man, had been a fading rock star, and was now one of God's children – apparently. She smiled again. He was either the latest line in prophets, or the greatest con-man the world had seen in a hell of a long time. The 17th would be an interesting day.

She leaned her head back against the chair and shifted her body, curling her feet up beneath her. Rachel Gold wanted the new chairman's PA to start as soon as possible, but Francesca would not be rushed. The girls she had seen were very good, but this was the first space she had had really to think about them. Even as she sipped the last of her brandy she knew she had made up her mind. Sometimes she was a sucker for sob stories, and besides Adam Gilmore ran a good operation and Samuels would need a PR set-up within the next year or so, and it was always useful to have inside information. Besides, she had liked her. There had seemed to be some empathy between them which was the most positive indicator one could hope for from an initial meeting. Interviews, or carefully edited c.v.s, hardly meant a thing in the long term. It was like almost everything else – chance.

Sighing heavily she dropped the pile of files to the floor.

The telephone sat mutely on the Italian marble side table. Her father's. She brushed the memory aside and reached for the receiver, her fingers finding each number mechanically, off by heart. It was late, and she didn't care whether her call would find Aidan busy or not.

'I'd like you to come over.'

There was a pause and she knew then that there was someone with him.

'You mean now, don't you?'

'Yes, I mean now, Aidan.'

The phone clicked softly and she took a deep breath. She needed him. Not tomorrow, or the day after. Now. And she pictured him making his excuses to the girl he had seduced, or was about to seduce. She wanted to make the most of him before he realized what was happening, because everything would be different then. And Aidan wouldn't like that at all.

# 2

The telephone rang, scalding her nerves, but she waited, immobile, until her mother answered it.

'It's for you – Samuels.' Sian looked into her mother's anxious face and wordlessly took the receiver from her.

'Sian? It's Rachel Gold.'

Even before Samuels' personnel officer told her the news, Sian knew the job was hers. No one in their right mind would telephone to tell you a job had gone to someone else; that kind of reply was relegated to headed notepaper and then the second-class post.

'When can you start?' Rachel continued enthusiastically.

'Monday?' Sian responded immediately. It was neither a cool nor a sophisticated reply – too keen – but she didn't care, in recent months she'd gone beyond that. God, it would be so good to get back to the real world! She thought of Petie then and felt a stab of guilt. But it would be better for him in the long term, more money, more security, she told herself, easily pushing any other arguments aside.

'That's perfect, Sian. I'll look forward to seeing you then. In the meantime I'll get a letter of confirmation in the post to you detailing salary, holidays and so forth.'

Relief hit her like a wave as she put the telephone down. Hugging her mother, she then turned to her son who was staring up at her from his carefully chosen place on the carpet. Sian lifted him into her arms.

'Well, Petie, you now have a working mum!' Her joy was suddenly his too and in his innocence he smiled and his tiny fists reached up to clutch at her hair. Sian's own smile melted slowly as she looked into his face. She told her guilt-ridden conscience that it would not be easy, that there would be a penance – times when she would probably wish she had stayed at home, but somehow at this glorious moment that eventuality did not seem possible. The year that had just passed came back with sudden and unrelenting clarity, nothing could be worse than that – nothing worse than the growing despair which had seemed to weigh her down a little more each day. Petie's plump eight-month-old hand touched her face and she looked into bright, liquid grey eyes and was reminded, inevitably, of Adam. She supposed sadly that her son would go on reminding her of Adam, like a lingering echo. But she cast the thought aside, determined now to be happy, and pulled Petie closer, amazed again at the fierce mother love which surged up inside her.

'From what I've read so far I would agree with you that Dunmar-Rock is the one we should go for. It would have been nice if they had been further up the worldwide rankings, although sixteenth is probably as good as we're going to get.' Francesca watched Geoff Buchanan's face carefully; he had done a lot of work on the potential merger and she realized quite suddenly that it mattered just as much to him as it did to her that it should succeed.

'Good, I hoped you'd say that.' Geoff shifted his gaze from the papers lying before him to the young woman who stood in front of his desk. He had tried to dislike her, tried to find some fault in the way she worked, her manner – anything – but only felt the emergence of a grudging respect. Vic was going to have a hard job on his hands, but Geoff felt a half-smile hovering just behind his lips; it was, after all, early days yet, but whatever happened the future promised to be an interesting one.

'Their international network is a little shaky,' she continued. 'It has definite weak points, especially in associate markets and particularly in the European sector. Didn't they acquire that through Bertholle and then drop the French association altogether?'

'Bertholle's was a pretty comprehensive European network, even had a few agencies in the Middle and Far East, but after a great offer from Rock they were swallowed whole and Bertholle retired. The entire outfit

31

came under Dunmar-Rock's umbrella – almost two years ago now.'

'They don't seem to have done much with it: thirty-one offices in twenty-two countries with no real link with the flagship agency, no direction, no corporate identity, no real growth. What the hell's Rock up to?' Her voice had risen slightly and Geoff saw dark Latin eyes go darker and knew intuitively that she had difficulty in controlling a temper that probably often got the better of her. She smiled suddenly and the darkness was gone, as if she were too aware of his thoughts. 'I just hate waste.'

'From what I can gather Rock has had a few internal problems,' he responded, 'their creative standards are not what they might be and most of the so-called high fliers have been with the agency for years. They treat it like a retirement home – solid, but dull – nurturing and relying on their blue chip clients and not really bothering to acquire any new business. They lost IBM to Saatchi's last year and you know how much that was worth. Even so, their total group billing still hovers around a healthy $750 million with pre-tax profits of nearly $12 million. But things are changing, I understand, and not before time. I believe you know of Philippe Sanchez; well, he's Rock's new bright-eyed boy and he's got some big ideas – like really shaking up the agency's creative approach and bringing in some new blood; like merging with a good UK-European agency, it's been rumoured. Should be interesting to watch,' he finished.

'But not for too long, Geoff. Now is probably just the right time to open negotiations. Why don't we look to the end of next month for an exploratory visit to the States?'

'Okay, and in the meantime I'll pave the way and get the rest of the material to you before we start on the framework of a purchase investigation.'

Francesca made no immediate answer, but turned away from him so that her eyes came to rest on the window and the grey horizon of London beyond, almost as if she were seeing a private vision of her own. 'This is a good opportunity, Geoff, too good to miss.' She caught a sharp breath before continuing. 'You may or may not realize that Samuels has the capacity and potential to be the world's largest and most successful advertising agency – and I don't mean in the same mould as our dinosaur big brothers who have lost something on the way to the top.' There was no emotion in her voice, she spoke as if it were a statement of fact. 'By 1990 there will be a worldwide market worth in the region of $200 billion, maybe more. Samuels must have the determination and vision to exploit that market, otherwise we shall go the way of all mediocre advertising flesh. . . .' She paused and then turned back to him. 'The world's getting smaller, Geoff – poorer countries are beginning to grow faster than the rich ones: look at Korea, Singapore and even Thailand for economic growth – and we could be in a prime position to take advantage of the situation, provided we get our global act together.'

'Not everyone in the advertising world is as enthusiastic about globalization as you seem to be,' he said carefully. 'Globalization means size, real size, which inevitably means more bureaucracy, more conflicts and probably at the cost of sacrificing some of our creative edge – losing our uniqueness.'

'You mean creating another dinosaur – a monster,' she replied evenly.

'Something like that.'

'It's too easy to stay small or moderately sized – perhaps relying on the creative and management style of a handful of people – to stay moderately successful, Geoff. But isn't that just a little old-fashioned and inward-looking? Isn't that stagnating? Good God! There's a whole world out there!' Her eyes were suddenly brilliantly black with excitement. 'With the massive improvements in com-munication across the globe over the last decade, more and more people are being exposed to the same TV shows, films and videos on the same machines, listening to the same music on the same stereos, styling themselves on and admiring the same sort of heroes – sharing the same dreams – and we can exploit these growing similarities and *without* losing the essence of our creativity, *if* we're forward looking and *if* we're smart. It won't be easy, but nothing worth having ever comes without real and sustained effort. It can be done, Geoff.'

'You're taking a hell of a job on your shoulders, considering we've yet to obtain the number one spot in the UK,' he taunted gently.

'Bullshit – Samuels could have been number one two years ago!'

He didn't say anything; knowing that what she said was true.

'We must believe that anything is possible – in growth and more growth; that we can deliver exactly what we say we can deliver, and never be satisfied with the average or the status quo. That leads nowhere – except maybe to stagnation and obviously mediocrity. Samuels has the capacity, the talent, to be the biggest and the best and there's no reason on earth why that can't be achieved.' Her features were tense, rigid, but then there was the smile again and a faint flush of crimson invading her cheeks as if she were surprised or embarrassed by the sudden intensity in her words.

But he believed her. Francesca Gaetini would be a difficult person not to believe. His eyes studied her with open admiration, awed still by the avid beauty, the wide wicked mouth and fiercely alert eyes – the sort of face that occurred rarely, the sort of face that could only ever be involved and hungry for something, something like power. He wondered if either Henry or Vic realized exactly the person, or visionary, that had been brought so unwittingly into their midst. Suddenly he wanted to laugh aloud; by the time they did realize it would be too late, far too late and for some inexplicable reason he found it incredibly amusing. Vic would wet his designer Y-fronts for sure.

The door was open and she stood uneasily on the threshold, waiting for him to look up and knowing that he knew she was there.

'He can be a real slave-driver, can't he, our Boomerang Ben?' Nick said at last and brought his gaze up from his desk to stare into her face.

Caroline smiled hesitantly, relieved that he had not mentioned or hinted at the words that had passed between them the previous day. Perhaps it had merely been the champagne, but even as the thought passed through her mind and she allowed herself to look into the lean, almost ascetic face she wondered at his capacity to make her cower, to make her feel that her existence was less than useless. It was foolish, she knew, but lately everything seemed a little foolish, or useless, or suspect.

'Well, he's naturally not too pleased that Vic Brunning has poached you; it's not exactly what he'd planned,' she responded, relaxing slightly.

Nick caught a breath which was not quite a sigh.

'I've outlined my ideas for all the forthcoming Baronets products. The campaign will use the same theme throughout, he already knows that; I've even given him a couple of alternatives that he might like to use – for Christ's sake, it's not as if I'm leaving the country.' Ben might make a feeble protest at his move, but that's about all it was. Nothing and no one was going to stop him working on the Matthias pitch. 'In any case Tony has the full brief and knows exactly how we were going to work the campaign; there shouldn't be any problems.'

'No, I suppose not,' she replied, suddenly aware of the dark smudges beneath his eyes and realizing intuitively that he must have stayed up half the night to get the draft outline completed. 'But you know what he's like,' she continued, 'he hates change.'

'Yeah – everything in Ben's garden has to be nice and rosy. Well, he should know by now that life just isn't like that, especially in this business.' He paused, studying her for a moment as if deliberating on saying his next words, and then shrugged inwardly, '. . . but he doesn't mind ringing the changes with the ladies, now does he, Caroline? Did you know the "boomerang" bit comes from the fact that they always come back for more? He must have charms that an unsubtle working-class boy like me is just too unsophisticated to see.'

'I really wouldn't know anything about all that, Nick,' she said defensively.

'No, I don't suppose you would,' he said softly.

She blushed, lowering her eyes, only half-understanding the implication in his reply. She would never be Ben Langley's type in a million years and, in any event, he had never made any move in her direction, as if he knew instinctively that it would be an up-hill struggle. There had been times when he would re-tell the same dirty joke, or graphically describe the sexual attributes of certain female employees of Samuels for all to hear, and she would feel the familiar hotness of a blush start to creep up from her neck to flood her face. Then she would make a feeble excuse and leave the room. And she always had the distinct feeling that the moment the door was closed behind her they would burst out laughing. It was the same with Nick; her shyness was a weakness which could be exploited, making her awkward and uncomfortable to be with. And she hated herself for it.

'I'd better take the file then, he's waiting for it,' she said finally, realizing suddenly that their working relationship, at least for the time being, was coming to a close and she would probably see very little of him. He had been elevated to Samuels' small and precious élite – Vic Brunning's new bright-eyed boy.

He thought he saw reproach in her eyes and felt the old irritation rise up because it seemed he had somehow injured her again. But he pressed the feeling down as she leaned towards him to take the proffered folder. She was close and his nostrils took in her sweet woman smell and he had a sudden crazy desire to pull her head down to his and rake her lips and face with his mouth and tongue. He met her eyes and saw how the violet had turned to jet, saw unguarded, softly confused expressions weave across her face as if she had read his thoughts, and he didn't know whether it was fear or desire. But she stepped back, too quickly, and stood once again alone in the doorway, and the moment was gone.

'You should wear that perfume more often, it's not bad . . . ,' he said in an effort to break the tension.

She blushed again and pulled the folder closer, tighter, as if it were a shield. 'I hope the pitch goes well,' she said, ignoring his remark. 'I'd better get this stuff back to Ben. He's probably wondering where I've got to.' She smiled tentatively and he heard a softly stammered goodbye as she disappeared from the doorway and made her way back to her account group and the realm of King Ben. Nick closed his eyes for a moment, suddenly swamped by tiredness, and then laughed soundlessly as he recalled how her eyes had widened in what could only have been sheer terror, and he wondered how he could have confused her reaction with desire – or lust. Caroline and lust just didn't seem to go together; the lust had been all his.

It was hot, claustrophobic on the tube. Sian's right arm groped uncomfortably over the head of a short, red-faced man to the safety of the plump black handgrip. Nothing changes, she thought, as the tube jolted into life and her body lurched to one side so that her face came too close to the man and her eyes were forced to flick over his seamy skin, laced with a thousand broken capillaries. But today not even the cloying, dehumanizing motion of travelling on the underground in the rush hour could depress the excitement which soared through her. It was ludicrously refreshing, even novel to be with the masses and back in the mainstream again instead of being at home day after day like an exile, without any real security, direction, or man to come home to her. Not even that.

Samuels beckoned, the sleek glass double doors glinting in the September sunshine. Sian felt her heart beating loudly, felt her feet quicken almost automatically as she approached the steps leading upwards to her new life. She was one of many to pass over the threshold of Samuels' famous entrance and fleetingly she envied the others who seemed so sure, so confident of their surroundings. But it took only a few minutes before Rachel Gold came to greet her in the bustling reception area and then take her up in

37

the lift to the awesome heights of the sixth floor, the sanctified realm of Samuels' senior hierarchy.

'Francesca's not around yet; why don't you use the time to familiarize yourself with your desk and the general geography of the floor?' She paused, frowning, as her gaze travelled to the other desk which sat just across from Sian's. 'I'd introduce you to Zoë except that she doesn't seem to be around yet. She works for Vic Brunning and in the short term for Geoff Buchanan until he gets someone else – they're the joint MDs. Anyway, help yourself to a coffee and I'll get back to my office before the rush starts. Give me a call if you need anything.' Rachel turned to go, but then added almost as an afterthought, 'Oh, and good luck.'

'Thanks,' Sian responded and felt sure that Samuels' personnel officer had been very tempted to add, 'You'll need it.'

As Rachel disappeared out of sight and the hum of a lift signalled her departure from the sixth floor, Sian turned her gaze to the silent typewriter which sat alone on one of the three working surfaces constituting her desk. She sighed softly, running her fingers lightly across the dead keys, and then smiled wryly; a year ago she had thought that she had left the slavery of the typewriter behind her for good. Her triumphant move to the role of junior executive at The Village had been short-lived, but how glorious it had been to leave the typing of her reports to someone else – actually to be considered to have a brain! But that was a year ago, she reminded herself decisively, trying to push the memory away, except that that long year somehow seemed more like ten.

'I'm afraid it's always this quiet first thing in the morning.' His voice cut abruptly into her thoughts and she turned to look into his face as he continued, 'I'm Geoff Buchanan – and I think you must be Sian; Rachel Gold told us to expect you.'

He was lightly tanned as most admen seemed to be, and she thought of Adam, but Geoff Buchanan's eyes were brown not blue. He was also a great deal shorter, with shoulders almost too broad for his size; his smile was also broad, displaying the necessary gleaming white teeth, and then she knew she had seen him somewhere before.

'I think we've already met – if a little informally. . . .' And she returned the smile because there was little other choice.

He seemed to think for a moment, deep frown lines suddenly forming, making him older.

'It was in the lift, actually – about a week ago,' she answered for him, 'but I think you were rather busy keeping your clients occupied. . . .' She smiled again, hesitantly, wishing she had forgotten about the incident as easily as he so obviously had.

'Of course – it was Bob Kornberg, wasn't it?' His eyes glanced over her face and he saw the doubt too clearly; after all how could she know who the hell Bob Kornberg was? 'Well, anyway, it's far nicer to have a formal introduction,' he said quickly, in an effort at changing the subject. '. . . May I offer you a coffee and in the process show you the complicated machinations of our pocket-sized kitchen?'

Before Sian could reply the hum of the lift made them both turn and Francesca Gaetini came towards them. The mass of dark curls had somehow been swept up and tamed so that only a few artful wisps lingered at the nape of her neck; a pair of David Morris earrings dangled heavily like pieces of fine steel as she walked; the black suit was tailored, almost severely, and Sian felt the first daunting nerves begin to dance wildly, felt the dark eyes flicker quickly over her.

'Good morning, Sian – and Geoff, too – it seems you've met already?' Her mouth was breaking into a smile and Sian felt some of the nerves cease fluttering.

'I was just about to make some coffee – would you like one?' Sian ventured.

'Thanks, just what I need – white, no sugar.' She watched Sian move away and then turned to Geoff. 'Have you got a minute?'

He looked briefly at his watch before replying. 'I have

about eight minutes, to be precise. I've got a client meeting in the small theatre at 9.30 – on the ground floor, for your information. . . .'

'Which client?' she said evenly as she moved towards her office.

'The MonCher group – the skincare range.'

'No problems, are there? I thought we'd got the pitch safe and sound,' she said warily, sensing his unease.

'They've found out that we've got a small outlet in cosmetics with Paynes. . . .'

'Someone's got a big mouth – in any case, the cosmetics don't conflict with their range.' She pushed the door of her office open and for a moment seemed to stand speculatively on the threshold.

'I know, but you know what the French can be like – the world has to revolve around them and let there be no compromise. . . .'

'I'm sure you can persuade them otherwise, Geoff; in any event it's probably just a question of their ego being a little bruised – pamper them a bit.' Her eyes were scanning the details of her office; they had all been attended to except the installation of her chair from GK. It was her father's and, she smiled dryly, the most important feature and it wasn't here. Fools.

'I intend to,' Geoff continued and she was snapped out of her thoughts.

'My question was the information on Philippe Sanchez. Have you managed to get it together yet?' She had dismissed MonCher from her mind, at least temporarily; it was Geoff's problem.

'I can probably get it to you by late this afternoon.'

'Fine,' she responded, and he knew from her clipped tone that he was now allowed to go.

'I'll see you later,' he said smoothly, and in a moment she could hear his steps take him back to his office and then, no doubt, to his coquettish client and some delicate massaging.

The smell of the coffee taunted her nostrils long before it

reached her desk and as the first mouthful slipped across her tongue she found it ridiculously refreshing.

'Have yours with me, please, Sian – we can talk.' She waited until the girl had sat down before continuing, 'I don't want today to be too arduous for you, or me; we're both new and of course that means learning almost everything all over again. Anyway, all in good time, but if you have any questions just ask.'

'Well, Vic Brunning's PA sits opposite, so she should be helpful, at least on the key people in the building, for instance, and where I can find things,' Sian replied, her eyes flickering quickly over the enormous glass bowl full of marble eggs which sat alongside the soft beige leather seating, the carefully monogrammed blotter so beautifully worn with age and then to the breathtaking painting hanging behind her desk.

'It is glorious, isn't it?' Francesca said quietly, following her eyes. 'It's a Matisse.'

'I hope the security is tight enough here!' Sian responded, smiling.

'So do I,' Francesca agreed. 'Well, at least the insurance company hasn't complained too much; I pay them enough. It could be safely installed at my home, I know, but it was a favourite of my father's and I like to have it close by, particularly as I'm likely to be spending more time here than I am there!' And then she turned quickly to her briefcase. The small dial in the lid resembled that of a safe, but in a moment it was open and Francesca pulled out two files. 'I'd like you to take a look at these – read through them carefully. There's one on a possible US acquisition, Dunmar-Rock, and the other is on Matthias, Europe's latest hero.'

Sian caught a short, inaudible breath. 'Are we likely to be doing work for him?'

'Perhaps, it seems a distinct possibility, but obviously I'd like you to treat everything I give you with total confidentiality.'

'Of course.'

'And if Mr Brunning should ask to see any of my files I

41

would like you, very discreetly, to inform me before you hand anything over, and that goes for Geoff Buchanan too, at least for the time being. Okay?'

'Fine.'

'If I'm not mistaken I think I hear his dulcet tones this very moment – I'll introduce you.' Francesca stood up and beckoned Sian to follow her.

Zoë had arrived and stood hovering over her typewriter, the mail in one hand and the morning papers in the other. She looked up immediately as Francesca and Sian moved towards her.

'Good morning – and you're Zoë, I presume,' Francesca said, smiling. 'I'd like to introduce Sian who'll be working for me. I'd appreciate it if you could give her as much assistance as possible over the next couple of weeks.'

'Yes, of course,' Zoë replied, only able to nod and smile tentatively as both hands were otherwise engaged, but then a voice boomed from within the confines of Vic Brunning's office.

'I'm dying of thirst – can't a man even get a cup of bloody coffee round here!'

Francesca moved casually past Zoë's desk and through the open door of Vic's office.

'Good morning, Vic; you sound on good form.'

He looked up abruptly from his desk and she saw the first signs of a blush creeping up in a pink wave from his neck. Amused, she wondered how long it had been since Vic had blushed so sweetly.

'I didn't realize you were there.'

'Obviously,' she said, a crooked smile on her face. 'Actually, I was a little concerned – thought you'd lost the use of your legs. . . .'

Francesca deliberately didn't wait for his response, but turned abruptly behind her and brought Sian forward.

'This is Sian Hart, my PA – Sian, Vic Brunning.'

He stood up awkwardly and then moved around his desk to shake hands. He was very tall, even good-looking, but there was no warmth, no feeling there, only a sort of resentment. Sian smiled dutifully and let his hand squeeze hers half-heartedly. She realized it was all a sham; he had no interest in meeting her, and there was that clear charge of dislike in the air as he stared past her to Francesca Gaetini. As he released her hand her eyes flickered once more back to his face and she was suddenly and utterly relieved that she did not have to work for Vic Brunning. That would be too much, even for her new found freedom.

'You used me!' Aidan's indignant, enraged voice shrilled at her from the telephone.

'How did you get the number of my private line, Aidan?' she asked quietly.

'You had no intention of getting me anything from the move to Samuels, did you?!' he continued, ignoring her question. 'You led me on – like a real patsy, knowing all the time you were going to leave me behind!'

'I didn't lead you anywhere, Aidan . . . ,' Francesca responded easily, 'you were the one who poked and pried trying to *use me* to further your own career.' The hostility was out in the open now, there was no need to be cautious any longer. 'It wasn't enough, was it, Aidan, to screw the boss, you had to have it all. Well, you did pretty well out of me and if you don't like your prime slot at GK which now appears suddenly to have become so mediocre, you know exactly what you can do.' There was a pause now and she could only hear his taut, sharp breathing. Aidan wasn't very good at faits accomplis, neither was he good at disappointment, so used was he to wanting his own way and getting it, and in his arrogance he had probably expected her to climb down. Did he really know her so little? Had there been no real communication between them at all? She sighed inwardly knowing that if there had been things would never have come to this. There had only been sex, good sex, yes, but now it seemed cheap, nasty, with nothing behind it. She had known that at the time, all the times, so why should it come as such a surprise now? She saw it all in a flash, as if for all time, its shallowness, emptiness – loneliness. Her father's face slid furtively into her mindscape as if encapsulating all the months, all the years of lovelessness that had slipped by so easily. But Aidan's voice claimed her as it broke in upon her thoughts.

'Perhaps we could have lunch and talk about things.' The arrogance had gone, and there was the other voice – the slick bedroom voice that she had heard so often before and she wondered how she had ever allowed herself to be persuaded by it.

'Perhaps, Aidan,' she said slowly, 'but right now I'm busy.' Francesca put the phone down with a soft click and stared at the closed door as if seeing a private vision of her own, but then she pressed her intercom and heard Sian's voice in response.

'Will you see to it that the number of my direct line is changed as soon as possible, Sian . . . and also that my chair from GK is brought over *today*. If there are any problems I want to know immediately.'

She reached for her briefcase and brought out the framed photograph of her father which had stood on every desk she had ever occupied. She caught a sharp, wary breath as his big handsome face stared back at her and inevitably the old dreams, lost dreams, which she had tucked away so carefully slid out of their hiding places; like worn-out, tired snapshots. Francesca closed her eyes in an effort to shut out the past; this was not the time. But the weighted silence was suddenly broken by an abrupt knock on her office door and before she could respond Vic Brunning was walking towards her, and for once she was glad.

'Matthias can't make it on the 17th now. The only date possible, unless we want to wait six months, is Friday.' He seemed almost out of breath as he walked across the room.

'I presume you mean *this* Friday. Has he got another tour lined up or something? Is that what this is all about?' Her father's image had been put to one side, her mind immediately and gratefully turning to this reprieve.

'Something like that. Anyway, he's going to be out of the country for a while, but he's cancelling a lunch appointment to accommodate us.' He was grinning.

'Have you actually spoken to *him* yet?' she asked quietly.

'Not yet – I've done all the contact through his personal assistant, a guy called Lucas Chant,' he replied.

'Lucas Chant? That can't be his real name – can it?'

'Christ knows – and who cares – he's been very cooperative and that's all we should be concerned about at the moment,' he responded tersely.

'I like to be concerned about *everything*, Vic, particularly when it comes to little details like people's names.' She paused for a moment. 'Did you ever hear of someone called Peter Allison?'

'No – should I have?' There was a touch of sarcasm in Vic's voice; she was going to say something he didn't want to hear.

'But you've probably heard of Ramm aftershave?'

'Naturally,' he replied. 'Colins-Gray have the account.'

'GK got it originally,' she said half-smiling, seeing a look of surprise flicker across Vic's face. 'We loused up.' It was nice to see more surprise on his face. 'As you are no doubt aware, Ramm is in the middle-to-downmarket range, aimed at the eighteen to twenty-five-year-olds – *very* macho. Anyway, we wanted a new face, a face that would catch the public's eye. The model agency sent us several good-looking guys and eventually, after a great deal of nit-picking, Peter Allison happened to win the prize. He not only had a good body – tall, muscular, etcetera, etcetera – but he had the sort of face you could remember, somehow unusual – ascetic, lean, and beautiful, beautiful tanned skin.'

'So what was the problem?' Vic asked impatiently.

'Peter Allison's real name was, is, Alison Peters. Peter Allison is a woman.' She was rewarded by a look of bemusement on Vic's face. 'Miss Peters had made the papers previously when she had been sacked from her job in a bank in Romford for coming in dressed as a man, but no one connected hunky Peter Allison with quirky Alison Peters from Romford. . . . Naturally, our clients didn't like it too much, particularly as they'd already pumped a hell of a lot of money into the campaign, so naturally we lost it – with costs.'

'You couldn't talk them round?'

'Come on, Vic – Ramm was supposed to be the successor to Brut, *the* macho guy's best friend. But instead of getting someone real, someone like good old Henry Cooper, we decided to change the world and do something different, invent a new face. It's just a pity that that face didn't know whether it was a man or a woman. Not very macho, Vic, and not very good for sales.' Francesca studied his face for a moment, surprised that such a self-involved, unsophisticated half-wit like Vic could have obtained such a position in one of Britain's best agencies. He must have a hell of a good mouth. 'After all,' she continued, 'our friend Lucas, particularly with Matthias' rather uneven past, shall we say, could have a record, could be dealing in coke, could be renting toy-boys, and so on. If Matthias is serious about all this he's got to be clean, and seen to be clean, which also goes for his right-hand man, otherwise we're just wasting our time.'

'Okay, I get the message – and I'll check it out,' he said wearily. 'Can we talk about the actual campaign now?' His words were deliberately designed to emphasize his boredom. There was no doubting what sex Chairman Gaetini was; just like a bloody woman to home in on unnecessary details with a presentation just about to blow them into orbit.

'I take it you're going to have to rush things now?' she said softly, aware of his irritation.

'Gareth Jones has been taken off it, we've got Nick Keogh on it now – the guy who did the Baronets campaign. He got the Best Launch of a New Product Commendation last year and also the Best Individual Colour Ad Silver Award just before joining us. He's good, even very good.' He wanted to add, 'He'd better be,' but pressed the words down.

'I'd like a meeting first thing in the morning.'

'I've already booked the main conference room for 10 a.m.'

'Fine.' Suddenly she felt very tired, it was beginning to turn into one hell of a day. 'I'll look forward to it.' It was his dismissal.

'Well, if there's anything else, I'll let you know then,' he finished lamely. He was not yet used to her abruptness, still unable to accept that she was sitting in the chair he had hoped to occupy. With a half-concealed shrug he walked out.

Her eyes followed him and rested on the door after he had gone. She wondered if he was aware that he wore his dislike for her like a heart on his sleeve. Poor Vic. Life could be a real pain in the ass sometimes.

'Friday! – I've hardly had a chance to tackle the draft yet!' Nick said aggrievedly. He wanted this to be *right*, not rushed or half-done and now he was supposed to wave a magic wand and produce something special for the brief tomorrow morning and then the actual presentation on Friday. They must be crazy.

'I haven't got time to molly-coddle you, Nick. If you don't think you can come up with the goods then I'll have to find someone else. . . .' Vic Brunning stood over him. The pale eyes had darkened and there was no mistaking the hostility in his words. Nick would do it because he *wanted* this pitch, *wanted* the prestige enough to stay up all night, and tomorrow night, until it was no longer necessary.

'Okay, Vic – I read you loud and clear.' He stared up into his MD's unrelenting face. He knew he had no choice. Caught.

'That's my boy,' Vic said carelessly, the cool and ruthless air had gone now, replaced so quickly by thin easy tolerance. 'I want the main conference room to be plastered with posters and photographs of Matthias. I want a couple of tapes of his last concerts and the tapes of his trips to Nicaragua and Beirut ready to play – I've already contacted projection about that. I want that idea we discussed about using a technique in which the background dissolves into a number of different shots while Matthias remains constant in the foreground clarified and put down on paper as a brief-stroke-script for distribution in the morning. I think a brainstorming technique is what we should go for and then it will probably only be a question of toning it down for the actual pitch. I don't want anything glitzy, or anything relating to his past – that's out, except if he wants to bring it up. The public generally has a conveniently short and inglorious memory; we want to keep it that way.' He seemed to pause for breath for a moment, and then added finally, 'Okay?'

'I'll see you in the morning . . . ,' Nick said in response, and found himself staring at the empty space where Vic Brunning had stood and saw a brief glimpse of his long, carefully tailored figure as he left his office. 'I hear and obey, oh master . . . ,' he murmured, hard put to keep a humourless grin from touching his lips; he had just witnessed the Brunning bulldozer in action and wondered fleetingly whether Vic used the same unsubtle approach with his clients, but mellowed, no doubt, by his flashing white teeth.

Nick sat in silence for a moment, brooding. Slowly he turned around to face the life-size cardboard image of Matthias standing incongruously in one corner. It had been taken from an old photograph, one of his live concerts; he wore only tight black leather trousers, his upper torso was naked but rippling with well-formed muscles – and sweat, the same sweat which poured down his face, making rivulets of the carefully applied makeup which ironically no longer mattered at that moment. It was the face that called his attention, a face that could say a thousand things. The expression he saw was not merely theatrical, it was complex, wild, compelling, as if it should somehow be censored. The lips smiled crookedly, wantonly, and the pale blue eyes seemed full of something like rapture, but it was not the rapture of divine light, not then anyway. Something else, something quite different. Dark. Nick studied the face and found it hard to align the Matthias he saw with the one who had now 'found God'. He had seen him once, at Wembley; the stadium had been packed and he had been so far away from the platform that Matthias remained only a tiny dot on the horizon, but they had rigged the place with giant videos and the face of the performer roared at them through the huge screens – a massive thing, not quite human, beautiful, all-knowing, child-like, omnipotent – all at once. Nick shook his head and blew out a slow cloud of smoke from the cigarette which hovered at his finger-tips. He wondered at the mind behind the face, behind the magnetic blue eyes which seemed to command by will alone; wondered at the visions this new Matthias claimed he saw. Shrugging his shoulders abruptly he turned back to his desk; he was wasting time.

'. . . and in addition to being slotted in at the end of the mid-day news to hit the housewife, it will also be screened at the end of the news on all channels in the evening.' It was a clear-cut idea, a short film of his recent tours with not too much of the religious overtone. Ultimately, of course, the effect depended very much on Matthias himself, but from the tapes she had just seen it seemed to Francesca that he had the charisma to do almost anything he wished. And what exactly did he wish? 'Do you think that politics might ultimately be his goal? If this was the States I could understand it, but the UK is a different ball-game altogether.' She frowned and then shifted her gaze back to the script. 'I like the script by the way, Nick, and I'm sorry about the short notice.'

'Thanks – well, at least the main bullet points are sorted out and anything else will presumably be thrashed out on Friday when you confer with him.' He sat across from her, still surprised that he should be sitting there with Brunning, with her – members of the High Council, the élite, Samuels' selected few. All he needed now was Henry Samuels and that would really put the icing on the cake, but he was sunning it in Antigua, and with an amazonian blonde so the gossip went; there was always a blonde with Henry Samuels somewhere, somehow in the background of his life – his not-so-secret obsession. Nick let his eyes linger over Francesca's partly bowed dark and lovely head; she had been left holding the baby, but it was obvious to anyone with any intelligence that she relished it and, he mused, that she couldn't give a damn if Henry in his infinite wisdom decided to take permanent retirement. It was easy to see that she knew what she was doing, even through the sleek Ferrari exterior. Nick pressed down a smile at his comparison, aware that his own preference with regard to the female sex would always lie with the more generous, stolid proportions of a Rolls.

'. . . I'm not sure even *he* knows exactly what he wants –,' Vic's terse voice broke into his thoughts and Nick switched his gaze back to his MD's face as he continued, '– maybe politics eventually, who knows? But right now it seems pretty clear that he needs to clean up the memory of his past before he's taken really seriously by the establishment, and that means exposure, and the right kind of exposure.'

'The TV chat shows can easily be arranged, as can the radio spots, and from what I've heard they're all practically lining up with their tongues hanging out.' Francesca caught a breath which was not quite a sigh. 'I'll feel happier once we've met him and then I'll be able to draw a few conclusions of my own. At the moment I feel as if we're groping in the dark.'

'So go ahead and grope – maybe that's what he wants, something weird and wonderful,' Vic said carelessly and grinned.

'You know, Vic, you're wasted here – you should have been a comic,' she replied smoothly and stood up. 'I think we'll wait until Friday, don't you?' She smiled dryly and turned to Nick. 'If you could get the script back to me with those changes, Nick, say by tomorrow morning, I'd be grateful.'

Nick nodded in response. It was over for the time being – his part in the big pitch, Matthias, the briefing; it had all been so much easier than he had imagined. But as he stood up and watched Samuels' new chairman gather paper and files together, watched as she pressed down barely concealed irritation, expertly avoiding Brunning and the air of hidden conflict, he somehow felt that he still wasn't quite in the real game. That was something else, something he wasn't quite prepared for yet and where there were no rules.

The message lay on her blotter, white and black against deep burgundy. She didn't want to speak to Michael now, didn't want the old memories to intrude once again into her life, but even as the thought passed through her mind her hand was reaching automatically for the telephone. It was a central London number and in a moment Michael's voice touched her as if he had been waiting for her call.

'What's the matter, Michael?' She had heard the hesitancy in his voice, remembered only too well her mother's call and wondered why she suddenly felt older, so much older than him.

'I was hoping you could lend me some money – as a temporary loan if you like. . . .' His voice trailed off weakly and she tried to picture him, wherever he was, but failed because this was not the voice of the Michael she had known, this strange voice that was distant, brittle, lonely all at the same time.

'Of course I can.' She paused, carefully choosing her words. 'Mother called me, she wanted to know where you were.' There was no reply. 'What *is* the matter, Michael? Have you had an argument with her?' He still did not respond and she felt curiously afraid for him. 'You're not in trouble, are you?' She wasn't even sure what she meant by that word; it was alien and somehow foolish, as if she had just read it in a novel.

'I just want some time to myself, that's all – breathing space, whatever you want to call it.' The words came out stiff and disjointed as if he had rehearsed them carefully. Like a child.

'Do you want to stay with me for a while? There's plenty of room.'

'No, no, I don't want to do that.' His voice was remote, weary, but then she heard his soft sad breathing and felt a sudden surge of longing to comfort him, to retrieve what was left of the golden brother she had known in that dim distant past when they were just two children and the adult world was only a vast seething other planet which had yet to touch them.

'Where shall I leave the money?' Her own voice came at last and then she added, aware of his unease, 'I could leave it at our reception desk – in an envelope.'

'Yes . . . thanks.' Again she heard that hesitancy as if he wanted to say more, but then there was only the thickness of his silence.

'I'll make sure it's there by 3 p.m., so you could come in any time after that.'

'I won't be able to see you,' he said tautly, defensively.

'Not now, anyway, Michael,' she said gently, 'but you know where I am if you should need anything.' She had meant to say 'me', but at the last moment exchanged it for something less vulnerable.

'Yes, I know,' he said neutrally, and then he was gone and she stared into the receiver just as she had done when her mother had called, as if it were an echo.

She sat in silence for a moment, then moved away from her desk to the window. The sky had darkened and rain was falling in big slow drops, spattering the roofs and ledges of the grey buildings, denting puddles, pouring thick tears of water down thousands of windows.

Francesca read his profile again. It was excellent, as she knew it would have to be. Philippe Sanchez was only thirty-six and yet he was now practically in control of one of New York's largest advertising agencies and one, moreover, with a pretty comprehensive network. It seemed as if he had been plucked apparently from almost nowhere. He had risen through the ranks with no degree, something that Rock had rectified and then came the Harvard Business School and ultimately the return to Dunmar-Rock like the proverbial prodigal son. It was all interesting, but perhaps not important at this stage. Francesca studied the photograph of the man she would subsequently have to bargain with. It told her nothing except that he was dark, and that his origins were undoubtedly Hispanic. He had risen indeed. She leaned across her desk to the intercom.

'Sian, could you see if you can get me a few minutes with Geoff Buchanan sometime today? Thanks.' He might not have anything more for her, he might not even have a date yet for the planned exploratory meeting, but she needed to talk; he had met Rock once.

'Zoë, I think you've got Geoff Buchanan's diary, haven't you?' Sian asked and then raised her voice when she realized that Zoë was deeply plugged into her audio equipment. The mop of honey-blonde hair shot up as if she had been stung and then she visibly relaxed when she realized that it had not been Vic, but Francesca Gaetini's new PA who had called her.

'Oh, yes, yes I have. . . .' She swivelled round on her chair so that she faced her desk and the piles of paper and files which sat in a disordered heap. Two *Economist* diaries the colour of her flamboyant red nail varnish sat one on top of the other.

'He'll be free after lunch, would 3.30 be okay?' Zoë looked up, her round, pretty face etched with a frown.

'Yes, that'll be fine.' Sian watched her write the appointment in and then turn mechanically back to her typewriter as if she were merely an extension of it. 'Can I help?' Sian added, unable to ignore any longer the chaos and the muttered curses which came at regular intervals from Zoë's set lips and which somehow sounded near despair.

'Really – it's okay,' she said with an effort, 'Vic doesn't like anyone else doing his work.' But her gaze shifted momentarily to her desk and Sian saw how she closed her eyes as if that would take away the unholy vision. 'I just wish sometimes I could have more notice when things suddenly become urgent; he's had the draft on his desk for two days now,' she said finally. 'I'm supposed to get this report finished by 5.30 *and* type all these private letters of his. . . .' Her glance moved from the file and the pile of papers to the girl who sat across from her and Sian could clearly see her hesitation. 'Well, perhaps if you could do some of these letters. They're all in longhand and really self-explanatory. . . .' Zoë stood up and walked across the room. 'But don't let on, will you? He'd kill me if he knew.'

'I won't breathe a word – and certainly not to him,' Sian replied wryly, but realized that Zoë had missed the implication in her voice. As she watched the girl return to her desk she wondered how she could work for such a man, how she could allow herself to be bullied in such a manner. She sighed inwardly, feeling doubt touch her. Perhaps Vic Brunning had virtues she was as yet unaware of, perhaps it was only his abrupt manner that had made her dislike him so quickly and therefore judge him too harshly. Her fingers reached for the letters and her eyes briefly scanned each one – holiday bookings, share-cheques to his bank, renewal of his RAC Club member-ship, an inquiry about an exclusive health club. Sian drew in a sharp breath and tried to push the furtive shadow of depression away. This was not really her work, but it was a reminder of the past, of the trivial tedium this role often became, and of all she had lost. She closed her eyes for a brief moment and then cast the memory aside as her hand reached for the on/off switch of the typewriter; the letters would take up very little of her time and then she would go again through the files that Francesca had given her.

'I met Rock about eighteen months ago at the Cannes Film Festival,' Geoff said, settling himself more comfortably in one of the deep leather arm chairs. 'It was an opportune moment – at least for us and particularly with what we have in mind now – because at that show we won several Gold Lions amongst other awards and Rock deliberately sought Vic and me out to congratulate us personally.'

'How did he strike you? And I don't mean just as an ad man,' Francesca asked, sitting across from him.

'Late sixties, seems likely to work till he drops, conven-tional American, very sharp but more of a manager than a

54

leader. Dunmar was the chief motivator, and when he died I think Rock lost a little direction. He's great with the nuts and bolts of the business – with doing things right, but lacks vision, hence Dunmar-Rock's current stagnation.'

'And this is where Sanchez comes in?' she responded.

'Well, it certainly looks like it; he might be a bit raw, but he's hungry and seems to possess that unique combination of skills – a guy with a vision and the practical ability to bring it about.'

'This "raw" bit interests me – he seems to have sprung from nowhere and then under Rock's sudden guidance was catapulted into a prime slot. . . .' She saw Geoff frown.

'I know, but I haven't been able to dig up any information on his pre-Rock days. Presumably he must have done something right otherwise Rock wouldn't have shown such an interest.'

'Yes, and I'd like to know exactly what. But perhaps this is just a little irrelevant at this moment in time.' She paused and reached for a cooling cup of coffee. 'I found some of the remarks on the other key people interesting too, if not amusing. . . .'

'Any one in particular?' he asked, returning her smile. It was pointless compiling a report on people without the human element. Some of Rock's people were potentially good, but had become stale, boring, even lacking the right sort of confidence in their own abilities. Some simply needed to be put out to grass.

'I liked the comments on Gerry Schwarz – "brought in as new media director eighteen months ago – good ideas, great potential, but he doesn't realize it and no one else does either."' She laughed and replaced the file back on the table. 'Have you got a date for the meeting yet?'

'Rock's secretary promised to get back to me by Wednesday. He's been on the West Coast for the past week and we're supposed to deal with him direct, at least initially.'

'Obviously doesn't want his golden boy to get too

power-hungry just yet. . . .' Francesca remarked with a smile.

'Obviously,' Geoff agreed. 'By the way I've got the finance boys already working on some draft figures. I'll let you have them as soon as they're available.'

'That sounds fine, Geoff.' She stood up and moved towards her desk. 'And while I think of it, how did the MonCher meeting go yesterday morning?'

'Better than I'd hoped,' he said, draining his cup. 'It was only a touch of French petulance and in any event, as it turns out, they're so in love with our creative work that they wouldn't risk moving anywhere else.'

'Great.' She paused for a moment and shook her head gently before continuing, 'I'm rather glad today is turning out a little better than yesterday.'

'Well, don't say that to Vic,' he responded, grinning as he stood up, 'He's just heard that General Breweries want to review their account with us.'

'Are you quite sure you should be grinning about this, Geoff – we're talking about a hell of a lot of money . . . ?' Francesca's face was suddenly shadowed.

'It's just a threat,' he said easily. 'Old man Swanson has taken a sudden dislike to our account manager.'

'Who is he, and why?' she asked abruptly.

'Mike Weinberg, an old friend of Vic's – he's been screwing Swanson's daughter. . . .'

'Oh, my God – doesn't he know that it's a little unwise to shit on your own doorstep?' she said impatiently. 'Apart from that, what's the objection anyway?'

'He's married.'

'Christ.' He saw circles of red anger colour her cheeks. 'So presumably we have a choice between moving Weinberg off the account or losing it.'

'I think there's a little more to it than that. . . .'

'He wants him fired,' Francesca finished for him. Geoff nodded.

'Well, tell Vic to fire him.'

'He's too good to lose, Francesca.'

'I didn't doubt that, Geoff – we'll just slip him into one

of our subsidiaries and bring him back proper in a few months when the heat has died down.' She saw the reinstatement of Geoff's smile. 'But I'll personally fire him, and for good, if he doesn't stop messing around with Samuels' profits.'

'Fair enough,' Geoff responded.

'But I'd rather you didn't tell Vic about our little conversation. I'd like him to work this one out for himself.' She matched Geoff's knowing stare and allowed the ghost of a smile to settle on her lips.

'Agreed,' he replied and then walked slowly towards the door. 'I'll see you in the morning.' He heard her soft, vague reply as if already her mind was concentrating on something else and he thought of Vic and almost felt sorry for him.

'You didn't do these, did you?' It was a statement rather than a question and Vic knew she would be too timorous to resist him. The offending letters lay white and perfect in between each page of the correspondence blotter. Too perfect. Could almost have been Zoë's work, but not quite. Not one spelling mistake, not one comma missing. Did she think he was really such a fool?

'I was afraid I wouldn't have time to finish everything . . . ,' she protested weakly.

'Finish everything by when? I usually expect you to stay late if you haven't managed to complete what I've given you.' He attacked her for her error because he was angry, disappointed, sullen that his own dreams had been thwarted and that now there was something else to plague him. 'I can't help feeling dissatisfied with your attitude lately, but I don't have either the time or the energy to discuss this with you now. I'll talk to you in the morning.' She seemed to hesitate for a moment as if expecting something more, but the weighted silence told her there would be nothing further so she walked, head bowed, towards the door and his eyes automatically followed. She was wearing tight, very tight trousers and he knew she wore nothing underneath because he had told her not to.

57

But she irritated him, just as the feeble batting of her big blue eyes had just irritated him. He wondered, meanly, if she had expected him to let his anger dissipate and then give her a nice little fuck. God, women were all the damn same. His mouth tasted dry and he longed for a drink. He got up and moved to the window and then abruptly walked to his office door. Samuels' local, the Drayman's Arms, would be open now; he'd think about Mike and the General Breweries mess over a pint. He smiled, suddenly realizing the irony.

Zoë was still sitting at her desk as he came up behind her.

'I'm just popping out for half an hour. Will you be here when I get back?' he said tersely.

'Yes,' Zoë replied hesitantly. 'I'll finish the corrections on the report.' It was already gone six, but Vic never asked – he only *told*, and in any event she would stay until he returned because she wanted to go home secure in the knowledge that he was no longer angry with her, that he still wanted her.

'I understand you helped my secretary with some letters this afternoon?' Vic had moved across the room and now stood by Sian's desk.

She looked up into his face, only too aware of how her good deed had gone wrong.

'I thought she needed a hand. . . .'

'I appreciate what you were trying to do, but I always insist that my work is done by Zoë, and Zoë alone.'

'That must make things a little difficult sometimes?' she asked, unable to remain mute, unable to stop the surge of dislike for this mean-minded oaf, this conceited fool.

'I think that's my problem, not yours.'

And she watched him walk away, heard the hum of the lift as he called it, felt the sudden loss of tension in the atmosphere at his absence. Sian looked at Zoë, but she had already turned back to her typewriter, intent on her corrections and the wishes of the man she seemed to serve with such humiliating obedience, apparently oblivious to what had just passed. Sian closed her eyes for a moment, suddenly wondering how her son was, how Petie was, and if he were missing her.

'He's had a bad day. . . .'

She turned at the sound of the voice, snapped out of her reverie, as Geoff Buchanan drew alongside her desk.

'I think he's the sort of man who would give you the impression that every day is a bad day. . . .'

The fleeting look of regret had gone from her face like a shadow and there was only that air of repugnance about her which made him want to smile; Vic had an amazing knack of getting on the wrong side of people.

'He just likes getting his own way, that's all, and when he doesn't get it, it makes him a little bad-tempered. Don't take him too seriously.' Her face was still set, still spoilt by the frown Vic had managed with such ease to put there.

'I wish I had your tact,' she replied evenly and looked up at last into his face.

'Forget it. Tomorrow's another day.' They were clichés, but at least apt, and Vic could be very forgettable sometimes. The tension seemed all at once to drain from her face and she was betrayed into a smile, and it was a nice smile, he thought absently.

'. . . It's time I went home, too,' she said finally.

'Where's home?' he asked politely.

'Wimbledon.' She was placing the translucent plastic cover over her typewriter.

'Do you share a flat, or a house?'

'Neither. I live with my parents.' She saw the mild look of surprise in his eyes – yes, I'm twenty-seven and living with my parents. Definitely a 'no-no'.

'Well, I think you'll have just about enough time to get home, relax and recover for another session tomorrow . . . ,' he said smoothly and swiftly to ease the awkwardness and then looked self-consciously at his watch. 'I'd better be off too – see you in the morning.' He smiled again, relieved, and she watched him walk towards the lift. She had successfully made him feel uncomfortable a second time and she wondered how she managed to do it with such ease. Perhaps in the year that had passed she had managed to acquire not only a child and a burden, but a different air about her – bitter, no longer having the softness, the charm which Adam always said made her so female. But she was tired, it had been a long day and she still had to get home. Sian shrugged herself into her coat and tried to put all such thoughts away, pressing them all down, out of sight, to think of later. They did not amount to much, anyway, not now.

He seemed bigger, much bigger than she had imagined. But none of the tapes, none of the interviews had prepared her for this man. An engaging half-smile hovered on his lips as he sat behind the simple black desk, which was the only substantial item of furniture in the otherwise empty room. Gone was the rock star, the raw wildness which had been his trademark. This new Matthias was dressed in black, the polo-neck sweater, the beautifully cut jacket and trousers; in total contrast to the white-blond hair which was cut short, emphasizing high cheekbones and piercing blue eyes. All his features seemed carefully planned and placed in flesh which was smooth, cream and so perfect. Ageless. Francesca studied him as he addressed Vic, saw how obvious, how apt was his description 'golden'. Even now he seemed to give off a glow, an easy, deceptively arrogant glow giving extra years to Vic, as if Matthias had drained off all the light.

'It could have an impact – this idea of yours,' Matthias said neutrally.

'Obviously, but only with the right, hard-hitting backgrounds,' Vic responded enthusiastically.

'And you think too much emphasis on God, as you put it, may not produce the effect I desire?' He leaned forward a little, bringing his hands together so that the finger-tips touched, and then stared into Vic's face.

'Well, God isn't exactly fashionable these days . . . ,' Vic said lamely, hard-put to meet the brilliant, unblinking gaze.

'Perhaps that's what the problem *is*, Mr Brunning.' Matthias spoke smoothly, and a small derisive smile came to rest on his mouth. Mocking.

'I think what Vic means,' Francesca interjected, 'is that until we have some sort of idea how the public is responding to the campaign as we see it now, it would be better to play it safe.' She paused as if expecting him to respond, but he remained silent, studying her, and she continued, 'The various shots of different types of global unrest or chaos within the short film we have in mind will be skilfully picked to touch people where it really hurts, shock them, make them think . . . and as each shot dissolves into the next one you will remain constant in the foreground – like an anchor.' She shifted her gaze from the briefing document to his face.

'I like that word, "anchor",' he replied quietly. 'There is nothing and no one in the world today which provides any sort of anchor, any sort of reassurance that there might be another alternative to our inept and pitiless way of life.' He stood up and moved across the stark room to stand in front of a huge framed photograph of a crying child with its arms outstretched against the background of a battered and bloodied Beirut. 'Bob Geldof had the right idea, but he didn't go quite far enough. It isn't sufficient to draw attention to a global problem and then hand round a collecting plate. The idea has to be perpetuated, strengthened, built upon. Otherwise, people forget.'

'Geldof did an excellent job,' Francesca said.

'I'm not disputing that – I simply want to go further.'

'How?' Vic asked sharply. 'Politics? You're hardly in a position to stand as a member of parliament. . . .'

'Perhaps not, Mr Brunning.' He smiled thinly. 'But there are other paths of influence which might suit my purposes better. After all, politicians, all generations of them, whatever their nationality or creed, have had no real answers; religion as we know it has had no answers and has been twisted by its glorious hierarchy to achieve quite the opposite of its true meaning.'

'And you have the answer?' Francesca asked carefully.

'I have no answer, Miss Gaetini, but perhaps I do have an alternative to what there is – an awareness of what there *could* be.'

61

'The British public are among the most critical, perhaps the most cynical in the world,' she said, after a pause.

'You mean that I might be wasting my time?' he asked evenly, turning back into the room.

'Perhaps.'

'You saw the reaction to my tours . . . ?' He was closer now, standing alongside her chair.

'That was the younger generation.' But she could see the supreme confidence in his face, so sure of his ability to control the conversation, the situation.

'Agreed – and don't young people learn appropriate and, unfortunately, also inappropriate attitudes and behaviour from other people? As I did, almost to my cost.' He leaned down towards her. 'You are probably aware that my video album topped the charts in twenty-eight countries, selling more than sixteen million copies worldwide.' She heard his soft even breathing as he paused. 'I am the perfect role model for young people, perhaps the most popular role model in a long time. . . .'

'More popular than Jesus, even?' Vic's voice cut in, hard-put to keep the cynicism out of his words.

'John Lennon is dead, Mr Brunning, and the anthem he coined died with him. But coming back to your remark, Miss Gaetini, I have also had a tremendous response from the older generation – large donations of money, support for what I am trying to do, suggestions where I should direct myself next; several offers from well-established organizations.'

'Which organizations?' Vic asked, barely able to press down the sullenness that was beginning to creep into his voice.

'Amnesty International and Greenpeace, among others.'

'Are you interested?' Francesca said.

'Interested, yes, but I don't want to be identified with one particular cause. Perhaps it is not beyond the realms of probability to imagine that these organizations and others like them could work together, beneath one enormous benevolent umbrella.'

'With you as its figurehead, I presume,' Vic asked with a trace of sarcasm.

Matthias only smiled.

'I have to build upon what I have achieved so far, Mr Brunning, and perhaps with careful management and the right sort of publicity I may achieve a great deal more.'

'And you like the idea of a massive satellite link-up?' Francesca asked, as his eyes slid so easily back to her face and she felt blood seep slowly into her cheeks as she matched his stare.

'Fantastic.' He leaned languidly against the desk.

'I thought the setting could be central Europe, even an Eastern bloc country, which would not only lend it an edge of originality, but make your message – shall we say – more readily accessible to those who perhaps wouldn't otherwise even hear it.'

'Very good, but I want it to be much more than just another rock-pop extravaganza; I want it to be an education – an experience.' His eyes were examining her slowly.

'That's where the film shots and the posters we are preparing come in,' she said evenly, visibly battling against a desire to look away; she did not want him to win.

'They must be massive pieces of pain, Miss Gaetini, *huge* chunks of misery and chaos to make them open their damned eyes.' He said the words almost softly, but there was no doubting the intensity he wished to convey and she swallowed slowly as he brought his face just perceptibly closer to hers.

'The technical difficulties and logistics of the operation will be something else,' Vic interjected suddenly. 'We have to discuss the project and get complete cooperation from the other artists we hope will contribute.' This was supposed to be *his* pitch and she only the onlooker; he should have known she'd have something sensational tucked neatly up her Jean Muir sleeve.

'It *will* be brought off, Mr Brunning,' Matthias replied impatiently, turning to look at Vic's pale face. 'People expect the impossible as they also expect that something should be done about our messy little world.'

As he looked away from her, Francesca felt her eyes drawn back again to his face, to the small vital veins in his temple and the thin, so suggestive mouth.

'There is a new awareness of the environment, of how small and limited this world of ours can suddenly seem if we do not take steps to counteract the consequences of our actions on the future.' His voice rose just slightly. 'Each country, each government must be held accountable for the effects of its actions – on its people and on its environment.' He saw the doubt in Vic's eyes. 'It may sound like an impossibility, Mr Brunning – a dream, but we have to start somewhere or otherwise we are lost.' He stopped and deliberately turned again to Francesca as if she had shared his vision. The searing blue of his eyes had darkened with excitement, like shadowed windows reflecting his own future. 'I am not afraid to try, if you are not, Miss Gaetini.'

'Does that mean you're giving us the campaign . . . ?' It was Vic's eager voice, unwittingly breaking in on the air of tension which had cut them off from him.

Francesca shifted her gaze, glad of the reprieve, of a reason to look away from Matthias. There was a tightness in her throat, a nerve throbbing at the back of her neck; his closeness made her uneasy – threatening, as if he had somehow managed to peel back her skin, all the layers, and leave her utterly exposed.

'It would seem so, Mr Brunning,' he said slowly.

'You were sailing a bit close to the wind in there, weren't you?' Vic said, loosening his tie. 'It seemed to me that at the outset at least you were trying to put him off! I thought we came to pitch for a campaign – not try and talk the client out of it!' *My* campaign.

'I think "our client" knew exactly what I was trying to do, Vic, I would have thought that was pretty clear.' Even for your addled brain. She drew a breath and turned towards him and was amazed to see tiny beads of perspiration nestling in the curve of his nose and along his brow; Vic had been really worried.

'About as clear as mud!' he said indignantly, as they neared the waiting car, and then continued with a sneer, 'but as you say, as long as you and our friend Matthias understand each other, that's all that matters. . . .'

'Not now, Vic,' she replied impatiently, as the door of the Mercedes was opened for her, 'I really don't need any of this.' She was not, somehow, quite in control and the knowledge made her uneasy, irritable. Now all she wanted to do was return to the sanctuary of her office, away from the disturbing interview and the dangerous shoals of thought which had begun to take shape in her mind.

'And I didn't need our pretentious friend's little lecture on the evils of mankind either,' Vic persisted in an attempt to nurse his bruised ego, 'or his patronizing attitude. Christ! After all, who does he think he's kidding with all that crap – everyone knows that this religious trip is just another way of getting the limelight after his years drugging it.' When Francesca did not respond, he drew in a sharp impatient breath. 'I suppose he's apeing that famous "forty days in the wilderness" bit – except he had to make it a hell of a lot longer while he got dried out. . . .'

'Maybe, just maybe, Vic, he might have a point, might actually be serious,' she said at last, surprising herself.

'Oh, *come on* – do I really believe my ears?!' He snorted contemptuously. 'I thought you were supposed to be smart.'

'Let's get back to the office, Vic.' She spoke dismissively, suddenly tired of him, and turned her face to the window.

'He's too cool to be real, too wild to be God-given beneath that smooth, suave exterior,' he went on insistently. 'He's a con.' She did not respond and he shrugged, letting his gaze focus on the Friday shoppers in Oxford Street, the masses of surging people on the pavements, clogging the roads, buying, buying. 'I'll organize a celebration drink in reception tonight in honour of our new prestigious client,' he said finally, sarcastically. But she did not hear him, she had cut him off, intent on a private vision of her own.

Caroline watched the video with fascination and let the music assault her ears. She could hardly remember Matthias as the rock star so many had worshipped, but now his image seemed to flood Samuels' vast reception area and she was entranced. She sipped champagne slowly, staring avidly at a face which seemed to promise pure and unsullied sensuality; and she thought, unfairly, of Guy and closed her eyes.

'Aren't you going to congratulate me?' He had seen her from across the room and she had reminded him guiltily of his past rudeness; now, happy, he could be kind.

'Nick – yes, of course,' she laughed then and he saw the fine whiteness of her teeth. 'Congratulations!' She was somehow relaxed and he realized, seeing the spots of red on each cheek and the telling glass in her hand, that it was the champagne. For a moment their gaze was pulled back to the huge screen, but then they saw the tall figure of Vic Brunning moving through the buzzing crowd and his outstretched arm pointing upwards to the enigmatic face of Matthias; he brought his other arm up so that his hands became joined in a gesture of victory and there was general laughter, cheers and ultimately quiet as he prepared to speak.

'Well – we did it!' More cheers. 'You can read all about it in tomorrow's press and in *Campaign*, etcetera, etcetera, next week. In the meantime we are going to celebrate, but first I'd like you to raise your glasses to Nick Keogh who was called in at the last minute for the pitch, but as you can see managed to deliver the goods well and truly.' The toast completed, Vic continued, 'One last thing – this win, with a little hard work, should make Samuels number one in the UK and then, who knows?' He smiled hugely as glasses were raised again and caught Nick's eye across the room as if they were conspirators.

'I must admit, he's good at this sort of thing,' Nick said, turning to Caroline. 'And they love it.'

But she was not interested in Vic Brunning. The easy atmosphere, the alcohol seeping through her limbs and the heady music seemed to open up a new world; it made her brave.

'Did you actually meet him?' she asked happily.

'Matthias? No. I'm generally a sort of back-room boy, at least so far.' He let his eyes flicker over her, warmed by her obvious innocence, surprised that she could be so easy to be with. 'But I feel as if I have: my office is covered with pictures, posters, drawings – even a life-size cardboard cut-out.'

'Why a life-size cardboard cut-out?' She was laughing now and his gaze settled fleetingly on her neck and the opening of her blouse, the creamy flesh beneath.

'I thought it would inspire me,' he said smoothly and leaned backwards towards a tray of champagne in order to refill their glasses. 'Would you like to see it?' He poured foam expertly into each glass.

'Could I?' she asked, and suddenly he felt the sure spectre of guilt as he looked into the wide violet eyes. She has no idea, he realized, but then he was moving and beckoning her to follow.

The office was small, at least it seemed so because it was still full of the debris of the pitch, but as Nick switched on a single desk lamp the magnificent image of Matthias was revealed standing alone in one corner. Caroline moved across the room, stepping over sheets of paper and newspaper cuttings to touch the two-dimensional figure. He heard her laugh quietly.

'What's the matter?' He walked slowly towards her.

'It just seems funny somehow. . . .' She turned around and watched Nick as he drew closer and suddenly felt the nerves begin to dance like wild things in her stomach. But he stopped, inches away, and they both stood like sentinels beside the cardboard deity until he took her hand, so easily, and pulled her gently against the wall. In the half-light her eyes shone and her lips seemed to tremble, but he brought his finger up to trace them, to still them. His mouth came down in agonizing slowness to cover hers and he felt her terror, but then there was warmth and eagerness as her lips parted and he felt her whole body shiver with pleasure.

The reality of Nick was not unlike her dreams, her imaginings, except that in her dreams she had allowed no boundaries. His arms glided over her back, so skilfully; his lips asked and promised so much that there was only a crushing desire to give herself to the maddening, feverish drive, but then his soft fingers reached the neck of her blouse and she shivered momentarily as each button was undone and he brought his mouth down to her waiting breasts.

He wanted to break her, drain that amazingly responsive mouth, make her cry out so that she would remember. He heard a soft moan and felt her wordless response as she pressed against him, and he crushed her breasts together so that he could feel their opulence all at once, moved his tongue across the dusky nipples and then down to the cushion softness of her belly. Perfect fragrant skin. Silently he began to lift her skirt so that his hands trailed along her thighs, his tongue still playing skilfully, distracting her. He ignored her first weak protest and thought that he had won, but then her hands joined in the resistance and tried to push him away. For a moment it seemed his persistence had been rewarded and he glanced up and saw that her eyes were clamped shut, but tears too heavy to hold back were forcing themselves past her eyelids.

'For God's sake,' he said impatiently, exasperated and confused by the fat tears coursing down her cheeks. He pulled himself into a standing position, feeling his erection irrevocably wither and die. 'What the hell's the matter?' She looked like a little girl now, no longer the woman who had kissed him with such obvious desire only a few minutes before.

'I think I'd better go.' She spoke quietly, desolately. She had come here with him full of excitement, her shyness for once in hiding, wanting to prolong the moment and her fragile happiness. Like thin sad clouds. A sob caught and stayed in her throat and she bowed her head in an effort to avoid his sharp scrutiny.

Suddenly he felt ashamed, guilty because she moved him and he didn't want to be moved; this was not part of the game.

'Well, well, well – hope I'm not interrupting anything?' Vic Brunning stood silhouetted in the doorway, cutting out the light from the corridor. Nick heard a small, terrified sound issue from Caroline's mouth and felt her fumblings as she clumsily tried to do up her blouse. In a moment she had moved past him and in her anxiety to leave knocked over the mute figure of Matthias. She seemed to pause as if to retrieve it, but surged suddenly onwards, only one thing important to her. Vic moved theatrically aside to let her pass and then turned back into the room, a broad smile stretched across his face.

'Not a thing, Vic, not a damn thing,' Nick said slowly, almost to himself, and then shifted his gaze from the space she had fled to meet the grinning clown's face of his managing director.

'I'm so glad that your creative talents are rather more successful than your manly charms seem to be, Nick!' Vic continued, enjoying the moment, '. . . And I was only doing my duty coming up here – thought the least I could do was thank you personally for all your hard work. . . .'

Nick closed his eyes for a moment in frustration, clamping his teeth shut on the words hovering just behind his lips, feeling his face grow stiff and tighten as if the skin would break. You asshole.

Her office seemed larger, emptier somehow. Francesca moved over to the coffee table and the enormous vase of lilies. Her hand gently touched and lingered on their sleek white beauty and then she started, was drawn back to her desk as the telephone rang, scalding her nerves.

She was surprised at the way her hand moved to the phone, apparently unaffected by the fierce pumping of her heart and the hollow sickness in her stomach. Sian's calm and collected voice had simply told her that Matthias was waiting to speak to her. His call was not really a surprise; there had been too much electricity in that strange, blank

69

room, and it had not been her imagination, that molten air, nor that lost schoolgirl sensation as she felt her knees literally grow weak. And he had known. Ridiculous. Francesca wanted to laugh out loud except that it did not seem funny. Memory seized her in its unrelenting grasp and she was fifteen again, innocent and foolish – he had been a skiing instructor, bronzed and rugged and utterly indifferent to yet another schoolgirl crush. She was twenty-nine now, supposedly older and wiser, too wise to fall for this golden, enigmatic man who seemed to promise so much, drowning her senses.

'I am flying to Paris on Sunday evening. There are a few further points I'd like to clarify – perhaps you could join me.' Soft, potent voice. That was all he said and she felt her lips pull into a half-smile at his directness. Invisible.

She drew a quick, sharp breath.

'May I call you back on this?' she replied evenly, amazed at the calmness in her words as if they issued from another voice and another mouth. And she could see him then with searing clarity, in that strange room, almost as if she could touch him, touch the high cheekbones, the pale blue eyes and that dangerous child-like mouth.

But she knew she would go.

# 3

The stark, clinical whiteness of the ladies' toilet made her eyes blink in rebellion. Caroline moved wearily to the nearest wash-basin and let cold water run into the bowl. She cupped her still trembling hands towards it and began splashing her face until her cheeks grew chill and almost numb. Mechanically she reached for a paper towel to pat the wetness away, but then heard footsteps and voices and laughter. Her immediate reaction was to hide and she stepped backwards and into the safety of one of the cubicles. She sat down on the incongruous seat, wretched, like an exile as the laughter of the girlish voices grew louder, turning to conspiratorial giggles as handbags were opened and closed and talk muted as lipstick was applied with practised ease. There was no escape, so she waited in silence until they had gone. Finally, she opened the door and was immediately confronted by the reflection of herself in the mirror directly opposite. A hot, burning flush soared into her face and her eyes closed briefly to shut out the vision: in her haste her confused fingers had slipped the wrong buttons into the wrong holes in her blouse and now a ridiculous gap laughed at her – an awry, sad hole where soft skin showed through like a wound. She remembered his lips then and his face as he had brought it down to meet hers; remembered sudden piercing dread at the loss of control. Tears slipped into her eyes again so that the white polished tiles danced in front of her and only then did she remember Guy, that he had planned to meet her, that he would be there now, waiting. She pushed her hair back roughly in a gesture of frustration and then turned with a sigh towards the door. Her coat was upstairs in the office with her handbag and the Marks & Spencer carrier bag hoarding the carefully chosen lambswool sweater that had so pleased her at lunchtime. A lunchtime

71

that now seemed to belong to another age, another place.

Samuels' reception still pulsed with euphoria, people still thronged the vast room with their champagne and their brittle laughter, but already some had trickled away. And the trickle would turn into a steady stream until only a hard core remained; those who were drunk or getting drunk, those who were lonely or who didn't want to go home, or both. Caroline slid furtively past groups of people, intent on the glistening double doors where Guy would be waiting. She did not look beyond that point, did not want to see or speak to anyone who might delay her escape. She felt the muscles of her stomach contract like tightening coils as she approached the glass doors, as Guy's familiar figure loomed up to greet her. Even as he bent down to kiss her and she felt his soft, passionless lips on her cheek, she wondered whether he would know, whether he would detect some vague, lingering smell of the other man on her skin and that therefore she had betrayed him. Caroline lifted her eyes to his face as he turned to go down the steps to the car, but Guy's face was impassive and safe, just as it always was.

Nick had watched her leave. He had seen her scurry through the reception area like a fugitive and longed to smile, but the smile stayed locked and stifled behind his lips. His eyes had followed her to the door and to the young man who kissed her so carefully. He had noted the dark pinstriped suit, the yellow silk tie which spoke of the City, of stockbroking or merchant banking, or perhaps it was estate-agency – that new 'profession', where even the brainless upper-crust could make a killing. A shadow momentarily dimmed his eyes and automatically he brought his glass of champagne to his mouth. No doubt she thought him crude and tasteless for engineering the little seduction that had gone so badly wrong. No doubt he had sullied her carefully nurtured, carefully planned, goldfish-bowl of a world. Impatiently he switched his gaze away from the blank stare of the double doors and looked across the room. The crowd was thinning considerably now and he saw Tina, good old Tina, leaning against one of the snowy white pillars. She looked bored as usual and the guy she was talking to could hardly stand up. Nick drained the rest of his glass and started to walk across the room towards her. Matthias' contorted face moved extravagantly above and behind him, like a graven image, his voice taunting, pleading, goading: '. . . the pain is worth the price . . . the price is worth the cost. . . .'

'I thought we were supposed to have a meeting this morning?' Vic asked aggrievedly as he moved passed Sian to stare into Francesca's empty office.

'As I've already explained, she telephoned me at home last night to say that something important had come up, to cancel all her meetings for the next two days, and finally that she would be calling the office some time today to enlarge on her movements,' Sian replied evenly.

'Christ! We've just picked up the most prestigious account going and she decides to do a disappearing act!' He sighed dramatically and then continued hotly, 'We were supposed to discuss the meeting we had on Friday and then write up a draft.'

'Actually I do have a draft here which Francesca sent in by hand this morning – it shouldn't take very long to type up and once it's done I'll leave a copy on your desk.' Sian shifted her gaze from his sullen expression to the papers in her hand. 'I think she would like your comments by the time she returns.'

For a moment Vic seemed at a loss for words; his mouth had dropped slightly open and his head nodded almost imperceptibly as if in sudden and silent agreement.

'Fine, fine . . . okay . . . ,' he said slowly, in an effort at casualness. She had not only covered her ass, but got him by the balls at the same time. He turned abruptly away and went back into his office, his hands clenched in fists of muted rage. What was so damned important that their beloved chairman felt able to absent herself for two whole days? Henry would be calling this afternoon and would no doubt find it curious that his protégée was not where she should be. Vic smiled inwardly, finding comfort in the fact that he would be the one to tell Henry that they had won the Matthias account and that it was the managing director he had chosen to overlook for the chairmanship who had masterminded the whole thing. But it was cold comfort and he swallowed slowly in the depths of his throat. The day had not begun well and there was still the General Breweries mess to sort out. Old man Swanson was adamant Mike had to go – exile for a few months as far as he was concerned, until the heat had died down and naughty, nubile Charlotte had turned her attentions elsewhere. But it still meant a good replacement had to be found for the account, it still meant that Mike would now be unable to supervise the launch of the Storm personal computer campaign next month, which meant more bullshit and explanations to another client. He paced restlessly across the room, pausing momentarily before the window, and moved abruptly back to his desk. It was only then that he heard the sound of a soft familiar footfall stop short of his office.

'Zoë!' he shrilled. 'Where's the mail, the morning papers and my bloody coffee?!!' He had switched to an easier target, finally, glad of an outlet for the resentment which was beginning to gnaw at his innards like acid.

The sky was darkening by the time the car reached the outskirts of Paris. She could hear the wind thud past the windows muffled by thick, heavy glass. Francesca leaned her head back against the soft leather seating and closed her eyes. She had not called him until late Saturday evening and even then had almost changed her mind, but she smiled wryly in the semi-darkness knowing that to have denied his request would only have put off the inevitable. He had flown on ahead and she had been met at Charles de Gaulle airport by a liveried chauffeur. Matthias had learned how to do things with considerable style. As his enigmatic face slid into her consciousness, her thoughts returned to their previous meeting and Vic's subsequent sour and cynical comments: 'He's too cool to be real, too wild to be God-given beneath that smooth, suave exterior. . . . He's a con.' Perhaps. It didn't really matter now, she would find out for herself. Her gaze turned to the window and the evening sky which was settling into a mass of black-blue metal. Almost directly above, a bald moon cast a pale-pearl light across the tops of the trees, the only light for miles. They had left Compiègne far behind and were now speeding down a road carved through dense woodland. It was almost like a magical mystery tour, a guessing game. She caught a breath which was not quite a sigh – and it had been so long since she had allowed herself any real games, or time, any sort of time. In any event, she told herself guiltily, things had been left reasonably tidy for the short time she would be absent from the office and, after all, this was supposed to be business; there would be another draft report for preparation on her return. Light and shadow fled across her face as a mocking smile began to tip the edges of her mouth. It might be that the report would not be totally honest, not totally encompassing all 'the business' which would pass between herself and Matthias. But that was her privilege, after all, and she had allowed herself few enough of those.

The car swerved smoothly and in the distance she saw the chateau glittering like a small jewel. The road was straight now, like an arrow, made cavernous by a tunnel of magnificent oak trees which caught the building in the bowed embrace of a hundred branches. He was not there to greet her. Francesca looked briefly about her before following a young footman up the terraced staircase. The house was huge and exotically beautiful, and seemed almost too lavish in the rapidly deepening shadows. She caught a glimpse of darkening corner towers, embossed columns, heavy voluptuous garden sculptures. It could not be his, Matthias did not have the means – or maybe that was a fallacy, too, that he had given the bulk of his fortune away – in any event he no doubt had friends in high places who had the means, he had said as much. As she stepped through the carved oak doors she wondered if his friends would be here, if they were waiting for her inside. Somehow she had not bargained on that eventuality. Francesca sighed inwardly, surprising herself at the sudden surge of disappointment. She did not want business, suddenly, did not want other people, only the aloneness he had implied so easily in their brief, burning conversation.

Her suite was a triumph, the glorious lush pomp of Baroque, yet the bathroom had none of this, as if the master, or mistress, of the house had had a sudden and inexplicable change of mood. It was almost exclusively Art Deco; the bath, wash-basin, floor all in siennese yellow marble, the walls covered with black Japanese tiles, Lalique moulded wall-lamps. But it was the bath in the centre of the room that caught her attention – delightfully enormous, like a huge beached whale, raised by three marble slabs to pedestal-like proportions. She stood in front of it for a moment, smiling, and then turned and caught her reflection in the ornate wrought-iron mirror over the basin. Her face was flushed and her eyes shining, and she realized that she looked like an excited child. She shook her head slowly, not knowing whether she liked what she saw. After all, what was she doing here – in this beautiful museum, this house that belonged to God knows whom? And where was he, this man she hardly knew? Was this part of his game, his image of the mysterious man who still somehow stood beyond normal boundaries? She closed her eyes briefly in exasperation. This whole thing, this weird and wonderful adventure, was so unlike her, so unlike the new dynamic chairwoman of Samuels destined, according to all the advertising propaganda, for greatness; so unlike the cool, disciplined woman people saw; and wasn't it she who was always in control, who had the answers, not anyone else – not *him*? She felt the familiar knot of tension gather like a fist in the back of her neck. Too late to turn back, but neither did she want to. She had never been very good at back-tracking, never very good at taking the easy way out, and the scars didn't seem to show. She groaned softly; dinner was in fifteen minutes, the luxurious bath she had promised herself would now have to wait.

Nothing had changed. He had kissed her finger-tips like a Viennese count and she had wanted to laugh because nothing seemed as it should be. Even as he showed her to her chair she had felt the magnetism, the heat which seemed to emanate from him. Matthias was dressed in black as before and he sat opposite her, down the length of the carved table studded with candle-light. They had talked of nothing and everything, but very little of the campaign. Her eyes had come to rest on his face and then slipped slowly, determinedly away to stare into the fire, and then to the paintings of eighteenth-century old-young men, and upwards, soaring, to the vaulted ceiling. She did not want to look at him, did not want to battle, yet; the warmth, the wine and the dream-like quality of this whole world lulled her senses like a sweet drug and she felt, ridiculously, that she would prefer to be suspended in time, like a tremulous, hovering bubble.

'And do you find our Mr Chant to your liking after your little investigation, Miss Gaetini?' His question broke sharply in upon her reverie and her eyes were pulled back to his face.

'It had to be done – we couldn't afford to take any chances with someone who might prove a liability.' She sighed inwardly, her mood broken; of course he would have known, sooner or later. 'And please call me Francesca.'

'What did your little investigation tell you?' He spoke smoothly, sarcastically.

'You already know the answer to that.'

'Lucas, or Kevin Crowley, as he was once better known and as you are no doubt already aware, has been off heroin for over five years. After leaving my backing group in '79 he began toying around with Scientology, followed up very quickly by Hare Krishna et al. Disillusionment set in, not surprisingly, and he then wisely decided to join me in my work, almost from its inception.' He brought a glass

77

of glistening yellow wine to his lips. 'He is as clean as he is ever likely to be – as clean, shall we say, as your average advertising executive.' He laughed softly and raised his glass to her. 'But this is your reprieve . . . ,' and he pulled his face into a small frown as he imitated the one that wove quickly across her own at his remark, '. . . your reprieve from life.' And he smiled, that strange, child-like smile as if he knew something that she could not, or would not, acknowledge, something which slipped furtively, exasperatingly beyond her grasp.

'Why should I need a reprieve?' Oh, but she did, she did.

'Because you are making this work of yours a whole life – a personal monument.' His pale eyes flicked slowly over her, penetrating.

'I was always taught that ambition was healthy,' she replied evenly, vainly attempting humour.

'You were taught wrong.' His hand reached to his glass and wound languid fingers around the stem. 'And why make yourself a slave to the brittle glitz of advertising, "the whore of the consumer"?'

'It's not all "brittle glitz"; it's a damned hard business run by a network of highly qualified professional people – behind that very necessary glamorous exterior!' She was glad of the mild flush of anger which rose into her cheeks. 'People need advertising, need a whore of Babylon – just as you do.' She matched his stare for a moment, watched his lips move almost imperceptibly before he spoke.

'Doesn't say much for people, does it?' he replied mildly. 'You make yourself sound like advertising personified, which I don't really think I believe, arrogant and so confident in your assessment of what "Joe Public" thinks he needs to function in this neatly packaged world. And so you go on perpetually selling him the fragile dreams your truly amazing – and I do not jest – creative people conjure up.' He twirled his glass between his fingers for a moment. 'Why not be more honest? Isn't it big business for you and your company, lots of mega-bucks to help make this pretty little world of ours spin a little bit faster?'

'Don't you mean "shitty" little world?' God, she was

getting drunk, but it was somehow a relief to say it, to move away from talk of the world she normally lived and breathed, and she heard him chuckle, throaty and rich. For a few long weighted seconds they both fell silent, gazing into their glasses until she looked at him again.

'Where do you really come from?' she asked softly. There had been nothing in his carefully prepared biography to tell her; it had all been safely tailored so that no holes showed, no private patches of shame for the public to fall upon and ultimately devour.

His features were suddenly passive, without expression, as if he were reflecting on what he would say.

'You know that I am half German, my mother's half; you know that I was brought to England as a bawling three-month-old brat, and that I am and have been for the past, almost forty years, a British citizen.'

'And your father?'

'A good sort, so I was told, maybe English, maybe Austrian – my mother was never sure,' he said slowly, cynically. 'She was a lady of the night . . . another whore from Babylon. . . .'

'I'm sorry.'

'There's no need, I forgave her a long time ago.'

She felt she had said too much, probed too deeply, but when she raised her eyes again to his she saw that an engaging half-smile hovered on his mouth as if he had read her thoughts.

'And you?' he said slowly.

'My father died when I was seventeen. I loved him very much.' There was a long dreadful moment as the memory shook her again and she wished she had not drunk so much. 'My mother and I have never got along – we don't see each other very often.' Ever. Familiar guilt made her insides contract and she was that child again, desperate to please, desperate to win some love from the icy, awesome beauty that was her mother.

'I believe I have opened a wound – I think it must be my turn to apologize.' His voice was quiet, almost coaxing. She had expected her curiosity, her probings, to sting him;

she had not expected the reverse to happen, the tables to turn, yet they had and so easily, as if *he* had engineered the whole conversation and not she.

'There is no wound.' She replied too quickly and she wondered why she bothered to deny it.

Matthias stood up and she heard his chair scrape against the floor as he pushed it back.

'Parents always leave wounds,' he said easily, finally. He began to walk towards her. 'It's late and you must be tired.'

She rose from her seat and let him take her hand. He turned it palm upwards, cupped, and caressed the soft flesh with his mouth. It was, somehow, frighteningly suggestive and she swallowed slowly as he withdrew, straightened, and stared into her face.

'I think you will sleep well here – the air is heady, like opium.'

'I hope so,' and she slowly lifted her head. 'It seems to have been a long day.' There was a pounding in her ears as she met his brilliant, unblinking gaze.

'This house, this chateau or whatever you wish to call it, is not real, you know . . . ,' he continued, taking her arm and moving toward the doors. 'It's hardly more than a hundred years old.' His mouth pulled into a grin. 'It's someone's fantasy, someone's dream – a lavish folly of Greek, Gothic and Baroque, and so on and so on.' He gestured absently.

'It could be a nightmare,' she replied softly.

'Oh, no, never a nightmare, Francesca – never a nightmare.' His voice was as soft as hers now, but there was a finality that encouraged no further discourse, and she obeyed the silent command because that was what she wanted and because she had, ultimately and willingly, been seduced by his words.

A fire was burning in the grate of her room and someone had pulled the heavy brocade drapes across the windows. She crossed the room and pushed a fold of the material back so that she could look outside at the darkness, at the bald moon and the heavy outline of the blackened forest. She let the curtain fall back into place and moved to the open door of the bathroom. Francesca leaned her neck back and winced at the tension which had returned to grip the top of her spine like a vice. Automatically she walked towards the yellow marbled bath, let her fingers run along its thick, fat rim until they found the taps. Water poured in a deluge filling the room with steam and she moved back into the bedroom to remove her clothes. She wondered where he was, whether he had gone to his own room and his own bath. There had been something elusive, unfinished, in the way he had left her; but she would not go to him.

The water was almost too hot and she groaned softly, luxuriously as she lowered herself into it. For long minutes she just lay there as the tension and tiredness seeped slowly out of her limbs. The large fifties showerhead rose above her head like a halo and she stood up, switching it on, so that first hot and then gradually cold water sprang at her like a burst water main, cascading down in a thousand whipping drops on to her skin until she gasped in delighted shock. It was only as she turned to switch the torrent of water off that she heard his soft footfall as he came close to the marble steps at the foot of the bath. Immediately she saw his outline through the translucent shower glass and she stopped, panting softly, hearing her heart knock frantically against her ribcage. Their eyes locked as he paused, slowly, beneath her. He *was* golden, she thought, god-like, and it did not seem shocking or even surprising that he should be standing there, naked, before her. There was about him a physical opulence, a promise of unspoken, unspeakable, pleasure. His lips moved inexorably into a smile of thorough sensuality, and he brought one long, languid arm up towards her and slid a finger down from the creamy hollow in her neck, down, down to the soft fur at the apex of her thighs so that her belly jerked and she shivered.

'I'm wet. . . .' And her voice was almost a whisper, not like her own voice at all.

'But I want you wet. . . .' And he held his arms out to her.

Nothing in her seemed to be functioning, but there was a crazy voice in her head telling her that she would always remember this moment, this yellow marbled bath, this room, and his dangerous beautiful face and the arms reaching out to take her. She moved mechanically towards him. He was already erect, huge and stiff, and he lifted her easily down on to him so that they melted together in one swift shuddering movement. Her legs closed and grew around the golden torso as his arms came up to slide, grasping, across her back and then down to the smooth round curves of her buttocks to pull her closer into him. But then there was only his hot rhythmic breath against her face and his wanton, child-like mouth closing upon hers so that their tongues joined and the feverish thrusting of their coupling grew stronger and stronger making her cry out as the terrible pleasure built and built rising up and through all the layers until she opened her mouth to scream, 'Yes, oh yes . . . oh yes. . . .'

It had been a quiet, uneventful day; even Vic Brunning seemed conspicuous by his absence. Sian shrugged herself into her coat and then turned sharply as she heard the photo-copying machine hum into noisy action. Curiosity getting the better of her, she walked towards the tiny room which housed both the telex and the photo-copier. Geoff Buchanan was feeding paper into the machine with barely controlled impatience.

'Can I help?' But she didn't want to help, she wanted to go home.

'I expect you want to get home. . . .' It was more of a statement than a question.

'No, really,' she lied, 'if you're stuck I can hang on a few minutes.' She felt her heart sink knowing she was caught.

'That would be fantastic.' The relief in his face was almost comical, like a man grasping at straws. 'With Zoë being off sick I left the presentation with the temp – she typed it up all right, but I need at least ten copies for a 9 a.m. meeting tomorrow morning and it's an eighty-page document.' He sighed heavily as the machine ran out of paper. 'I did call personnel, of course, and they're getting back to me, but it's a bit late now. I thought you'd already left. . . .'

'Not quite.' She smiled with an effort, and then added, 'If you give me half I'll go down to the next floor – they have a much bigger machine and it won't take so long.'

'That's marvellous, I really do appreciate it.'

Her smile was warmer now in response because she realized he really meant it and she was touched by a twinge of guilt.

It took longer than she had anticipated and she began to feel a growing irritation. Her mother would wonder where she was. So far she had managed to be home in reasonable time, although she realized that Francesca had not yet got into her stride and late nights would probably become a necessity at some point, particularly with the merger coming up. Sian caught a breath which was not quite a sigh. Of course her parents loved Petie, doted on him, and were doing everything they could so that their daughter could start life afresh. But nevertheless her mother had to have Petie all day and usually Sian tried to get home for at least a few minutes with him before he was bathed and put to bed. His sleeping pattern was erratic at the moment and she had known him sometimes still be awake even at 10 p.m., but she was always there then. Life was beginning to form some sort of acceptable pattern at least, but it had all been a strain, a terrible strain, and Sian knew that her parents were deeply disappointed, deeply hurt. Except, of course, they would never say so. She sighed again, her eyes shifting accusingly to the papers in her hand; at the rate things were going she wouldn't be home until midnight. If Francesca had needed her to stay, that was one thing, she thought aggrievedly, but Geoff was not her boss even if he was one of the joint MDs.

When she returned to the office he was still there struggling to finish his half of the documents.

'I think you'd better give the remainder to me. It's getting rather late,' she said tautly.

'It's okay . . . ,' he said smoothly, carefully, sensing her irritation. 'I'm sure I can manage the rest.'

The guilt came again and she sighed inwardly.

'No, really, I'll be far quicker.'

He paused for a moment and she felt his scrutiny.

'If I let you finish these documents you will allow me, of course, to arrange a taxi to take you home – on the company, naturally.' The little speech was rounded off with a mocking smile and she could only respond in kind.

'Thanks – I really would appreciate that.' Her cheeks blushed pink with embarrassment knowing that he had sensed her resentment.

'Good,' he said easily and handed her the remainder of the documents with obvious relief. He watched her turn away and wondered whether it was just his demand on her time that had made her look so bruised, or perhaps there was something more meaningful troubling her and he was merely an added irritant. He shrugged softly. She seemed a nice girl, maybe a little too serious, but nice all the same. He could ask Francesca about her – *when* Francesca got back. He shrugged again; he was just as curious as Vic about their missing chairman's whereabouts, but managed to keep that curiosity under wraps, unlike Vic. Geoff moved away from the now silent grey machine and walked back into his office. There was the best part of a bottle of white wine nicely chilled in the small fridge of his drinks cabinet. He had opened it at lunchtime when he had heard of the Matthias success; strange of Francesca not to be around at the time of triumph. When he had spoken to her later in the day she had skilfully avoided being drawn on her movements and spoke in a tone that discouraged any further questions. He smiled slowly; they would all, no doubt, know soon enough.

Geoff was sitting thoughtfully in his office chair rolling a glass of wine between his hands when Sian returned.

'They're finished, collated and bound . . . ,' she said neutrally.

'Wonderful.' He poured wine into an empty glass. 'Drink some of this while I call reception and order you a car.'

The offending documents were put to one side and she sat down, glad of the glass of wine, glad that the responsibility and aggravation of getting home were being taken out of her hands.

'Ten minutes,' he said, putting the phone down.

'That's fine.' She felt herself visibly relax.

'I'm sorry if all this has messed up your evening – I had no idea it would take so long.'

'Really, it doesn't matter now.' She suddenly realized that that was true; it really didn't matter any longer.

'How are you liking Samuels?' Geoff asked easily.

'I think once I know my way around a little better, I shall probably like it very much,' Sian replied, 'and Francesca can make life seem very interesting . . . ,' she added, her mouth lifting into a smile.

'She certainly can . . . ,' he agreed. 'But what did you do before Samuels?'

'I worked at The Village. . . .' It was only half a lie.

'PR – Adam Gilmore's company?'

'Yes.' She could feel the right answers beginning to dry up in her mouth. Her eyes strayed to her watch.

'Were you doing the same sort of thing?' He saw the shadow momentarily flee across her face.

'I was an account exec for a while –,' she paused and then added quickly to staunch the inevitable question that would follow, '– it didn't work out.'

'Well, it happens . . . ,' he said smoothly, and he saw how her well-shaped fingers trembled as she reached for her glass. 'Part of life's rich tapestry . . . ,' he added and thought how inane that must sound.

'Part of life's rich tapestry,' she repeated in a remote voice and stood up. 'I'd better make my way down to reception; the car will probably be arriving at any moment.'

'Of course,' he said, but they both knew she had plenty of time. 'Well, thanks again. . . .' He followed her into the outer office and reached for her coat which was lying as she had abruptly left it, deserted across a desk. 'Allow me.' She was betrayed into a smile and he felt a sudden, inexplicable feeling of relief as if he had redeemed himself. Sian's arms slid smoothly into the coat and as she moved backwards to make the ritual a little easier he caught the lingering sweetness of her perfume, but she moved again and the sweetness was gone. He watched her walk to the lift and wished her a vague goodnight as she disappeared behind slick, smooth metal; and if someone had asked him why he did not immediately move, why his eyes remained on the cool closed doors after she had gone, he would not have been able to tell them.

The air *had* been heady like opium. Francesca drew a swift soft breath in remembrance and fastened her seat belt as the plane began its descent. Matthias had not disappointed her, he was like no one she had ever met; there had been something uneasy, something intangible in him that she had been unable to touch. Even at the height of passion he was controlled, in control, and she, somehow, his toy. She winced inwardly at her own description and turned to the window. Clouds embraced the plane, white-grey sullen shoals pouring over the wings and sweeping past windows. Last night had been his triumph, and she wondered whether he had planned it all from beginning to end, like the perfect showman. They had dined, incongruously, in the ballroom and she had laughed because it was an almost perfect replica of the one she had seen in Vienna's Schönbrunn with her father, except that Chateau de la Chênerie's version was rather smaller. As they had started on their cognac, music, his music, seeped from each corner of the ornate room and he had swept her towards gilded archways on the far side and into a hall of mirrors. He had stood behind her, his hands on her bare shoulders staring down the infinite corridor of images as if they were seeing innumerable choices of their own future. She remembered shivering momentarily as he undressed her and how they had made love with all the other endless images until the whole world had seemed one glorious, greedy reflection of desire. Francesca shook her head slowly and felt the jolt of wheels as the plane touched down; she leaned her head back and closed her eyes letting the memory slip away. For all its carefully contrived glory his finale in the ballroom could not compare with the beauty of siennese yellow marble.

She was not prepared for the flash of cameras once she had passed through customs, or the deluge of questions aimed at her like shots out of a gun. The press surrounded her in a small buzzing swarm and she swore softly.

'Miss Gaetini – where is Matthias now? Is he returning to London at a later date?'

'Miss Gaetini – when does the campaign officially start?'

'Miss Gaetini – how much will the campaign cost?'

'Miss Gaetini – where exactly was this chateau in which the meeting was held?'

Francesca swallowed deep in her throat. He must have known about this all the time – *he* was the only one who could know.

'If you would like to be at Samuels' offices at 9 a.m. tomorrow morning, gentlemen, I should be glad to answer all of your questions – right now I'm a little tired.' She flashed them a brilliant smile and started quickly towards the exit doors.

'I have a car waiting for you, Miss Gaetini.'

Francesca turned her head sharply in puzzlement.

'I'm Lucas Chant. Of course, we haven't met. . . .'

'Was this little circus your idea – or *his*?' she asked tersely.

'It's good for publicity,' he replied lamely.

'You still haven't answered my question, Mr Chant.'

'We usually discuss everything before implementation.' His voice was neutral.

'How very wise. Indeed, I'm rather surprised you need the services of the best advertising agency in the UK at all,' she said hotly.

'The car's over here . . . ,' his voice began to trail off as she rejected his arm and he saw her intent.

'Thank you all the same, Mr Chant, but I prefer to take a cab.' She smiled humourlessly and for the first time looked fully into the thin unappetizing face so in contrast with the man he served. Turning impatiently aside she moved towards the glistening blackness of a nearby cab. Even in her anger she just wanted to get away, and as soon as possible, before the hounds of the press could come any closer and discern that something might be wrong. As the cab moved off she breathed a heavy sigh of relief, but her hand clutched the leather handgrip too tightly as if she were fighting to control the angry disappointment whirling dangerously inside her.

Michael was curled up on the step when she opened the small latched gate of the cottage. Francesca felt a weary thickness gather in her throat as she stared down at her brother.

'Michael . . . ,' her voice sounded somehow distant in the gathering dusk, low and remote as if she were afraid to wake him and find out why he should be here, crouching in the shadow of her doorway like a waif. But immediately his head shot up and she smiled tentatively, and he returned her smile, almost innocent, as if for him everything was as it should be and there was nothing wrong with him half-sleeping on her cold marble step with darkness creeping up soft and thick. He allowed her to take his arm and she led him into the house as if he were a child. As the glare of the hall light fell unkindly across his face she wondered, sadly, how she had compared him with Matthias. Fire and water. And as memory pulled her back she realized with surprise that her anger had dissipated, that now there was only disillusionment and the knowledge of her own weakness. Matthias had seen all the advantages of their meeting before she had, had used those advantages; she had only used some of them, and all for herself because she had wanted it that way. Perhaps she was losing her touch. She smiled inwardly, derisively, at her attempt at self-deception. With searing clarity she recalled how his hands had skimmed so expertly, so possessively over her body, how her own had reached up to bury themselves in his white-blond hair. Even as she carefully shut out the vision something inside her rose rashly in eagerness and she wondered when she would see him again.

'Sorry about this . . . ,' Michael said gently, sheepishly, mistaking her abstraction for confusion.

'It's okay – really. I was miles away for a moment.' Her gaze shifted back to his face and she saw how tired he was. 'You will stay, won't you? There's plenty of room.'

'I sort of ran out of money . . . ,' he replied, avoiding her question.

'I'll give you some more, but in the morning when you've rested properly.' This time he would not get round her.

'I hadn't planned on that,' he said slowly, lowering his eyes so that he would not have to look into her face.

'I'd like to know what exactly is going on, except that somehow I don't think you're going to tell me . . . ,' she said quietly. 'Would you like a coffee, or maybe something stronger? Have you eaten?'

He shook his head negatively to all her questions and she felt impatience rising into her throat. Pressing it down she moved over to the drinks cabinet and poured two cognacs.

'Drink this. Maybe it will help loosen your tongue,' she said in an attempt at humour. Still he didn't reply. 'I told mother I would call her if I saw you again.' Baiting him, but almost true.

'I don't want you to do that,' he said at last. 'Isn't it perfectly clear that *I just want to be left alone!*' His voice rose, suddenly stinging her and she wanted to recoil, but there was quick resentment, too, at his anger.

'You just want to be left alone . . . well, that would be a hell of a lot easier, Michael, if you'd planned your little escape from mother's ivory tower with more care – asking me for money and more money is hardly achieving the result you say you want!'

'I'm sorry . . . sorry.' He shook his head desolately and immediately she regretted her impatience because there had been the old jealousy there too.

89

'She'll be very worried.' And she thought of Livia pacing the long low terrace overlooking the sea.

'I know, I know.' He lifted his head. 'I telephoned so that she wouldn't come – I couldn't have borne that.'

'Does she ever. . . .' Francesca's eyes slid away from her brother's, the question caught and held in her throat.

'No, Fran.'

The words had slipped out too easily and she felt her cheeks burn as he saw her hurt and at the use of the sudden heart-wrenching childish name he had always had for her. Of course Livia would never speak of her, why should she?

'She only thinks about me.' There was no arrogance in what he said, it was simply a statement of fact. 'There is no one else in her life except me – no real friends, no men – only acquaintances or business people.' He smiled sadly. 'And that's just the way she wants it.'

'I've always felt, somehow, that closeness – except with you, of course – was just not her style,' she said with an effort at humour.

'It's not even "closeness" with me – we hardly touch – it's more like a supreme possessiveness.' He let his eyes rest on her face. 'I don't believe that she likes men in the physical sense, if she likes them at all, of that I'm sure. And I think the thought of sex revolts her.'

'Poor mother,' she said without emotion and thought inevitably of her warm, affectionate father and wondered how she and Michael had ever been born.

'Poor me,' Michael replied and brought the snifter of cognac slowly to his lips. 'You know, I've never had a woman,' he said abruptly, and the words seemed to stay in the air for a long moment.

'You didn't have to tell me that,' she said softly.

'I know – but I just did, didn't I.' He closed his eyes, remembering, because he had almost had one, once. The young widow in Menton; she had tried to seduce him and he had almost let her. Indolent, melting Chantal. Her big strong body so ready, so easy. But his manhood had betrayed him even as her eager fingers had closed around

90

his hardness and everything had died. The memory made him cower and the glass in his hand suddenly seemed very cold.

'Look,' she crouched down beside him and saw how his lips trembled, saw how the lank fair hair, too long, hung over the high forehead obliterating his face, 'you can stay here as long as you like, I don't mind in the least; I'm not really here that much so you'd have the place almost to yourself.' He did not reply and she felt the words die in her throat as she paused, helplessly, beside him. 'I wish you'd let me help you, Michael,' she said, finally, almost to herself.

In the morning she did not disturb him, letting him sleep. But for a long moment she stood in the partially open doorway watching him; his body was curled up, foetal-like, with one arm thrown across his face, and she thought of their mother and what she had brought him to. She thought of the past as unhappy, unbidden memories came back in a flood and she was that same bewildered child again, neither accepted nor accepting. She thought bitterly of the thousand times through those thousands of days how she had wished and prayed her hair could be blonde – a beautiful silvery sheet of blonde. Like Mummy and Michael. As if changing her black curls to gold would have made her easier to love; would have made Livia love her.

Vic was in a good mood; he had finally cajoled a potential client to go salmon fishing and looked forward to a thoroughly self-indulgent and, in all probability, a rewarding weekend; although, of course, James Barra-clough could hardly be termed a walkover. But Barraclough whisky was not the name it used to be; it had fallen well down the tables in the whisky stakes. James Junior was supposed to be carrying the family flag and if he didn't do something pretty quickly, Barraclough's might find themselves falling off the edge of the world. At least, Vic thought easily, time is on our side and no self-respecting Scot could resist the sort of weekend he had in mind on the Tweed. The salmon would be at their peak and he'd even managed to rent the Duke of Roxburghe's stretch. At £2.5 grand for the two days, it wouldn't be a bad investment for the company if all went well; he'd have young James eating out of his hands in no time. Vic smiled to himself and reached for the morning papers – and hadn't he heard that Barraclough had a bit of a thing for busty blondes? Maybe he could find an excuse for Zoë to come along too, only as his personal assistant, naturally. . . .

'Christ!' his voice flashed, as his eyes came to rest on the front page. The newspaper shook noisily in his hands and he brought it closer to his face as if, somehow, he would find himself mistaken; but there was no mistake. Francesca's lovely face laughed at him from the front page of the *Mirror* – 'Matthias names rising ad star as confidante in campaign. . . .' There were similar lines in the *Sun*, the *Express* and the *Mail*, not quite so explosive, but still prominent enough to make him cringe, and all with variations of the same, sickening photograph. He didn't need any explanations on where she had spent the past two days now, it was all perfectly clear. What a cool, conniving bitch. He gritted his teeth, only too aware of how Henry would react to this smart bit of publicity, because it *was* smart, he had to admit. Vic winced as he remembered the telephone conversation he had had with him, how he had attempted to make Francesca seem wanting, irresponsible even – now it would be his turn to seem wanting, and not only wanting, but ridiculous, because he hadn't had a clue what was going on.

'Vic. . . .'

He looked up sharply and was startled to see her standing in the doorway of his office.

'If you've nothing else that's immediate – and I think this should take priority – I'd like you to take over the little press reception I've arranged in the large conference room. . . .' She walked towards him and his eyes were drawn automatically to the roundness of her hips as they moved beneath a silk sheath of peach and black, but then she caught his gaze and he felt a blush creep up from his neck as if she had seen all too clearly what was going through his mind.

'Press reception . . . ?' he asked, puzzled. 'I thought you'd already had one.' Vic shoved the morning papers towards her.

'That was – shall we say – rather too spontaneous for my liking,' Francesca replied easily. 'It made a good shot, certainly, but naturally more details would be appropriate.' She smiled thinly into Vic's upturned face. 'I've given them some information on the meetings with Matthias, now it only needs you to enlarge on the campaign and how we see it developing.'

'I see. . . .' He was hard put to keep the sarcasm out of his voice, hard put to keep an angry sneer from settling on his face. What the hell did she mean by 'meetings with Matthias'? There had only been one as far as he was concerned and she knew it. Now he was supposed to go along with her little scheme of things like a good boy because it suited her to tell him only half the story. He writhed inwardly, cursing Henry once again for his betrayal.

'Okay – fine,' he replied smoothly, pushing the bitterness down; to refuse would not only look churlish, but it would be stupid too, and there would be time enough later to pin her down on her little magical mystery tour. Right now he needed to be seen to be in on this account, and a press conference could go some way to restoring his bruised ego *and* his credibility with Henry. Vic stood up and straightened his tie, suddenly realizing that there could be a photograph in this – it had been a while since he had graced the gilded pages of *Campaign*. . . .

'How are you feeling?' Sian asked as Zoë walked past her desk with a flourish. She looked exceedingly pretty. Maybe the black leather mini skirt was a bit much, but the large blue eyes framed by her rosy autumn skin and mop of blonde curls gave her an air of innocence even so and Sian felt somehow reduced by such a vision; it was, after all, not much after 9 a.m. It didn't seem fair, but Zoë wasn't the sort of girl Sian could resent, she was too gullible, too vague to be aware of life's unremitting potential for complexity or pain.

'Much better thanks,' she replied, smiling broadly. 'It was only an infected wisdom tooth, but really painful while it lasted – a good dose of antibiotics and it's almost cleared up.' Her eyes scanned her desk which was uncharacteristically tidy. 'How was the temp?'

'Fine,' Sian responded. 'Almost too efficient for my liking, except that she was the only temp I've ever come across who didn't seem to like the idea of working late!'

'Was she attractive?' Zoë asked quietly, switching to the subject which mattered to her most.

'Attractive?' Sian repeated. 'Not particularly. Why?' She stared curiously into Zoë's expressionless face and wondered why it should matter so much.

'Oh, nothing really, I just wondered . . . ,' she replied, lowering her eyes as if Sian might see there the real reason for her question. 'Well,' she continued uneasily, sensing that some explanation was called for, 'it's just that Vic had a temp once who was rather unattractive, at least so I was told, and he doesn't think it's good for the image. . . .' She finished weakly.

'His – or the company's?' Sian asked tersely, suddenly annoyed.

'Oh, come on, Sian –,' Zoë said in an attempt at humour, ' – you know what men can be like sometimes, and there's nothing wrong in preferring to work with people who you find more pleasing than others, is there?'

'I suppose not,' Sian conceded begrudgingly. 'But what are these "others" expected to do – go around with buckets over their heads or commit hari-kari to save us the inconvenience of having them disrupt our aesthetically perfect little world?' She sighed inwardly knowing she had said too much and that probably Zoë had no idea why her apparently innocent remark should have irritated her so much. 'Oh, never mind, Zoë, it doesn't really matter,' she said finally.

'But don't you like working with people who are, at least, physically attractive?' Zoë persisted.

'I suppose so,' she replied with barely concealed impatience and began reaching for the morning mail which lay in a ragged heap beside her desk, 'I've never really thought about it.' But she wondered uneasily if Adam had been less attractive whether she would have allowed herself to be so easily dazzled by him.

'Well, I never would have taken this job with Samuels if I hadn't found Vic so attractive,' Zoë said resolutely.

Sian caught a sharp breath and shifted her gaze from the envelope in her hand to Zoë's blank, pretty face and wondered how it was that they even came to speak the same language, but there was something so serious in the tone of Zoë's idiotic words that somehow she found herself smiling despite herself.

'But he is sort of "sexy", don't you think?' Zoë continued, as if in need of reassurance.

'I've never really thought about that either,' Sian replied dismissively, unable to equate the coarse, large-lipped, loud-mouthed MD with the word 'sexy'. She shook her head gently, almost in disbelief; it certainly takes all kinds to make a world, but perhaps these days, she thought wryly, she wasn't really in a position to judge. But as the sullen vision of Vic slipped from her mind it was effortlessly replaced by that of Adam and she wondered how he was, what he was doing and if he often thought about her. And she cursed herself for being such a fool.

It was one of those bloody days. Caroline clamped her lips tightly shut as another lacerating gust of wind tore at her skirts and whipped back her hair. The train had not only been late, but had also not completed its usual journey and she had been forced to get out a stop too soon which meant a long, tedious walk up Tottenham Court Road. It *would* be today of all days that Fate should make her late; in his infinite wisdom Ben Langley had decided that she should attend a client meeting with him in Croydon. Generally she enjoyed client meetings because nine times out of ten they were interesting, even stimulating, but Chetwood Cheeses, the chairman Humphrey Sullivan, Ben Langley and Croydon were not in any way stimulating. The account was steady but dull, as was Sullivan; Langley made her nervous, and Croydon was, well, just Croydon; and the meeting was planned to go into lunch, so the whole day would be gone. She sighed heavily and pulled her coat more tightly around her as Samuels loomed up, and she had the sudden desire to turn and run, but even as the thought took shape she knew she was too much of a coward. The lifts were just closing as she stepped through the doors, but someone had seen her and held it so that at the last moment Caroline squeezed in with more late-comers. It was only as the metal doors closed behind her that she realized with a hollow sinking feeling that Nick was pressed into one corner and it was too late to pretend that she had not seen him. Not now – not when she was such a mess with her hair dragged and pulled by the wind and her eyes stinging from its ferocity. She closed her eyes briefly in relief as she realized that he must get out at least three floors before her. She felt her mouth go dry as his floor approached. But he did not make a move to get out, and each time as the lift halted with painful slowness she expected him to leave, but he remained quietly, almost patiently, in the corner and as the fifth floor drew level she knew instinctively that he would get out with her. Even as the doors opened and she moved out, she slowed her pace and felt his hand tentatively touch her arm as other people filed passed her.

'Caroline. . . ?'

She turned slowly, her head lowered so that she would not immediately meet his eyes.

'I just wanted . . . ,' she heard the sharp intake of his breath, '. . . well, I wanted to say sorry about last week.'

'It's okay, really,' she stammered too quickly as the memory came flooding painfully back and she recalled the agonizing moment only a day later when she had seen Vic Brunning in reception and had literally run back up the stairs to escape his eyes. He had probably not even seen her.

'I was drunk,' he lied, and her gaze was pulled finally to his face and rested there. She wondered whether he realized how finely his thin ascetic face was made, how it was firmed and made strong by the squaring of his jaw, how well the lips were shaped, how long his dark lashes were, which had brushed her face and skin as he held her so expertly against the wall. She could hardly believe that he had nearly seduced her in classic advertising fashion; wondered why he had bothered to try.

'It's okay,' she repeated, for want of something better to say. As always he seemed to paralyse her initiative. There was a pause then, long and awkward, until she said, 'I have to go, I'm late.'

She began to move away, but his voice followed her.

'Are you going to The Birthday Party?'

She turned sharply, for a moment unable to comprehend.

'The Birthday Party?'

'You must have had a memo – Henry Samuels' birthday, the social event of the year . . . ,' he said sarcastically.

'Oh, yes – I'd forgotten,' she replied vaguely.

He briefly studied her puzzled face and wondered why he was making such an uncharacteristic effort, she was obviously not interested.

'Maybe I'll see you there,' he said finally, impatiently.

Her smile was tentative in response and he watched her turn and go, longing, all at once, to take her by the shoulders and shake her. But instead he shrugged resignedly and his hand reached out to press the button for the lift.

Caroline walked slowly along the corridor. She didn't really care, somehow, that she was late now; Ben would rant and rave anyway. But she cast any thoughts of him aside to concentrate on what had just happened. Was Nick really asking her if she intended to go to the party? She had forgotten about it, or rather dismissed it from her mind, because normally she didn't go. It was a strictly Samuels' affair and no wives, husbands, girlfriends or boyfriends outside the company were allowed to attend; Guy had grunted his usual disapproval when she had half-heartedly mentioned it. Caroline smiled inwardly, suddenly feeling an eager and unaccustomed surge of rebellion as she thought of the coming party. It has been two years since she had attended her first one and from what she could gather from the gossip each one that had followed easily superceded any that had gone before. The Samuels Birthday Party was becoming almost legendary. Guy wouldn't like it if she were to go, but perhaps, after all, she wouldn't tell him. And as she reached her office she realized all at once and with some surprise that she had already made up her mind. When she slowly pushed open the door there was only the monotonous sound of a typewriter and the clatter of the telex machine as she stood tentatively on the threshold, but Ben's voice was conspicuously absent and for one wonderful, fleeting moment Caroline dared hope that he had decided to go without her.

'I brought the meeting forward,' Geoff said slowly. 'I know we said the end of next month, but Rock and Sanchez are doing a round trip to the Far East and then Europe and I didn't like the smell of it, so I pressed them – not too hard – for a date before they left.'

'I presume you mean they may be looking for offers?' Francesca replied.

'Something like that,' he said evenly. 'I know it means that they could try and sting us, but it was a chance I thought worth the risk.' He paused for a moment knowing that she was waiting for him to go on. 'They need us, Francesca – just as much as we want them.'

'I'm glad you said "want" rather than "need"; it makes us sound less, shall we say, vulnerable . . . ,' she added sarcastically.

'Okay, okay.' He sighed inwardly, she was obviously not in the most cooperative of moods. 'They are stagnating, they need strengthening, they need new blood, they need our high profile to offset their own and they know as well as we do that by merging with us, more than any other UK shop, conflicts will be minimal.'

'When do we go?' she asked and her lips moved into a slow smile.

'The end of next week,' Geoff replied, with a sigh of relief.

'Do you want to make the travel arrangements, or shall I?' she asked, reaching towards the telephone.

'I've already booked the flights and made appropriate hotel reservations,' he said quickly and chuckled sheepishly as she returned her hand to the desk top, raising one cynical, surprised eyebrow in response.

'Are you sure you really need me, Geoff?' she asked, as her smile turned into a broad grin.

'I wouldn't dream of going without you,' he replied seriously and then added, 'I've booked the Mayfair Regent, but if you have any objections. . . .'

'No, no – the Mayfair will be fine. I take it we'll be staying the weekend?'

'Well, I thought it might be a good idea; at the moment we don't really know what we're dealing with and it may give us more opportunity to get to know our future colleagues.'

'Don't speak too soon, Geoff. I have the feeling that Sanchez may be the one to put a spoke in the works if anyone does, so let's wait before tempting Fate.' But she was pleased, glad that things were moving so fast. If they'd caught them after their world trip no doubt Dunmar-Rock could still find an excuse for driving a hard bargain, maybe a harder one, particularly as they would have ensured visits to other European networks in their schedule. It was all in the game.

'Can you let me have the draft figures, full client list, etcetera, etcetera, by the beginning of next week?'

'Sure – I might even manage it by the weekend if we're lucky,' Geoff replied easily and then started to move out of his chair, but she gestured to him to remain sitting.

'Has Vic sorted out the problem with General Breweries? She recalled Vic's pale face as she had stood in the doorway of his office only two hours before. He had looked as if someone had just severed his vitals and she supposed with a thin sinking feeling that it was because she had apparently taken over his account *and* beaten him to the front page of the national dailies. She sighed wearily knowing that he would try and make her life more difficult because of it. The irony of the situation was that she had known as little about Matthias' plans as Vic had, and that still stung, but it was a sting she realized she could live with – provided he didn't do it again, and provided that he didn't think he could use her so easily – again.

'You'll be pleased to know that he solved it in just the way we discussed,' Geoff said laughing, and Matthias' blond face slid slowly out of her mind.

'Great. That's what I wanted to hear. Where has he decided to put Weinberg?' she asked, but it didn't really matter in the short term.

'Egypt.'

'Christ!' And she laughed.

'I think Vic decided the further away the better. Besides, I understand Mike has never been to the Middle East and, in any event, he might even discover that he misses his wife. Amazing what a bit of distance can do.' He was smiling, but Francesca saw a vague shadow fall briefly across his face.

'You're married, aren't you, Geoff?' she asked.

'Separated,' he replied, letting his eyes rest on her face. '*My* wife found distances amazing too; she found someone else to fill in the gaps – couldn't stand the advertising world.'

'Sorry. I didn't mean to put my foot in it.'

'It's okay – seems a long time ago now, anyway.' But, God, it still hurt. And he stood up to go, suddenly tired. He looked at his watch and groaned under his breath; it was only just 11 a.m., maybe it was the dreaded lurgey of middle-age creeping up. Sometimes he felt about ninety as he walked through the agency; it seemed full of kids – bright, witty, attractive kids with their whole lives ahead of them, all dazzled by the glamorous gleam of advertising. Like moths around a flame.

He was gone. Francesca walked slowly, inevitably around the empty house. There was a note standing neatly against the oval mirror in the study – he could not stay; he needed time to himself . . . to find out who he was. She sighed heavily and gazed into the mirror.

'Bullshit, Michael, garbage,' she cursed softly. 'You've run away from mother and now you've run away from me.'

Suddenly she felt let down, rejected, used. He had had it all and she had had to fight every inch of the way. Did it ever occur to him that she might have need of him – that she might have wanted him to stay just for herself? A humourless smile tipped the edges of her mouth as she thought of the foolish plans she had allowed her mind to conjure up. There could have been a job for him at Samuels – she could have made one, slipped him in somewhere. He could have stayed with her until he'd sorted himself out, and then mother would eventually have come and there would have been a reconciliation, with Michael at least, and maybe a door would have been opened, just a fraction, for her. Maybe it could have worked. But it hadn't begun to work, and it wouldn't work. Ever. They always managed to burn her someway, somehow, in the end, and she still hadn't learned.

The phone rang sharply and she was jolted out of her thoughts. Even as she approached the telephone she wondered if it would be Livia. The doting mother looking for her lost and wayward son. Sometimes over the years she had wanted to scream, 'What about me? What about me?' But she never had and she supposed she never would.

It was Matthias.

'I thought you might want an apology.'

'Only if you want to give one,' she replied smoothly, but she was glad, so glad he had called; glad that he had pushed the spectre of her mother away, glad that his voice had the power to do so. She smiled to herself because his

101

voice had that quality of saying nothing and everything, disturbingly intrusive – intimate, taking her back, so that she would remember.

'Can I see you?'

'Is this another piece of the Matthias publicity machine at work . . . ?' she asked sarcastically.

'It wasn't like that.'

'What was it like?' Her voice was controlled, cool.

'It was beautiful, Francesca.'

She drew a sharp, quick breath and swallowed deep in her throat. He was good, very good, even the quickening of her pulse told her that. She wondered if he realized just how good he was, but she was sure that he knew.

'I'm preparing for an important trip to the States at the end of next week,' she said carefully.

'I didn't mean next week – I meant tonight.'

She laughed. 'I thought you were supposed to be in Paris over the next few weeks.'

'Paris can wait for a few days.'

'Can *you* wait – at least until tomorrow night?' She was tired and, as much as she wanted him, she would not jump when he called.

'That might not be possible.'

'That's a pity,' she said evenly.

'But they do say that anything's possible. . . .'

'Yes, they do.'

'Tomorrow night. So be it,' he said finally and she knew that it had cost him.

# 4

'We want you to go.'

'I don't know – I really haven't given it a lot of thought,' Sian replied evasively.

'Why, if you hadn't given it a lot of thought, did you even bother to mention it?' Her mother stood over her, a small smile touching her lips. 'Sian, you haven't had a proper night out in months and if you want to go to the Samuels Birthday Party, then you shall.'

'It all seems such a lot of bother . . . ,' Sian answered finally, turning her gaze from the fire to her mother's face.

'Hardly . . . ,' her mother persisted. 'Your father and I will be here to look after Petie – our social calendar isn't exactly over-booked for the next few weeks.' She laughed softly.

'Exactly,' Sian responded in exasperation.

With a sharp sigh her mother sat down beside her.

'Do you think this sort of attitude helps? Do you think it helps Petie, or us for that matter, if you stay home night after night because you feel some sort of irrational guilt if you treat yourself to a good night out?' She paused for a moment before continuing. 'You have to start living properly again – you can't go on blaming yourself forever for what's happened. . . . I want to see you happy again, really happy. I know it won't be like before, perhaps, but you've got to give it a try.'

'Everything's so . . . different now,' Sian said softly and she felt the maddening prickle of tears filter slowly into her eyes.

'I know, I know – but it won't seem different forever.' And her hand reached up to push the thick honey hair back from her daughter's face just as she had always done, reached across the adult shoulders to take the child that was still there into her arms.

Vic walked across the room and Francesca drew an impatient breath knowing that he intended to discuss more than the Matthias report. She thought with amusement that there was something vaguely predatory in the way he approached her desk and she wondered if he was aware of it and whether it was aimed at her or the chairmanship. She suppressed a smile as he pulled out a chair.

'Glad to find you at your desk,' he said sarcastically.

'Duty called, I'm afraid, Vic,' she parried.

'You could have let me know about the Paris meeting with Matthias.' He spoke sulkily and she sighed inwardly.

'I didn't know anything about it until Friday evening and even then didn't actually decide to go until late Saturday.' Her voice was tight as she reached across the desk for the report.

'You still could have let me know – I could have come with you. . . .'

'He didn't ask you, Vic – he asked me – it's as simple as that,' she responded sharply. 'Now let's forget it, shall we? We've got a lot of work to do on this account and the sooner it's all agreed and put under way the better.'

He swallowed hard, bitterly, watching each movement of her head as she glanced over the first page of his dutiful comments on the campaign. His campaign.

'This all seems fine – I didn't really think there would be much that we wouldn't agree on,' she said, looking up.

'Good,' he replied and wondered why he didn't choke on the word.

'Have you already decided on the account team?' She spoke agreeably, but knowing it was useless. Vic's resentment seemed to lie thickly in the air and there was nothing she could do about it.

'You'll find the names listed at the back . . . ,' he said dryly. 'I thought Pete Morgan could handle the day-to-day running – get the satellite link-up off the ground, contact the artists, arrange the television and radio interviews. He'll keep me posted at every stage, obviously.'

'Could you refresh me on what he has done before?'

'I thought you'd been given all the information on the key Samuels people?' he asked derisively, glad to find her wanting.

'Even *I* have my limits, Vic,' she replied impatiently. 'Perhaps you'd be good enough to tell me.'

'Pete was the account director for the launch of *Glitz* magazine early last year – it was a brilliant campaign. He's also done some work for the Film Council and did most of the organization and direction on the UK tour of that Latin American priest, José Parenté, a couple of years ago – could have parallels.'

'What's he doing at the moment?'

He sighed dramatically before continuing, '"US Fashion in Britain" and a series of press ads for *Tatler*'s international innovation.'

'Sounds like our man.'

'Unless you have a better idea,' he said resentfully.

'I'll leave it up to you then,' she replied, ignoring his remark. 'Let's say we'll have an account group meeting in a week's time, or just after Geoff and I come back from the States, to see how the campaign is getting off the ground.'

'I didn't know you and Geoff were going to the States – I thought that was next month.' He sounded aggrieved.

'You would have known soon enough, Vic. I'm surprised Geoff hasn't told you already,' she said wearily and paused for a moment before adding, 'It's the merger, we've had to bring the meeting with Dunmar-Rock forward.' She stood up and handed him the file on Matthias; it was a gesture of dismissal.

'Thanks,' he said slowly. For nothing. As he walked out of her office he had the distinct impression that he was being elbowed aside. Geoff was making a nice cosy little nest for himself, so it would seem, and she was busy taking over his prize campaign. It had been a long time since he had felt uneasy; up until now he had had everything his own way, practically Samuels' top dog, practically the golden boy. Not now, not since Henry had gone haywire and appointed a woman over his head.

*

'Are you coming to lunch?' Sian asked as she watched Zoë looking desperately across her desk. 'What's the matter?'

'I can't find a pen.'

'Here, borrow this.' Sian walked across to her with the proffered pen. 'Why do you need it now, it's gone one o'clock?'

'Vic wants to do some dictation,' she said lamely, noting the disapproval in Sian's eyes.

'Doesn't he know what time it is?' she replied angrily.

'It won't take long – and I really don't mind – honestly.'

'Oh, Zoë . . . ,' she said in exasperation, knowing that it would be useless to argue. 'Do you want me to bring you some sandwiches?'

'Yes – anything will do. Thanks.' And she waited until Sian had slipped on her coat and disappeared into the lift. The sixth floor was thick with quiet now, as she expected it to be, and she sighed with relief. Sometimes, but only sometimes, she allowed herself to think what would happen if they were found out – if someone came into the office . . . but Vic always had an answer for everything, she thought comfortingly, and, anyway, didn't she love him and didn't that mean she would do anything for him? He needed her. She supposed it was as simple as that.

He was leaning against his desk as she walked into the room and he was angry, she could feel it. For a long moment he stared at her, then he leaned across and took the pen and pad wordlessly from her hands. He turned her around so that he would not see her face. Their sex was dry, arid, unforgiving, but he drove into her again and again until he was empty.

It had all been arranged very discreetly. The management of Le Suquet had even planned for Matthias to take an unused side door to the alcove table he had chosen for their meeting. She had dressed with consummate skill and as she moved through the tables of diners Francesca knew by the eyes that followed her that she had indeed succeeded. Scarlet silk. It had always suited her and now she wanted

106

it to work for her again, because she wanted to draw some of the light away from Matthias, wanted to bathe in her own light, not in a reflection of his. She wanted him to want her. More than anything else.

'You look wonderful.' His voice was soft, silky.

'Thanks,' she replied easily, but there was a thickness in her throat as she sat down and his face suddenly seemed so close. He had, she thought, the sort of smile that is completely irresistible, and she had resisted many.

'There can be seclusion – even in a public place – if one is careful . . . ,' he said gently. '. . . You don't mind?'

'Not at all.' But then she smiled. 'Provided the press aren't suddenly going to appear from out of the wood-work.'

'Ah, . . . my little surprise at the airport.' He poured wine slowly into her glass. 'A miscalculation and I take full responsibility – but I did apologize,' he paused again, '– and it was worth it to see you in all your glory on the front page of the national dailies.' He lifted his eyes to her face. 'Am I forgiven?'

She watched him for a long second. So sleek, so smooth, like a magnificent wild cat. There was that soft half-smile again and she thought how easy it would be to trust him, implicitly.

'Until the next time. . . .'

'Touché.' And he laughed.

'I think I was a little abrupt with your Mr Chant,' she said. 'After all, it wasn't really his fault.'

'He did mention something to that effect. But he's had worse and Lucas is nothing if not a survivor.'

'He seems so . . . fragile, somehow,' she remarked.

'Not what you were expecting?'

'No. I imagined a too clever whizz-kid or a laid-back Bohemian type – sure of himself, but Lucas is almost waif-like.'

'A lost, lonely waif . . . and I found him.' He smiled and brought a glass to his lips. 'But he's good, and I can trust him.'

'Do you want to talk about the campaign?'

'Not now . . . later . . . next week.' He laughed again and handed her a menu. 'I am tired of the campaign – and sitting here with you in this little bubble I have created is a luxury which I want to enjoy for as long as I can.' His face seemed to lose its animation, its glow, for an instant, but then he smiled and the shadow was gone. 'Let's eat. And I suggest we share an enormous platter of sea food. It's excellent here – sometimes I can close my eyes and imagine I'm sitting in a restaurant on the harbour at St Malo . . . sometimes I think I can even smell the sea.' And he smiled with a trace of sadness.

'Do you come here very much?' She was curious now.

'Not enough; there's never enough time,' he said. 'I usually ask them to bring it to me at my home.' He turned his face to the window and Francesca followed his gaze to the street outside, heard him murmur again, 'Never enough time.' There was a long pause before he shifted his eyes to her own and for a split second their gazes locked and they were both very still, remembering.

'Chateau de la Chênerie seems very far away,' she said quietly.

'Too far . . . like a dream . . . my Chateau of the Oaks,' he said wistfully. As if it would never come again.

Her eyes swept over his face as he looked away from her, finally settling on the half-tilted unhappy mouth that reminded her so much of a thwarted beautiful child. But then he was staring back at her as if he had sensed her thoughts and there was no trace of that child she had seen in the man who watched her with such deliberate longing.

'Shall I ask them to bring St Malo to my home again?' His fingers stretched across the small chasm of the table to touch hers and she realized quite suddenly what it was to feel a jolt of human electricity pass between two people.

She shuddered for a moment as he tightened his hold around her fingers.

'It's already been decided really, hasn't it?'

'Shall we go then. . . .' He slowly released her hand and stood up as if she hadn't spoken and for a moment watched her beneath half-closed lids. 'Unless you want to change your mind?'

'No, I don't want to change my mind,' she replied expressionlessly, too aware that once again the situation had gone beyond her control; knowing that he knew she wouldn't resist. But she pressed any doubts down as they walked into the darkened streets to the waiting car because there was little point in pretending. It was too late for that, her own body told her as much; there was only this dizzying, crushing need. She wanted him too much, more than she had ever wanted anyone. And the knowledge frightened her, because she knew instinctively that Matthias had never really needed anyone in his whole life.

Aidan looked aimlessly around at the white roughened walls and the dusty chianti bottles which dangled wearily at intervals from ropes of plastic vine leaves. On two long horizontal walls someone had painted lurid Mediterranean seascapes, but the sea was too green and the sky too blue. He sighed, realizing that Brunning was obviously not planning to be over-generous on this lunch, and neither, it seemed, was he planning to be punctual. Aidan closed his hand around the plump bowl of the wine bottle and let his eyes slip once again to the open doorway. He had almost cancelled their meeting at the last moment, but then he recalled the repeated humiliations at trying to call her and his resolve came back with renewed strength. Francesca had changed her direct line number at Samuels and if he tried to come through the normal channels her bloody secretary always said she wasn't available. He felt foolish now for not insisting on having her number at home whilst things had still been going nicely. It was ex-directory of course, but she had managed neatly to avoid the issue each time he had brought it up and with hindsight he realized that she must have seen how their relationship would end all along. She was a smart bitch, that was true enough, and that was one of the reasons why he had been attracted to her in the first place, that and, of course, her goddamn beautiful face. But she had used him and then cast him aside because that usefulness had been over. Everyone knew in the agency, everyone – as she would have known that they would if she'd bothered to stop and think about it for just one moment of her precious time. Aidan winced inwardly, still not used to rejection, still not used to losing. His ego had been badly bruised, wounded, and as if intent on turning a knife in the wound he allowed the image of her lovely laughing face to taunt him again from the pages of the national dailies. He had been suspicious immediately once the shock had worn off, and all his suspicions had paid off when Fate had at last been kind and allowed him the opportunity of seeing her leave that restaurant in Draycott Avenue with the 'Golden God' himself – oh, *so* discreetly, but it was difficult to be discreet in one of the most fashionable parts of London. They were screwing, that was for sure. He felt it, he knew it – how could two of the 'beautiful people' resist each other? And hadn't he known Francesca long enough? There was no one else as far as he had been able to tell, and for all her damned ambition she was a woman and the sort of woman who needed a man around somewhere . . . he knew that only too well. Even as he tried to push the memory away a furtive picture of her naked body slid into his mindscape and there was that slow aching in his loins. She could always do that to him. He closed his eyes for a moment as if to shut out the vision and then smiled humourlessly, his hand reaching mechanically for the dying glass of wine. He thought of Brunning, and wondered whether the advertising grapevine had done its usual work and he already knew about his new chairwoman's little rendezvous and the possible implications. But somehow Aidan doubted it. This was a nice juicy little number, hot off the press, which had fallen right into his lap. It was a bit of a long shot and he'd have to choose his words very, very carefully, but the information might prove useful, particularly as he'd also managed to glean from the grapevine that Vic felt distinctly put out by their new chairwoman . . . nothing ventured, nothing gained. And if necessary he would prove it, he wasn't quite sure how, but he would think of something. Maybe Francesca had over-stepped the mark at last. Of course there was nothing wrong with screwing, even a client, but Samuels' new ad star and the glorious apparently stainless Matthias? Wasn't that just a little bit unprofessional? Aidan poured himself another glass of the thick red wine and practised patience.

The weather had stayed fine for the weekend as she'd hoped, but Francesca felt a chill in the air which spoke of the coming winter. It was quiet, even for a Sunday, but it was supposed to be quiet that she needed in order to pore over the Dunmar-Rock file. Well, most of her research was done now and the autumn sun in the garden had pulled her away from her desk and, with an inevitability that unsettled her more than she cared to admit, her thoughts came back to Matthias. She shook her head wryly, wondering at herself for being so easily drawn into his web, because whichever way she looked at it somehow that's exactly how it seemed. The spider and the fly. He fascinated her, had done from the very beginning, but instinctively she knew that he had deliberately set out to seduce her and had succeeded only too well. Francesca swallowed slowly, let her hand trail across the sureness of a low brick wall.

Seduction and the new Matthias were not supposed to go together, as she had teased him the other night, but he had merely replied, 'Seduce means "lead astray", or "tempt into sin" . . . doesn't it?' She remembered then how his hand had drifted idly to her breasts before he continued, 'But I haven't led you astray or made you sin . . . what we do, we do because we wish, because we want, because we need each other.' He had smiled that slow easy smile and added finally, 'I have never said that I am God, or some sort of holy prophet . . . I'm only mere mortal man, and live and love in the way that I see fit.'

He had silenced any more questions with his hot open mouth, overcoming her, obliterating any more thoughts, but she was still left with a dull, nagging feeling of unease as if he had evaded her once again. A cloud passed over the

111

sun and suddenly the garden was cast in shadow and she shivered. As she turned to go back into the house the telephone rang angrily, snapping her out of her reverie.

'Francesca,' – it was her mother's voice – 'I have to know where Michael is.'

'I don't know where he is, mother.' It was true, but she knew from the tone of her mother's voice that she didn't believe her. She was a child again as if her mother had just waved a magic wand, and the unhappy effect never ceased to amaze her.

'I have never liked games, Francesca, and I don't intend to start now.' She paused. 'Please tell me where he is.'

She felt the familiar spot in her neck begin to ache with tension. 'He stayed with me one night at the beginning of the week and left the next morning. He left me a note, but didn't tell me where he was going.'

'I know he wouldn't do that.' There was that old familiar sharp edge to her mother's words; it had always been saved for her and Francesca felt the vague saving-grace of anger.

'Well, he did this time.'

The words seemed to hang in the air until Livia finally broke the awkward silence.

'I still find that hard to believe,' she persisted. It was like old times.

'He said he'd phoned you and told you he wanted to be on his own for a while.'

'This is all so ridiculous . . . ,' she said, not wanting to listen, casting Francesca's words aside. 'He's ill; I want him to see a doctor.'

But *you* want him, isn't that it?

'I think it's better if he's left alone for the time being.' Was she really so blind?

'I didn't ask for your opinion, Francesca.' Livia's short sharp reprimand.

'It might surprise you, mother, but I care about Michael too – he is my brother after all.'

The silence was palpable then and slowly Francesca looked down at her hand holding the telephone; the knuckle was white with tension and she wondered why she allowed herself to be reduced to this. Her mother had been the only one ever to do it.

'Just tell him to call me.' No goodbye, only the cool sound of a click as she replaced the receiver. Livia had terminated the conversation in her own inimitable way.

Francesca stared into the mouthpiece and listened to the sudden throbbing quiet. 'Mother, you truly are a bitch.'

'Garbage and glamour . . . ,' Philippe Sanchez muttered as he looked out over New York. He knew plenty about the garbage; he had been born into it. It always made him want to laugh when he heard the song 'Spanish Harlem'. There had never been any roses for him there except perhaps his mother and she had withered and died long ago. Of Honduran extraction, she had arrived in New York just after the Second World War with his grandmother. His grandfather, a nomad Frenchman, had disappeared in search of some mine 'which would change their lives' and died somewhere north of Ecuador, apparently, at least that was the story. Philippe closed his eyes for a moment as memory prompted him, and he saw the old blurred photograph of a thin tall white man that his mother had cherished for too long. Philippe Alain Poirier, his namesake – a dreamer, a drunk who had left his grandmother too many times to recall, until he had forgotten to come back altogether. And his mother had loved him because she would not know how to do otherwise. On her death he had torn the brown and white photograph up – he never had believed the story and dreams were no good to him.

Rosa Sanchez had married at fifteen; too young, perhaps, but it was like that then, and Bernardo Sanchez had had need of a young wife because his first wife had died and he had three sons to raise. He was a trucker, large, red-faced but kind, and for a few years Rosa had known security, but then came the accident and Bernardo couldn't truck any more, in fact Bernardo couldn't do anything any more, and by the time Rosa had paid for the

113

funeral there wasn't a great deal left for his widow and children. Fortunately for Rosa, Bernardo had given her no babies so she could work, but the money was slow and painful coming in and she grew tired and lonely and desperate; she was still young and it was alien to her blood, to her culture to be without a man to love and serve.

At first there weren't many men, just one or two – just to help, just to keep her bed warm and maybe pay a bill now and then. There were some who were kind, loved her cooking, would come back again and again, but always somehow they were married. She was very careful, douching herself each time with vinegar or lemon, but there was a part of her mind which doubted whether God had intended to bless her with children anyway. Bernardo had failed, and for the first few years of her widowhood nothing happened with the others either, and in her heart she felt thankful and guilty because there was no room in her life, or her purse, for another child.

But then came Philippe. He had known without his mother ever saying anything to him that he had been the turning point in her life; his birth had changed everything. There came a point when there were no more men and no more money, and if Rosa had been asked how she felt she would probably have replied that God had given her both a reward and a punishment which, under the circumstances, was more than she deserved. When Philippe was sixteen, and had asked quick, probing questions about his father, she had tried to tell him that he was the last son of Bernardo Sanchez, but it had been easy to find out that Bernardo had died too soon and he had been born too late – he had known that before he asked her, his step-brothers had been pleased to tell him as much. That was one of the few times she had made him angry.

Philippe shifted his gaze to the streets miles below as yet another police siren shrieked its way down the heady length of Fifth Avenue, eventually no doubt plunging into the outer realms of Harlem; Little Spain. He smiled humourlessly; most New Yorkers avoided it even more than Black Harlem. The sound of the door opening behind

114

him made him turn and his eyes came to rest on a much smaller man, a George Burns look-alike – Ed Rock, his boss, his guru – his father? The thought made him want to smile again. Never his father; not Ed of the big mouth, big cigar, big wallet. Sometimes the thought made him want to throw up and he still couldn't figure out why.

'How's tricks?' It was Ed's favourite opening gambit.

'Okay, Ed,' Philippe replied. 'It's all set for 3 p.m.'

'I'm looking forward to this . . . ,' Ed said, smiling lecherously, '. . . she's supposed to be some broad.'

'Yeah,' Philippe said neutrally and wondered why he insisted on using that corny old word for women as if he were a dog on heat. Ed was like a museum-piece, a character out of some old movie. 'I'm more interested in what she, and therefore Samuels, are going to offer us.'

'Sure, sure – I just thought. . . .' Ed's voice trailed off. It was only a joke, for Chrissakes. He sighed and sat down. 'Remember, we don't take anything less than seventy-five big ones – fifty up-front.'

'I know, Ed, I know.' Philippe drew a sharp, impatient breath. 'We've been through all this before.'

'Well, it's just that I want it right, that's all,' Ed said defensively. 'No harm in going over things.'

'Three thousand times?' Philippe said tersely.

'This deal means a lot to me.' Ed's voice was tinged with reproach.

'If you're that worried about it, why the hell don't you do all the talking yourself?' he responded harshly.

'Because I want *you* to do it,' Ed said evenly. 'And if I didn't think you had what it takes, you wouldn't be sitting in that chair.' He sighed inwardly, wondering why it always came to this. 'I'm an old man, goddamnit, can't you humour me just once?'

It was a plea, but Philippe turned away, shifting his gaze back to the window.

'It'll all go according to plan, Ed – you don't have to worry about a thing,' Philippe said finally with exaggerated patience.

Ed looked up at the lean, long back of the young man

who stood at the window. He didn't doubt his words; Philippe always got his way in the end. It was the way he got it that sometimes worried him. And did he have to treat him as if he were half-way to the funny farm, like a piece of shit? Ed gritted his teeth and bit back the fatal words hovering on his tongue. All because of Rosa; all because he screwed his spick mother. But Rosa had been some spick – even then. And for a moment Ed's rheumy old eyes misted over and he thought of all the 'might have beens', but then he started to smile at the schmaltz which seemed increasingly to flood his brain. He was getting old. Maybe Philippe was right, and he was already half-way to the funny-farm. . . .

The boardroom was conservative, even to the extent of being almost traditionally English in flavour, but curiously the wood panelling was sprinkled with excellent examples of American folk art, and Francesca wondered whether it had been Rock or Dunmar, or some obscure interior designer who had decided on the ultimate effect. Her eyes returned to Rock who was pouring some drinks and the plump man, Cornwell, who was the agency's chief finance guy. Sanchez seemed conspicuous by his absence. Even as the thought passed through her mind the door opened and he walked in. There was no mistaking him and she realized that the photograph she had seen hardly came close. Sanchez was much taller than she had imagined, well over six feet, dark, slim, with a square, almost handsome face. As he leaned towards her to shake her hand she noticed, too, that his eyes were not that deep liquid brown she had come to expect in Hispanics, but a sort of amber. He was, she decided, interesting, if a little too cool.

'Let's all take a seat before we start getting down to business. I hate starting on the heavy stuff when I'm standing up.' Ed chuckled and winked at Francesca. For a moment she was taken aback, but then good humour asserted itself. Rock was obviously an ad man of the old school, nearly forty years in the business as far as she could gather, and it showed; she wondered why he hadn't retired. There was another joke and some more small-talk – all at his instigation – before Sanchez drew their attention to the papers he had laid before them.

Her eyes swept swiftly over the summary page.

'I take it this is a negotiating figure?' she asked evenly.

'We think it a reasonable sum,' Philippe said, avoiding a direct reply.

Francesca heard the sharp intake of Geoff's breath beside her.

'But not negotiable?' she repeated.

'You'll go a long way before you find an international network which could fit so nicely with your company – that's why you're here, isn't it?' he said smoothly.

'We're here to *discuss* a proposition, Mr Sanchez,' she replied smiling thinly, 'and from what I can gather, you need us as much as we want you.'

'Touché. . . .' Rock interjected, and Francesca realized he was enjoying himself immensely, but she saw the warning glance from Sanchez and Rock quietened like a chastened schoolboy.

'We're not just selling one agency, Miss Gaetini, but a network with total billing in the region of $800 million.'

'$750 million,' Francesca responded tersely and was surprised to see a small smile come to Sanchez's mouth.

'We'd like $50 million as a down-payment and the remaining $25 million linked to an earn-out formula, to be paid over the next ten years based on performance.' He had said it now and he watched her face. She was 'some broad' as Ed had so crudely put it, younger than he had imagined, and no doubt used to getting her own way.

'Is the earn-out formula negotiable, Mr Sanchez?' she asked sarcastically, trying to sound unimpressed by his directness.

'Of course.' He replied too reasonably. They were over-stretching it a bit, he knew, and Samuels might wriggle and squirm, but they'd come to some arrangement in the end. He had his own contacts on the London agency scene, and he'd heard about her ambitions with regard to globalization and which direction she wanted the

117

agency to go. And Francesca Gaetini couldn't do it on her own, not without an international network. There would be a couple of other candidates in her sphere of thinking, but neither of them were as clean when it came to conflicts as Dunmar-Rock.

'Before we come to any sort of decision, either way,' Geoff interrupted, 'we would, of course, need to carry out a detailed purchase investigation . . . accounting policies, profit and loss accounts over the last three years, budgets, assets, and so on.'

'Naturally,' Philippe replied.

'And naturally –' Francesca said tautly, '– if we still wish to talk, the figures may have to be subject to negotiation.'

'*If* that is the case, then perhaps we'll get together again once Ed and I return from our Far East trip.'

'Perhaps, Mr Sanchez,' and for a moment her eyes rested darkly on his face. She had looked forward to this trip and the anticipated challenge, but somehow this short, jagged meeting and the over-confident, smug man in front of her had merely left her irritated and subdued. 'Let's leave it for the time being,' she said at last, 'there's still a great deal of ground to go over – it seems sensible to wait and contact you on your return.'

'You will be attending the dinner we've arranged for you this evening?' Ed asked, slightly alarmed at the finality in her voice.

'I'm afraid not,' Francesca replied, lying, 'I have to return to London, but Mr Buchanan is looking forward to it.'

'Oh.' The old man was obviously disappointed, but she felt, somehow, that she had scored a point. Except that it was childish of her to refuse so suddenly at this late stage, but the thought of the evening ahead and all the double-talk almost made her stomach turn and Geoff would cope, he might even enjoy it.

'You pushed it a bit in there, didn't you, kid?' Rock said uneasily.

'No more than you would have done once,' Philippe replied sharply. 'What's the matter, Ed? Are you letting a pretty face get between you and business?'

'You really got under her skin, you know that?' Rock went on, almost to himself. 'If she'd had a bazooka, I bet she would have blown your ass half-way to Denver.'

'It's called business, Ed – she knows it as well as I do. Maybe I got her on a bad day,' he finished wearily; Ed was getting on his nerves.

'She's sharp though – don't underestimate her, kid,' he continued.

Philippe sighed, he hated it when Ed called him 'kid'.

'I know she's sharp,' he replied tautly. 'Let's hope she's sharp enough to contact us with the right answer.'

'Oh, she will, she will,' Ed said with authority. 'But this is only the first round, don't forget that . . . she might surprise you yet.'

'You sound as if you're on her side – not mine,' Philippe responded impatiently.

'Oh, you know me, Phil . . . I just like to see a few sparks fly now and then, keeps me young,' he mused good-humouredly.

'Yes, Ed.' Philippe said without enthusiasm and looked up from the sheaf of papers in his hand to the old man standing before him. Ed was seventy-two and should have retired years ago; he'd been married three times, drank too much scotch, smoked too many havana cigars, dreamed too much and had a heart that threatened to blow any second. He didn't give a goddamn. For a fleeting, reluctant second Philippe was touched by a vague feeling of admiration, but the shrill voice of the telephone scalded his thoughts and the moment was gone.

'I've decided I will be going to the party after all,' Sian said smiling, but Zoë was leaning over her desk, head down, and didn't hear her.

'Zoë?'

The blonde head leapt up with its customary anxious jerk.

119

'Sorry, Sian, what did you say?' A soft frown wove across her forehead.

'I'm going to the party.'

'Great!' Zoë exclaimed, and the inevitable question followed. 'What are you going to wear?'

Sian smiled dryly and an image of the familiar and uninspiring clothes in her wardrobe came into her mind.

'I'm not quite sure,' she replied slowly.

'Well, you've only got two more days – you'd better make up your mind pretty quickly.' Zoë grinned suddenly and pulled open one of the drawers of her desk. 'Have a look through *Vogue*. It might give you some ideas.'

'It'll probably make me depressed!' Sian retorted, laughing, but allowed herself to be cajoled into flicking through the rich pages of the magazine and found herself, unexpectedly, beginning to feel excited about the coming party.

'We could meet up before it starts?' Zoë asked enthusiastically. 'I know a wine bar not far from the Grosvenor House.'

'Okay, sounds like a good idea – I'm not sure I'd like to walk in stone cold sober, anyway,' Sian replied easily.

'Great – that's settled then,' Zoë said and hurried back to her desk as she heard the lift doors opening. Vic had been out for most of the afternoon and was due back at any moment. He would be at the party too, but she knew that it would really mean that they wouldn't see much of each other for most of the evening because they would have to keep up their usual pretence – perhaps they would have the occasional dance if she was lucky. But she consoled herself with the image of how attractive she would look in the new dress she had bought and the fact that maybe, just maybe, Vic might take her home afterwards. She also consoled herself with the thought that probably by Thursday her period would have started. There was nothing to worry about, she knew, because she hadn't forgotten to take any of her pills and had even checked the pack to make sure, so there couldn't be anything really wrong. But even as the thought passed through her mind,

Zoë's hand strayed to her handbag which leaned against her desk and reached in to find the empty packet of contraceptive pills which lay in the zip pocket. She had taken every one, there was no mistake. So there couldn't be anything really wrong.

Nick leaned heavily against the bar as a crush of people surrounded him. Once he had secured a large gin and tonic he squeezed himself through the crowd and found a good position above the dance floor to survey the scene. Henry Samuels was as good as his word: the drinks didn't cost a penny and the buffet in an adjoining room could only be described as 'sumptuous'. He wasn't here in person, of course, he never was, but a massive birthday cake was still made year after year as if he were going to be there to cut it. Juliana's discotheque blazed in one part of the enormous ballroom, roaring to an ever-expectant crowd. At intervals a Chinese sword-swallower would pass through the throng of people, followed closely by a woman with several snakes wound about her opulent body. There were also balloons, streamers and the odd clown who occasionally pulled weird and wonderful objects from a gargantuan pair of silk trousers. Nick shook his head gently and then scanned the deepening crowd on the dance floor. It was strange watching people he saw every day in a working environment actually dancing – jerking, twitching, literally throwing themselves about in a feverish frenzy, like beings from another planet – even Vic Brunning, who surely must have had one too many to be dragged up on the floor writhing in seeming ecstasy to an old Rolling Stones number. Nick almost laughed aloud. But the laugh faded as his eyes came to rest on a dark head just visible behind a row of people at the edge of the dance floor.

Caroline moved tentatively away from the blast of the music and towards the nearest bar; she felt nervous and totally lost, and anxiously searched the crowd for a familiar face, but instead found herself pushed against a table and against the back of a waiter who was about to take a tray of drinks from the bar. In a few moments she

121

was standing in his place and trying vainly to catch the eye of one of the bar staff. As she patiently waited, her eyes were drawn to the highly polished mirrors behind the selection of spirits in front of her and she saw her reflection. She was pleased with what she saw, if a little shocked. Somehow the dark blue strapless dress suddenly seemed to reveal a great deal more of her breasts than the image she had seen in the mirror at home, as if it had taken on a life of its own. Perhaps she could hitch it up a little in the cloakroom. She tugged the gold locket which hung around her neck as if it might cover some more of the exposed flesh and as she looked back into the mirror she saw him only a few feet from her own reflection. Caroline swallowed slowly as her stomach churned, but he smiled and asked her what she would drink and then he was suddenly standing next to her.

'I didn't think you were coming.' Nick tried to keep his eyes on her face, not on the glorious neck and shoulders which made him want to reach out and touch her.

'I didn't either – it was a sort of last moment thing,' she said lamely and took a long saving gulp of the gin and tonic he had put into her hand.

'Let's move away from here, it's too crowded.' He seemed to take it for granted that she would follow, and he moved back up the stairs to the spot from which he had first seen her.

They stood side by side for a few minutes, saying nothing, simply watching the hundreds of other faces below. Caroline's hold on her glass began to relax and she allowed her eyes to lift up to his face. She tried to remember the first time she had realized that she was attracted to him, but it only seemed a vague distant memory. He was so completely unlike Guy in every way that it made her smile.

'What's so funny?' He had turned back as if he had sensed her eyes.

'I don't know really . . . just being here, I suppose.' It was almost the truth and she felt a blush creep up from her neck as he stared into her face.

'Let's dance.' And he removed the glass from her hand and guided her to the dance floor. The music had slowed and Phil Collins was lamenting over 'Separate Lives', but it was what Nick needed; Caroline had a way of unnerving him and she wasn't even aware of it. Dancing would be a safe step forward, but he wasn't sure where the step would lead him. He pressed any thoughts down as he brought her against him; he could think of that later, right now all that mattered was that she was here and he was holding her, and she was warm and sweet and so, so soft.

'Francesca – glad you could make it!' Vic Brunning called jovially.

She turned abruptly to find Vic leaning lazily against a private bar and her eyes narrowed as she realized the man standing beside him was Aidan.

'I could hardly miss Henry's birthday party – even if he couldn't make it himself,' she said smoothly.

'You know Aidan O'Donnell, *of course*,' Vic added, a broad grin stretching across his smug face.

'Naturally,' she replied coolly and wondered exactly what Vic meant by 'of course'. It wouldn't be difficult to imagine. She drew a sharp wary breath sensing instinctively that Vic was up to something, but did he have to make it quite so obvious? Her eyes switched to Aidan's face and the knowing smile which seemed to hover on his lips.

'What's this . . . ?' Geoff came up behind them. '. . . A gathering of the clan, or something?'

Francesca sighed inwardly with relief at the sound of Geoff's voice and didn't really know why, but she did know that she didn't like the idea of Vic and Aidan suddenly appearing to be such good friends. One thing was for sure, neither of them would have her welfare at heart.

'Why don't we have a walk-about, Geoff?' she offered easily. 'I'm sure Vic and Aidan have a lot to discuss.' It was a retort of sorts and she would have to content herself with that for the time being.

'Sure, why not?' Geoff responded. 'See you later, boys.'

They walked back into the crowd and the music and the lights, Francesca feeling uneasy, Geoff suddenly feeling old; it got worse every year. He caught sight of Zoë dancing wildly in the middle of the floor and wondered whether he was old enough to be her father. Perhaps he was getting obsessed with the age thing, he told himself comfortingly, after all he was only *just over* the forty mark. His glance moved from Zoë to the girl dancing in front of her, Sian.

'You seem to have made a good move with your secretary, Francesca,' he said, as they came to the other side of the room.

'Yes, I was lucky there – she's also a very nice girl.'

'Maybe a bit on the serious side?' he added, suddenly finding himself interested.

'Well, she's got problems like the rest of us,' Francesca said slowly, glad that the music was less raucous now.

'Like . . . ?' he probed.

'Maybe you should ask her,' she replied.

'Oh, come on, Francesca,' he said impatiently.

'Like I said – ask her,' she responded firmly. 'Look, Geoff,' she continued, changing the subject, 'I think I see Peter Morgan over there. I'm going over for a few words.' With that she gave him a smile and moved away, swallowed almost immediately by the crowd. He was left alone suddenly in a sea of people and wondered for the hundredth time why he had come. He turned aimlessly to the bar; a drink wouldn't go amiss, it might even dispel the strange mood of self-pity he seemed to be in. This was a party, after all.

Caroline lifted the empty glass to her cheeks hoping that the ice still lying in the bottom would cool her burning skin. Nick approached bearing two more drinks and she looked a little wary as he placed the glasses on the table beside them.

'You don't have to drink it,' he said, noting her expression, '– I'll get you an orange juice or something if you'd prefer.' He wasn't going to make the same mistake as last time.

'It's okay, I think I can manage it without falling over,' she laughed and suddenly realized that she was relaxed, finally, that Nick was no longer the remote being he had been a week or even an hour ago. But did it really have to take two large gin and tonics to chase away her feeble timidity, her awkwardness?

'Would you like to dance again?' he asked as his gaze followed hers to the floor below.

'No – thanks,' and she turned back to him, 'it's too hot and it's nice up here . . . just watching everything.'

His eyes settled on her upturned face and the careful, shy smile which seemed able to move him with such astonishing and unexpected ease. His hand came up automatically to cradle the soft roundness of her cheek, tilted the chin and brought his mouth down to hers. There was no hesitation because she had known, just as he had known, that this was inevitable. And her lips parted in eagerness, her heart beating painfully as his hands glided slowly across her back, her delight deepening as he pressed his face possessively against hers, because she had been so sure that he had found her lacking, that he would not want her again; so sure with the disproportionate tragedy of youth that they had had their moment and she had lost it – that it would never come again.

Sian felt her face flush crimson as Zoë stood coyly before Vic.

'Oh, *please* Vic. . . .' Her voice whined and was both flighty and playful at the same time.

'Look, love, I've already said "no" once,' he said, with barely concealed impatience. 'I've made other arrangements and taking you and your friend home is not one of them.'

Sian winced and wished that some kind deity would whisk her away, anywhere but here.

'Wait a minute,' Vic exclaimed suddenly, '. . . there's Geoff, and he looks as if he's at a bit of a loose end.'

Geoff was subsequently called over and Sian felt her embarrassment deepen at the awkward situation he had been forced into.

'Well, it's not exactly what I had in mind . . . ,' he said lamely, but knew he was caught.

'Won't take long, Geoff,' Vic said generously, slapping him on the shoulder and as if in compensation, 'I'll buy you a drink in the Drayman's. . . .'

'Thanks a million,' Geoff replied sarcastically and turned to the two girls.

'I'm sorry,' Sian offered quickly. 'I really didn't want anyone dragged into taking us home.'

'Oh, it's okay,' Geoff replied and sighed gently. 'I haven't got anything better to do.'

Zoë had lapsed into silence, crestfallen at Vic's attitude; she had had one dance with him at the beginning of the evening, which seemed a lifetime ago, and had hoped at the very least that he would finally take her home, but he had pointedly avoided her and she supposed that he did not want anyone to get the wrong idea about their relationship. She drew a brief, unhappy breath and wondered, perhaps, if she was becoming too demanding.

Apart from the traffic on Park Lane and the surrounding area, the roads were comparatively quiet, and Sian found herself luxuriating in the comfort of the back seat of Geoff's car. Zoë had ensconced herself in the front as she was to get out first. Her usual cheerfulness had returned and she was chattering away to Geoff as if the evening had been one of excitement and triumph.

'And did *you* enjoy yourself?' Sian realized the question was directed at her.

'Well, I must say that Henry Samuels certainly knows how to do things in style,' she responded.

'You haven't answered my question,' Geoff persisted.

'It was fun,' she answered finally. 'But I think, maybe, I'm a bit out of touch with this sort of thing.' And as the words slipped out of her mouth she wished she hadn't said them.

'Why "out of touch"?' he probed, and she heard the interest in his voice and wished that she had had the foresight to say something else.

'Oh, I don't go out all that much . . . I'm a sort of a homebird, I suppose,' she lied.

'And it's difficult with Petie, anyway,' Zoë's voice interjected, 'isn't it, Sian?'

Sian felt her heart sink, wondered why she had never told Zoë that she preferred to keep her private life *private*. Why, she wondered too late, had she told her in the first place? She was suddenly amazed at her own lack of judgement.

'Who's Petie?' Geoff queried, although he had guessed. And he knew she wasn't married; he had already found that out from Francesca.

'My son,' Sian replied tightly, and wished for the second time that evening she could be spirited away silently and quickly to some nether world where people minded their own business. But Geoff chatted smoothly on as if all was well with the world, seemingly unaware of her inner turmoil.

'How old is he?'

'Almost nine months.'

'Must be quite a handful.'

'Yes, he is.'

'How do you manage for babysitters?'

'My parents are very good.'

This was like an interrogation and she was getting tired of it.

'We should be coming up to South Ken tube now, Geoff,' Zoë's voice piped up and he turned his attention back to the vagaries of finding Roland Gardens and the flat which Zoë shared with three other girls. 'It's straight on and the second or third turning on the left,' she continued.

As they drew up outside the large Victorian house Zoë turned her curly blonde head around to bid Sian good-night, totally unaware that she had inflicted a blow upon her friend's pride.

'Good night, Sian,' she said gaily. 'See you in the morning.'

'Goodnight, Zoë,' she replied, only just managing to conceal her irritation.

'Why don't you get in the front seat now, Sian?' Geoff said. 'Otherwise I shall feel like a Samuels chauffeur, or something.'

She dutifully obeyed and the car turned southwards in the direction of the Fulham Road. There was a surprisingly balmy silence for a few minutes, and Sian felt the exhaustion of the evening and her anxieties slowly and inevitably beginning to surface.

'It must make things difficult for you sometimes,' Geoff said. And she sighed inwardly, weary of his questions.

'You mean my son?' But she knew he did.

'Yes. Well, I mean working – the added responsibility,' he replied awkwardly, wondering why he was pursuing the subject with such unaccustomed curiosity.

'Sometimes . . . but I've got used to it.' She turned her head to the window and realized with relief that Putney Bridge was only just around the corner and that Wimbledon and therefore home was now not too far away.

There was another silence then, but no longer balmy and she thought how excrutiatingly long minutes could seem when you wanted them to end. For a moment she stared into the distance and then shifted her gaze enough to take a furtive, curious look at his now quiet and steady profile.

'Will your parents be waiting up for you?' He probed again as if her eyes goaded him, and he heard the sharp intake of her breath as if he had caught her out.

'I am over twenty-one, Geoff,' she replied impatiently; this was getting *too* much.

'Sorry . . . sorry,' he said carefully. 'You should tell me to mind my own business. I get carried away sometimes.'

'Let's just drop me as a subject of conversation, shall we?' She said more sharply than she intended and turned her face back to the window and the comforting sight of Wimbledon Common and deliverance.

*

Geoff watched her walk hurriedly up the path to her home and closed his eyes in frustration, only too aware that she must think him a clumsy and inept fool. He shook his head wonderingly; it had been a strange and unsettling evening from beginning to end and he had been unable to improve things one iota. If anything he had made matters a hell of a lot worse, for some inscrutable masochistic reason. Maybe there was such a thing as the male menopause, after all. He smiled half-heartedly. Then his thoughts turned back to Sian and the 'problem' he had been so eager to uncover. Petie . . . cute. Perhaps, he mused, if Joanne and I had had some kids, or even a kid, we wouldn't have split up. But even as the image of his almost ex-wife passed through his mind and the purr of the car jolted him back to reality he knew he was kidding himself. Joanne would never have risked her model-like figure for the sake of a child; she had always loved herself . . . and other men . . . too much. Geoff sighed heavily as he turned the car out of the long road and back in the direction of the West End. He realized quite suddenly that he was tired, bloody tired, and that there was still Friday to be got through before he could kiss goodbye to a bad week.

'So Rock's not such a bad old guy,' Francesca said, her words laden with cynicism.

'Like I said when I came back from New York on Tuesday, he couldn't have been nicer,' Geoff pointed out again, sensing that he was wasting his time.

'Did Mr Sanchez grace you with the honour of his presence over the weekend?' she asked bitingly.

'He came down by helicopter on Saturday morning,' he said weakly and saw her eyes roll to heaven.

'Of course . . . I forgot . . . ,' she said dryly, 'it's almost impossible to get to The Hamptons unless you sprout wings.'

'Yes – I was being buttered up – I accept that,' Geoff said defensively. 'But neither was I bombarded with any more details on the deal.' He drew a weary breath. 'It was interesting, Francesca – really. Rock still holds the reigns, even if Sanchez is waiting hungrily in the wings.'

'Caught between "a rock and a hard place" – isn't that what they say, Geoff?' And she smiled humourlessly.

'This could be a *very* successful merger,' he persisted, 'even allowing. . . .'

'I haven't changed my mind, Geoff,' she interrupted him before he could go any farther, 'if that's what you're trying to say. What I said to you when you came back from New York still stands.'

'But you haven't said "yes", either,' Geoff added, not satisfied.

'Look, nothing has altered my opinion as regards Dunmar-Rock's suitability in the merger stakes.' She sighed. 'You know Sanchez irritated me and I shouldn't have allowed myself to be irritated . . . I just don't want him to think that he has us in the palm of his hand.'

'He's trying it on.' He turned from his stance by the window and watched as she moved from her desk to the table and the silver cigarette box. He had never seen her smoke before.

'I know he's trying it on,' she repeated and blew out a slow cloud of smoke. 'I've done it myself often enough.'

'Even if we went for the $50 million we could still come down on them hard on the performance targets,' he said evenly. She would come round; she just didn't like being beaten at her own game. Sanchez might be difficult, but he was already turning around Dunmar-Rock's dull image and was anticipating the future and the inevitable rise in the company's billing and ultimately the share price. He was being smart, maybe not very subtle, but then Francesca would have done no less herself. She would simply have done it with more style.

'I've already worked that out, Geoff.'

'Okay, okay,' he said, realizing that he had pushed far enough.

'But that son of a bitch won't get another cent if Dunmar-Rock's precious earnings don't grow by twelve per cent over the next ten years!' Her eyes were black with anger although her voice had hardly risen. And Geoff nodded stiffly in agreement knowing that this was not the time to mention that he had considered ten per cent an acceptable figure.

'Maybe we can get together early next week and clarify the details,' he said finally. 'In the meantime, I'd better get back to my office. I've got an account group meeting in five minutes.'

'Which account group?' she asked curtly, still endeavouring to press down her temper.

'Claire Hewitt's. It's that new brand assignment for Chico cigarettes; she's having some unsettling vibes from the lobby for anti-smoking.'

'Why, particularly?' she asked, suddenly aware of her own cigarette still held between her fingers; she thought she'd given up two years ago. Slowly she ground it out in the thick marble ash-tray.

'The manufacturers want it aimed specifically at the eighteen to twenty-five-year-olds; the lobbyists say it's immoral.' He shrugged his shoulders. He didn't entirely agree either, but as long as smoking existed and kids wanted to smoke, that's exactly what they would do, however much the anti-smoking lobby protested. If it wasn't Chico it would be some other brand. It was not a very convincing argument, and he knew it, but he pressed any worthy thoughts down; a guilty conscience wouldn't help his client.

'In that case we'd better stop advertising alcohol, motor bikes, glue and sexy underwear . . . God, even sex kills now!' Soon the righteous would remove all temptation and would then find themselves in the position of having no one to pillory in their brave, sanitized new world. 'Maybe they should find out why some kids smoke and others don't; maybe they should find out why some of us so-called adults imbibe so much; maybe they should just concentrate on finding out what it is that creates inherent human weakness so strongly in some people that they seem to nourish their own self-destruct button. . . .' She shook her head gently, knowing she had gone over the top. 'Forget it, Geoff, just do the best you can,' and as he

131

began to walk towards the door of her office she added slowly, 'We have a business to protect, let them take care of the moral issues.' Even as he closed the door behind him she shut down any more thoughts on the matter. The world had always been full of dangers; remove one and it would simply be replaced by another. Part of life's rich cruel tapestry.

It had been almost two weeks now. Perhaps she was ill – perhaps there was something really wrong with her. Zoë stared into the brown steaming liquid of her coffee. She had felt slightly nauseous this morning, but the feeling had gone now and she wondered, hopefully, whether she had some sort of virus. There was always the doctor, of course, but somehow she didn't want that; Dr Andrews had been the family doctor for years. Perhaps she could go to someone else, just in case, although she knew there couldn't be anything to worry about. Zoë lifted her head from the untouched coffee cup and stared across the room at Sian.

'Sian . . . ?'

'Yes, Zoë?' There was a sheaf of papers in her hand and a paper-clip stuck between her teeth as she turned her attention to the pale face of her friend.

'I'm almost two weeks' overdue.' She was surprised how easily the words slipped from her mouth, but even as she said them there was a soothing sense of relief.

Sian took the paper-clip slowly from her mouth.

'You mean your period's late – is that what you're saying?'

'But there can't be anything to worry about, Sian,' she said quickly.

'What do you mean?' There were two dots of red on Zoë's white cheeks. Sian watched her for a moment as strange disquieting echoes from the past rose up to greet her.

'I'm on the pill –,' she said almost defiantly, '– and I know that I didn't forget to take any.'

'So you can't be pregnant,' Sian said neutrally, wonder-

132

ing why she didn't feel reassured. Vivid memories seized her as she recalled how she had tried not to believe what was happening to her even as Petie was growing inside her.

'Well, I can't be, can I?' Zoë said easily.

'Perhaps you should go and check all the same,' Sian replied.

'There's *nothing* to worry about, Sian – there can't be,' Zoë retorted with unaccustomed sharpness and it was then that Sian realized that she was, indeed, worried.

'There's a woman's clinic just off Tottenham Court Road. They're very discreet and you get the results very quickly,' Sian continued firmly. After all, she should know.

'Thanks, but no thanks, Sian; I know I don't need to go, it's just a sort of hiccup, that's all.'

'I hope you're right, but if you change your mind I can give you the number.' But Zoë shook her head. 'Have you told your boyfriend?' Sian said finally, and wondered why Zoë had never mentioned him to her.

'My boyfriend . . . ,' she replied clumsily, 'no, there's no need.' And Vic's face slid inevitably into her mind. She had never thought of him as 'her boyfriend'; somehow the description just did not seem to fit. For the first time Zoë felt a flicker of fear. If, by some impossible quirk of fate, she was pregnant, there would be no turning to Vic. He had never even asked whether she was on the pill. She supposed he just took it for granted, as most men seemed to. That had been one of their unspoken rules: that there were no questions, that she would make no claims on him, that she would just be there.

Caroline purchased her fare card as usual, then passed through the turnstile of Richmond station as usual, but other than that nothing was 'as usual' at all. There had been a row after her return from the party; she had been home far too late and apparently Guy had called in her absence and her parents had had 'the unpleasant task of telling him where his fiancée was'. She had countered with the uncharacteristically brave reply that 'she was not his fiancée – yet'. Now her mother was hardly speaking to her and Guy was still sulking. Caroline found a seat in the train next to the window and brought her book out from its hiding place in her large shoulder bag, but it remained unread. Her eyes absently scanned the familiar advertisements which ran the length of the tube, trying to sell everything from holidays to secretaries, but she shifted her gaze back to the window and the face which she saw reflected there. Nick had arranged to see her at lunchtime which would be the second time since the party. She had managed, so far, to avoid any evenings because that, somehow, would put everything on a different footing and there were still her parents – and Guy – to contend with. It was only a matter of time before Nick became insistent, of course, and then she wasn't sure what would happen. Caroline sighed heavily and watched her breath make a soft white circle on the glass of the window. He was what she wanted and she had never really admitted it to herself until the party. Nick had always seemed beyond her reach and she could never have imagined him wanting her in the same way. But he had, he did. Caroline swallowed slowly and felt a thickness gather in her throat as she remembered. They had sat in his car for ages and he had caressed her exquisitely – and there had only been gentleness; but they had done nothing she felt was wrong, and she knew that that had been deliberate on his part and she wasn't sure she understood. A hot sweet blush crept into her face as she recalled her own responses, how much she had wanted him and how he must have known. Her heart seemed huge inside her, like a rock, and it didn't matter that it had begun to rain, that great fat drops poured frantically down the window to form puddles in the cracks and crevices of myriad station platforms; it didn't matter at all.

Francesca cast a trained eye over her mail and then reached for the large cup of coffee sitting by the telephone. It had been a quiet, uneventful weekend except for the call from

134

Matthias which came at an unholy hour on Sunday morning. The sky had still been tinged with dawn as the telephone had blasted her so unkindly out of sleep. It seemed to her that he must have been up for most of the night, yet he still sounded fresh and alert. Maybe 'Golden Gods' didn't need sleep. She sipped the hot, strong coffee and let it slide down her grateful throat. There had been a party – some of sort of promotion which Lucas had arranged – so many people that he couldn't refuse, couldn't *afford* to refuse. She had smiled then, knowing that Matthias would be drawn like a magnet to the right party and the right people; she knew him that much. He had called her because he needed to speak to someone 'sane', that she was the only one he knew and why didn't she fly to Paris. For a moment she had been startled by the need in his voice, but then his tone had abruptly changed and he was the old Matthias, and she wondered if she had imagined the fleeting plea in his voice. But she was snapped out of her thoughts by a sudden knock on her office door. It was Vic.

'Can't stay long, Francesca, just wanted to keep you up with events.' He sat down.

'The Matthias campaign?'

'Yup.'

'No problems, are there?'

'Oh, no – I think Pete Morgan's got everything beautifully under control,' he said confidently.

'Yes, I spoke to him on Thursday evening at the party,' she replied. 'Incidentally, I didn't realize you and Aidan O'Donnell were such good friends.'

'I wouldn't say that exactly. We only just met recently in fact.' He smiled. 'Talented guy, but then, I'm sure you know all about that.'

'Yes, I do, Vic,' she too smiled thinly, looking directly into his face and wondering why this jovial new Vic should be so much easier to dislike than the sullen old one.

'Anyway, back to Matthias,' he said easily. 'This satellite link-up's going to cause some real headaches, but then we expected that.'

'The response Peter's had from the other artists seems to be pretty good so far. Of course the technical details are not exactly going to be easy, but we seem to be getting the sort of cooperative response that we want from most of the countries already contacted. And naturally there's been no difficulty at all arranging spots on the major TV and radio chat shows and breakfast television.' She tapped her desk slowly with one finger. 'Is there anything else?'

'Not really. I just wanted to ensure that you were clued up on everything,' he said smoothly.

'Peter will update me on every new development as it happens; that's already been agreed.'

'Good, that's what I told him to do.' He smiled again as he stood up and adjusted his pink silk tie. 'There is just one other thing that might cause a few ripples.'

'What's that?' she asked, looking up into his pale, early morning face.

'Well, it might be an idea if you told Matthias to cool it a bit with these parties – I mean, it hardly fits in with his new image, now does it?' His large hands rested briefly on the back of the chair as he made to go.

'What are you getting at?' So this was what he had been leading up to all along. 'In any event he's supposed to be in Paris,' she added quickly.

'Well, he wasn't on Saturday night. He was in deepest darkest Buckinghamshire,' he said, hard put to keep the triumph out of his voice. 'You obviously haven't seen today's *Mail*.'

'No, I haven't.' And automatically her eyes strayed to the coffee table strewn with the morning papers.

Vic followed her gaze and walked slowly over to the pile of papers, flicking through them until he found the one he wanted.

'Nigel Dempster's done it again,' he said, smiling broadly as he placed the paper in front of her, opened at the appropriate page, the society gossip column.

In a prominent position was a picture of Matthias, beautifully attired in black tie, his arm draped languidly across the back of a chair inhabited by 'the breathtakingly lovely Melissa Barton–Carr . . . racy blonde daughter of Fleet Street magnate, Sir Richard . . .'. She hated gossip pulp, hated the hype jungle that her mother had always loved and yearned after so successfully for herself: charity queen, beloved of all good causes. Now it was Matthias who stared up at her from its pages, still with that same crooked, all–knowing smile that she had come to know so well. And she wondered if he had thought of her seeing it, wondered if he could know how her stomach would lurch with humiliation and something unexpected, called jealousy.

'How did you know about this, Vic?' He was loving every minute of it and she felt her pulse begin to race with anger.

'The paper, of course, but I had the tip–off from a friend.' He put a certain emphasis on the word 'friend' and she knew without doubt that he meant Aidan. 'Apparently our pretty prophet's been seeing lovely Melissa for a while now.'

'And you also found this out from your "friend"?' she said dryly.

'That's right.'

'I see.' She spoke neutrally, pressing any emotion down. 'Well, what are you going to do about it?'

'Me?' he asked sharply.

'As you obviously feel so concerned about "our client's" behaviour . . . ,' she continued, '. . . perhaps you'd better be the one to discuss it with him.'

'I thought you'd be the person to do that,' he said, frowning.

'Oh, no, Vic . . . you can have this one.' She was smiling. 'After all, it was really yours to begin with.' And she turned her attention to the mail which lay still unread on her desk, but then added slowly, 'Of course, the whole thing may probably be a misunderstanding. You know what our greedy friends, the press, are like . . . I should make sure you get your facts right before you do anything at all.'

'My sources are totally reliable,' he said with an effort.

'You mean "your friend",' she said sarcastically and smiled again before turning her eyes from his face to the letters in front of her in a gesture of dismissal.

'I've got to get to a meeting,' he said finally, lamely. As he turned to go he was suddenly unsure how the meeting had gone, but he had the unhappy suspicion that once again she had somehow turned the tables on him. Yet, there had been something when he had shown her the paper, – a certain redness in her cheeks. Hadn't there?

She didn't respond to his remark and just watched his retreating back as it disappeared through the door, waiting for the soft slam as he closed it.

Francesca rose from her chair and moved instinctively to the window. So, Matthias had lied, or so it seemed. She would have to check it out, of course, but Aidan wouldn't stretch the truth very far because too much depended on it. And did he really think she wouldn't find out? Obviously she had been too lenient with him. Maybe she should have just got rid of him in the first place, but it didn't make any difference now. For a moment she lifted her head back and brought her hand up to rub the sharp ache in the nape of her neck. She would deal with Aidan later. Now there was only Matthias. He *had* been to a party on Saturday evening, she knew that much herself, but he had implied that it was taking place in Paris. Buckinghamshire. She would have laughed except that her lips would not move and her mouth had gone strangely dry. Vic's words came back to sting her with unrelenting force: 'He's too wild to be God-given beneath that smooth, suave exterior. He's a con.'

And as Matthias' perfect face slipped inevitably into her mind, she closed her eyes as if to shut out the vision. Because she had wanted to believe him.

# 5

It was nearly three weeks before he called her again. The interview with Vic had passed off easily without repercussions, and she had casually allowed him to take any initiatives regarding Matthias; he would be the direct contact now because that was the way she wanted it to be. In the intervening period Francesca had engrossed herself in other work, pulling a smoke-screen over her anger and hurt, and referring any calls from the rock star to Vic's office; there had only been one and she had managed to avoid it. But he had found her at home, finally.

'You are conspicuous by your absence,' he said evenly and at the sound of his voice she felt all the feelings she had submerged begin to come dangerously alive, like wild childish hope.

'Am I? I've been busy,' she replied, knowing that her words came out practised, like stage dialogue.

'Why am I always put through to that buffoon, Brunning, now?' he asked with barely concealed impatience.

'I've got an important deal on my hands at the moment and several other campaigns to direct – I can't be everywhere at once,' she replied tautly, as anger began to seep through at last. He had betrayed her, hadn't he? 'Besides, Vic is very competent. . . .' She never thought she'd say that. 'Is there a problem?'

'I don't like dealing with buffoons.'

'Perhaps you could tell me exactly what is wrong?' she said evenly, pressing her temper down.

'I was going to ask you the same question.'

'I told you – I've been busy, there's a lot going on.'

'Bullshit.'

There was a long, long moment then and she closed her eyes.

'Will you have dinner with me tomorrow night?'

'In Paris . . . or are you still in Buckinghamshire?' The words slipped out so easily and she hated herself for them.

'Ah – now, I see.' He sighed dramatically and she felt anger again. 'It was only a publicity shot – and certainly not the sort of one that I wanted.'

'I wish the world we lived in wasn't so small,' she said slowly.

'What does that mean?'

'It means that *you* can't bullshit *me*.'

'I fly to Munich the day after tomorrow. I'll see you when I get back.'

And he was gone.

She replaced the receiver carefully, surprised that her hand was so steady. There was no release or relief, as she had hoped there would be. Instead there was only weariness and desolation, and she wondered if her judgement had left her altogether because it seemed, somehow, that she had handled it badly, that she had, in the end, only injured herself.

Zoë stared into the gleaming white abyss of the toilet bowl; she felt sick, but nothing happened and she felt tired, so tired, almost as if she could fall asleep standing up. For a moment she leaned her head against the cold formica wall of the cubicle; it had gone on long enough, tomorrow morning she would make an appointment at that place Sian had told her about. But it still didn't seem possible; she had been so sure, so careful. As she made her way back to her desk she suddenly remembered that she had promised Vic that she would set up new files on the Matthias campaign. At the moment all the data was in one overflowing box-file. She glanced at her watch, realizing that it was well past five; he wouldn't be back tonight, but nevertheless he would expect to see them completed by tomorrow morning. Zoë sighed heavily in frustration and gave a half-hearted smile as Sian caught her downcast face.

'What's up?'

'I've got to finish some things for Vic and I really don't

feel like it now, particularly as it's almost time to go.' She sighed again.

Sian watched her expression for a moment and noted the absence of the usual glow to her cheeks. Zoë was pale and definitely not herself.

'Is everything okay?' she enquired, not wanting to put the real question she longed to ask into words.

'I think you'd better give me the number of that clinic you talked about,' she said carefully and her eyes slid away from her friend's scrutiny.

'Oh, Zoë . . . ,' Sian said softly.

'I don't understand – I've been so careful, I know I can't be pregnant.' She felt suddenly bewildered.

'Are you absolutely sure you took your pills every day?' Sian probed.

'Yes . . . I've looked at the packet so often, I'm almost cross-eyed.'

'You weren't sick or anything, were you? Sometimes you can bring the pill you've already taken back up if you vomit.'

'No, no, nothing like that,' Zoë replied sharply. 'The only thing I've had wrong with me recently was that infected wisdom tooth.'

'But you took antibiotics, didn't you?' Sian asked as realization began to sink in.

'Yes, why?' Zoë caught the look in Sian's eyes and felt a hollow sickness in her stomach.

'Are you on a low dosage pill?'

'Yes . . . but what are you getting at, Sian?' Panic seemed to seep into her voice.

'I read somewhere, ages ago, that if you take antibiotics when you're on the pill you should use another form of contraceptive at the same time.' She lowered her eyes for a moment. 'I think antibiotics weaken the effect of the pill or something.'

'Oh, my God.' Even as she spoke she still wondered if there could be some mistake, whether she really was ill, and the nausea, tiredness and lack of a period were related to something else, some strange malady. But she knew, just as thousands of women before her had known.

141

'I'll give you that number,' Sian's voice sounded suddenly remote. 'I'll come with you as well if you like.'

'No, it's okay, Sian,' she said tightly.

'Why don't you go home? I'll finish up for you.'

'No, I don't feel like going home just yet.' She felt tears seep into her eyes and tremble so that the whole room danced.

'Anyone want a drink?' Geoff's voice suddenly broke in and Zoë turned sharply away. 'What have I said?' He looked hurt.

'She's not feeling too well,' Sian said quickly as Zoë disappeared into Vic's office.

'Oh, damn . . . ,' he stammered, 'I know it sounds corny, but it's my birthday and I thought my office colleagues might like to share a drink with me. . . .' He held a bottle of white wine in one hand and several glasses in the other.

'Of course – and happy birthday, Geoff,' Sian said cheerfully, with an effort. Since the unfortunate drive home from the Samuels' party Geoff had gone out of his way to be tactful and considerate almost to the point of irritation.

'Actually, these days I try and forget birthdays – but, what the hell!' And he poured the chilled wine expertly into the waiting glasses.

'I take it I'm not allowed to ask how old you are?' Sian asked, looking into his face.

He caught a breath which was not quite a sigh and suddenly she felt sorry for him for some unfathomable reason.

'Forty-one to the day. . . .'

'Really? I wouldn't have thought it.' And she meant it and was rewarded by a dazzling smile that was almost child-like in its openness.

'Hold on a moment and I'll just take a glass in to Francesca.'

'She's still on the telephone, I'm afraid,' Sian remarked as he moved to go.

'Doesn't matter, I'll only be in there for a second . . . ,'

142

he said, walking towards the closed door, '. . . we're supposed to be having dinner together as a sort of celebration.' He sighed inwardly knowing that Francesca, for all her obvious attributes, had been a last resort; they made good business partners, and maybe even friends, but that was as far as it went, which was probably just as well.

As he disappeared into Francesca's office Sian picked up a glass of wine and carried it in to Zoë who was leaning over one of Vic's filing cabinets.

'Drink this and let me give you a hand,' she said slowly.

'Thanks.' But Zoë didn't look up and Sian drew a sharp weary breath as she realized she had been crying. 'It'll be okay, really it will, Zoë, and in any event it's yet to be confirmed.' But they both knew.

'I know, I know – I just don't want to think about it, that's all.' She sniffed and Sian thought that at that moment she didn't look much more than fourteen.

'Oh, so that's where you're hiding. . . .' It was Geoff. He looked from one girl to the other and attempted a half-smile. 'I wondered if you'd like to join me for dinner?'

Sian swallowed hard, it was the last thing she felt like.

'Zoë . . . ?' She turned her gaze to Zoë's half-bowed head.

'No – no thanks, Geoff, I'm not feeling too good.'

'Well, how about you, Sian?' He saw the doubt in her face and felt compelled to add, 'Francesca's going to be delayed for quite a while . . . I just wondered. . . .'

She was caught. It was his birthday, after all, and in all probability Francesca wouldn't make it at all.

'I'll have to make a phone call – and I'd also like to help Zoë finish off these files . . . ,' she said guardedly.

'That's okay, there's plenty of time.' He spoke too quickly. And she watched him return to his office, glass in hand, and wondered why on this, his birthday, he should be brought to the level of taking the office secretary out to dinner because there was no one else.

'He's a nice guy, Geoff,' Zoë said suddenly.

'Yes, he seems to be,' Sian reluctantly agreed, but wished she wasn't the one to fill the empty space at his table, wished somehow that she was going almost anywhere else but with him.

Caroline watched Nick as he pushed his way through the early evening crowd of the Drayman's; it was full of advertising people, mainly from Samuels and she was crushed into one corner.

'Sorry I'm late,' he said as he drew close.

'It's okay, I've only been here a couple of minutes myself.'

'I thought we could go for a meal.' He was pushed against her as someone slid behind him and there was the round swelling of her breast burning him through the thin fabric of his shirt. And for the thousandth time he wondered why she, of all people, should have this effect on him.

'Oh, but you said we'd just be going for a drink. . . .' Immediately his eyes darkened and she knew she had said the wrong thing.

'You have to get home?' he asked dryly.

'It's just that I hadn't mentioned I'd be late to my parents,' she answered lamely.

'How old are you, Caroline?' He spoke tightly.

'Twenty-three. . . .' Her voice was very small.

'Don't you think it's time you started living a life of your own – or is it that you'd rather be somewhere else than here – with me?' His eyes flicked over her awkwardness, and he felt impatience climb into his throat and stay there.

'You know I want to be here . . . ,' she replied and lifted her great soft bruised eyes to his, but he was unmoved.

'Well, phone them then,' but she didn't respond and he longed to shake her like a rag doll.

'Is it Guy?' he asked sharply.

'No. I don't know. . . .' Her words trailed off weakly and her eyes slid away from him.

'Maybe we should forget this evening altogether.' She had put him off too often.

'It's just that everything seems to be happening so fast. I just want to take things slowly, that's all.' It was a plea, but she knew he would not be satisfied.

'Take *what* slowly? Me? Telling Guy? Your parents?' he said hotly and then added quickly, 'I'm tired of waiting for you to make up your mind, I'm tired of you trying to put me off. Is it such a big deal to go out with me just for one whole evening, for God's sake, or would you hurt darling Guy's feelings or something?' He sighed heavily. 'You can't have it all, Caroline, not with me, anyway.'

'I don't want it all. I'm just trying to take things one step at a time,' she said reproachfully. Her parents would never understand, Guy wouldn't understand. The situation seemed like a nightmare and she was stuck in the middle like a confused idiot child.

'That's just it – you haven't taken *any* steps, not one, and I'm supposed to be happy with seeing you at lunchtimes, or sneaking a quick drink after hours.' He drew a sharp breath as he tried to suppress his impatience and choose the right words. 'That's not enough, Caroline!' and a too vivid picture of her took shape in his mind as he recalled how she had cleaved to him in the safe womb of his car, how his lips had raked her neck, shoulders, breasts. He closed his eyes for a brief, stinging moment.

'I'm sorry . . . ,' she replied feebly, powerless.

'I don't want you to be sorry; I want you to do something,' he said, exasperated.

She wanted him to tell her what to do, she wanted him to take all the problems away so that she wouldn't have to face them and then they could start again. Instead, she looked automatically at her watch.

'Christ!' He snapped as he caught her glance.

'I'm sorry.' It was a thoughtless and clumsy thing to do and she wondered if she were capable of doing anything right where he was concerned. He was like another planet, wild, unexplored, and she was both frightened and fascinated by him. She hardly understood her own feelings any more.

'For God's sake, don't say sorry again – and if the time is

worrying you all that much, then you'd better go.' He looked away from her, angry and disappointed, not daring to speak. He swallowed hard and realized his throat was unbelievably dry. 'I'm going to get a drink. Do you want one?' he asked icily, and then moved off without waiting for her reply.

For a lost, fleeting moment she watched his retreating figure and then without looking back she eased her way through the crowd of people and out into the street.

Nick felt a cold waft of wind as the door opened and closed and turned to see the space where she had stood momentarily empty, only to be filled by someone else as if the corner, the place where they had stood and talked had never existed.

Langan's. Adam had brought her here once to celebrate the winning of an account. But Sian pushed the memory down as Geoff, following the waiter, guided her to a table by the window.

'It can be poser's paradise here, but I like the atmosphere,' he said easily, and he gave her a smile of encouragement as if he suddenly expected her to change her mind and decide to go home after all.

'Yes, I know,' she replied, 'but it's been a long time since I last came here.' And he saw a furtive shadow flee across her face.

He sighed inwardly, sensing instinctively that she was thinking of 'the man', Petie's father.

'You won't know it, but you're sitting exactly where Michael Parkinson was sitting two weeks ago.' It was a tedious thing to say, but anything to break the mood. Christ, it was supposed to be a birthday celebration!

'I can't stand Michael Parkinson,' she replied slowly, but her mouth was tipping at the edges with a smile as she realized suddenly how much effort he was making.

'Neither can I.' And he laughed almost with relief, but his eyes came to rest on her face and he was reminded how attractive she really was when she smiled. 'Now let's order some champagne because I'm sure we're both ready for it – and it seems appropriate.'

'You don't need an excuse if it's your birthday, do you?' she asked gently, meeting his gaze.

'No, I suppose I don't,' he replied and was surprised to feel himself blushing as she studied him.

Her eyes followed him as he turned and nodded to the waiter, noting the slight trembling of his hands as he held the wine list. He was trying so hard, and he was lonely, and it was his birthday, and she had almost left him to celebrate in soulless, solitary splendour.

'Krug Grande Cuvée, never fails . . . ,' Geoff said jovially as he turned back to face her, and he was caught by her stare and the tilt of her wide sweet mouth. He swallowed very slowly and thought fleetingly how different things would seem if Francesca was sitting there. She probably wouldn't come, and it didn't really matter, not now. It was going to be all right.

The air was damp and full of the smell of November, there was even a vague mist ghosting up from the ground and clinging to the edges of cars. Francesca wondered briefly how the bonfires which had no doubt been put together with loving care would fare tonight, because it was the 5th, Guy Fawkes night; she had almost forgotten. She shook her head gently as she made her way up the marble steps to Samuels. Her father had always insisted on a bonfire party when they were in England. He had revelled in it, for all his Italian blood, and for once Livia had stood back, taken second place because Michael had insisted that his father should have his way. And she had stood on the terrace in black fur, removed and silent, like an exile.

The sixth floor hummed quietly, waiting, like a perfectly oiled machine, as Francesca stepped out of the lift. She liked this time of the morning, just before the rush, the noise and the people. Sian was already sitting at her desk and Francesca raised her eyebrows at her upturned face.

'Another early bird.'

'It was Petie's idea, not mine. He decided he wanted to get up a lot earlier than I did,' Sian responded, laughing.

'How are things?' Francesca asked, letting her eyes come to rest on Sian's face.

'Fine . . . really,' Sian replied, aware that she was under scrutiny.

'Good,' Francesca said, smiling, and then added, 'but actually I didn't really need to ask. I can tell by your face.'

Sian's features puckered in puzzlement as she watched Francesca move on into her office, but she cast her curiosity quickly aside as the shriek of the telephone abruptly interrupted her brief reverie; things were starting early and she'd hardly had time to touch her coffee. Even as she put the call through to Francesca the sound of the lift doors opening made her look up and Samuels' joint managing directors came walking towards her. The short and the tall, the spider and the fly, beauty and the beast. Sian smiled to herself. Yet despite their obvious differences Vic and Geoff seemed to work well together, at least as far as the world could tell. . . .

'Where's Zoë?' Vic asked petulantly, his eyes drawn automatically to his absent secretary's desk. No 'hello', no 'good morning'. . . .

'Hi!' Geoff interjected before Sian could respond to Vic's abruptness. She saw the gleam of humour in his eyes as he walked into his office and took a deep breath before turning back to Vic.

'She's not in yet, Vic.' She spoke evenly. 'It's only just past nine.'

He grunted.

'I was just about to make some more coffee; would you like some?' It was a lie, but anything to remove the sullen expression from his face, although she wondered how she stopped herself from telling him to take a quick jump off the nearest bridge.

'Oh . . . thanks,' he stammered, and as she stood up she almost laughed because it sounded as if Vic was going to choke on the word. *He knows I don't like him and he can't understand why I'm being so civil. Neither can I.* But she drew a sharp, wary breath as Zoë's face slid into her mind.

★

'When are they arriving?' Francesca asked as Geoff sat down.

'The day after tomorrow.' Rock had called him from Amsterdam; he and Sanchez intended rounding off their trip by a few days in London and basically wanted to look Samuels over at close quarters.

'I take it we'll have a formal meeting. Do you think a credentials presentation would be in order?' Naturally Dunmar-Rock had seen what Samuels could do, but the new showreel of ads was beautifully put together: original, youthful and dynamic. If anything could start their mouths watering, that could.

'Definitely. They want a look around, they want to see what they *could* be getting – we should give them the works.' Geoff smiled crookedly. 'Dunmar-Rock won its first Clio award in three years with that futuristic office ad, so they've been preening their feathers a bit . . . but they know our record in creative awards takes some beating, even worldwide, so I think a little reminder should leave them fairly chastened by the end of the presentation.'

'Good.' She felt the beginnings of optimism. It was a bonus that Rock and Sanchez would be stopping over before going on to New York. This time she would play down her annoyance at Rock's golden boy's presumption: this time she would be charming and out to make a killing. She smiled inwardly; maybe they could have the merger document put together and signed by Christmas.

'But they would like Henry to be around,' Geoff said, sighing heavily.

'He's not back from Antigua yet, is he?' Francesca shook her head gently. She had almost forgotten the existence of Samuels' president and founder.

'Last night,' he said carefully. 'I took the opportunity of phoning him and telling him how things were going. He's only interested in meeting Rock when the merger is finally settled, i.e. at the formal joining of the two companies.'

'We'll have to manage without him then . . . ,' she replied easily. Henry might seem like the icing on the cake to Rock, but for the time being it would be better to keep good old Henry in the background until his signature was needed on the dotted line. Like bait. In any event, this merger was her baby, her brainchild, and she didn't want him breathing down her neck, no matter how benevolently.

'He seems content to leave it that way,' Geoff added. 'Anyway, he's sixty-two now and obviously wants to take it a bit easy. . . .' Geoff laughed silently. Henry had been wiling away his time for well over six weeks with a voluptuous blonde who could by anyone's standards be his daughter; Henry was a debauched old bastard. '. . . Especially as he can see that Samuels is in capable hands,' he finished, and grinned.

'Flattery will get you everywhere . . . ,' Francesca grinned back and then her face became serious again. 'I'd like a draft document drawn up on the figures we discussed – nothing changed.'

'Still twelve per cent earn–out?' he asked.

'Still twelve per cent earn–out,' she repeated in response. Sanchez could have his $50 million, but she would have her pound of flesh too.

'Okay, have it your way,' he said, getting up. 'I'd better get on with things and leave you to it.'

'Fine . . . ,' she replied, reaching for the phone. 'Oh, and Geoff – sorry about last night and your birthday.'

'No problem, Francesca. It turned out to be a most enjoyable evening, after all,' he said mysteriously and grinned again.

She watched him go with curiosity, realizing from the look on his face that there was a woman involved somewhere. He was a nice guy in the real sense of the word and not the sort to live alone happily, or to be satisfied with a string of meaningless affairs. He was, she realized, smiling to herself, completely marriageable and there weren't many men like that around. She wished him and whoever she was luck. But as the door closed softly behind him her thoughts switched almost immediately back to the merger talks. It might be a good idea to arrange a discreetly lavish dinner, perhaps at the Dorchester's Terrace restaurant. There would be no expense spared, nothing left to chance this time, too much was at stake. Samuels had been a big step in the right direction and she had still managed to keep her father's creation, GK, almost intact just as he would have wanted; Samuels was now number one in the UK since the Matthias' win, but it needed Dunmar-Rock's international network to make it a real force to be reckoned with in the worldwide stakes. Francesca swallowed deeply and then suddenly realized she still held the silent telephone in her hand. She began dialling the number her brother had left over two hours previously, but there was no reply. She sighed heavily with impatience; he would think she had forgotten and she had, but there was nothing she could do about it now. But she cast any guilt aside because there could be no room in her life over the next two days for thoughts of Michael, or mother – or Matthias.

'They think I'm probably over ten weeks,' Zoë said in a small voice.

'Oh, God, Zoë . . . what are you going to do?' Sian stared at the pale cameo of her friend's face.

'I can't have it – it's impossible, – I just can't,' she said, almost to herself. The woman doctor had been efficient but kind, and her probing fingers had told her everything the clinical test would later confirm. Zoë felt a taut thickness gather in her throat, heard a silent scream in her head: it wasn't fair, it wasn't fair.

'What exactly did they say?' Sian asked.

Zoë looked up at last, her features drawn, her eyes bright with fear.

'If I decide to go ahead with an abortion, I have to have something called pre-abortion counselling, to make sure that I know what I'm doing, I suppose. . . .' Her voice trailed off weakly. 'Tomorrow evening.' As the words slipped out, stilted and afraid, a vivid picture of her father came into Zoë's mind: a staunch church-goer, a member of the town council; she had often heard him describe abortion as 'murder', and always within her hearing as if he were brandishing a flaming sword in front of his only child. She closed her eyes to shut out the vision and was snapped roughly out of her thoughts by the intrusive buzzer of Vic's phone. Her hand shook as she reached for the receiver; she listened to his abrupt instructions and then placed the telephone mechanically back in its cradle. She knew instinctively that there could be no telling him, he wouldn't understand, and then she saw in a rare, painful flash of insight that Vic would only be repelled, disgusted, that her attraction for him would automatically be gone and her position at Samuels made impossible.

'Would you like me to come with you?' Sian's voice seemed to come from far away.

'No – no, it's okay.' Zoë shifted her blank gaze to her friend's face. 'I've made up my mind and nothing will change it,' she said firmly and with more conviction than she felt.

'Are you really sure? Don't you think you might like to, at least, *tell* your boyfriend?' Sian asked gently.

'No,' Zoë said sharply. 'I don't want to *tell* anyone, Sian – not anyone.' She didn't want to be made to think about it, didn't want to be counselled. She just wanted it over; wanted the nightmare that had suddenly disrupted her life to be finished.

Sian watched her turn away and gather up the papers beside her desk with unaccustomed care; it was a dismissal. She wanted to turn back to her own desk, but her eyes seemed to slide of their own accord to the window and to the white sky beyond as memory claimed her. Maybe she had loved Adam more than she should, more than Zoë obviously did her boyfriend, perhaps . . . and maybe in her naivety she had thought that Adam would stand by her because for so long she had woven intricate dreams of a future life with him. But they had only been dreams, and he had failed her just as she had failed herself. Now, ironically, she was faced with this uncomfortable parallel which carried with it all the echoes of pain and doubt she thought she had submerged so successfully. Sometimes, even now, she wondered how she had gone through with it all, how she had withstood Adam's bullying of her and his insistence that she leave a job she relished before the scandal broke, the months of unique loneliness which followed, and then the final humiliation at having no man, except her father, to visit her in hospital – and he had come, carrying a huge bunch of white daisies in his arms and that sad smile on his face; and she had cried. Sian blinked hard as the picture faded and she was made captive by a huge surge of mother love as she thought of Petie. Adam could ignore her all he wished – but not Petie, that was cruel, and it had been nearly two months now since the last time he had called. She swallowed slowly and wondered whether it had, after all, only been his bronzed handsome face and his undoubted charms that had captured and blinded her and whether, maybe, underneath all the glitz, there was really nothing special at all.

Fizz. Caroline grimaced; surely they could come up with a better brand name than that. She stared at the long, slim can, carefully coated in a deep metallic cornflower blue and thought that at least the packaging could almost be called elegant. If only it wasn't just a tin can containing an insipid cold drink. Ben had glibly remarked that the public would eat, drink, or slap on anything that looked pretty if you sold it hard enough and in the right way. She returned her eyes to the blank page of the advertising brief lying in front of her. Apart from the client's name, the brand and the date, all the other boxes on the page remained empty and she had promised Ben that it would all be nicely completed by tomorrow morning. She sighed heavily; he would probably only tear her effort apart when he got his big pastry fingers on it anyway. At that moment those same fingers were no doubt busy holding a large glass of wine and mauling some of the goodies the company kitchen had arranged for Diana's leaving party. They expected her to join them sooner or later and Caroline supposed that she would, provided she could get the damn brief completed, and provided she could get Nick Keogh out of her head.

She had messed everything up where he was concerned, that was clear, and he had obviously been totally fed up with the situation anyway. She sighed again. It was probably not meant to be; they were too different, worlds apart – 'not cut out of the same wood', her mother had said when she had managed to cajole what she could from her daughter. But there was an underlying unease in all these white-washed thoughts, a sort of careful pretence, because nothing her mother could say, or anyone else for that matter, would change the fact that he made her feel like no one had made her feel, that every time she thought of him she was swept by a crushing need which almost made her feel dizzy. Caroline closed her eyes and wondered why she was so incurably wet. Only last night Guy had hinted about an engagement ring, no doubt prompted by her mother, and she had said nothing in response, pretending she had misunderstood. And tonight he was meeting her in reception to take her home after the party, even though she had asked him not to, but he had insisted and she had inevitably given way. Incurably wet. Her eyes came to rest again on the blank sheet of paper, with all its carefully designed blank boxes and then she lifted her gaze to the equally blank, empty office and abruptly decided that the brief could wait. She would take it home and work on it tonight. She stood up and slid the papers back into the waiting Samuels folder. At least the brief would give her an excuse not to invite Guy in, which would mean that she could curtail the expected embrace with almost a clear conscience. She shook her head gently; why couldn't she just tell him that she felt nothing any more, that she hated the thought of him touching her, that their long tedious relationship was only habit, – that it was over. But she knew she wouldn't. And as she moved towards the open door she pressed any more thoughts of Guy down to think of later, or tomorrow, and let her mind switch to the party and the thing that mattered to her most. Nick would probably be there.

He was leaning languidly against a wall, glass in hand –

blue jeans, blue shirt – his equally blue eyes seemingly fixed on the brunette he was speaking to. Caroline glanced at him briefly as she walked into the room and discovered that her hands were trembling as she reached for one of the glasses of wine carefully laid out in rows for the waiting hordes. For several minutes she made smalltalk with her account group, but always with half an eye on Nick's lean blue figure on the other side of the room. As the minutes slipped by with agonizing slowness and glasses of wine were refilled and filled again, she began to realize with searing clarity that he was not going to come over, that he intended keeping his distance as if he had decided that she was, after all, a waste of time. Her heart began to beat painfully as a speech was made, as gifts were presented and she found herself clapping and cheering with everyone else as if all were well with the world and nothing was wrong. And then she saw him move, very slowly, as the applause began to fade, and she closed her eyes with relief because she knew, at last, he was coming to her. But even as the last hand-clap withered and died, he had passed her, brunette in tow, and disappeared through the open door. She told herself that long dreadful moments always pass, but the dread seemed to go on and on and on, sinking into the hollow pit of her stomach like a lead weight, and she wondered wretchedly how she still stood there with the same glass of wine in her hand, a fixed smile stretched across her face . . . waiting for Guy.

Nick watched Tina slowly undress: she thought she was teasing him, being provocative, but he remained totally unmoved, like a thing apart, like a spectator watching a performance. He had let himself be seduced by her, that had been the easiest part, but now he was tempted to tell her not to bother, just to put her clothes back on and go home. A small, humourless smile tipped the edges of his mouth as she turned towards him clad only in a red G-string, her long pendulous breasts swinging gently together like two old friends. He had planned to avoid the party altogether, but had somehow found himself there as usual with all the others hoping for a free drink and a good time; he had had nothing else better to do. Of course he had known that Caroline would probably be there and he had thought at the time that Tina coming along and chatting him up again was a gift from the gods. And he had meanly enjoyed the waiting game he had played and the wounded expression on her face as he had left the room with Tina trailing dutifully behind him. But now it all seemed childish, empty and pointless; he had gained nothing, but neither had he gained anything by their equally pointless and brief relationship because she had been afraid to make a decision and probably because she was also afraid to trust him. And, of course, he had proved her right. He drew a sharp, impatient breath at his own impulsiveness, but she had left him little choice with her feeble hesitations and qualms, and he did not need those sort of burdens. She was too shy, too vulnerable, too weighted with sensitivity and the millstone of her too middle-class background – *that* he certainly did not need. He became aware of Tina's intrusive fingers as they glided across his chest, but he remained immobile waiting for his body to react as he knew it ultimately would. And she would have to work for that reaction because he did not want or desire her white willing flesh, did not want that thick curling mass of chestnut hair tumbling so possessively across his belly, but even as the thought took shape and fled furtively away her eager tongue had betrayed him and she was claiming his erection like a prize.

'You've heard of sweet-talking, haven't you?' Ed said with exasperation.

'I know what you're saying,' Philippe retorted sharply, 'now let's talk about something else, shall we?' He turned his face away to the world beyond the window of the car, his eyes fastening on Piccadilly Circus and the seething mass of cars and people which seemed to choke it.

'Okay, okay – so I'm driving you crazy – I just want things right, that's all.' Ed took a long drag on an outsize cigar and let the smoke pour out slowly from his mouth so that for a moment his grizzled features were shrouded in a pall of grey. 'You've done the hard sell bit, now it's time to show them,' but he meant *her*, 'that you're really a nice guy and you want this deal just as much as they do.'

'Do you want to dictate to me exactly what I should say?' Philippe said sarcastically as the window rolled down with a soft purr; Ed thought of everything, even what to do with his filthy cigar smoke.

'You know what I mean, Phil,' Ed closed his eyes in an effort at pressing down his rising irritation, '. . . for Chrissakes, why do you always have to be so goddamn unreasonable?'

'I was just made that way, Ed.' He looked carefully into the old man's face and returned his gaze to the window with a finality that encouraged only silence.

Ed did not like that look; pitying, yet pitiless. It conveyed too many things, too many dangerous memories. Sometimes he wondered if Phil really did dislike him as much as he thought he did. And sometimes that dislike was more like hatred. Ed brought the cigar back to his lips; he didn't want to think about that. The trouble was, of course, that he loved the son of a bitch; even loved the hostility and the brooding ice in his eyes when he looked at him, like a breath of something he had lost somewhere too long ago. But there was also warmth there, there had to be, and he *was* Rosa's boy after all and she had been one of the warmest women he had ever known. It was a pity that she had only been a spick and his housekeeper, otherwise he might have married her. His forehead creased into deep frownlines as memory prompted him, but Etta had still been around then, still trying to wring out some more bucks from him with that silly smile of hers and that lurid overdone swing of her big round ass. But Rosa had kept everything going, kept him sane. It had been inevitable that he should move from relishing her mouth-watering cooking to relishing the glorious earthy quality of her body; so ready, so willing to receive and enjoy. He smiled inwardly with remembrance and

157

glanced sideways at the young man beside him. Rosa's boy. And Phil was all he had.

The credentials presentation had gone well; Geoff had surprised her with his adroit sense of timing, his humour and the way he had drawn in the American market alongside the UK and Europe with such subtle ease. Rock had clearly been impressed, but Sanchez had remained a little aloof, even during the lunch which had equally been designed to impress. Francesca gave a pre-arranged signal and the lights of the small theatre began to dim and Samuels' prize showreel began to roll. She knew there was not one mediocre ad, not one that came a jot below a brilliant creative standard that was beginning to become Samuels' trademark. Not even Saatchi's, for all its size and power, really had the edge over them in this area. Francesca felt a small smile touch her lips: every dog has its day.

'Fantastic,' Rock said enthusiastically as coffee was handed around.

'I'm glad you liked it,' Francesca responded.

'And I assume real results accompany the excellence of your creativity?' Sanchez asked carefully.

'Naturally.' Francesca spoke easily. 'Take the ad on Stempel China and Glass: a huge company, but under-valued and certainly its image was less than dynamic. We began a campaign in the press and later moved into TV, and almost immediately there was a considerable change in attitude. Share prices improved ahead of the FT index and over nine thousand new shareholders were added to the register.'

'But are big budget accounts your speciality? What about the small guy?' Philippe found his eyes locked in silent combat with hers as she looked steadily into his face.

'We try and tackle everything, Mr Sanchez . . . we like to think that we can make *any* product a speciality.' He was definitely interested, definitely hooked; Sanchez was just playing hard to get. She felt a surge of relief. He would be a difficult bastard to work with, that was clear, but at least he was sharp and ambitious and at least they would both be aiming for the same goal, along the same road.

'Of course, we're still talking about the same figure. . . .' He began to smile, just a little crookedly, and she found herself doing the same.

'Of course.' She began to walk towards the door. 'Perhaps it would be more comfortable to talk further in the conference room opposite.'

Philippe watched her move, his eyes reluctantly drawn to the body weaving gently beneath black cashmere. It had been a long time since he had really wanted a woman, but suddenly he knew that he wanted her and the knowledge did not please him. She was so much all rolled into one – too sure, too perfect – that it unnerved him, and he had grown used to being the sure one, the one who held all the cards.

'So it is agreed that the $50 million initial payment still stands,' she said neutrally. 'And we think an earn-out figure of twelve per cent over the next ten years for the additional $25 million fair.'

There was a pause.

'Okay,' Philippe replied, and he heard Rock draw in a sharp wary breath. He had hoped for ten per cent, but they had got the $50 million upfront so it was inevitable that he should give in gracefully and now he would just have to ensure that the earnings would grow just a little faster than he had planned. In any event, hadn't he orchestrated the winning of that Clio award? Wasn't it he who had persuaded Pizza Palace to try them over Orwell-Stein to create ads for its $80 million campaign? And it had been he who had slashed the old guard in the agency, the has-beens who were sitting on old, safe blue-chip accounts like withered buddhas, and brought in young, aggressive creatives straight out of art school. He had broken the stale mould that Dunmar-Rock had set into; Ed had had tunnel vision for too long. But then Ed was old and didn't want the risks any more.

'Fine,' Francesca said evenly. Just like that. For a moment she wondered what game Sanchez was playing, but then realized that he had got what he wanted and could afford to be generous. But she would make sure he worked for it. 'I'll get any other details sorted out and down on paper for a draft document.' She turned to Rock. 'Perhaps you would like to name a date for signing, Mr Rock?'

'Ed – please,' he said, grinning. 'Now that it's all going to be in the family.'

Philippe winced.

'How about the 20th December . . . a nice time for a Christmas present?' He laughed and Francesca could not resist doing the same. And it would be some Christmas present: there would be about 150 employees of Dunmar-Rock who held stock in the company, the biggest shareholder being Rock himself with twenty per cent. He stood to become a much richer man out of the deal. Even Sanchez with less than one per cent would make a great deal of money, plus the fact that they were joining up with the UK's most creative hot-shop. It was a good deal – for both sides of the Atlantic.

'I think that will be in order.' She turned to Geoff. 'Maybe we could arrange for some champagne?' Geoff nodded and smiled. It had all been planned beforehand: three bottles of Roederer Cristal nestled neatly in Francesca's drinks' cabinet, all ready and waiting for the big moment. Her instincts had been right, and he wondered fleetingly as he slipped outside the conference room whether she had ever been wrong.

'I hope you will still be able to join me for dinner this evening?' she asked, as the door closed softly behind Geoff.

'Yes, of course,' Philippe replied automatically.

'I'd really like that . . . ,' Ed said, but shaking his head, 'except that I think all this travelling has eaten into my old man's bones.' A sad expression of inevitability seemed to settle on his face and he felt the full and uncomfortable studied gaze of Philippe.

'Are you feeling all right?' Francesca asked immediately, suddenly remembering that, after all, Rock was over seventy.

'Oh, sure, sure – just tired, that's all, but you and Philippe go ahead, I'll be fine.'

'Are you really okay, Ed?' This time it was Philippe, and Ed found himself suppressing a smile as he shifted his gaze from Francesca's face to his protégé. He wanted to say, 'I didn't know you cared. . . .'

'I told you, I'm fine – just need to get my head down, that's all; this has been a pretty big day, after all.'

The conversation was terminated as Geoff came into the room bearing a tray of the promised champagne. Philippe's eyes remained searchingly on Rock for a few moments before he was obliged to take up his role in the celebration. It was not like Ed to turn down a dinner invitation and certainly not *this* dinner invitation; maybe he was tired – and maybe he was up to something. Philippe pressed the thought down, this was not the time, but he would find out sooner or later, he always did.

This was not quite how she had planned it. There had always been Rock and Sanchez when she had imagined this dinner, now it was suddenly only Sanchez. It would have been easier with Rock. Francesca had not yet made her mind up about Sanchez; she neither liked or disliked him. He was cold, he was smart and he was also unreadable. She lifted her eyes from the depths of her gin and tonic and saw him coming towards her from the other side of the bar. She decided he was also good-looking if you could get beyond the icy quality of those eyes, and suddenly she was glad that she had decided to wear something a little less than severe and the clinging moss-green velvet seemed an ideal choice; maybe Mr Sanchez would thaw out a bit, and she smiled to herself. But as he drew closer and her eyes came to rest on his face she checked herself for her almost-arrogance. He was so very cool, so very controlled, and she recalled Aidan's bitter description of her, 'like the ice-queen or something. . . .' Francesca stood up as he drew beside her and wondered silently whether the description had boomeranged on her and she was meeting the ice-king. Eyes like chips of yellow glass.

'I didn't think I was late?' he asked, as they sat down.

'You're not – I'm just a little early.'

For the first half-hour the small-talk was almost painful, and Matthias' face slid furtively into her consciousness and she wondered what she was doing there, with this difficult, complex man, but she swallowed the longing – it would pass. Yet there was the merger, and it was going through because he had accepted her twelve per cent, her pound of flesh. Her father would have been pleased and he would have handled this dinner, this 'celebration' without a thought. She knew instinctively as she had known years before that if she had been a man everything would have been easier – wouldn't it? But over dinner Sanchez seemed to begin to relax and Francesca felt the old tension in the back of her neck start to fall away. Maybe he was human, after all.

'How did you come into advertising?' he already knew the answer, but he wanted to hear it from her.

'My father: he owned Gaetini & Kemp, the agency I was running before I joined Samuels.' She looked down at her glass for a moment before continuing. 'He died when I was seventeen and left my brother and me equal shares; he always wanted at least one of us to go into the business.'

'What about your brother?' He had seen the soft shadow behind her eyes and wondered.

'He's into rather expensive antiques, or was. . . .' Michael. He had slipped from her mind just as quickly as he had slipped out of her life, but he would come back to her for something, for money, wouldn't he? That, at least. Perhaps she hadn't tried hard enough with him. She took a deep breath, forcing herself to concentrate. 'Anyway, it seemed the most obvious thing for me to do and as it happened it was exactly what I wanted – and so I did my training at GK – watched over by an extremely benevolent and patient MD who retired once he felt I was able to manage on my own.'

'Which didn't take very long. . . .'

'And you?' she asked, pushing aside the compliment, eager to change the direction of the questioning.

'Me?' He almost laughed. 'My rise to power within the sanctified realms of Dunmar-Rock reads like something out of a comic book. . . .' He twirled a glass slowly in his hand. 'Ed seemed to see something in me that no one else had and plucked me out of obscurity.' It was almost true.

'That was . . . more than just a little fortunate for you,' she said quietly and saw how his eyes were suddenly veiled, saw that he was not telling the whole truth.

'Oh, Ed likes to play the philanthropist sometimes and a poor Hispanic kid who maybe had shown himself to be a bit smart, but with no chance of reaching the board, seemed an ideal choice.' He tried to push the bitterness away, but knew that she had picked it up.

'He seems very fond of you.'

'Ed seems fond of everyone.' He lifted his eyes back to her face and scrutiny.

'Do you have any family?'

'Nope . . . only a bunch of step-brothers.' He began to smile. 'They think I'm going to be the first spick president of the US of A. . . .' He shook his head gently and then slowly refilled their glasses; he was, he suddenly realized, beginning to enjoy himself. And he didn't mind her scrutiny, somehow he felt he could handle it now, and he found instead that his gaze matched her own, sweeping her face and her hair, but stopping carefully at the dusky skin at her neck where the sleek, tormenting beginnings of moss-green velvet began.

'Your parents?' Maybe she shouldn't ask, but he made her too curious with his guarded answers.

'My father died in a trucking accident years ago – I never knew him.' That *was* a lie, but there was no way he was going to confess all, no way Ed was going to rear his ugly head. 'And my mother died after a mugging, of a heart attack.'

'Oh, God – I'm sorry.'

'That's what I mean when I said "my rise to power reads like something out of a comic book" – a corny comic book. She was a cleaner, a "profession" highly populated by spicks and blacks as you might imagine, and she started

163

real early in the morning, when it was dark.' He looked into his glass. 'She was alone when it happened and I suppose it was a miracle that it hadn't happened before.' He had been nineteen then, a typical lowly office boy at Dunmar-Rock; running errands, making tea, doing the mail – with no real vision, only the raw, fragile seeds of ambition of which he was hardly yet aware. There had just been him and mama left at home, but he had enjoyed her clucking and fussing when he got back at night, and the hot spicy meals waiting to be served on the red and white checked cloth, and the familiar mother smell of her with that cheap scent she still wore even though her looks had left her long before. He had wanted to kill someone. He still wanted to kill someone because he could never make up to her for what was lost, for what might have been, never replace that cheap scent for a crazy two hundred dollar bottle on Fifth Avenue. He took a long sip of wine. 'Anyway, that was a hell of a long time ago.' And Rock had heard about the unfortunate death of Rosa Sanchez through the agency grape-vine and had put two and two together. It had been nearly twenty years since she had been his housekeeper, but he had remembered and Philippe had wanted to forget. But mama had told him everything about the man who had once employed her and who Fate had decreed would do the same for her son – almost everything. Rock's benevolent eye turned its full force on Philippe. There was the funeral which he had paid for, then the gradual grooming and absorption of Philippe into Rock's inner circle of young favourites, and finally and ultimately, Harvard. Rock had grinned from ear to ear. It took several years before Philippe figured out why.

'I shouldn't have asked.' If there was a question, she always had to ask it, even if it hurt; she sighed inwardly.

'I don't suppose your mother ever got her hands dirty cleaning other people's garbage.' He knew what the answer was because he'd checked, as he'd checked everything.

'Not my mother, no,' she replied dryly. 'My mother probably wouldn't know what garbage was.'

164

He glanced at her curiously.

'Is it nice being born with a silver spoon in your mouth?' How often had he damned and envied the Harvard and the Yale set, never really part of them, and the rich, spoilt, privileged preppies and their effortless superiority.

'It's not always quite as simple or as charming as it sounds.'

'But it helps.'

'Naturally.' She studied his face for a moment: the wide mouth, the well-shaped nose, the high, intelligent forehead, and wondered if the huge chip which he carried on his shoulder hurt as much as it seemed to. 'It's getting late.'

'I'll see you home.' He stood up and she realized again how tall he was.

'Thanks, but I have a car waiting outside.'

'Until the signing, then.'

She took his outstretched hand and felt its long smooth coolness, looked into the old-young eyes and tried to imagine him as a boy, a child, but nothing would come.

Philippe watched her walk across the room and he was reminded of another time, another place when he had been just seventeen and thought himself in love with an exotic Puerto Rican dancer called Carlotta. She had laughed at his wide-eyed adoration, but Carlotta had kissed him – once – and he would always remember the rich taste of her thick rosy-red lipstick, remember the slight, sensuous swing of her buttocks as she walked and that wonderful mass of dark, dark hair which framed a face carved by the gods. Like Francesca.

He swallowed slowly, painfully, and reached for the final drops of his wine. It was time to go and Ed would be waiting; he could bet a thousand dollars that the old bastard would be sitting up in bed with a great fat havana in one hand and a scotch in the other. He lifted his eyes to heaven in exasperation. Ed would want to know every word that was said, but this time he would be disappointed, he was definitely in no mood for an interrogation. Philippe sighed heavily realizing with sudden searing clarity that he was in the mood for a woman, he even had the number of a good escort agency. But he knew he wouldn't use it, not now, because there was only one that he wanted and she was just a little beyond his reach, and at least he had always known just how far that reach could stretch. He was like a lone wolf crying for the moon. He shrugged and smiled to himself and added an additional five pound note to the tip; it had been a good meal.

'When do you go in?' Sian asked quietly as Zoë placed a cup of coffee on her desk.

'Next week.' She didn't want to think about it, didn't want to think what they would do. The woman who had given her counselling had been very understanding and she hadn't really tried to make her change her mind, which was a relief. There was no choice, anyway. She stared blindly at the square piece of sky framed in the window. In any case whatever she decided to do, her father would have branded her either a whore or a murderer. She closed her eyes. And there was her job, wasn't there? And Vic. And the rest of her life.

'If you want me to do anything. . . .' Sian's voice trailed off lamely. There was nothing to say. It was a terrible decision to make alone, as it was, and in any event mother nature didn't exactly give much time to agonize over what should or should not be done. Her eyes rested on Zoë's immobile profile and she wondered why she was so adamant about not telling her boyfriend. Maybe she was afraid she would lose him, which would naturally mean that he was worth losing, but Zoë probably wouldn't see it that way; maybe he had been a one-night-stand, which would explain her reticence. Sian caught her breath and then thought of Adam. She wondered how many men had ever used a woman's body and walked away. No looking back, no questions asked.

'A penny for them?' Geoff asked cheerfully, as he came out of Francesca's office.

'Too deep and meaningful, Geoff, I'm afraid . . . ,' but he had betrayed her into a smile. '. . . I think I should take a crash course in "how to be light-hearted".'

166

'I'll do something about that tomorrow night,' he said grinning and then, without waiting for her reply, disappeared into his office.

She watched his retreating back with curiosity; still surprised with herself that she had accepted a second invitation to dine with him. He was exactly what Zoë had said, 'a nice guy', maybe too nice if that was possible, and he was also charming, attentive and generous. It all made her feel peculiarly guilty because she knew somehow that she could hurt him, that strangely Geoff was more vulnerable than she was. Sometimes she wondered whether she had buried her feelings somewhere too deep to retrieve because there was a sort of numbness inside. And there was still Adam, of course – his face effortlessly stealing into her mind with unrelenting regularity. But she pushed the thought of him aside because thinking about him was pointless. In any case, Geoff seemed able to make her laugh – Adam had never even tried.

It was late and she had promised herself an early night. Francesca poured the steaming sweetened milk into a mug and topped it up with a large tot of brandy; a remedy of her father's when he couldn't sleep and there were only long, restless nights. And she thought sadly that there must have been many of those for him. Her mind swept backward to the awakening years, to the discovery that the icy silence between her parents was augmented by sudden, frightening arguments, that theirs was not a marriage at all, but a savage charade of separate rooms and days and nights of absence by her father, until she thought he had finally abandoned her and that great mausoleum of a house in which her mother ruled. But he always had come back. Francesca blinked the images away and brought the milk to her lips. It was too hot, and she placed it back on the white surface just as the sound of the doorbell pierced the quiet. She pulled the loose white folds of her robe more tightly about her and walked through the hall to the front door. The spy-hole only told her that the man was blond and immediately she thought of Michael, but as she opened the door her brother's face faded abruptly and it was Matthias who stood there, immobile and expressionless, his eyes locking without hesitation on her own.

'I thought that, as I was passing, I'd call in . . . ,' he said softly and his mouth slid into a slow, mocking smile.

'And Munich?' she asked, trying to put business between them, trying to crush the surge of eagerness which arose at the sight of him.

'Munich is past – I'm supposed to be in Paris, but London seemed a better idea.' His eyes looked back at her, pale, suggestive, saying too many things. 'May I come in?'

She opened the door wide and he passed through, and she wondered why she had not told him to go as she had promised herself – it was late, she was tired, he presumed too much. Yet she allowed him to lead her just as he had known she would.

'Did you want to talk about the campaign, the ad?' she asked, looking away from him and walking towards the drinks cabinet in her study.

'I could have found out how things were going from Brunning the buffoon if I'd wanted . . . you know that's not why I'm here.' He took the proffered cognac from her automatically and then scanned the room carefully until he slowly returned his gaze back to her face.

'Why *are* you here?' The picture of him in the *Mail*, which Vic had so kindly guided her to, slipped unhappily into her mind: that crooked smile, the arm draped provocatively across the back of Fleet Street tycoon Richard's daughter, the low, low neckline of dear Melissa which left little to anyone's imagination. Francesca took a deep gulp of her cognac and let the burning liquid spread warmth and hopefully calm through her limbs. She had followed Aidan's unsubtle lead and discovered all she needed, even the fact that Sir Richard's family owned the chateau where Matthias had seduced her with such studied brilliance. He had been seeing the young socialite for several months, among others.

'I wanted to see you – isn't that enough?'

She let the words fall into silence, not wanting to reply.

But he came towards her, so close she could smell him – that searing, musky smell that made her head swim.

'I'm tired . . . really very tired,' she said finally.

'Was it that precious photo?' he asked wearily

'I really don't need this, not now,' she said softly.

But his hands came up to cup her face and she shivered as they slid down her neck following the line of her shoulders so that her robe began to slip and fall at his touch. She clamped her eyes shut as his hot mouth found her breast and her head went back in silent agony. He thinks he can seduce the world; he thinks nothing living is beyond his reach and the dizzying manipulations of his golden fingers. She clutched his head, stroked his hair, letting her hands gently pull white-blond strands through the slits of her fingers, and then desolately pushed him away.

He straightened himself and watched her pull the white robe back over her shoulders to cover her nakedness. There was a sad sort of smile on his face, like a child.

'Why are you doing this?'

'I can't do anything else.'

He sighed heavily. 'Why do you want everything?' His forehead creased into unaccustomed lines of bewilderment.

'It is not I who want everything, but you.'

'I needed her . . . I needed the contacts.'

'Like you needed me – a sort of business deal?' Francesca replied sarcastically.

'It wasn't like that. . . .'

'It was beautiful . . . remember?' she said, with a derisive smile on her face, his own words coming back to sting him like a bad echo.

'You don't think it's possible to have sex with someone and love someone else . . . ?'

'Oh, don't give me that old, worn-out excuse of the famous lustful male.' She felt the anger suddenly rise out of nowhere. He would have touched her – them – just as he had touched her, Francesca, caressed them in the same perfect way, performed all the special little tricks that he had performed on her in just the same way because he could not help himself. And he had that gift, that way of making you believe that each gesture, each touch was for you alone, that he had never done it quite that way with anyone else before. She clenched her fists. 'It's called self-indulgence – it's called having it all.'

'And you've never wanted it all, you've never tried to have it all?' And this time it was he who laced his words with sarcasm.

'I've never pretended to be some God-holy prophet, some new species of man who's going to change the world!'

'I didn't give myself that label. . . .'

'But you've never denied it – you've loved it all, every damned minute!' She shook her head. 'You must have really seen me coming.' Her voice was low then, lost. 'And I believed in you, that's what's so sad, so damned stupid. . . .' She lifted her eyes to his face. 'There are thousands of people, young people who want to believe in you, who probably do, and you're going to cheat them.' Just like me. 'Like all the others before you – shattering their innocent illusions, breaking their little dreams – because all this will come out, every party, every girl – sooner or later.'

He stared at her for a long moment and she felt tears of rage slip traitorously into her eyes.

'Don't you care?'

'I care.' And he still stared. 'But it's not those thousands of little people that you really care about, is it? It's yourself and your own broken dream, that I was some reformed mystic who wanted to change the world, but still wanted you and only you at the same time.'

She shook her head, but he continued, 'You can't bear the thought that I might be human, might want someone else when you're not around. I never committed myself to you, never told you that I was everlastingly faithful. Did I? And I can "make love" or "make sex", or whatever you want to call it to others and still love you, or need you more than them. . . .' He saw the grief held in her eyes and knew that his words were wasted. 'But that isn't good enough for you, is it?'

'No. . . .' It could never be; and there would be no compromise for her, no going back because she had never been any good at learning to live with half-truths, games, wondering where he was, who he was with, fooling herself.

'I thought not.' His eyes seemed lighter, more expressionless, more empty. 'And I can't change, Francesca, not now – it's too late for me.' It was a warning, a plea, as if he expected her to do what he could not. But she did not respond and he turned his face away from her so that she would not see the extent of his disappointment.

He swallowed slowly, in the depths of his throat, hating the uncomfortable, timeless silence, until he was unable to look away any longer and his gaze came back to settle on her face. 'And please don't concern yourself as to whether I intend cheating the innocent thousands of their dream. It is what I *achieve* that will count in the end, not who I sleep with,' he said with great deliberation. 'That seems to be *your* probem.' But he still wanted her, still couldn't understand her rejection of him. 'And what of the great god "Advertising" . . . ? What of the promises and pretty dreams you weave for staggering amounts of money – offering the little people a dream world which you know is a lie, and capitalizing on those dreams: the perfume that will make every man want you; the cigarette that supposedly improves your image, yet kills you at the same time; the car that makes you feel like a king, but the little man can hardly afford to buy . . . ?' He laughed then, a wry despairing laugh and stopped so abruptly that the sound was rough, raw, like a sob. '*You* accuse *me* of breaking dreams – yet you sell them every day of your glitzy, glossy existence.'

'That's enough.'

'It's called "business", isn't it?' he said finally, sarcastically.

There was a long, dreadful moment and they both stood woodenly, staring at each other, wrapped in silence.

'I'd better go. . . .'

She said nothing as he drained the last of his cognac, as

171

she watched the broad darkness of his retreating back leave the room, but still found her steps following his as he reached the half-lit hallway. He turned to face her and she was caught by the look of bruised regret.

'You'll let me call you sometimes?' he asked softly, all anger and bitterness suddenly gone and she was moved once again by the strange child in him.

She forced herself to smile, forced down the longing.

'Of course. . . .'

His arm lifted to open the door, but with his free hand he reached out for her.

'Just for me – this. . . .'

And he pulled her close so that his hands could come up to bury themselves in her hair, arching her neck back so that he could rake her face and skin with his mouth. And she wanted to cry out, but instead her hand came up softly, slowly, to cover his lips so that he would stop.

He lowered his eyes and she saw a passing unhappiness flee across his face like shame.

'I've seen things you've never seen, done things you'd never dream. . . .' But then there was that smile again, crooked, wanton, as if he were remembering. 'I'm not a good man. You know that, don't you . . . ,' he whispered sadly, finally, and traced the outline of her mouth with his finger, '. . . but I would be if I could.'

# 6

She leaned her head against the closed door, clamped her eyes shut as she heard him pause on the path and then the inevitable sound of his footsteps as they began to fade, fade and die. Her shoulders sagged with an enormous sadness and she wondered briefly whether, if he should return, she would have the courage to turn him away again. There was still somehow a feeling of the essence of him on her, lying thickly on the air like a heady, musky scent as if he still stood beside her, still provoking that familiar crushing need and the searing remembrance of the dizzying pleasure he could give her. The telephone rang and she thought for a moment that it would be him because she wanted it to be, but instead Michael's voice broke the silence and she wondered at her ability to confuse them both with such stinging ease.

'Francesca, can I see you?'

'It's very late, Michael,' her voice said wearily.

'I thought perhaps you could come to my hotel.'

'With some more money . . . ?' she asked shortly.

There was a pause then and she sighed.

'I don't really need much. . . .'

'What are you doing with it, Michael? I gave you more than enough to last until the end of the month.'

'I'll pay you back – you know that.'

'It's not the money I'm concerned about, it's you . . . and it would be nice if you wanted to see *me* and not just my money.' He didn't respond. 'Mother called me again shortly after you left, she thinks I'm keeping you from her and her temper is, to say the least, fraying.' She didn't want this conversation, not now.

'I don't want to see her.'

'God, Michael . . . what do you want! I'm really tired of all this – it would be nice if just once I got a little

173

consideration.' She drew a sharp, impatient breath. 'Have you ever wondered what I might be feeling, what I might want?' And Matthias' sad, silky face stole tormentingly into her mind. Just for the warmth of him.

There was another long pause and she closed her eyes, willing patience.

'I need a thousand pounds . . . as a sort of down-payment.'

'A down-payment for what? What have you got yourself into, Michael?!'

'It's legal – I promise you it is legal.' She heard him sigh and knew that he was trying to decide whether to confide in her or not. 'I want to rule my own life, get my own thing going – without mother, without anyone.'

'But you want *my* money.'

'Only temporarily, only as a loan – I've told you that.'

'I suppose you're not going to tell me what this "own thing" of yours involves . . . you know, it's just possible I might be able to help.'

'I want to do this on my own.'

'Okay – well, do it your own way, and in that case you won't expect me to come to you at this rather late hour. Get a cab, Michael.' And she put the receiver down.

It was good, very good. Nick ran through the closing seconds of the reel once again, more than satisfied with the final shots they had chosen for the campaign. Matthias had yet to be inset, of course, but Nick was sure he would be impressed by the slices of film they had selected. It was divided into four parts: the Israeli/Palestinian conflict with shots of the crisis in the Gaza Strip; Beirut – and a brilliantly handled film of the aftermath of a car bombing; environmental – the gruesome effects of illegal dumping along the eastern seaboard of the US and heart-wrenching shots of the seal disaster off the polluted coasts of the British Isles; and finally the growing worldwide drug problem with a skilfully mixed combination of the abused and their abusers. The reel came to a close and Nick turned his attention to the draft script which still had a few rough edges, but was coming along nicely, another few days and the sound track could be prepared. He stood up and stretched; he had been sitting in the same position for over an hour and his long legs were stiff, he was also thirsty and a picture of a brimming cup of hot coffee slipped easily into his head. Nick glanced at his watch. Brunning wanted to see the completed reel in half an hour; he had just enough time to get back to his office and relax for a few minutes before meeting him.

Samuels seemed quiet somehow for a late Friday afternoon. Nick laughed soundlessly as he caught glimpses of half-empty offices; no doubt most account groups were still drooling over their long, long lunches, or boozing it up behind the locked doors of the Drayman's. He turned into the narrow corridor of the third floor, the 'prize' floor, the one where the largest accounts seemed to take seed and grow along with the egos of their managers. He shook his head gently and then slowly became aware that someone was coming towards him from the other end of the empty corridor. Even from a distance of fifty yards or more he could see the blood drain from her face at the unexpected sight of him and as the gap inevitably closed between them he slowed until she was only an arm's length away.

'Hi.' His eyes flickered over her.

'Hi,' she repeated lamely and felt a hated tide of crimson flood into her face.

'How have you been?'

'Okay,' she replied and her fingers seemed to tighten around the file she was carrying. 'How's the campaign going?'

'Great – I think.' A smile began to tip the edges of his mouth as he looked into her face. 'I have to show Big Bad Vic the draft in about twenty minutes . . . I was just going for a sneaky cup of coffee to sustain me in the coming ordeal.'

She nodded dumbly and prayed silently for a clever reply, but her lips remained excruciatingly mute and seemed to acquire a dry, dustless rim which would probably crack if she opened her mouth.

He sighed inwardly. And wondered again at her capacity to move him. She was hopeless, but he still wanted her.

'Could you make it for a drink tonight?' He watched her carefully and was surprised to see the lovely soft mouth broaden into a smile.

'Yes . . . fine.'

'I'll see you in the Drayman's – about 6.30?'

'Okay.'

He glanced at his watch. 'Look, I've got to go . . . I'll see you later.'

She watched him walk away from her and closed her eyes briefly, happily, savouring the moment. Perhaps it would be all right now, perhaps she would handle things better. Caroline tucked the file she held more tightly under her arm and continued on down the corridor. A picture of Guy's miserable face stole unwillingly into her head. She had told him, finally, that it was over, that she no longer wanted to see him. Even as she told him she had wondered why it had taken her so long when it all suddenly seemed so easy. He had been angry at first, then sullen and then angry again, until she had grown tired and had tried to get out of the car and he had suddenly become contrite and sad. He had ultimately attempted to kiss her, half-smothering her with his long wet tongue and pinning her to the car seat in a painful embrace of probing hands and pointed elbows until she had pushed him away in disgust. There had been several anguished telephone calls since and her mother had become involved, siding with poor darling Guy. . . . Caroline took a deep, determined breath; whatever her mother might say or contrive, she would not go back on her decision even if she and Nick did not work out. She thought of the ring Guy had said he had bought her – a solitaire – how very predictable, how very like Guy . . . and 'how ungrateful she was to turn him away now after all they had meant to each other'. . . . Caroline reached the turning in the corridor and a window which overlooked a small paved square. She paused for a moment and leaned her head back in a gesture of relief.

Oh, God, how glad she was that she had not taken his damned solitaire, how glad that Guy's ring did not sit possessively on her finger like a bribe!

'I managed to get away on time,' Sian said half-smiling, and awkwardly placed a crumpled bag of grapes on the bed-side table.

'You shouldn't have bothered,' Zoë replied without expression.

'Do you feel okay?' Sian responded, ignoring her remark.

'It's over, that's all that matters – I don't want to think about it.' But tears too heavy to hold back brimmed into her eyes and began to fall slowly.

'Oh, Zoë, I'm so sorry. . . .'

'It doesn't matter, it really doesn't matter,' she protested weakly, 'I know I couldn't have gone through with it, I just couldn't. Not on my own.' She shook her head. '. . . Better to be like this than end up like . . .'

The words stopped abruptly on her tongue and her eyes lowered guiltily as she turned away from Sian.

'I made a different choice, that's all, Zoë,' she responded quietly.

'I'm sorry, I didn't mean to be rude . . . it's just that I'm not strong like you, and I couldn't have gone through all those months and then have a baby alone,' she said, with remembered fear. 'And my parents aren't like yours – I think my father would have either killed me or himself rather than endure the scandal.'

Sian stared at the mass of blonde curls, heard the little-girl stifled sobs. It would have been a disaster.

'Then you've done the right thing. As long as you feel like that you'll be okay.' She forced herself to look about the blank room with feigned interest, hating the moment.

'I didn't want it to be like this . . . I didn't want this to happen . . . it wasn't my fault.' Zoë lifted her face up and knotted the handkerchief gathered in her hand in slow twisting pain.

'No, it wasn't your fault,' Sian answered. 'In any event,

I don't care what anyone says, I think it's cruel and selfish to bring into the world a child that is not really wanted.' She felt strongly that what she said was true, but somehow her practised little speech sounded hollow in the small white room where Zoë sat and cried. And she was stung suddenly as she thought of Petie and the secret times she had wondered what her life would be like without him. Free. She closed her eyes to shut out the vision and turned back to Zoë.

'Was it very expensive . . . how have you managed to pay?'

'I borrowed a hundred pounds from a friend – I said it was to help me with my overdraft, but that only covers about half of the expenses; the rest I have to pay back over the next few months.' She spoke mechanically and brought the sodden handkerchief back to her eyes and then shifted her gaze to a small window. It was dark outside.

'You still haven't told your boyfriend?'

Zoë laughed abruptly and then the laughter died just as suddenly into a rough, choking sob.

'Oh, no. And I don't intend to.' She lifted a closed fist and wiped away the dampness from her face. 'I never told you who he was, did I?'

'You don't have to.'

'Vic,' Zoë replied in almost a whisper. 'It was Vic.'

Sian stared at Zoë's rigid profile for a long moment and wondered if she had heard correctly.

'I know you don't like him . . . ,' Zoë continued uneasily, 'but he's not so bad when you get to know him.'

Obviously.

'And he knows nothing about this at all?' Sian asked with difficulty.

'Oh, no . . . no,' and her voice trembled into a brittle laugh. 'Vic doesn't know anything, and he's not going to.'

'You shouldn't have told me.'

'Why not?' Zoë said with surprising sharpness. 'I had to tell someone, I couldn't keep it to myself any longer.'

'Are you going to go on seeing him now?' It was none of her business, but the question slipped out unguardedly.

'I suppose I should cool things a bit, maybe,' Zoë said in a weak attempt at sophistication. 'Or perhaps I should get myself another job. . . .' It was all talk, because she knew she wasn't going to do anything of the kind.

'Maybe he'd want to know . . . ?' Sian said lamely. But Vic was the sort who would get up and run – he wouldn't see the connection between sex and a baby.

'Don't make me laugh, Sian . . . ,' Zoë replied bitterly.

'If you feel like that, then why do you. . . .' Her words trailed off.

'I don't know . . . ,' she said awkwardly. 'I just can't seem to help myself.' There was a taut little silence before she added, 'Sometimes I think I love him.'

There was nothing she could say. Sian closed her eyes in exasperation. But he doesn't love you. . . .

She stayed for a few long moments more before her eyes were drawn inevitably and guiltily to her watch. She stood up to indicate that she was about to leave.

'I shouldn't think too much about it all for the moment; just concentrate on getting back to normal and that will probably take longer than you think.' She slipped her coat back on. 'Do you need anything else?'

Zoë turned her flushed damp face finally back to Sian. 'No, I'll be fine now.'

'Okay,' Sian responded as her eyes flicked sadly over the younger girl, who seemed so much younger, younger than her. 'I'll see you on Monday, then.'

Zoë nodded and turned her blank face slowly back to the window.

There was a soft drizzle turning the pavements to silver outside. Sian walked quickly across the narrow cobbled road and towards the lights of the main high street in the distance. She shivered suddenly as a chill gust covered her with pinpricks of rain. Vic. Zoë and Vic. What a fool she was! How many times had Zoë made feeble excuses for being with Vic when it was not really necessary, how many times had she left her 'working' in the office when there was really no need. She'd been walking around with her eyes closed. But slimy, conceited, big-mouthed Vic! She tried to imagine the two of them together, but failed. Sian shivered again. And, of course, there was no chance that Zoë would ever tell him about the abortion, that wouldn't suit him at all, it would sully his super-adman image and, no doubt, his feelings, whatever they might be, where she was concerned. Suddenly Geoff's grinning and somehow innocent face slid into her mindscape and she sighed softly with relief. He was nice, he was easy to be with and, for the time being at any rate, she would settle for that. The deep-throated roar of a bus chugging up the hill made her head turn and Sian started to quicken her pace; if she managed to catch it she would be home in time to put Petie to bed. Pulling the collar of her coat up higher around her face she started to run.

The TV screen was a mass of black and white fuzz; there was no real sound except a mild, irritating hum.

'Shit!' Ben Langley pulled the tape from its black slot and stared manically at the label which had been so carefully stuck across the front. 'Clarence is an ass-hole! How many times have I told you that that boy is an A1 ass-hole?!!' Ben threw the offending tape across his desk, watched it slide and then fall off in a cascade of paper. 'I asked for PAL – not NTSC – P . . . A . . . L.' He glared at Caroline who hovered uneasily in the doorway. 'As the little boy wonder seems to have hopped it – *you*'ll have to go back down to projection and make sure that it's done by 9 a.m. tomorrow morning.'

Caroline nodded dumbly, well aware that there would be no one available to change the tape at this time of the evening. It was already 6.30 and Nick would be waiting, but he would have to wait a little longer because there was no alternative to Ben's demand. It was just unfortunate that she happened to be the only one around to make sure it was carried out. She moved to the back of the long, open-plan office, well away from Ben's domain and the clink of the booze bottles as he pulled one out from the cupboard accompanied by a further stream of profanities. The job would have to be done by an outside source and she knew she didn't have a number for any of the companies she had heard so often bandied about the office. With a sinking heart she reached for the fat volume of Yellow Pages . . . maybe it wouldn't take too long.

But it was almost 7.30 by the time she found herself pushing through the inevitable crowd at the Drayman's. At first she couldn't see Nick, but then she saw the sure shape of the back of his head in a corner of the bar. She sighed inwardly with relief and made a path around a large group of people before coming within just a few feet of him, but she stopped there and felt her legs go strangely weak as she saw that he was not alone, that his arm reached past her to the wall and a girl stood coyly beneath the curve of his arm. She was very pretty, very female, the girl he had left the party with. Caroline swallowed hard, thought she would fade, die from the painful beating of her heart, but instead she found her feet taking cautious steps backward even as she stepped on someone's curiously hard foot and he groaned.

Tina stared interestedly at the girl just behind Nick, caught by her strange pale face.

'What is it?' he asked as he followed her gaze. He turned his head slowly and saw Caroline's retreating figure moving awkwardly through the tightly knit crowd. 'Christ,' he muttered and raised his eyes to heaven in frustration. She was late, bloody late, and he had thought she had stood him up. 'Look, excuse me, Tina, there's some business I have to sort out . . . ,' and he began to move away from her.

'You'll come back though, won't you?' Tina asked indignantly and looked at her nearly empty glass.

Nick didn't bother to reply. The door had already closed behind Caroline's dark head and he was afraid that by the time he made his way through the squeeze of people she would be gone. The rain bit into his face as he opened the door and he cursed softly as he saw her scurrying up the black, wet street. He called, but she did not reply and he didn't know whether she had heard him or not; he found himself running.

'Caroline?!'

She stopped, but didn't turn around. He caught her arm and pulled her gently towards him so that she faced him.

'You could have waited.'

'Why?' She lifted her head up and he realized that she was crying.

'I didn't think you were coming . . . ,' he said lamely.

'So you decided to chat up "Miss Flavour-of-the-Month" again. . . .'

He wanted to smile at her unaccustomed witticism, but pressed it down as she looked away from him.

'You haven't exactly made things easy for me.'

She shook her head and he thought he heard a small anguished sound escape her lips.

'You didn't make things easy for me, either,' she said abruptly, 'you had to have everything at once. . . .' Tears began to stream down her cheeks. 'I'm tired of everyone pushing me into corners, bullying me. . . .' Her lower lip began to tremble and her body began to shake, slowly, with great sobs. Nick watched her for a long moment as she stood in front of him, watched as the lights from passing cars illuminated then fled across her contorted, desolate face. He reached out for her, locking his hand gently on the back of her neck and pulling her into his chest, and moved them into the protection and darkness of a nearby shop doorway. He leaned against a wall holding her, stroking the bowed, unhappy head; amazed again at the way she seemed able to slip under his skin with such unexpected ease.

'I want you to come home with me,' he said at last.

And she didn't protest as he led her back out into the rain.

Aidan had been waiting patiently for over an hour. The rain had driven him to the tomb-like shelter of Samuels' underground car-park and he stood leaning against a pillar, his gaze fixed on one of the few cars that were left, a gleaming red Ferrari: Francesca's. He heard the solid hum of a lift and the inevitable opening of the doors followed by

182

the sound of her shoes echoing, as she walked unwittingly towards him. His eyes followed her as she moved past the pillar, travelling down the length of her body, familiarizing himself once again with the contours so discreetly defined by the beautifully tailored suit. Her hair was pulled severely back revealing the curving perfect bones of her face and he was struck again by how black her eyes could seem as they looked up and focused on his own.

'Are you trying to frighten me, Aidan?' And he had, the blood was shooting through her veins.

'If Mohammed won't come to the mountain, the mountain must come to Mohammed. . . .'

'I didn't know we had anything to discuss.' She began opening the door of her car.

'Oh, but we have.' He folded his arms.

'Really?' she replied dryly. 'But unfortunately I don't think I have the time to talk to you right now.'

'Do you always entertain Matthias at your home, at midnight, when he's in town?' It had been easy to get to know the little girl in his press office; she had been impressed by the Samuels' connection and totally goggle-eyed when he had asked her out for a drink. He hadn't even had to buy her dinner. She had opened her pink little mouth so sweetly, so compliantly, telling him everything. It hadn't been difficult to guess that Matthias' sudden decision to fly to London would include a visit to Francesca. All he had had to do was wait.

'My, my, you have been busy, Aidan . . . but I would have thought spying, even for you, was just a little bit below the belt. Stop wasting my time.' She made a move to get in the car.

'The press might be interested. . . .' It was his last shot. Brunning had backed down at the last minute. He 'didn't want to take any risks where the campaign was concerned . . . there was too much at stake. . . .' Instead he had only led Francesca's nose to the 'Golden God's' infidelities. Big deal. It might have hurt a bit, but she was a survivor where men were concerned, as he'd found to his cost.

'Oh, my God, Aidan, what sort of game are you trying to play?' she said tiredly.

'You want your precious campaign to work, don't you? You want all the prestige that goes with it, don't you?'

She watched him steadily as he sauntered over to the car and leaned on the roof.

'I asked you, what sort of game are you trying to play?'

'I want some respect, that's all, just a little bit of good old-fashioned respect. . . .'

'Is that really all?' She laughed humourlessly. 'And you think rubbing shoulders with the likes of Vic Brunning and hiding in dark and murky corners to spy on me is going to earn respect. . . ? And anyway, aren't you talking about spite, about revenge?' She shook her head in mock sorrow. 'You never could get it right, you know, Aidan – always just a little bit off the mark.'

He tried to ignore her words, her face.

'The press would pay me a lot of money for this story.'

'Is that what this is really all about – money? And in any case, what story?' she snapped. 'Perhaps if you'd stayed a little longer the other night you might have discovered that Matthias stayed approximately ten minutes . . . and I didn't see the flash of your camera as he stepped over the threshold into my eager, outstretched arms. . . .' She smiled contemptuously. 'The press like pictures, Aidan, didn't you know? Nice juicy pictures to thrill their readers with.'

She stepped into the car and slammed the door. He moved silently to one side as the engine roared into life, defeat pulling the handsome face down into almost comic lines so that he took on the look of a foolish, bungling clown. But she hadn't finished, and one of the windows of the Ferrari slipped down silkily and she leaned over towards him.

'And don't worry, Aidan, I'm not going to fire you. I had thought of that already, of course, but surprisingly you do have talent – you're not bad in bed and you're a good art director.'

'You bitch. . . .'

'Bitch, or no, if you stick your fingers in any more sordid little pies I *will* fire you, and just for good measure

I'll make sure that no one else in our wonderful world of advertising will want you either.'

The thickness in his throat tightened as the car moved smoothly away and he felt bile rise up into his mouth. Aidan scowled uselessly, hopelessly and spat the bitterness into a pool of silvered oil.

'Bitch, bitch, bitch. . . .'

Caroline surveyed the room cautiously and realized that it was like nothing she had imagined. Nick's taste, she thought guiltily, was surprisingly elegant, touched with careful splashes of bohemia. It had an uncluttered look, with muted colours, huge patterned cushions and plenty of light and space. Some strangely beautiful prints in deep, deep blues and burgundies broke up the white-washed walls and she smiled at the massive marble figure of some ancient mythical goddess standing arrogantly and nakedly in one corner. She moved over to the bookcase and neatly stacked columns of cassettes, her hands trickling slowly along each one, totally absorbed in discovering this new part of him.

'I've mixed two superb gin and tonics – although I say so myself.'

Caroline turned shyly as he came into the room bearing the drinks and some cashew nuts on a tray.

'Are you warmer now?' he asked, as she sat down.

'Much better, thanks.'

She had shivered nearly the whole time it took him to drive them to the King's Road, but now she sat quietly controlled, almost all evidence of her crying gone except for two feverish red circles still burning her cheeks and a dewy brilliance darkening and brightening her big doe eyes.

'Have you lived here very long?' she asked, so politely. And he wanted to laugh.

'About six months, but there's still quite a lot to do,' he replied, equally politely.

'It's lovely.' And she smiled, and he was caught.

'Take a long swallow of that g and t you have in your

185

hand.' He held her gaze as she stared at him, watched her as she lifted the glass dutifully to her mouth, then he slowly moved around the small table that divided them and sat beside her. He gave her a long, searching look and with a barely audible sigh pushed a strand of her dark hair back from her face. 'For some unfathomable, crazy, ridiculous reason, I want you, Caroline. . . .' Maybe it was more than that, he didn't know, he didn't care, he only knew that he was giving in to the aching need, the longing which would creep up on him at odd times of the day. Nick took the glass from her hand and placed it back on the table and pulled her into a standing position. He wound her fingers into his own and drew her away from the safe confines of the living room and into the arena of his bedroom. He brought her to the side of the bed and carefully took her face between his hands and kissed the tilted mouth. 'You can tell me to stop, and I will . . . ,' he said. She shook her head slowly and wordlessly began to undo her blouse, but he pushed her hands gently away. 'I want to do it.'

Caroline watched his partly bowed head, felt the touch of his fingers on her skin as he pushed the blouse from her shoulders and down her arms. She shivered momentarily as he unhooked her bra and let it fall to the floor. She closed her eyes for a brief burning moment as he removed his shirt and then pulled her against him. But her arms seemed to come up of their own accord to press his head into the curve of her neck and she felt the surprising warmth of his skin melt and mould into her own, his fingers stroking the tender skin of her outer breast, and the searching softness of his lips as they grazed her cheek, her ear, her neck. She heard herself whimper as he pushed down the remainder of her clothes, trailing his hands along her thighs until they came back to rest on her waist. He drew back the covers on the bed and pushed her gently down into the white coolness, and she lay waiting, watching, immobile until the whole length of his body slid beside her and she moved against him.

She was suddenly no longer afraid, no longer hesitant as she felt his warmth seeping over her, around her, his

186

hands, fingers gliding down, down. Under the heavy covers his mouth found her breasts, the nipples rising to his lips, rolling delightfully across his tongue. She sighed and moaned softly as his mouth caressed her belly, as his fingers slipped slowly between her thighs and to the silky sensitive core within so that his tongue could follow. And she stiffened automatically in trepidation at her own inexperience and his greater knowledge, but then there was his voice encouraging, loving, followed by a slow, vast, nerve-tingling wave of pure pleasure. Her body jerked in delighted shock, her eyes closing tight in dizzying expectation as her hands reached down to caress his head, his hair, in wonder as they came together and she was no longer alone.

It was late and he still slept like a baby. Caroline glanced down at Nick's half-hidden head cradled in the crook of her arm and started to smile. He snored gently and intermittently, almost snuffling, unlike her father whose huge, hog-like utterings reverberated through the night like a klaxon. She sighed heavily, sadly, knowing that if she did not leave soon there would certainly be a row awaiting her when she eventually got home. Richmond was hardly just around the corner from the King's Road and it would take an hour to get there. Guy would probably have telephoned again, and there would naturally be more words from her mother about her future and whether she knew what she was doing with her life. Caroline sighed again. Of course, she didn't really know what she was doing with her life, except for the fact that for the first time in months she felt happy, unburdened, free.

'You shouldn't think so much, it makes you frown. . . .'

Her mouth widened into a grin as Nick stared at her with one mischievous open eye.

'I have to go. . . .'

'I know.'

'I'm sorry.'

'Don't keep saying sorry.' He slid his hand possessively over her breast. 'Next time you'll stay all night. . . .' And he pulled her across him so that she looked down into his face, so that she could feel him, take him, again. 'Won't you. . . .'

'Could you come into my office for a few minutes please Sian?'

Even though Francesca smiled, Sian felt flutterings of mild panic as she left her desk and walked into the office.

'Take a seat.'

Sian sat down and her eyes followed Francesca as she moved behind her desk and opened a buff-coloured folder.

'We're going to diversify. . . .'

Sian felt a combination of relief and curiosity.

'The merger is about to be announced and there will be a lot of interest from the press and a great deal more of talk. I know you'll be able to deal with that . . . ,' Francesca opened the folder, 'but I don't intend stopping there, Sian.' She smiled and pulled a piece of paper into her hands. 'I want Samuels to move more convincingly into below-the-line activities like public relations, sales promotion, direct mail and so on. I know that as far as many of the big agencies are concerned these types of advertising are considered unglamorous or even uninteresting.' She looked up and caught Sian's interested gaze. 'I want you to familiarize yourself with each company, maybe through the annual reports I've left beside your desk, and then contact the secretaries of the heads of the following PR agencies and try and arrange meetings over the next few weeks.'

Sian took the proffered list and glanced at the names Francesca had circled in red pen. It was easy to recognize names she had known off-by-heart only a year before, easy to spot Adam's particular name because it seemed to jump off the page in a blaze of illuminated brilliance to sting her eyes. He would come, she supposed, and she would see his tanned, lean face after almost six long months.

'I think, if there's nothing else, that I'll get on with this.' And she smiled with an effort and began to stand.

'Good,' Francesca said evenly as her gaze came to rest searchingly on Sian's face. 'Sian. . . ?'

'Yes?'

'It doesn't matter. . . .'

The words had stuck in her throat as she caught the shadow of bruised regret in Sian's eyes; that look had said it all. In any event, it wasn't really any of her business. Francesca drew a weary breath as the door closed behind Sian. She could have made the appointments herself, spoken to the PR heads directly, but Sian would have had to find out sooner or later and deal with all the details. Maybe it was easier to soften the blow this way. The Village, Gilmore's beloved company, and another on the list, Prime PR, were both interested in expansion and both, she knew, were strapped for cash. It was not likely at this time that they would choose to go public, so it would mean selling out to an appropriate purchaser, which would naturally mean several meetings with that potential buyer. Francesca shifted her gaze to the photograph of her father standing on her desk. She was going to take the first real steps in Samuels' diversification strategy to ensure the growth she had planned was maintained and driven to even greater things. Her lips lifted gently into a sad smile as she stared back at the big handsome face of Carlo Gaetini.

'You would have enjoyed playing this game, papa. . . .'

The sadness did not leave her as she closed the open folder and turned to other things. Because if there was not papa, there was Michael, or mother, and then ultimately the aching for Matthias' dangerous beautiful face. They were gone, weren't they? All of them, to all intents and purposes, melting into and then abruptly fading out of her life. She sat staring, not seeing, touched suddenly by emptiness.

Sian placed the list next to the telephone and let her eyes skim slowly down until she found his name again. It was as well she knew, maybe she could make herself scarce when he came to see Francesca, but she laughed silently, wryly, knowing she would do nothing of the kind. Even Adam's name on a piece of paper brought the memories flooding back and what might have been, except, of course, there had never been 'any might have beens', or promises, or plans. . . . She glanced at Zoë who was bent over her desk. She had been silent about her feelings since she had seen her in the hospital; there had been no mention of Vic, or the abortion, as if she had wiped her mind clean of the recent past. Sian sighed heavily; Zoë had come to terms with the situation in her own way, just as she had. But even now she wondered why she had taken such a difficult road, why she had made her life so endlessly complicated. Because she resented her lack of freedom, the casting aside of her career, living with her parents . . . resented it all, and it had all gone, forever. Except for Petie, except for Petie. Tears of frustration suddenly spilled into her eyes and she thought with grim humour that if Adam had been standing directly in front of her at that moment she would have gladly brought her hand up to leave a stinging red weal across his beautifully tanned cheek. She closed her eyes and pressed the useless vision down. Tonight she *was* free, Geoff was taking her to see *42nd Street*, and at the weekend he wanted to see her again, and Petie. He was pushing too far too fast, and whatever common sense might tell her about Adam the thought of him still made her stomach leap with wild, foolish hope. But that scalpel-edge of pain had retreated, hadn't it? And she supposed it would go on retreating from her life, just like Adam had.

Vic rubbed the back of his neck harshly with a towel. Sweat poured between his shoulder blades, down his legs, ran in perfect drops almost into his eyes. He really punished himself when he played squash, but somehow the agony was worth it. And he had won. He glanced at his long body in the club mirror. Lifting his chin up and tapping the barely loose skin beneath – hardly a spare ounce of flesh and his dark hair touched with only a few, but acceptable strands of grey. The girl at the reception desk had looked at him just a little longer than she should and with barely concealed approval. Vic watched himself smile with satisfaction, checking his teeth; she seemed to have legs that disappeared up to heaven and a good body, as far as he could tell; she was also, apparently, a part-time masseuse. He brought his face close to the mirror and examined the flesh beneath his eyes. Maybe he would give her a shot at lunchtime. Zoë had been morose lately and, in any case, she had begun to bore him.

'Had any more fun and games with de Vico Sherry . . . ?'

'I haven't been having fun and games with anyone, let alone de Vico Sherry . . . ,' Vic said sourly and turned to Andy Kidd, his long-time squash partner, '. . . what the hell are you talking about?'

'I just heard that Julian Baring was sky-high on a shoot, that's all.' Andy grinned, he loved winding Vic up.

'Are you talking about coke?' Vic countered with disbelief.

'Yup,' Andy replied triumphantly. 'He's been hooked for some time.'

'Julian Baring!' Vic swallowed hard. 'That old guy – every kid's idea of Santa Claus without his reindeer – Christ!' A picture of the staid, plump TV personality slid into his head as he looked into Andy's pallid middle-aged face. 'Do you realize how much that campaign is worth?'

'I'm only a freelance producer, remember . . . ,' Andy replied smugly, 'and de Vico Sherry isn't one of my numbers as you well know.'

'That bland, mediocre sherry is worth in the region of four million to us, if you include de Vico Port, and Julian Baring, for your information, is being paid a nice fat fee of £25 thousand for each of the campaigns. . . .' Vic stalked angrily towards an empty shower cubicle. 'What the hell is Pat Shearer up to?'

'Well, usually Pat's as high as a kite too, so he wouldn't even notice if Baring's nose fell off from snorting. . . .' Andy's grin became even wider.

'Shit . . . ,' Vic muttered under the force of a jet of water. Why the hell couldn't they leave the stuff at home. Sure, he'd had a few sniffs himself at various parties, but that's as far as it went, yet a good part of the creative department sucked the stuff up as if it were a creative laxative. So far it had pushed out some good ads, but maybe it was turning their brains to shit in the process. He sighed dramatically as he thought of Gareth Jones and his pathetic attempt at the Matthias account. . . . He'd have to have a word with Shearer, and even Baring if things were getting out of hand. The billings tables were coming out again in January and they didn't want to lose any accounts at this stage of the game. The Matthias account had just pulled them ahead in the UK tables, but Saatchis were hot on their heels and if they lost de Vico his head would roll, and no doubt Chairman Gaetini would just love that. He swore softly and switched off the current of water. Thank God, he thought comfortingly, he was a man of simple, uncomplicated tastes – the odd smoke, a nice pint or a g and t at the Drayman's, . . . and last, but by no means least, a good lay. Vic sighed dramatically again; people had a way of sticking their heads up their own backsides and then wondered why they were wandering around in the dark. He glanced wearily at his watch and realized that he was running late, he'd hardly have time to read the morning papers and have the first coffee of the day. His mind switched automatically to Zoë and then back to the long, beckoning limbs of the club receptionist . . . it had been quite some time since he'd had a really good, mind-blowing massage.

A copy of the press release on the merger had been faxed to Rock's office and with satisfaction Francesca read again the final wording of the document. Samuel-Rock. The names knitted together well and the line-up of executives on either side of the Atlantic would hardly change for the time being, which was good for the morale within both companies. Sanchez had really cleaned up the old guard of Dunmar-Rock well before the merger and Henry had never allowed the Samuels' hierarchy to get too complacent or breed too fast. There was certain to be a little friction from some clients, but nothing, she was sure, too drastic. Rock had told her that Sanchez had the Midas touch where clients were concerned and she would have to take his word for that, although sometimes she wondered how because he had always been almost reticent the few times they had met. But Francesca found herself smiling as she remembered the dinner they had had together. Hadn't she seen a glimpse of that Midas touch then? He had been shy and then charming and then shy again, but she didn't doubt the ruthlessness that lay just beneath the surface and she was still curious about the relationship he had with Rock. She replaced the press release absently in its shining scarlet folder. There would be time enough to find out about that once she got her feet under the table in New York; in any event maybe Rock would eventually confide in her himself, he seemed the type somehow. And he was also totally alone – no wife now, no children, no relatives to speak of. But he did have a dog, apparently, a massive St Bernard called Peanuts which he doted upon. Francesca laughed soundlessly; one thing Rock certainly did have and that was a sense of humour.

The phone buzzed and her hand reached out automatically.

'Hi.'

Matthias.

'Where are you?' She betrayed herself again with that sudden surge of desire.

'I'm on your precious shoot . . . with your precious producers and camera crews. . . .'

'Is there something I can do?' She tried to sound removed, neutral.

'There is nothing you can do – except be there.' He laughed softly, mocking, as if he could see inside her. 'I just wanted to hear your voice.'

'Is everything going smoothly?' she responded evenly, with an effort.

'You know that nothing in my life ever goes smoothly –

it is full of delicious hills and valleys that first lift me up and then bring me down. . . .'

'Is this a down?' she asked gently, seeing his face.

'Perhaps,' he replied expressionlessly. 'I'll let you know next time I call.'

The click of the telephone as he put the receiver down made her blink and her eyes came to rest on its stark whiteness and stayed there long after he had gone.

Covent Garden was seething with people. A lone saxophonist played a haunting version of 'Imagine' in the boulevard as the tide of faces swept to and fro between wine bars, restaurants and the many shops still open for the benefit of souvenir hunters and early Christmas shoppers. Sian paused in front of a brightly lit window depicting Santa's grotto, except that all the nodding plastic pixies busily wrapping presents seemed to be wearing different types of men's underwear and she realized with a grin that it was, in fact, a menswear shop.

'That's good,' Geoff said from over her shoulder. 'I suppose Petie's a bit young to give Santa a visit . . . ?'

'Just a bit, Geoff.'

They walked slowly along the cramped street, warmed by the milling crowds and the white foggy air which seemed saturated by the glittering breath of Christmas. The Italian restaurant where Geoff had arranged for them to eat had already painted the words 'Happy Christmas' in artificial snow across its window and fine strands of gold and silver aluminium had been draped haphazardly over plants, pictures and menus.

'They seem to be getting into the spirit of things,' he said smiling as he opened the door.

'It's not even December yet.'

Geoff glanced at her profile as she passed him. She was brooding, had been all night. In the safe dark womb of the theatre there had been no need for conversation and during the interval he found himself dragging up any amusing line he could think of just to try and snap her mood. And she had been polite, of course, laughing or smiling in all the right places, but it had only been skin deep, and he had felt relief himself when the bell had chimed for the resumption of the second half. His hands were clammy as he helped her out of her coat and he wondered why he was trying so hard. Physically she wasn't even the type he normally went for. Sian was slightly taller than he was, wide-hipped and almost blonde with that thick straight helmet of honey-coloured hair. Joanne, like most of his other girlfriends, had been overly thin and brunette – they all tended to be fine-featured gym fanatics with long sinewy arms and concave chests. Sian definitely did not have a concave chest. His eyes flicked swiftly over her as they sat down and he sighed inwardly.

'You seem a bit preoccupied tonight.'

She lifted her eyes to his face and gave him a half-smile as if in apology.

'Sorry. I've been like this the past few days – don't take any notice.'

He nodded uselessly in response and handed her a menu.

'I've been thinking . . . ,' he said slowly at her partly bowed head, '. . . about the weekend.'

She brought her head up and he saw the wariness held in her eyes.

'I'm afraid that I've had to make other plans.' It was a lie, but he was stung to see relief flood unwittingly into her face.

'Oh, really. . . .'

'My wife wants to talk over a few things, so it means that I'll be driving up to Yorkshire early on Saturday morning.' Not quite true. Joanne was going to be in London over the weekend and was going to call him at some point to discuss the divorce.

'Maybe we could take Petie out some other time,' he said finally.

'Yes, that would be nice.'

He thought, as she smiled, that it could almost have been genuine. He had looked forward to the weekend. Petie sounded a cute kid and going to the zoo or wherever they decided to go appealed unusually to him. But he was pushing too hard, that was clear, an old habit that wouldn't seem to die; maybe he should cool it for a while and let her sort herself out. In any event, his ego seemed rather delicate these days and he didn't need another rejection at this moment in time; he had to leave himself a little dignity where the opposite sex were concerned – for survival purposes alone. But she drew him somehow and he wasn't ready to give up just yet and, of course, there was bound to be the guy who had fathered Petie hanging around somewhere in the background which wasn't going to make things any easier. Geoff pulled his attention reluctantly to the menu and skimmed lightly over dishes that usually made his mouth water; suddenly he wasn't very hungry.

His face had dimmed as he had spoken of his change of plan and Sian felt strangely guilty as if it were somehow her fault. But she was relieved; now she didn't have to rebuff him herself. She had almost made up her mind to go through with the weekend because, she had told herself sternly, she might actually enjoy it, but then she had made the call to Adam's office and been put directly through to him and things had somehow irrevocably changed. Even as she heard the first, so familiar tones of his voice something inside her had risen in eagerness and she found the coolness she had practised melting as his gilded charms began to stroke the days, weeks, months away. Sian caught a soft breath and switched her gaze back to Geoff's face which was now half-hidden by the menu. Adam had asked to see her, and Petie, and for better or worse she had agreed. She lowered her eyes and thought of the anger and resentment she had pressed down and wondered if she would have the courage to throw it back at him, but somehow she doubted it. Adam had always been able to seduce her with just a few words and it still seemed that he could, for all her fine words and resolutions. And she remembered the last time with sudden, searing clarity. He had taken her with him to a conference and they had made love in one of the thousand anonymous hotel rooms. The bedcovers had been pale blue, the walls a staggering white

– a cool room. But he had made it warm, and close and loving. Adam could to that.

'The *Wall Street Journal* thinks the merger is terrific, but some of the clients are more than ruffling their feathers . . . ,' wetting their pants would be a better description, Ed thought sourly, '. . . that's why I'd like you to come over.'

'To meet them?' Francesca asked.

'Yeah.'

'When do you want me to come?'

'I'm trying to set up some meetings for the beginning of next week. Maybe you could fly in over the weekend and come to my place for some brunch on Sunday. I could have you picked up from New York and flown down in the morning.'

'Sounds fine . . . but before you go you'd better let me know which clients we're talking about.'

'Oh, sure, sure. . . .' He closed his eyes for a moment. 'A couple of the big guys to start with – PRS don't like Samuels' connection with LoGold, they say it's a rival brand.'

'That's crazy, PRS can't pretend that LoGold hits them anywhere where it hurts – they only have one line in pharmaceuticals, Shepherds Cough Drops. . . .'

'And that new acne cream to hit the teenage market. . . .'

'But it's hardly been tested yet!'

'I know, I know,' he replied wearily. 'But the Marketing MD, Klein, has always been a pain in the butt.'

'And the other?' she asked impatiently.

'Sachs & Kenyon – they say their power tools clash with Autogen.'

'They might have a point, except that most of their products are for the outdoors market; Autogen concentrate on domestic appliances.'

'Yeah, well you come over here and explain everything as cutely as you know how because I'm beginning to feel my age.'

She suddenly found herself smiling as she pictured him frowning with frustration.

'What does Philippe say?'

'Oh, in his usual inimitable way, he says it will all blow over.'

'He's probably right.'

'I don't like my bright-eyed boy to be right all the goddamn time!' he said meanly, but she heard him begin to chuckle.

'I'll be there. I'll get my secretary to call you with the details later this afternoon.'

'Good. You've made an old man very happy . . . see you Sunday.' He replaced the receiver with a loud bang; he never could learn to do it gracefully. Once the mouthpiece had fallen out and it had dangled disconsolately from the receiver like a long, sullen tongue. But that had been years ago and telephones didn't seem to do that any more. Ed lifted the remains of his cigar from a nearby ash-tray and relit it, puffing out thick plumes of smoke in practised rings. He was very pleased Francesca was coming over. Sure, she would prove useful in the meetings, but he had exaggerated just a little. Naturally clients looked on mergers with suspicion – it was common knowledge that no client liked to advertise their brands through the same agency as commercial rivals, but they had foreseen and avoided any real confrontations; Philippe had seen to that. And no one could compare the Samuel–Rock merger with the near fiasco of the Saatchi/Bates takeover when clients panicked and left in droves, yanking some $500 million out of the new dinosaur. But even that had subsided eventually and they had now more than offset their losses by gaining new business worldwide. It was all part of the game. Ed shook his head; no, there were no real problems, and the ones that might exist Francesca could be seen to smooth over. He wanted her in New York for Philippe. The kid would never tell him, of course, but he really had the hots for her, it had been more than clear during their London stay. Ed smiled to himself; he might be old, but he hadn't lost it all. Why else did the schmuck think he had let him have her all to himself over dinner? He had even tried to avoid him when he arrived back at the hotel, but he had easily heard the key turn in the adjoining room and gone in to find out how things had gone. Philippe had told him to get lost. That was good enough. Goddammit, the kid was thirty-six and he hadn't even gotten close to marriage. A man needed a woman, especially a man in his position, a good, steady woman – not a line of tramps. Oh, he knew what Philippe got up to, he kept close tabs; they were always lookers, usually well-stacked too, Ed thought absently, but tramps, or real dumb cookies. He was just taking the easy way out – no involvement, no emotion, no pain. Schmuck. Ed stared out beyond the window as memory prompted him. Philippe's eyes had turned almost black when he had first laid eyes on Francesca in the boardroom and coincidentally, since they had come back from the London meetings, there had hardly been any dumb cookies hanging around. It was being a spick, of course. Ed shook his head impatiently. He still let it put him down, still let it make his guts squirm remembering; you only had to look into those weird amber eyes and you could see it. But for Chrissakes, he was half-white, wasn't he? Half-mine, wasn't he? Why wouldn't he let that knock the other on the head . . . ? A vision of Francesca slipped easily into Ed's mind . . . a broad like that, beautiful, rich. How the hell could he miss the opportunity of a life-time? And he's always the first one to accuse me of losing my touch and not being willing to take risks. Ed puffed long and hard on his havana cigar. Schmuck.

'I don't want you to see this boy. . . .'

Caroline looked steadily at the ramrod straightness of her mother's back as she rummaged in the roll-top desk.

'He really is very nice.'

'And what exactly is wrong with Guy?' her mother said haughtily and turned sharply, locking her daughter's gaze.

'Nothing . . . ,' Caroline replied. 'We just outgrew each other, that's all.'

'Guy doesn't think so.'

Caroline looked down at her hands and wondered why she ever bothered to argue with her mother.

'And he bought you that wonderful ring – how *could* you not accept it?!'

'I don't want to marry him.'

'Why on earth not, pray tell?!' her mother asked sarcastically and then continued without waiting for an answer, 'Goodness gracious! Eton-educated . . . he has a good job in the City – Lloyds – good prospects . . . he's *most* presentable . . . comes from a good family . . . old money.' She sighed dramatically. 'What more do you want?'

'I just don't see myself spending the rest of my life with him, that's all.'

'Well, what do you see yourself doing?' her mother retorted. 'Spending your life with that person from your advertising agency?'

Caroline almost wanted to smile then because her mother always had a habit of calling people she disapproved of 'that person'. . . .

'I don't know what I really want at the moment.'

'What sort of an answer is that . . . Good heavens, I was married to your father at twenty and had had Robert by the time I was your age.'

'I don't think I want to get married yet.'

'I see. So you want to go on working – and in advertising, I suppose?' her mother responded with distaste.

'You know I have quite a good job, mother. . . .'

'I always wanted you to go into Fine Art . . . or nursery nursing – something feminine.'

'But advertising is perfectly respectable.' Caroline thought how hard she had worked for her degree, how hard she had fought for a place in the agency.

'I would hardly call it a profession – and I was always brought up to believe that men in advertising were certainly not gentlemen.'

'But that's so old-fashioned, mother,' Caroline protested.

'Old-fashioned or not, I can't help feeling that it's still true.' Her mouth puckered into a sour frown and she turned back to the roll-top desk and the pile of invitations she had prepared. 'And what sort of work does this "Nick person" do?'

'I've already told you – he's an art director.'

'What does that mean?'

'He writes copy for advertisements, advises on the creative work. . . .' It didn't sound very impressive, even to Caroline's own ears.

'Really . . . ,' her ·mother's voice drawled cynically. 'But I'm still no wiser, Caroline.'

'He's working on one of Samuels' most prestigious accounts at the moment,' she said pleadingly to her mother's back.

'And what is this "most prestigious account"?'

'It's a sort of semi-political account – for Matthias – you must have heard of him . . . ?'

'Of course, isn't he a drug addict or some such person?' she retorted disdainfully as if something foul-smelling had just entered her nostrils.

'That was all a long time ago. You know very well he's been trying to change society, the world, for the better.' It was useless, why was she trying?

'He's what your father and I would call "a nine days' wonder", my dear.'

So patronizing.

'At least he's making an effort . . . ,' Caroline responded weakly.

'Yes, well, we're rather side-stepping the issue now,' her mother said tautly. 'When are we supposed to be meeting Nick, or whatever his name is?'

'Keogh.'

'His name is Nick Keogh?' There was that foul-smelling disdain in her voice again as she emphasized the last word. 'Isn't that Irish?'

'I've no idea. He doesn't sound Irish.'

'Thank God for that.' She shuffled the invitations into a neat pile and turned finally, irritably, back to her daughter. 'Well – when do you suggest?'

'Perhaps it's too soon.' Never would be too soon. Caroline felt her stomach sink. She couldn't see Nick here, in this house, in this room, with her mother and father, sipping orange souchong tea.

'Not at all,' her mother replied sharply. 'If you insist on seeing this Nick Keogh, then I think you owe it to your father and me at least to let us meet this apparently amazing young man who has so easily vanquished any feelings you may have had for poor Guy.'

Caroline gave no answer, her gaze returning to the twisting, turning of her fingers as her mother swept past, out of the room.

Francesca moved quickly aside to let the messenger go past as he ran out of the Samuels building, a tape of ads just perceptible under his arm. She smiled to herself; it always made her feel good to touch the raw pulse at the bottom once in a while, and as she passed through the revolving doors and into the main reception area she was caught by the steady buzz of activity and in particular by two overalled maintenance crew who were replacing some of the ads blazing across the walls with the agency's latest creations. She crossed the luxuriously carpeted floor to the lifts with almost a light-hearted air. The meeting with Henry had gone very well. He had agreed to all the conditions of the merger, with only a few very minor alterations, and had even promised to arrange to be in New York for the signing. He looked very well too, tanned and fit, but perhaps a little too plump, and the famous head of thick white hair had been swept back skilfully like a lion's mane. They had lunched at the Connaught and after the meal was over he had finally leaned back in his chair, port in hand, with the casual authority of an aristocrat or a well-fed cabinet minister. It was quite clear to her, if to no one else, that he intended taking a less fervent role in the running of the company and that there would be no full-time Henry Samuels to be seen about the agency in the future; it appeared that he wanted to sit on the side-lines for a while, maybe for good.

Francesca lifted her head with a trace of arrogant self-confidence; that would suit her just fine.

Michael was already sitting in her office as she stepped into the room and she sighed inwardly. He was early. She had hoped that he would give her some breathing space after the meeting, but at least he looked surprisingly well, she thought, as he rose too eagerly to greet her. The last time she had seen him he had been pale, unshaven, almost haggard . . . the night Matthias had come and then gone. She pushed the memory down as he moved towards her, concentrating on the gleam of enthusiasm in her brother's eyes and the obvious newness of the carefully cut navy-blue blazer, trousers and silk cravat. At least he was trying.

'You seem pleased with yourself,' she said, pulling off her gloves and leaning towards him as he came softly to kiss her cheeks.

'I've been recouping my losses,' he said, grinning and helping her off with her coat.

'Ah, I see,' she said slowly and moved across the room to sit on the long leather sofa. Her eyes flicked over him as he followed her, and her thoughts took her unwillingly back to their father, the big dark Italian, and how very unlike him his son had grown to be, her brother – this blond, sheepish, almost-man.

'In fact . . . ,' he continued quickly, 'I've got the thousand pounds I borrowed in my pocket, plus the interest of course.'

'You know you don't need to go into all this, Michael.' She caught an inaudible, weary breath. 'It's not the money I'm really concerned about. . . .'

'I know, I know,' he replied impatiently, 'it's what I'm doing with it.' He leaned a little towards her, hands clasped. 'That's why I'm here. I wanted to tell you a little more about it.'

Immediately she knew he had come to ask her for more money, probably a lot more money.

'Would you like some coffee?' she said evenly, putting off the moment.

'Well, actually I already took the liberty of asking your secretary to arrange coffee once you arrived – it's probably on its way right now.'

'Thanks.' And she raised one cynical dark eyebrow.

'I'm into stocks and shares. . . .'

'With whom?'

'He's marvellous, a real find. . . .'

She knew then that he wasn't going to tell her.

'A sort of tipster?' she said dryly, knowing that the tipster, or whatever he was, had probably found Michael.

'More than that, Fran, really . . . I mean, he knows what he's doing.'

'He's not just making calculated guesses, then – he has, hopefully, reliable inside information?' She found her gaze resting on his intent face, examining him too sharply.

'Oh, yes – of course.' He flexed his fingers nervously so that the knuckles shone white-red. 'It's just that there's a real big one in the offing. . . .'

'And you need big money?'

'£20 thousand.' He at least had the grace to blush, she thought wearily, as blood soared into his face. 'It's the only way to get really started – thinking big.'

'Oh, Michael . . . ,' she said helplessly and with a trace of pity, 'you almost sound as if you were talking about Monopoly money. . . .'

His face suddenly darkened and she knew she had said the wrong thing and in the wrong way.

'I do know something about the stock market, Francesca,' he responded with brittle arrogance. 'And you don't have exclusive rights where business deals are concerned, you know.' For an instant she saw a pale copy of Livia's insolent spirit.

'I didn't mean to insult you, Michael,' she said patiently, 'but we both know that you don't really have a lot of experience at this sort of thing.'

'And what do you think I've been running with mother all these years – an ice-cream stall?' he said defensively.

'Perhaps you could tell me some time, because I've really no idea.' They played with antiques. It was a hobby, a rich, meaningless hobby, to keep him to all intents and purposes busy, but obviously not happy. A bird in a gilded cage. Usually 'the business' consisted of going to auctions on the continent and occasionally Sotheby's or Christie's; usually it meant buying a few things Livia wanted for her own collection. Only once had Michael ever mentioned 'a client' and then it was an old friend of their father's in Italy who was under the mistaken impression that Livia or Michael would be prepared to act on his behalf at a prize Regency auction in London. But surprisingly Livia had allowed him to attend, and alone.

There was a tap on the door and the difficult silence was broken. Sian came in bearing a tray of coffee.

'Well, will you lend me the money?' he asked as Sian left the room. Francesca thought there was a trace of defiance in his voice, but from Michael's lips it sounded more like a plea. She reached for the coffee pot and mechanically started to pour, silently choosing the words she would use.

'You want me to lend you £20 thousand on a gamble, on a tip. . . .'

'It's a certainty. . . .'

'A tip from a man I have never met and whom you hardly know.'

'He's an old pal from Eton.'

'Eton was a long time ago – the least you can do is let me check it out.'

'You don't trust me, do you . . . ?' He stood up and walked angrily across the room to stare out of the window, hands thrust deep into his pockets. 'You think I'm an unworldly fool.'

'I would be the unworldly fool if I didn't ask you these questions, Michael.'

'You'll get it all back – every penny,' he said desperately. 'You know I've got plenty of money of my own . . . I just can't get to it, that's all. . . .' His voice trailed off sadly. Livia still pulled all his strings. 'I just want to do this one thing – on my own.' He stressed the last three words as if she hadn't understood him.

'I know, Michael, and I do trust you – it's other people I don't trust.'

'I even called mother before coming back to you,' he continued, as if he hadn't heard her. And naturally she had refused him in that gentle, patronizing, 'only I know what's good for you' voice. He had surprised himself then by almost sounding angry.

'I know.'

'How do you know?!' He turned sharply back to her.

'She called me.' It had been very late, but that would not matter to Livia. As far as she was concerned Francesca was 'conspiring to keep Michael from her by lending him money'. There had been the old contempt in her voice, designed to wound, and finally Francesca had closed her eyes, moving the telephone away from her ear until the voice had stopped.

'God . . . ! Why can't she mind her own business, just once?' His shoulders sagged with exasperation.

'She thinks you are her business, Michael.'

He made no answer.

'You look so like her,' she said quietly as the words slipped unchecked from her mouth. 'I sometimes think that I was pushed out of her affections because I remind her so much of father.'

He shook his head slowly.

'What do you mean?'

He blinked hard as if her voice had stung him out of his own misery and his face filled with a guilty flush.

'Nothing . . . I didn't mean anything.'

She watched him for a long, dreadful moment, wrapped in silence; afraid to press him because they both knew only too well that he obviously had meant something.

'So you won't lend me the money,' he said at last.

'I never said that, did I?' She wanted him to go now, to end this disquieting interview. 'You must have known I wouldn't turn you away.' She walked across the room to her desk and wrote a cheque and a short note to her bank. 'There shouldn't be a problem, but if there is, just ask them to call me.'

206

'You'll get it all back, I promise – with interest, naturally.'

'I don't need any of that, Michael, I've told you,' she responded gently, looking into his pale features. 'And we are family, aren't we – brother and sister – after all.'

'Yes . . . of course.'

But he looked away from her and she knew, somehow, that she hadn't imagined the shadow which seemed to flee across the fragile beauty of his face.

# 7

It could be called a luxurious hotel room, even beautiful, but somehow, like all hotel rooms, it still lacked any feeling of warmth; there was no feeling of the scores, hundreds of people who had lain here, lived here for a short space in their lives. Francesca lay across the bed and stared at the pale yellow ceiling, but at least there was comfort, at least she could put her feet up for a few quiet hours. She was glad now that she had taken up Ed's offer to meet his clients, even if it might mean sorting out conflict problems which was something she hated. The little meeting with Michael had left her uneasy and unhappy and she couldn't seem to shrug the mood off. There was obviously something she had missed, something which seemed to slip furtively away from her each time she brought her mind to focus on him, on mother, on herself. Her eyes slid to the travelling alarm beside the bed; two hours. In the end she had decided to go straight to Ed's place after a brief rest at the hotel and not wait until the following morning; it would mean less sleep, but in her present frame of mind she knew that that would hardly matter. She needed people, not more time in which to think, time which hung like a weight around her shoulders. There had been too much of that recently.

It was not to be The Hamptons, not now winter had caught up with New York and snow covered the high and low peaks of the White and Green Mountains. Francesca was picked up from the hotel and taken by Ed's private plane to his country place on the edge of Berkshire County. The drive to the house took her through narrow back-roads and small villages, and it was clear, even in the gathering dusk, that silver-veined streams carved their way through the dense woodland, and she thought for a moment that she could hear them as they ran parallel to the road. Francesca leaned her head back against the seat and was reminded too easily of the long drive she had taken from Paris to Chateau de la Chênerie and Matthias. There had been no tinkling streams or charming villages then, only a vast expanse of black forest with a golden god weaving golden dreams at its core.

The portico of the white square house glowed amber in the darkness and as Francesca stepped out of the car she found herself shivering beneath the soft fur of her coat. A path of light was thrown down as the main door to the house was opened and with surprise Francesca saw Philippe and the massive, wobbling shape of a St Bernard come towards her.

'If I'd known you were coming tonight, I would have picked you up, but I've only just got here myself.'

'That's okay,' she said, bending down to stroke the probing head of Ed's famous dog, '– I didn't really know myself until a few hours ago.'

He seemed more relaxed somehow and she found her eyes skimming over him quickly with approval. Philippe wore dark blue jeans and a thick heavy sweater in black wool that could have been designed for him alone. He guided her into the house and she was struck immediately by the warmth and colour of the beautifully constructed interior. It was obviously Georgian in inspiration, but also charmingly New England, and she saw again examples of the same exquisite American folk art she had seen at the Dunmar-Rock building. These were unmistakably Rock's inspiration and a smile began to tip the edges of her mouth as her eyes fastened on Ed who stood grinning broadly, havana in hand, in front of the sort of fire she had not seen since her childhood.

'Glad you could make it,' he said cheerfully as Philippe helped to remove her coat and Peanuts padded over to take his place at Ed's feet.

'Well, it seemed a good idea to come a little earlier than planned – hotel rooms can become rather tedious.'

'You can say that again . . . I seem to have spent half my

life in them.' He beckoned to her to sit down, his eyes passing over her as she took a seat near the fire. Class, he thought with satisfaction, every inch class; from the Blahnik boots to the shape of her chin. He shifted his gaze to Philippe who was walking slowly back into the room. His boy had class too and the schmuck didn't even know it. 'Would you like a drink now and then see your room, or would you prefer to go straight up?'

'I'd love a drink now to warm me through . . . I'd forgotten how cold it could get here at this time of year.'

'Scotch and soda?'

'Yes, why not – but just a small one,' she replied smiling.

'I'll have the same, Ed,' Philippe interjected as he sat down. 'You've had quite a trip,' he continued, turning towards her.

'I know what you mean, but I think I need the change of scene – if only for a couple of days.'

'I'm glad you said that, because I really don't feel these conflict problems are quite as bad as Ed seems to think and I'd hate to think you'd had a wasted trip.' His eyes narrowed slightly as he looked up at Ed passing the drinks around. As far as he could tell there had been no need for Francesca to come at all and he couldn't understand why Ed had insisted on it.

'Now come on, Phil – be fair – this could just be the tip of the iceberg and, anyway, don't you agree that it's a good idea for our blue-chip clients to meet our British partner?' He shrugged genially and took his place in front of the fire. 'Great public relations.'

'Sure, sure . . . ,' Philippe responded evenly, '. . . but it just seems a hell of a long way to come for Francesca – and only for a couple of days at that.'

'But, really, I don't mind,' she interrupted, forcing a smile as she sensed the beginnings of tension between them and then turned wearily to the glass of scotch in her hand, drinking it slowly, letting it spread warmth through her tiredness.

'You see, the lady doesn't mind, Philippe. I think she

even feels it's a good idea, just like I do . . . in any case, while we're on the subject, I don't want any shop-talk this weekend; we can do what's necessary Monday morning,' he said, pressing his impatience down and attempting to smile as charmingly as his guest. What the hell was wrong with the kid? For Chrissakes, from the way he was acting you'd think he didn't want her here at all.

'Well, I think I'll go and unpack my things and freshen up before dinner, if you don't mind.'

'Sure, go ahead. Philippe will show you the way.' He watched her walk out of the room followed by Philippe and then allowed himself to frown. Wonder-boy was going to louse things up if he wasn't careful. Ed sighed and took a long swallow of his scotch. Phil had been relaxed, almost cheerful, before she arrived, but now – now he was coiled up like a spring with that hard-nosed look. He'd always been a difficult son of a bitch ever since Rosa's death, when Ed had stepped in to try and guide the boy, taking over where his mother had left off, but Phil had never learned yet the wisdom of how or when to thaw out. Ed drained his glass irritably and shook his head in a gesture of hopelessness at the dog lying sleepily and totally unmoved at his feet. Sometimes he wondered whether Philippe needed a plug of dynamite up his ass to help him see straight.

'I've just done a roast – nothing fancy,' Ed exclaimed, wheeling a trolley into the room. 'I like to do my own cooking these days when I get the chance.'

Francesca glanced appreciatively at the huge side of beef lavishly decked with roasted potatoes and onions, and felt her mouth begin to water.

'It looks marvellous.'

'One thing Ed is really good at is roasting meat . . . ,' Philippe said with a sarcastic smile.

'In my book –,' Ed retorted immediately, '– that is called a back-handed compliment.'

Philippe put his hands up in mock protest.

'Okay, okay. . . .'

'Just for that, you can carve. . . .' And Ed handed the carver theatrically to Philippe.

211

Francesca studied them silently, relieved that the tension had slipped so neatly away from them both. Her eyes focused on the short, frail old man as he sat down and then shifted to the long darkness of Philippe as he stood at the end of the table. Whatever he chose to believe about Ed, it was quite clear that the old man doted on him and she couldn't understand why Philippe should be so grudging, but then there were always more sides to people than the ones they opted to show you; perhaps she might discover a few more by the time this weekend in New England was over.

The roast was delicious and Ed followed it with home-baked apple-pie and cream. There were no more clashes between the men and by the time the port was handed around the old man's head had begun to sag and Francesca realized that his eyes were closed.

'Is he okay?' she asked quietly.

'Sure . . . ,' Philippe replied smiling, '. . . this often happens when he drinks too much port on top of scotch.' His eyes examined Ed's half-bowed head and then turned back to Francesca. 'He'll wake up again in a few minutes.'

Francesca slowly finished her own port, but found herself only able to half-concentrate on what Philippe was saying; Ed's tired old head seem to draw her. She noticed with a touch of pity that it would shudder, sway slightly and then grow still again, and the process would be repeated. But Ed looked up suddenly, eyes wide open, cheeks glowing almost purple with rough seams of broken capillaries.

'That goddamn port . . . always sneaks up on me,' he said sheepishly. 'Well, I don't know about you two, but I'm going to hit the sack.' He saw Francesca's gaze as it settled on the soiled plates and dishes. 'Now don't worry about the mess. I've got a woman coming up from the village tomorrow morning – give us some time to take a walk first thing.'

They stood up as he walked a trifle unsteadily past them.

'Take the port and go sit by that great fire. Otherwise it'll be wasted,' he said and waved a hand in the direction of the sitting room. 'I'm just going to let the dog out a minute for his nightly. . . .'

'Will he be all right?' Francesca asked softly, so that her words wouldn't carry.

'Yeah, he'll be okay and if I offered to take him upstairs on his way back he'd probably get a gun and shoot me – I tried it once before.' He shook his head in remembrance as a picture of the first time slipped into his mind. Ed had practically bitten his head off. 'Peanuts is, of course, the exception to the rule . . .', he added with a dry smile as they watched the huge dog pad happily down the hall after his master. 'Come on, let's do what he says and go through to the fire.'

It was easy to relax with the warm weight of the food and drink lying in their stomachs and in the downy elegance of the fire-flecked room. Francesca leaned forward nearer the fire as Philippe piled more logs into the hearth. She felt curiously at ease in Ed's house, in this room with its soft feather cushions, its smell of pine and dog.

'It's a beautiful house.'

'I like it the best of all his places,' Philippe said, sitting across from her and following her eyes to the fire.

'Does he manage to get down here often?'

'Not as often as he'd like.'

'Why doesn't he retire?' she said, looking at him. 'This place is ideal.'

'Ed – retire?' He shook his head. 'He'll work until he drops . . . I sometimes wonder whether he dislikes the idea of me holding the reins while he's still around.'

'Maybe he just doesn't want to be on his own, maybe he likes your company and the buzz he obviously still gets from advertising.'

'Yeah, yeah. . . .' He looked down into the glass he was holding. 'I don't know why he wants me hanging around his neck so much; I never make his life any easier.'

'Yes, I had noticed,' she replied wryly.

'The story goes back a long way.' He paused, reflecting, then lifted his eyes cautiously to her face. 'He screwed my mother too many years ago to count . . . and he's convinced himself that I'm his son.'

She swallowed slowly as he continued looking at her, waiting for a reaction.

'Couldn't he be right?' she said at last, willing him to look away because there was something in the clarity of his stare that made her uneasy, like seeing half-way to someone's soul.

He laughed contemptuously and drained the last drops of his glass.

'Ed?!' His eyes seemed to grow round with derision, as if she had said something faintly ridiculous. 'Do you see the slightest resemblance between us?'

'No, but that doesn't always mean anything. . . .' And she found herself reluctantly thinking of the striking difference between herself and her mother; like an echo.

'And doesn't it seem strange to you that Ed did not produce children from any of his three marriages? I don't think he's even got any bastards as far as I can tell and he's had plenty of mistresses, I can assure you.'

'Why are you so determined *not* to be his son – is the thought so bad?'

'Sometimes it makes me almost want to throw up,' he said bitterly. 'My mother was his housekeeper and then ultimately his mistress before he grew tired of her and left her to rot.' He had never been able to stand the thought of anyone touching her, even now. He had taken enough taunts and cat-calls as a kid never to let him forget that his mother was 'the *puta*, Rosa Sanchez'. It was only as he grew old enough to understand and realization had crept over Rosa's once fine face, that the men had stopped coming.

'Men have a habit of doing things like that . . . ,' Francesca said carefully, '. . . Why should Ed be any different?'

'You like him, don't you?' He wanted to change the subject now because he could feel the old, paralysing darkness creeping up on him.

'Yes, I do.'

214

'He's quite a character, I'll give him that,' he said, trying to keep the grudging note out of his voice. But he looked away from her, into the fire, as if he didn't want her studied gaze any longer.

She watched him for a long moment as light and shadow fell across the taut, rigid features, his shoulders hunched as if the load was very heavy. And she found herself wanting to lean over and push the thick black hair backwards from the bitter sadness of his face, because for an instant she felt as if she were looking at a reflection of herself.

He stayed silently where he was until the fire folded down upon itself, long after she had said goodnight and gone to her room. Philippe sighed heavily as the room grew slowly darker and wondered why he had allowed himself to be drawn on the subject of Ed. It always seemed to open old wounds; maybe if he let them bleed long enough he could exorcize the pain altogether. He leaned slowly back in the chair, stretching his legs and closing his eyes. A picture of her sitting across from him slid like a balm into his consciousness, but this time his hands did not stay wrapped, impotently, around his empty glass; instead they reached across to touch and peel away the tiny jet buttons so that the rosy silk of her blouse fell from her shoulders. Philippe opened his eyes and laughed sound-lessly. 'You've got it bad, kiddo, real bad,' he whispered to the empty room.

The sky was achingly clear, an icy winter blue, and for a moment Francesca thought there had been a light fall of snow, but realized that the blanket whiteness was only a thick layer of polished frost. Her eyes scanned the view from her window and she saw that Ed had indeed chosen well. The big white house lay in a shallow valley surrounded by a gentle range of wooded hills. She could see no other house or farmstead and it seemed that to all intents and purposes they were alone in a pretty wilder-ness, except that Ed had talked of 'the village' as if it were only a short drive away. She turned her back into the room

215

and reached for the scarlet sweater which she had unpacked the night before and pulled it roughly over her head. The colour went beautifully with the blackness of her slacks, as she had planned, and fortunately there was even a pair of matching scarlet socks tucked in one of the suitcase pockets, so that at least her feet wouldn't get cold. She looked into the mirror of the pine-wood dressing table and liked what she saw – not too polished, not too much of the advertising executive. Finally, she sat down on the bed and pulled on the almost new walking boots she had purchased too long ago to remember. They were not exactly elegant, but in all probability were the most comfortable piece of footwear she'd ever owned. Francesca smiled as she stretched one unfamiliar, but freshly booted foot out before her . . . *Vogue, Elle, Tatler*, eat your heart out.

'We'll eat when we get back, if that's all right with you?' Ed said, as he slipped his arms into a huge sheep-skin.

'Fine,' she said.

'Philippe's gone down to the village to pick up a couple of things, so we'll go on ahead.'

They walked down the polished hallway and into the flag-stoned kitchen which was now spotless. Peanuts lay against the kitchen door, but immediately arose as Ed walked in.

'Guess where we're going, you big galoot . . . !' Ed asked the upturned slavering face of Peanuts as he wriggled ecstatically before him. He let the dog wriggle just a little more in anticipation before opening the door and allowing Peanuts to hurtle out through at a speed which almost took Francesca's breath away.

'That's a very big dog you have there . . . ,' she remarked, laughing.

'He's just a big baby, maybe a bit dumb, maybe a bit on the fat side, but you can't have everything. . . .' Ed followed Peanuts' progress as long as he could before the dog disappeared amongst the freezing undergrowth. 'Of course, he's getting old now . . . ,' he said finally, with a trace of sadness.

They walked through what winter had left of the garden and into a narrow forest road which led directly from the house. It was cold, a brittle cold, and their breaths came hot and white as fog as they passed under the trees.

'This will all be Phil's one day, of course. . . .' He glanced at her face and saw the surprise. 'You mean you hadn't guessed?' If she had guessed he would have been more than a little surprised himself.

'Actually, Ed, I'm not sure what I'm supposed to be guessing at. . . .' She did, but at that moment she preferred to let him think that she remained in ignorance.

'It's not legal or anything, but he's my own flesh and blood.' He reached into his pocket and drew out a cigar.

'Your son?'

'Well . . . as I say, it's not actually been proved, but his mother and I knew each other pretty well, if you know what I mean.'

He winked knowingly and she found herself wanting to smile.

'In any case, I don't need all that blood-testing stuff . . . I can *see me* in him, that's all that counts.'

'What does Philippe think about all this?'

'Oh, I know he thinks I'm an old fool . . . I also know that it breaks him up that I never had the decency to marry Rosa, his mother.' He lit up the cigar and they walked in silence for a few paces. 'Can't say I blame him, really, no son likes to think of his own mother doing a turn with the boss.' He chuckled softly. 'She was my housekeeper at the time and as it happens I was already married when he must have been conceived – and then Etta, my second wife, started suspecting we were jumping in the sack together and Rosa had to go. You see, Etta was trying to get a helluva divorce settlement out of me and I just couldn't afford her finding out for sure.' He took a long pull on his cigar and blew smoke out in a thick grey cloud. 'She was some woman, was Rosa, – but I've got to be straight with you, I would never have married a spick, it just wasn't done.' He shook his head gently. 'Of course, things are different now, times change,' And he thought of Phil.

'Did you ever see her again?'

'My divorce came through, I moved out – we lost touch.'

'Did you know about Philippe at the time?'

'Nope . . . but it came as quite a shock when I put two and two together twenty years later.' He paused for a moment, scanning the woods for a sign of Peanuts and then, satisfied, moved on. 'You know, I never believed in Fate and all that crap, if you'll excuse the expression, but when I discovered Rosa Sanchez's kid was working in *my* company and was probably my own flesh and blood after all those goddamn years . . . it really started the old brain cells buzzing like crazy.'

'Why are you telling me all this?' she asked curiously.

'Oh, I guess I just wanted to clear the air,' he lied, 'after all, we're probably going to be seeing a lot of each other.' And he'd make sure of that. He hadn't practically told her his life story for nothing; he wanted her to know what Philippe would come into when he was six feet under, wanted her to understand that he wasn't just some jumped-up smart-ass spick. He was his son and he would be a rich son of a bitch. Suddenly Ed felt the sting of tears as they seeped furtively into his eyes. He cursed silently, this sort of thing was happening too often lately. Quickly he brought the cigar back again to his lips and prayed wordlessly for the saving grace of smoke. Shit . . . maybe Phil was right and he *was* just an old fool.

They met Philippe after they had circled the small lake at the foot of the forest road and were on their way back home. Francesca watched him as he came striding easily towards them; he was smiling and as he drew close she thought he appeared bright, almost breezy, and there seemed to be no trace of the Philippe she had left sitting alone in the fading firelight of the night before. They walked back in companionable silence and when they arrived at the house Francesca realized that all but the eggs were already prepared for their long-awaited breakfast which was now brunch.

'You can cook too . . . ,' she said good-humouredly and looked at Philippe.

'I can vouch for that,' Ed interjected, 'he's great around the house too.'

'Oh, shut up, Ed!' Philippe replied, but he was smiling, Francesca noticed, even if his eyes had darkened just a little.

The afternoon passed off with a series of card games and draughts tournaments until dusk came down, and a simple dinner of steak and salad was prepared followed once more by Ed's apple-pie.

'I'm going to catch an early night,' Ed said, as he collected the plates, 'but you two go ahead and help yourselves to the port.'

'Not for me,' Philippe responded. 'I need an early night too, it's going to be a long day tomorrow.'

Ed gave him a searching look, wondering if he'd heard right. He hadn't just offered to sacrifice his long languid glass of port so that they could be left alone, only for Philippe to throw it back casually in his face.

'Oh, come on, Phil . . . the night is yet young, as they say.'

'No really, Ed – we've got that meeting with Klein in the morning and that's after an early start,' Philippe stood up, '– and I want to be as fresh as I can to see him.'

'I think Philippe's right.' Francesca interjected.

Ed looked at both of them for a long moment, barely managing to push his exasperation down.

'Okay, okay . . . have it your own way.' He shrugged his shoulders irritably, picked up the plates and walked out of the room.

'What did I say?' Francesca asked after Ed had disappeared down the hall.

'You agreed with me, and that's a big "no-no",' he replied, smiling and then added finally, 'Come on, let's help the old tyrant clear the table.'

From her bedroom window Francesca could just make out the hunched figure of Ed as he stood stoically in the garden waiting for Peanuts to finish 'his nightly'. It was already beginning to freeze, that glacial freezing sharpness that made the sky seem brittle, as if it would break at a touch. She turned from the window with a trace of sadness; she would miss this house, these woods, Ed, Peanuts and even Philippe. But she was snapped out of her reverie by a knock at the door.

'Sorry to disturb you,' Philippe seemed to tower over her in the semi-darkness, 'but I thought it politic to warn you to set your alarm for 6 a.m., otherwise you might have a rather unpleasant awakening.'

'Thanks.'

'Well . . . ,' he said a little awkwardly, '. . . I'll say goodnight then.'

'Goodnight, Philippe,' she said gently as the familiar shadow of his shyness wove across his face.

There was another awkward moment before he stepped back from the doorway, his long slow stride taking him away from her, into the half-light of the narrow, beamed passageway.

In the end Adam had cancelled their weekend meeting so she had resorted to taking Petie to the local park. The weather was cold and murky, and a threat of drizzle hovered in the air. She had walked for a long time, pausing at the almost deserted duckpond with a few stale pieces of bread, so that Petie would at least have the pleasure of watching the stubborn remnants of the bird population before winter really set in and the pond became a world unto itself. Adam had apologized too profusely for his absence and she had listened silently to his excuses, finally allowing herself to be talked into agreeing to see him after his meeting with Francesca on the following Wednesday afternoon. He had never seen Petie, not once, and she thought that at last he had decided to acknowledge his son's existence . . . but he already had one son, William, and he had made it clear that that was obviously quite enough. And, after all, Petie had never figured in his scheme of things and, if Adam had really had his way, Petie would never have figured in her own either. But she had traitorously allowed her thoughts to sweep danger-ously back to their affair when The Village had inexorably become her whole existence, and now she had found tremulous hope in just hearing Adam's voice after the agonizing silence he had permitted to pass between them.

Sian blinked hard as the shriek of the telephone roughly intruded on her thoughts; Zoë was not at her desk. With an impatient sigh she got up and moved across the room to answer it. After taking a brief message she turned in the direction of the sixth floor kitchen; the coffee percolator would be almost empty now and Adam was expected in fifteen minutes.

'Hi.'

Geoff stepped out of the lift and walked towards her.

'You wouldn't, by any chance, be intending to make some coffee?' he asked, smiling mischievously.

'You'll be the first to know, Geoff.'

He watched her walk into the tiny kitchen and then tentatively followed.

'I was wondering whether you might have time for a quick drink this evening . . . ?'

She closed her eyes briefly at his question and tried to seem busy as she endeavoured to pry a filter paper from its wrapping.

'I'm sorry, Geoff, I've already got something arranged for tonight . . . ,' she thought she heard a faint weary breath escape his lips, '– Thursday or Friday would be better.'

'Let's make it Friday then,' he offered. 'We could have dinner. . . .'

'Yes,' she said, turning to face him, 'that would be nice.' Sian cursed silently, wondering why she should sound so ungracious, so patronizing.

'Fine,' Geoff responded, and he was still smiling. She wondered suddenly why he was being so patient with her. 'See you later.'

She watched him retreating back as he walked across the room and into his office, glad that he would not be standing by to see Adam arrive and in all probability the tell-tale surge of a blush creep into her face.

He was late, five minutes late, and as he made his way

from the lift she was immediately struck by how little he had changed and realized all at once that she had expected him to be different, to look unlike the person she had loved because she supposed it would have been easier somehow. A dark overcoat was slung casually over his arm. He wore a cashmere blazer that she recognized: black-blue, gold buttons. There was that familiar polished air he always managed to convey, and a trace of the carefully chosen after-shave stinging her nostrils as a painful twinge of memory touched her with astonishing ease; saying so much, saying so many things, but then he was winking familiarly as she stood up to show him into Francesca's office. The door closed too quickly behind him and Sian moved slowly back to her desk. She wished he hadn't winked.

Vic studied Gower carefully. Stu was making him an offer that was almost too good to refuse and he had obviously done his homework before approaching him, even to the extent of discovering how much he resented Francesca. Of course, he hadn't put it directly into words, but had hinted obliquely at the rumours he had heard through the ad-land grapevine. Stu Gower was founder and chairman of GKP, Gower & Kid-Porter, one of the most admired of the London agencies and about ninth in the agency tables. GKP had had a very successful period of growth and for some time had been looking around for appropriate new blood to boost their stretched management resources, and, no doubt, to swell their coffers with the accounts these 'new resources' would bring along with them.

'Naturally you don't have to give me any sort of an answer now – think it over, take as long as you like.' Stu leaned conspiratorially towards Vic, his big red jowls wobbling, growing crimson, under the light of the table lamp. 'But the timing is excellent. News of the Samuels' merger has upset a few of the clients – not too much, but just enough – and before the dust settles some of them will only need to hear a whisper that you're considering leaving before making up their minds and going with you. . . . With, perhaps, a little persuasion on your part, of course.'

Vic rolled his glass slowly between his hands, allowing a half-smile to curl the edges of his mouth. What a satisfying coup it would be! He could give Henry and Francesca a kick right where it would hurt and do himself some good in the process. Now that the merger was about to be finalized there would eventually be talk of managerial changes and that would, of necessity, have to include some of the Yanks. It might not affect him initially, but sooner or later Chairman Gaetini would run another little ring around him. Things were okay at the moment, just, but for how long? Long before she had joined the company he had enjoyed being one of the heavyweights in advertising, wallowing in the spotlight as Samuels' bright-eyed boy. Now that spotlight had insidiously moved to cover 'Samuels' dazzling new chairman', eclipsing him. There was Geoff too, boring, run-of-the-mill Geoff, carving out a nice little niche for himself. . . . Samuels had changed, irrevocably, and Vic didn't want to be around to see any more of the so-called changes. The idea of moving to pastures new had begun to take root as soon as Henry had brought in Francesca over his head, but he had held on in the hope that she would fall flat on her designer face and Henry turn back to him in consolation – and apology. But he knew now that would never happen, she was too clever for that. The timing of Gower's offer was, indeed, excellent, but he wouldn't let him know too soon. Vic sighed inwardly with satisfaction. Stu was a generous man, but he hadn't been generous enough so far and there was still Christmas to consider and the annual bonus. Vic had no intention of giving up £10 thousand for the sake of a few weeks.

'When shall I call you?' Gower's voice broke into his thoughts.

'The 20th.' Vic shifted his gaze back to the older man's face.

'That's the day of the merger, isn't it?'

'As it happens,' Vic replied noncommittally, but there

was no denying the implication of his words. He got up to leave.

Stu shook hands thoughtfully with his potential colleague, his eyes following Vic as he crossed the bar of the club. Brunning was a sly bastard, a bit too obvious maybe, but he had a wide wicked mouth which clients seemed to like, and he had plenty of experience and connections where it counted and that, he knew only too well, was worth its weight in gold. The icing on the cake, of course, was the fact that it was highly likely that he would be bringing a nice juicy little wedge of Samuels' clients with him, which would naturally mean a jump in the profits and even a move upwards in the agency rankings. Stu pulled at the plump lobe of his ear, felt the familiar outcrop of wiry red–blond hairs tickling his fingers. Reluctantly he supposed he would have to relinquish GKP in favour of GKPB, but perhaps it would be a small price to pay in the long run. Gower & Kid-Porter-Brunning . . . it was a mouthful and there would be a few lacklustre objections from the board, but naturally Vic Brunning would love it and Stu knew instinctively that such a move would clinch the deal if all else failed. The size of Vic's ego was almost legendary.

'Any messages?' Vic asked as he walked nonchalantly past Zoë's desk.

'I've left them on your desk. . . .' She lifted her eyes hopefully as he disappeared into his office. 'Shall I come in?'

There was silence for a moment before he replied.

'Okay – but bring me a cup of coffee at the same time. My mouth tastes like the inside of a camel's armpit.'

She laughed dutifully and made her way to the kitchen. He seemed to be in a good mood, she thought with relief. For the last two weeks he had practically ignored her and she had grown almost desperate. Eact morning she had dressed carefully, as provocatively as she dared, but Vic had hardly noticed. There had been no lunch hours, no late hours in his office when everyone had left; he was treating her as if she were no longer of interest to him. But nothing had changed, not really, she told herself, too easily. He had no knowledge of what had happened to her, so in theory everything should be as it was. But it wasn't, for whatever reason. Vic had a way of freezing people out of his life with consummate skill; she had seen him do it often enough, particularly with women. . . . Zoë shovelled three spoonfuls of sugar abstractedly into the steaming black coffee, not noticing that her fingers trembled as she did so. Mechanically she placed a spoon in the rim of the saucer and made her way back to his office.

'Just what I need,' Vic greeted her with a smile.

And she smiled too widely in response.

He watched her as she walked out of the room to get her notepad and pen and thought, meanly, that she was like an anxious puppy trying to please its master. Naturally he had not been immune to the obvious longing in her eyes each time he had left the office, each time when in the normal course of events she should have been slipping discreetly into his room and he would then switch on the 'Do not disturb' notice. She bored him; he had known that for a while now and Cherry, the girl at the squash club, made a nice change, but now she had gone on some kind of course for two weeks and would not be available until after Christmas. Vic's eyes examined Zoë casually as she came back into the room. She was wearing those stretch pants again, so that virtually nothing was left to the imagination. He took a large mouthful of coffee and watched her small pale hands as they placed the notepad and pen on his desk. She had nice hands. But then they returned uneasily to lie in her lap where she stared awkwardly into the slow twisting knot of her fingers until her gaze shifted to his face, looking at him with those big doleful blue eyes. Pleading. Vic stretched his hand across the broad expanse of his desk and pressed a small red button which would illuminate the notice outside his door. The meal with Gower had been boozy and heavy, but he was left with a pleasant feeling of lethargy and a languid need for sex. He looked meaningfully into her now flushed face and swivelled his chair around, slowly undoing the zip of his trousers.

'Let's have a little fun, shall we, Zoë . . . ?' He was too tired to exert himself and as she came eagerly around the desk towards him he took her hands and pulled her down into a kneeling position directly in front of him. Immediately she knew what was required of her and only with a trace of disappointment did she lean downward towards him. Vic reached out to hold her head between his hands as she took him in her mouth and groaned with satisfaction deep in his throat as her head began moving rhythmically to and fro. Perhaps he would miss this, after all. Perhaps. But there would be other girls just as willing at GKP – and there was no question of Zoë going with him.

Geoff's eyes flicked sharply over Adam Gilmore. He was just the sort of media man that made him feel uneasy – so cool, so perfect in his sleek sartorial splendour, it was almost uncomfortable sitting in the same room. He wondered with a trace of envy how long it had taken Gilmore to cultivate his immaculate media-man image, the flashing white teeth and the so-golden tan. He drew a sharp breath and endeavoured to press his thoughts down; this was a business meeting and Francesca wanted his opinion on the possibilities of a Samuels/Gilmore union of some kind. As long as Gilmore ran a good operation that was all that should matter. Geoff brought his attention to bear on the paperwork in front of him. There was a copy of their latest annual report, a gleaming ebony-covered tome with the name of the company written in gold across the front. The Village always managed to produce something eye-catching without going over the top and touching on tinsel-town. He sighed – just like Gilmore himself. There were also budget reports, information on accounting policies, client lists and updates of the revenue tables of different PR consultancies; The Village had managed to sneak into eleventh place in the rankings according to *PR Week*. Despite his private misgivings about Gilmore, Geoff knew that Francesca was making a move in the right direction and whatever PR company they brought under their wing would be a sound investment for Samuels. Only recently he had read somewhere that the PR industry had grown in the region of forty per cent last year and that was *fast* growth by anyone's standards. His broad forehead wove into lines of concentration. Of course there were also other profitable areas in which they might choose to invest: sales promotion, direct mail, packaging and design. In fact he had a pile of information on his desk on each of those categories. PR was really just the tip of the iceberg. He brought his attention back to focus on the meeting which was beginning to wind up amicably enough. Gilmore stood up finally; they shook hands and Geoff noticed how tall he was, a good head taller than he was himself, and he wondered briefly why it should bother him so much. Francesca walked slowly with him to the door of her office to make her goodbye and then returned to her desk, pouring another cup of coffee for them both.

'Well?' she asked.

'We already know it's a good outfit. Gilmore built it up practically by himself, he wants to expand, and he needs cash. . . .' Geoff said mechanically and matched her stare. 'That's where we come in, isn't it?'

'Perhaps – but I want to meet Derek Richie before I make up my mind.'

'Prime PR?'

She nodded and looked down at the rough notes she had jotted on a piece of paper.

'I think Richie would be prepared to be wholly owned. I'd like at the very least fifty-one per cent to Prime's forty-nine per cent.'

'And Gilmore doesn't want a sell-out; *he* wants the fifty-one per cent.'

She nodded again and said with a wry smile, 'I think he might just dig his heels in a bit.'

'Well, they both run good operations. . . .' Geoff pushed his chair back and drank the last of his coffee. 'Let me know when Richie's coming in.'

'Of course – and maybe we could find time to have lunch this week, or early next . . . ,' she said to his retreating back.

'I'll get back to you on that,' he responded over his shoulder as he opened and closed her office door. Geoff glanced at his watch as he stepped into the corridor. It was getting late and after Sian had turned him down he'd managed to scrape up a squash game with Pete Morgan, but if he didn't hurry they'd miss the court altogether. He moved across the corridor, and the sound of voices made his head turn and he saw Gilmore helping Sian on with her coat. At the same time they both looked up as if they had felt his eyes and he found himself squeezing out a smile that stayed fixed on his face as they walked away from him. Geoff's gaze followed them automatically, saw the arm Gilmore brought up to guide her gently into the lift slide across her back. He stood staring, not seeing, as bitter thoughts converged in his mind. Of course, Sian had worked at The Village before Samuels – before the baby, but he had not made any connection between her and Gilmore because he had seen no reason to, not even when he had asked her about her past and her face had immediately darkened, fingers practically trembling at the very mention of Gilmore and his beloved company. Now, it was all too plain, and he felt a mocking blade of jealousy pierce him as an all too vivid picture of Gilmore slid insidiously into his mind. Suave, silky, flawless Gilmore – he was even tall, Geoff thought, with a further pang of envy. He shook his head with weary inevitability and walked over to a bookcase where his squash racket lay across a row of outdated creative reports and old *Economist* diaries, their bright blood-red covers veiled with a thin layer of dust. He pulled the racket impatiently into his hand, suddenly feeling unreasonably angry. Sleek he might be, impeccable he might be, but Gilmore was no knight in shining armour. He hadn't married her.

It was late and the office was almost eerily quiet when the telephone rang. Francesca put her coat down in exasperation and picked the receiver up.

'I knew you'd still be there . . . at your precious office, with your precious papers. . . .'

She had thought she could grow immune to his voice, but there was that old power again.

'I was just about to leave.'

'I missed you. . . .'

'I was in New York – you know that.'

'How was it?' he asked smoothly.

'Fine,' she replied evenly. 'Where are you calling from?'

'Paris, of course . . . my refuge . . . full of tiny holes where the press have poked and probed the Matthias machine. . . .'

'The film went well, I hear.'

'Reasonably . . . but nothing is ever perfect.'

There was a pause then, weighty.

'I thought I might see you tonight. . . .'

She sighed inwardly, sadly, and made no answer.

'May I?'

'That's not really a good idea, is it?' she said at last.

'Why do you always make things so complicated?'

'Haven't we been through this before?'

'Only once. . . .'

And she knew that small crooked smile had settled on his mouth.

'In any case, you're in Paris.'

'I intend to fly by my own fair hands; I could be at your door almost before you are.'

'I can't . . . not tonight . . . I have a dinner engagement.' Liar, coward.

'I'll wait for you.'

Before she could reply he had gone and she closed her eyes in frustration at her own weakness.

Caroline lifted her eyes to Nick's face, a frown dimming her features.

'You're torturing your face,' he said lightly.

'What do you mean?' she asked, still frowning.

'Frowning.' He started to smile and brought his hand up to smooth the creases which ran across her forehead.

'Mummy . . . ,' but then she corrected herself, '. . . my parents would like to meet you.'

'Isn't this a bit premature?'

'Yes, I know,' she said awkwardly, 'but it's just the way they are, I'm afraid.' She felt too warm suddenly and the crowd in the Drayman's was getting thicker, if anything.

His face grew serious.

'They want to look me over, isn't that what you mean?'

'You really don't have to. . . .'

'Why not? I've got nothing to hide.' He had a momentary vision of what the 'interview' would be like and inhaled deeply, impatiently; he knew instinctively that they would not like what they were going to see – he was not dear old Guy, he was not public-school, and finally and worst of all, no doubt, his family did not have money, any money.

'I could put it off quite easily,' she said anxiously, as her own vision of their meeting soared uncomfortably into her mind. It would be agony.

'There's no need . . . I don't mind at all.' And he didn't. They might scare Caroline with their cloying prejudices, their blinkered, suffocating views, but not him. There was no point in putting the interview off, because it would have to come sooner or later if he and Caroline stayed together. If. He looked down into the softness of her uneasy upturned face and felt that familiar thickness gather in his throat. It had not been like this for him before, not this subtle seeping happiness which touched him at odd times of the day and night – this need.

Caroline took a sip of her drink which somehow seemed flat, tasteless, and thought of her mother's long, unforgiving face. The meeting would be a disaster, she was sure of that, and she was also sure that her mother would make certain that it was. Nick was already damned even before her parents had met him and then, she knew, there would be recriminations and 'threats' if she decided to go on seeing him against their wishes.

'I wish they were different sometimes . . . ,' she said suddenly, vaguely.

'I wish mine were different sometimes, too.'

'Do you?' she asked hopefully.

'Of course.' And he loved his parents, even enjoyed their company, but knew that he would inevitably grow away from the world they lived in. It was already happening; his father had noticed – wise, witty, horse-backing Jimmy.

'It's just that mine have a way of making life very difficult somehow . . . ,' she said lamely.

'You're trying to tell me that they could make things difficult for us, aren't you?' He shook his head and smiled. 'They don't have the last word in all of this, you know.' The bewilderment in her face moved him almost to pity. 'You could always move in with me. . . .'

Her eyes grew round with amazement.

'Are you serious?'

'Perfectly.' But he hadn't realized how much until now. A frown had reappeared on her face and he knew he was probably forcing her into making another choice again and Caroline wasn't used to choices.

'You're torturing your face again . . . ,' he said gently and once more his hand came up to smooth the creases away.

A Barbra Streisand tape was playing somewhere in the background and the same barman was still serving the same drinks. Sian smiled with a trace of sadness; it was as if nothing had changed at all.

'We used to come here a lot,' Adam said.

And she wanted to say, 'Did you think I could forget?' But instead the words stayed muted and unsaid behind her lips.

'I'm sorry about the weekend.'

For a long moment she studied the tanned face. Petie did have his eyes, she thought with a touch of pain, dark grey, the eyes of his father, but somehow Adam didn't seem like Petie's father at all.

'That's okay.' But it wasn't.

'You look great,' he said, with only a touch of awkwardness.

'Do I?' God, how she had agonized on what she should wear! How she had studied herself in the mirror for any traces of the bitterness which never seemed too far away – sometimes.

'There's something different about you. . . .' He smiled that old easy smile as his gaze swept effortlessly over her.

'Perhaps it's maturity – the joys of motherhood,' she said with a sarcasm she was unable to resist.

'Don't, Sian – it doesn't suit you.'

Her face darkened at his rebuke, no matter how gentle.

'It's been easier for you, Adam. . . .'

'I've thought about you a great deal,' he responded defensively.

'Sometimes thinking isn't enough.'

'I know, I know. . . .'

'You've never seen Petie – do you realize that?'

'Okay, okay. . . .' His tan deepened under her uncompromising gaze. 'But if you remember it was *your* decision, ultimately, and you know I didn't want you to put yourself through all this.'

'Don't you mean *yourself*?'

'All right, if that's what you want to think . . . but also remember that I have children already, three of them, and I never said I intended to sacrifice them for the sake of our relationship – did I?'

No, that had been *her* dream . . . a silly, selfish, schoolgirl dream which had been thwarted, smashed and broken into a million brittle pieces. Suddenly she found herself wanting to cry, felt tears of secret rage force themselves into her eyes as his hand closed over hers.

'Don't, Sian, don't, please. . . .'

She looked away from him, blinking back the maddening tears, hating herself for the way they betrayed her pain with such ease.

'It's okay, I'll be okay. . . .'

'Maybe this wasn't a good idea,' he said lamely.

'Aren't you used to a woman's tears, yet?' And she smiled with an effort; not wanting it to end like this.

'I never get used to it.' And he thought of his wife, of the

232

scores of times she must have cried during their married life and how uncomfortable it always made him feel. Once he had thought it a woman's secret and final weapon; these days he was not so sure, but he was still no wiser, still no closer to understanding. He shifted his gaze back to her face. The tears had miraculously gone, but her eyes had grown large and luminous and he was stung by a twinge of memory, by her flushed, glowing skin as if they had just made love. He wondered if she was aware how eagerly, how naturally she gave herself. Sian was instinctively tactile, instinctively uninhibited, and he had missed that over this last year. But she had changed, inevitably; although motherhood quite obviously suited her whether she were aware of it or not. If he resumed their relationship it would be different. There was the child, and he had enough children, and his career, . . . and, of course, his wife.

'I'd like to set up some kind of trust for Petie,' he said suddenly.

Her eyes looked back at him warily.

'You don't have to. As you said, it was my decision.'

He closed his hand more tightly over hers and she felt lost, caught, like a butterfly pinned to a board.

'I *want* to.'

And she wondered if that would be all, because his soft smile could say so much, so many things. For a brief heady moment her eyes held his and they were both very still, remembering. But then there was a furtive image of Petie slipping into her mind, followed strangely by an unsettling picture of Geoff's marooned face as they had left him standing alone outside his office.

It was one of those December days in England when it was not really cold, only wet, miserable and damp, and the sky a measureless expanse of grey lying like a weight overhead. Francesca lifted her face to the pinpricks of rain as she crossed the street to Samuels; Christmas was less than three weeks away, yet it seemed more like October or November. As she passed swiftly through the reception

233

area she caught the tremulous gaze of the receptionist watching her with more than usual interest. She smiled slowly, automatically, in response and stepped into the waiting lift forgetting the girl's expression almost immediately. Sian was already seated at her desk as she made her way across the room to her office, and she greeted the younger girl with her customary 'Good morning' and request for coffee, but Sian's reply seemed muted somehow, lacking its usual enthusiasm, and Francesca frowned briefly as if there was something somehow she had not quite grasped yet. But she pressed the thought down as she approached her desk and the pile of mail lying on the burgundy blotter.

'Francesca . . . ?'

Sian watched her from the frame of the doorway.

'What is it, Sian?'

'Haven't you heard . . . ?'

'Heard what?' There was something in Sian's set, rigid expression that suddenly made her afraid.

'About Matthias.'

'Matthias?' she repeated stupidly. As if she had never heard the name before.

'He was killed . . . last night . . . in a plane crash . . . ,' Sian said woodenly.

There was a long dreadful moment before Francesca spoke again.

'How do you know?' she asked slowly.

'Someone from his office telephoned first thing – it hasn't hit the papers yet.'

'I see,' Francesca said expressionlessly. He had not been waiting for her when she arrived home last night, and she had covered her disappointment with a vague feeling of relief because he would not make her have to choose again. And she had taken a further precaution by leaving the phone off the hook in case he called. But, of course, he hadn't called; he couldn't call.

'I'll get your coffee,' Sian said quietly.

Francesca stood up and moved to the window, staring at the grey stone walls with their hundreds of windows as if they did not exist.

'Have you heard?!' Vic's outraged voice snapped the silence in two as he walked across her office.

'I heard. . . .' She turned to face him.

'Christ! What are we supposed to do now with his bloody campaign?!' Why couldn't this have happened later, some other time, when he wasn't here any longer? He had wanted to leave in a blaze of glory, bathing in at least some of the prestige which would have come out of the Matthias campaign once it had hit the air waves. Now it was a lame duck . . . a dead duck . . . literally.

'Could you leave me alone for a while please, Vic,' she said slowly and saw how his large mouth dropped comically open.

'But we've got to talk this through. We'll have to give some kind of press statement. . . .'

'Not now, Vic.'

'For God's sake!' He responded impatiently.

'I said – *not now*.'

For a split second their gazes locked and then he was cursing softly again before turning finally, angrily, away from her and in the process almost knocking Sian over as she walked in with the coffee.

'Would you try and get me Lucas Chant please, Sian,' she said quietly, ignoring Vic as he made his sullen exit.

'Of course.'

'And will you also see that I remain undisturbed except for any calls regarding more information on what has happened.'

She watched Sian leave, heard the soft click of the office door as it was closed behind her. 'What has happened?' she cried inwardly. Somehow she couldn't bring herself to say the actual words – not that he was dead, that he no longer existed. It did not seem possible. Her hands came up to cover her face and for a few moments she remained motionless as the reality of what had happened began to sink in. When she finally allowed her hands to slide from her face, her eyes shifted slowly to the tape of his last concert at Wembley five years previously, which sat on a shelf along with scores of others in her office. Francesca stood up, moved across the room, took the tape down and switched on the power to her video. Automatically the machine whirred into life as she slipped the black cassette into its mouth. She pulled one of the nearby chairs up, close, and waited for the screen to break into life. The stadium was swarming with people. Huge video screens stood at either side of the raised platform where he would perform and her eyes came to rest on the empty stage; waiting. Matthias made his entrance from the back, his blond torso outlined beautifully against black leather. He walked languidly towards the waiting crowd and a camera picked up his face, immediately transferring it to the massive screens, and she found herself abruptly looking into his pale blue eyes, but the camera pulled back and his figure diminished as the crowd roared and both his arms rose into the air in a gesture of triumph. He belonged *there*, she thought with sudden clarity, not in any sort of political arena, not in Munich or Paris, or in the arms of some tycoon's daughter, but *there*. And he had never realized it. She switched the set off and leaned back in the chair. There was a dull ache somewhere inside and she closed her eyes as his face slid painfully into her consciousness, and there was that crooked, mocking smile fixed on his lips. As it always was – as it always would be.

'He decided to fly to London . . . I don't know why.'

Francesca stared down at the long pale face of Lucas Chant. His eyes were swollen and sore, but they stared out at the world through a haze of brilliant tears which cascaded uncontrollably down his cheeks. And his crying was pitiful, ugly, shaking his thin sad frame.

'Do you want me to go?' she asked softly.

'No, no – I don't want that.' He reached for the handkerchief which he had twisted into a knot of anguish. 'The girls in the office don't know what to do with me.' He laughed brokenly and then stopped as a rough sob caught in his throat. 'He was very good to me – always.' He shook his head gently and tried to smile. 'And he was –

*different* – you know?' His eyes came to rest on her face and they seemed to plead with her to understand.

'I know.'

'He did some pretty wild things and not always good things, but he had a way of making them not so bad . . . he could make you forgive him so easily. . . .'

She knew that too.

He fell silent for a moment, his crying reduced as he looked about the almost empty room.

'I was nothing before him, just nothing.' He swallowed deeply and then brought his eyes back to her. 'Look at me – the ass-end of nowhere –' He turned away helplessly, his shoulders sagging as if the weight were very heavy.

She moved to sit down beside him, her gaze suddenly falling on the massive black and white photograph of a crying child framed against a battered and bloody Beirut. How long had it been since she had sat here, in his office, in this strange stark room where it had all begun?

'He had such great dreams of what he would do, what he would achieve. . . .' Lucas' weary words continued.

'But he did achieve a great deal,' she added, but her voice was dim. And she supposed that he had; it just didn't seem to matter any longer.

'Not enough, not nearly enough – he wanted so much more.'

Oh, she could believe that.

'But I don't think it will all end with his death.'

'No, no – perhaps not – and he wouldn't have wanted that,' he said, as vague hope momentarily defeated his misery and there was a ghost of a smile on his face. 'And he wouldn't have wanted to live, either, not the way he would have been once they'd finished with him.' He shook his head slowly and then added with surprising venom, 'You might find it hard to believe, but I was glad when they couldn't revive him, glad that none of their tricks could do anything for him.'

'He was alive?'

'Barely – and they kept on trying nearly all the way to the hospital, but he was just fading away. By the time I arrived he had gone and when I saw him I wanted to rejoice, because there was nothing left of his beautiful face, nothing left of my golden god.' He stared back at her, the stunned, puffy, grief-stricken face filled with pain, and he put his arm up against his face as if he would hide it.

She stood up and placed a hand on his fragile shoulder. 'I'll go now.'

He didn't reply and she walked slowly, quietly towards the door and turned back only when she heard his weak shaking voice follow her.

'I loved him . . . you know?'

She could only nod in response as her hand reached with relief for the handle of the door. She wanted some air now, cool clean air, release, and she made her way quickly and silently past a weeping receptionist, down the marbled hallway to the main door where the press would be waiting, but they would get nothing from her, not now. That would all have to come later.

She drove to Richmond and walked along the river. It was drizzling and there was no wind, but the persistence of the soft rain quickly made her clothes damp and she shivered as she sat beneath one of the black lifeless trees. There were many boats moored along the flat river: houseboats, rowing boats, even an old lifeboat, as her eyes passed almost unseeing down the brown length of the water. Francesca leaned her head back against the tree and closed her eyes. So there had been nothing left of his beautiful face. She could not imagine that . . . it was a travesty . . . death should be enough. A tightness began to climb in her throat and her eyes grew tired as she pressed the craving for tears down. And Melissa, poor, racy, blonde Melissa; she supposed there was nothing left of her beauty either, but there would be plenty of tears – Sir Richard would see to that.

# 8

'Why don't you just come out with it, for Chrissakes?!' Ed sighed heavily in exasperation. '. . . What's the big deal?'

'Mind your own business, Ed,' Philippe said icily.

'I know you've got the hots for her. . . ,' he persisted, 'you might as well wear a neon sign around that thick skull of yours for all the difference it would make.'

Philippe made no answer and turned to the waiting files on his desk.

'Goddamnit! Do you think you can hide that sort of thing from *me*?!' Ed felt his temper begin to rise and attempted to smoke the cigar which dangled uselessly at the end of his fingers; it had gone out. 'What's the matter with you, anyway? She's only a woman; sure, maybe a bit classier than you're used to, but a woman all the same. . . .' He lit up his cigar with an angry trembling hand and sharply scrutinized Philippe's partly bowed head. 'Afraid of a real challenge – is that it?'

'Drop it, Ed – just *drop it* – okay?' Philippe straightened to look at the stubborn, deeply lined face which stared back at him. Sometimes it seemed that that face had always been there, somewhere, somehow, ready and waiting to probe and interfere like a meddling, worrisome guardian angel . . . or a clinging leech, he thought unkindly, maybe that was a better description.

'Look, kid –,' there was a conciliatory note in his voice.

'And don't call me *kid*.'

'– I just don't want you to miss out on a golden opportunity,' Ed continued stubbornly, but Philippe had returned his gaze to the papers lying on his desk in a gesture of dismissal. 'I've just got a gut feeling about this one . . . maybe if I'd met someone like her when I was your age I wouldn't have got stuck with three useless broads who were only interested in beauty parlours and

239

my goddamn bank account.' Ed took a long drag on his cigar as if he were considering carefully what he would say next. 'I'm an old man, kid. I want to see you set up with a lady who's more than just well-stacked – someone with the right credentials – before I meet my maker.'

'Oh, quit it, Ed, will you?' Philippe retorted sharply, his eyes brilliant with subdued anger. 'Do you want me to start bawling now – or later?'

'All I'm saying is think about it . . . and while you're about it, how about developing a sense of humour and getting rid of that goddamn chip you've got on your shoulder?!'

With careful deliberation Philippe began to gather the files on his desk together.

'You're a stubborn son of a bitch . . . you know that!' Ed's voice started to rise as he realized that Philippe was about to walk out on him. 'I bet your mother never stood for any of your horse-shit. . . .'

'Leave my mother out of this!'

'She knew all about giving, all about caring and sharing *and* when to draw the line. . . .'

'And you'd know all about that, of course.' Philippe moved around the desk towards Ed.

'She was a good woman.'

'But you never married her . . . did you, Ed?' Philippe said slowly, softly, bringing his face low and thrusting it forward so that it was only inches away from the older man's.

'And you can't ever forgive that, can you? Can't ever stop turning that knife round and round in that old festering wound you love so goddamn much!'

'And you can't ever keep that big mouth of yours shut, can you . . . ?' Philippe hissed.

Ed stared into the cool pitiless amber eyes and wondered why he didn't do just that, but it would be like trying to ask Peanuts not to piss.

'She scares you, doesn't she?' Ed retorted. 'For a smart-ass spick, you're being amazingly dumb. . . .'

'For the last time, Ed – leave my private life alone. Do

you understand? You're trying to live your own pathetic dreams through me – well, just forget it!'

Philippe moved abruptly away from him towards the door.

'You're an ungrateful bastard . . . ,' Ed shouted after him, finally losing control, 'if you weren't my own flesh and blood I'd . . .'

Philippe whirled around like a snake.

'And I'm not your fucking flesh and blood . . . not your kid . . . not your goddamned son!'

'Schmuck!' Ed threw back at him.

The door slammed and Ed stared unseeing at the dark polished wood, then slowly down to the remains of his cigar which still smouldered. He lifted it to his lips and blew out a long cloud of smoke.

'You're still an ungrateful bastard . . . kid,' he said to the empty room.

The restaurant was half-empty and Geoff wished he had booked a later time when more people had climbed out of their drinking holes. He had decided on Chinese in the incongruous setting of an old canal boat moored at Camden Lock, but now he wished that they had stayed in town for the warmth and safety in numbers of the city. Instinctively he knew that this evening was not going to be one of life's greatest; Sian sat across from him endeavouring to be charming, but obviously wishing she was anywhere else than in a Chinese restaurant, on a barge, in December, sitting opposite a man she did not, really, want to be with.

'Have you spoken to Francesca?' he said.

'She hasn't called since yesterday afternoon,' Sian replied quietly as she recalled Francesca's ashen face. She had sensed almost from day one that there had been more to her relationship with Matthias than purely business, and now it showed.

'But she'll be in on Monday?'

'I think so – at least, she only mentioned that she was taking Friday to work away from the office.'

'It's been quite a shock.'

Sian nodded. 'And obviously under the circumstances I think Francesca got to know him well . . . ,' she replied carefully.

'And I wonder what we'll do about the campaign?' Geoff responded without noticing her veiled reply.

'Vic's going a little crazy about that,' she remarked, smiling.

'It doesn't take much for Vic to go crazy,' he said easily and realized all at once that they really didn't see much of each other any more. They had been neatly prised apart by Francesca's coming and he no longer seemed to walk in Vic's shadow with such easy grace. There had been more changes than anyone was aware of.

'How was Gilmore?' he said suddenly, unable to press down the question he had been longing to ask all the evening. Her face reddened and immediately he wished he hadn't asked.

'He was my boss,' she replied, as if that would explain everything.

'I know that.'

There was an awkward silence.

'We just went out for a drink.'

'For old times' sake?' There was a trace of sarcasm in his voice.

'Something like that.'

'He seems to be doing very well.'

'He's very ambitious,' she said almost defensively.

'Most people in this business are.'

'Are you?'

She was trying to change the subject.

'Probably not as much as Mr Gilmore.' There was that sarcasm again, but he couldn't help himself. It was like digging a hole and letting yourself fall into it bit by bit.

'You obviously don't like him.'

'I wouldn't say that – I hardly know him.' That part was true.

'He's a very good PR man . . . ,' she said uneasily, searching for something neutral to say.

242

'That's very clear.'

Sian stared fully into Geoff's face as the first stirrings of anger began to move inexorably, but then she softened, realizing all at once that he was jealous.

'It's getting late.'

He glanced impatiently at his watch.

'It's not even ten yet. . . .'

'I've got a busy day tomorrow and, in any event, Petie's always up far too early for my liking.' She smiled thinly and then felt foolish because Geoff could see through the facade too easily.

'I'd better get the bill, then.' He looked away from her, the jealousy and irritation suddenly evaporating into a slow sad feeling of defeat.

They drove south in silence, through the heart of London and the Friday night traffic. Sian stared unhappily beyond the window of the car. Christmas laughed maliciously back at her as they passed thousands of shop windows – grinning jovial Santas; nodding snowmen; plastic prettied trees and the garish brilliance of the lights strung across Regent Street. She sighed inwardly, knowing that she had hurt Geoff and never wanting to. Perhaps it was simply that he had come along at the wrong time – that she wasn't ready for someone else – or perhaps they just didn't go together somehow. But ultimately it was Adam, wasn't it? Nothing had really changed; she still wanted him. And he was Petie's father, she thought defensively, and that should mean something.

'I suppose you're going to be busy up until Christmas. . . .' Geoff's voice seemed to come out of nowhere.

'I have a few things to sort out.' Mainly myself, she thought humourlessly.

'Which means we probably won't be seeing each other, at least outside the office.' He thought wryly that he could have said nothing, asked nothing, but the answer would have been just the same, except perhaps less painful, and he wondered why he was so intent on deepening the wound.

'Maybe it's better that way, Geoff,' she said gently.

'If you say so.'

They sat in the ensuing quiet, feeling exposed and awkward, unable to reach each other. Sian closed her eyes as if the action would shut out the long, uncomfortable moments and when she opened them saw with relief the vague outline of Wimbledon Common and knew that home was only minutes away.

'It's just that things are a bit difficult right now,' she said at last, anxious somehow to make amends.

'I know.'

She glanced at Geoff's implacable profile and knew there was nothing she could say that would make any difference. She turned her face back to the black face of the window and they remained wrapped in stony silence until the car drew up outside her house.

'Thanks . . . ,' she said softly and found her hand reaching out to touch his arm as if in consolation.

'There's no need to thank me – after all, it wasn't exactly a successful evening, was it?' He shifted his eyes to her face and saw that she was half-hidden by shadow, that there was only the outline of her lips which seemed to have any real substance. He had always liked the wide sweet curve of her lips and at that moment he wanted to kiss them, just once, just to see how it would feel. But instead he leaned across her to open the door.

'You're a very nice guy, Geoff,' she said finally and then moved to get out of the car.

He stopped and looked back at her and she saw with surprise the beginnings of anger in the over-brightness of his eyes.

'Don't say that, Sian, *that* I don't need. Sometimes I wonder if it is really even a compliment,' he said sharply. 'And I don't need your kindness – like a pat on the head because I've been a good dog.'

She seemed about to speak, but then climbed quickly out of the car and he thought he heard her call a brief goodnight, but later when he recalled his harshness he was no longer sure.

Somehow she could have been Joanne at that moment. Joanne had always said in her smooth cynical way what 'a nice guy' he was and he had hated it, wincing inwardly, but he had never told her and for some irrational, illogical reason he had waited until now to let the world know . . . at least Sian, because she had managed with just a few words to flood him with all the pain of that carefully hoarded bitterness.

Geoff turned the car back in the direction of central London and as the car wove through countless streets of countless homes – maybe even happy homes – he wondered fleetingly where his portion of 'happiness' was and why so often it seemed to slip furtively and unkindly beyond his grasp. He looked briefly to one side as he passed over Putney Bridge and tried in vain to glimpse the dark reaches of the Thames before the outlying tentacles of the city claimed him. He felt suddenly and overwhelmingly tired which was preferable to the creeping demon of self-pity which was hovering only just out of sight. Inevitably he thought of his painfully empty flat and the knowledge that he had no further plans for the weekend which seemed to stretch out mercilessly before him. Maybe he would go into the office and work on those research papers, or of course he could go over the figures of Gilmore's precious PR company. But maybe he would simply take a long walk off a short pier, which would just about solve everything nice and neatly. He shook his head gently and felt the beginnings of a sad mocking smile touch his mouth. No, he simply wasn't the type.

She had left her briefcase open, but the thick wad of papers would remain there untouched. Francesca had pulled a chair close to the fire and sat hunched, legs drawn up with her chin resting on her knees, as she stared blankly into the blue-red of the artificial flames. The room was saved from total darkness only by the light from the fire and there was no sound except the sough of the wind outside and her own breathing. After Richmond she had driven around a long time in the mournful drizzle before returning home. The day had worn inexorably on and on, and now she was curled up like a child, caught by a wave of fatigue which seemed to weigh her down, exhausting her heart and her mind.

He had never belonged to her, of course – and never would have – but the knowledge brought her no comfort. And yet in a few short months he had managed to slip beneath her skin with such ease that it had been frightening – and she had withdrawn for her own safety, because she had known that however much he might have protested, she would never have been enough. She pushed her hair back in a gesture of anguish, dragging her mind back in order to make some sense of the past. He had accused her of complicating things, of wanting it all, but it had been he who had demanded too much. But she wondered with a curious sadness whether she would have seen him, slept with him, that night if he had ultimately come, and once, no doubt, lovely Melissa had been slickly dumped and bypassed for the evening. Francesca drew a long weary breath because there was still that scathing self-knowledge of her own weakness – that she wanted him, still wanted him. But he had allowed the plane and his own impulsiveness to put paid to any foolish dreams she may have harboured. Even he must have known that the weather was too bad for such a flight and yet he had risked it, because that was the sort of person he was. And she tried for an ugly moment to picture his face in the terrifying darkness as realization struck him that he was no longer in control and that his god, finally, had taken over. But the image she saw was somehow not afraid, and she thought that that strange wild smile would have slid inevitably across his beautiful mouth. After all, golden gods are immortal, aren't they?

The morning dawned colder and Francesca could see a light frost dusting the leaves in the garden as she stared disconsolately through the window. She had hardly slept and what sleep she had had was erratic and full of wretched dreams. As her eyes swept over the enclosed garden she was reminded of a white house in New England where the frost had looked like snow and she was suddenly stung by a longing for Ed's easy old-man humour, for his refreshing New York banter and that simple room she had occupied with stripped pine and chintz curtains. She smiled with a trace of self-pity at this sudden vulnerability and closed her eyes in an effort to bolster her ragged spirits. Even as she did so the door-bell screamed and she thought her nerves would snap, but instead she found herself automatically pulling her robe more tightly about her, automatically pacing towards the sound of the bell.

It was Michael.

'I know it's early, but I tried to call last night. . . .'

'I left the phone off the hook . . . ,' she replied wearily as he stepped past her.

'Oh. . . .'

'I'm really not feeling up to much, Michael – perhaps we could arrange another time. . . .' But there was no strength in her voice, and as she turned to face him she realized that he had had little sleep too and that he had hardly heard what she said so that her protest slipped away unnoticed.

'I need your help –'

'More money?' she replied without expression.

'Not much, not really. . . .'

She sighed heavily. Not now, Michael.

'I really would appreciate it if we could talk about this on Monday.' Without looking at him she sat down.

'That's too late . . . I need something now.'

'Michael . . . ,' she said in an effort at patience, 'I have had hardly any sleep, it is very early on a Saturday morning and in case you are not aware, there are no banks open today.'

'A cheque would do.'

'What happened to the £20 thousand?' She lifted her eyes to his face and saw defeat. Reluctantly she found her interest begin to awaken and an awareness seep through, pressing down the momentum of her misery.

'It'll be okay, it's just taking longer than I thought.'

'What is?'

'Recouping my investment. . . .'

'Sometimes and quite often shares go down and not up, Michael,' she said slowly, sarcastically, and saw how his fists clenched. 'People lose money all the time, a great deal of money – and this has not been a good year.'

'This was a good tip,' he protested.

'But it hasn't paid off?'

'Not yet.' Nigel had told him the news in the murky depths of a City cellar bar full of pinstripe suits, his fat face pulled into an appropriately apologetic expression. 'It's just going to take a bit longer than I had anticipated . . . ,' he had said lamely, '. . . the sale of the shares hasn't taken off very well against all expectations and predictions. You'll just have to hold on to them.' But for how long? his mind had screamed. Too damned long.

'But you are sure it will.'

'Pretty sure,' he replied, not meeting her eyes.

'That isn't good enough.'

'I've told you – it was a good tip!' His voice began to rise.

'Whose tip? Why don't you let me check it out?'

'No.' Because then she would find out that he really was a simple fool.

'And you want more money on that basis?' she said coolly.

'Yes.'

Her eyes examined his pale empty face sharply and she wondered how she had compared him with Matthias, how he had been born her father's son.

'No.'

'That's not fair!'

'We're not talking about being fair, Michael – we're talking about business and about a lot of money.'

'I don't want that much,' he retorted sullenly.

'I'd be a fool to lend it to you.'

'And I'm a fool asking for it, I suppose!' His face twisted into a childish frown. 'God – you'd think I was asking for the bloody moon! Just one more loan – just one more, and I know things will start working for me.' He walked across the room to the mirror above the mantel-shelf and looked fleetingly at the white face that stared back at him. '*I've got to get this right, Fran,*' he said with sudden intensity.

'I have to prove to mother that I can succeed on my own.'

'Why don't you come in with me?' she said quietly, knowing what his answer would be.

'I don't want that – it's got to be something I've thought up myself, something that only I can lay claim to.'

'Only with *my* money.'

'But it was father's business . . . wasn't it?' he said meanly, in desperation.

'You gave up your share without a qualm and not once have you ever shown the slightest interest in the business,' she replied too sharply, longing to add that he had never shown any interest in their father, either.

'That wasn't my fault!'

'Whose fault was it?'

He looked away from her. Mother, it had always been mother; deriding and gnawing away at what respect there might have been for the man who had been his father. He had never known him. Michael cringed inwardly with sudden self-loathing; his own father had frightened him and it had not needed the mocking innuendoes of his mother finally to alienate him. Carlo Gaetini had always seemed so loud, so big – larger than life – that it only seemed natural to back away from those enormous wide-open arms until they had opened for him no longer.

'This is all pointless. . . .'

'I'm sure father wouldn't think so,' she said suddenly.

'Give me the money – please, Fran,' he replied, ignoring her remark.

'Come in and see me on Monday, and we'll talk it over more sensibly.' She had had enough now, more than enough.

'No – I want an answer now!'

'I'm not ready to give you an answer now,' she said with weary impatience and a flicker of anger.

'You're supposed to be my bloody sister. . . .'

'When it suits you.'

'That's a rotten thing to say.'

'But it's true.'

'We've always kept in touch . . . ,' he said feebly.

'Barely,' she replied dryly, as all the old devils of her memory began to crawl out of the woodwork. 'You let mother see to that.'

'That's not fair,' he said again. But it was true.

'I've never thought things have been very fair where I was concerned, Michael.' It was out in the open now and she found herself looking at him with sad curiosity.

'Oh, for God's sake. . . .'

'You don't agree?'

'It really always comes back to darling mother in the end, doesn't it?' he remarked impatiently. 'Well – what the hell can you expect when . . . .'

He studied her for an instant, his face reddening.

'When what?' she asked carefully, and saw how he lowered his eyes and then brought them up to rest reluctantly on her face.

'Forget it.'

'When what, Michael?' she persisted.

'It doesn't matter – it was just something to say.' He spoke without conviction.

'I want to know.'

'I said I would never . . . say anything.' His voice shook, but somehow he wanted to tell her because suddenly she seemed to have all the things he wanted and he had never realized before.

'Tell me.'

'But you must know . . . surely?'

She stared back at him in the wrapped weighted silence.

'Tell me.'

His shoulders sagged and she saw how he fixed his gaze on the twisting knot of his hands. He had gone too far and now his courage was failing.

'*She* should have told you . . . or father. . . .'

'You tell me,' she said softly.

He seemed to hesitate for a moment and then the words came out disjointed and afraid.

'You're not mother's daughter . . . you're not even father's, come to that. . . .'

She stared fixedly at him for a long moment until she

thought she would drown in the utter stillness, drown in the panic which began to take shape in the pit of her stomach.

'What do you mean?' And she realized her voice was almost a whisper.

'I shouldn't have said anything – I said I wouldn't,' he said helplessly as he saw the ashen upturned face.

'What do you mean, Michael?' she repeated each word carefully as if her resolve might waver.

'I am their son . . . ,' he said uneasily and she thought that his words seemed to shake, 'but you are not their daughter.' He paused and she thought she saw tears of fear standing in his eyes. 'I think father adopted you – or they both did – I don't know.'

'You think?' she asked quietly.

'Look, Fran . . . .'

Somehow she thought 'Fran' sounded wrong now, like something distorted. Unsuitable.

'Look . . . ,' he continued, 'I can hardly remember; mother told me years ago. Father wanted another child and mother wouldn't give him one.'

'So I was conveniently brought in,' she said in a remote voice.

'I don't know – I don't know!' There was something in the set calmness of her face that frightened him.

'I think you'd better go now, Michael.'

He stood hesitantly watching her, but unable to move. It had all gone horribly wrong and with sudden searing clarity he realized he had no one else to turn to.

'But what about the money . . . ?'

She made no answer for a moment, but then slowly lifted her head and he was stunned by the desolate soul-chilling face that looked back at him.

*'Get out, Michael! Get out!'* Her voice screamed at him. And she was shocked by the scream which raked the silence, as if somehow it came from someone else, from another mouth. Later she remembered hearing his long desperate sigh and did not care, only finding herself thinking numbly of the countless times she had been

struck by the curious differences between them, but most of all by his stark fairness and her darkness, and how as a child she had been trapped by that familiar surge of despair at Livia's obvious love for Michael . . . and her furtive childish dream that one day, somehow, her mother would turn to her with her arms held open and that special smile she always saved for Michael soft on her face. Perhaps in the most secret part of her heart she had always known about mother.

But papa . . . not papa. She had been his, hadn't she? They couldn't take that away from her. From somewhere far away she heard a door close and knew that Michael had left, but it didn't seem to matter any longer. The pain, the searing bitterness of what had passed between them was beginning to sink in. Her heart knocked frantically and she could hear a pounding echo in her ears as her hands came up to close over the sound. Odd disturbing images from the past slipped unhappily into her mindscape, claiming her through the years, and she thought she would die from the pain of it. She felt the old childish aching for papa creep up on her as tears of bewilderment surged into her eyes and rolled down her cheeks.

It was as he had expected. Nick looked disinterestedly about the room, noting with dry amusement the modest display of silver, the invitation cards carefully placed along the broad marble mantel-shelf, and the meticulous positioning of the latest copy of *Country Life* which lay across an occasional table directly in his line of vision.

'. . . And you've been at Samuels how long, Nicholas?' Caroline's mother asked as she resumed her seat on the other side of the room. He loved the way she said 'Nicholas'; it must have been over ten years since the last time anyone had called him that.

'It will be about a year in March.'

'And before that?'

'McCann's.'

'McCann's?' she asked, pulling her face into a mask of exaggerated confusion.

'McCann-Erickson . . . ,' he replied patiently, '. . . yet another advertising agency.'

'Ah, I see. And why did you choose advertising as a career?'

He sighed inwardly; did she have to make their meeting quite as excruciating as an interview . . . ?

'There are not many careers open to art graduates and what opportunities there are are open to competition of the keenest sort. I was lucky in that I discovered I could write copy. . . .'

'Copy?'

'The text in advertisements.'

'You mean, the jingles, as they say?' she said with a small laugh.

He decided it was not a nice laugh, a smirk, she was making fun of him.

'Sometimes.'

'So you joined an advertising company.'

'They pay very well,' he said deliberately, knowing that she would find his wording unsubtle, vulgar – but she liked money, that was more than clear, only the *right kind of money*.

'And your father . . . ?'

'My father?' he repeated vaguely as if he did not understand.

'What does he do?'

'He's in the rag-trade.'

'The rag-trade?'

'He sells clothes.'

'He has a shop then?' she probed.

'Not exactly.'

'I don't understand. . . .'

He had been waiting for this.

'Market stalls – he has several of them,' Nick replied and found his eyes pulled to Caroline's. Her face had reddened. He shifted his gaze back to her mother.

'Market stalls.' The words slipped slowly from the pursed lips as if she were regurgitating something unpalatable.

'He does rather well, actually.' And he did, but she would never appreciate that, and he wondered why he had been so intent on telling her because any barbed pleasure he had hoped to gain somehow evaporated in the awkward silence which followed.

'Something stronger . . . Nicholas?' Caroline's father interjected uneasily. 'Sherry?'

'I'd prefer a gin and tonic. . . .'

'Fine, fine. . . .' And he stood up, obviously relieved and quite obviously ignoring the sharp unforgiving glance of his wife. 'Anna?' There was no reply and Nick thought that she did not look like an 'Anna', the name was too kind.

'I'll have the same, daddy, please,' Caroline asked quietly and he knew that she was risking their disapproval or, at least, their surprise. Nick gave her a searching look and then turned back to the older woman who was now staring rigidly through the large bay windows as if the unnecessary interruption of a gin and tonic had thwarted her aim.

'I'm retired, of course, as Caroline may have told you,' her father said as he handed Nick his drink. The older man moved back to his seat and drew a soft weary breath. True . . . this was not Guy, not safe rather boring Guy who his daughter had apparently been destined to marry through no more than habit. And he was glad that she had decided against such a trap, surprised that she'd even had the gumption to break it off. He'd always thought privately that Guy was a little wet and that Caroline wasn't far off it either, but perhaps he had misjudged her. But Anna, Anna wouldn't give up easily and it was a pity the boy had felt compelled to mention his father's circumstances; it would have been much easier in the long run if he had evaded the issue or told a little white lie just for the time being. He let his eyes study Nick once more and wondered if Anna hadn't bitten off more than she could chew, but she would never admit defeat, not Anna, and he closed his eyes fleetingly in exasperation as an image of the argument that would surely follow took shape in his mind. But there was

254

always the club later, he thought with some relief, and then brought his gin and tonic up to his waiting lips. God . . . all he wanted was a little peace.

'Do you still want to see that film?' Nick did not let his eyes leave the road as they drove through Richmond, unsure of how she would respond.

'No, I don't think so,' Caroline replied quietly and wanted to add, 'not now.' Her mother had said very little once her father had thankfully intervened with the gin and tonics, but the atmosphere in the room had been almost unbearable and she had grown more and more tense as the awkward silences became longer and more frequent, until finally she had been unable to stand it a moment longer and had stood up indicating that they would go. And all she wanted to do now was run and run . . . and to keep running.

'Dinner, then?'

'That would be nice.'

'You don't sound very enthusiastic.'

'No, really, I'd like that.'

They drove for a few heavy moments wrapped in silence.

'I take it I shall be "out of bounds" from now on. . . .'

'Mummy is very set in her ways . . . ,' Caroline said lamely.

'I didn't help much – she was goading me and I took the bait.'

'She thinks that she will persuade me to go back with Guy. . . .'

He swallowed slowly.

'And will she?'

'I suppose if I really wanted a safe, boring, dreary marriage like my parents', that's exactly what I would do.' The words came out so easily that she felt as if she had suddenly been released and she almost wanted to smile.

He glanced at her with surprise and saw how her face was beginning to relax and he was touched by relief.

'Your father doesn't seem too bad.'

'Daddy's the long-suffering type.' She had never said that before.

'Does he drink?' If he hadn't guessed by the florid complexion it had been made more than obvious from the way he gulped down his very large g and t.

'Sometimes.' Too much, she thought sadly, especially over the last year or two.

'You know what he ought to do?' Nick said seriously.

'What?'

And she turned to look at him, her eyes tracing the sweep of his forehead, each reassuring curve, the fineness of his jaw-line, as if she had never seen them before.

'Give her a "good tamm". . . ,' he drawled in a broad West Indian accent.

She started to laugh.

'What's a "good tamm"?'

'Translated from the Greek – "a *good time*"; translated from Nick Keogh's book of idioms – "make mad passionate love to her", preferably with a whip and wearing a black leather G-string. . . .'

She laughed again as the farcical image took shape in her mind in glorious technicolour. Not her father, never – and certainly not with her mother. And suddenly she felt touched by sadness. Nick's ludicrous scenario wasn't all wrong; take away the lurid trimmings of his 'good time' and he was probably nearly all right. Except that it was probably too late.

'Hey – it was only a joke.'

'I know . . . and I adored your accent.'

And she smiled quickly at his worried face so that the sadness slid easily away.


'The press conference is tomorrow,' Vic said sharply. 'I promised Pete Morgan I'd get back to him by this afternoon.'

'Okay, and how do you think we should handle it?' Francesca looked back at him.

'Perhaps you should tell me – after all you've had plenty

of time to think the whole thing through.' Let her eat her way out of this one.

'Well, I don't see why we shouldn't continue with the campaign as it stands . . . he would have wanted that.'

'And *he's* hardly going to be around to appreciate it, is he?' he retorted sarcastically.

She closed her eyes with impatience, expecting this.

'That's not what I meant. We can still draw on all the publicity the campaign might have had and probably still make an impact – maybe an even bigger one.'

'I thought the idea was that the TV spots, the talk shows, the satellite broadcast were all supposed to launch him as a cross between Mahatma Gandhi and John F. Kennedy. What's the point if we're only left with a ghost to play around with?'

Francesca winced inwardly at his tactlessness, at his lack of imagination.

'Several good reasons, Vic: one, it's never been done before; two, Lucas Chant wants us to go ahead with it and he is paying us so we lose nothing; three, we change the concept to a tribute to a potentially great man . . .'

'I think I want to throw up.' Vic interjected.

'. . . four, people love tragedy and tragic figures,' she continued, ignoring his remark, 'and because of this I am certain the campaign will attract maximum attention which will mean our name in big red lights; and finally, the money raised from the satellite broadcast and any other spin-offs will be used to form the basis for some kind of charitable or educational foundation in his name – which, of course, will also receive maximum publicity.'

'Whose idea was that?' he asked cynically.

'Mine.'

'And you think all this will work?'

'There's no reason why on earth it shouldn't – unless you can tell me otherwise.'

He shook his head with feigned disgust, his large mouth pulling into a sneer.

'Christ, I've heard it all now!' But it would work, just as she said it would, and somehow the knowledge made him bitterly angry. 'He was a load of balls from beginning to end – all that crap about caring and sharing – you didn't really believe him and I certainly didn't.'

'That's not what we're here to discuss, Vic,' she said with barely concealed distaste.

'He was a first-class, ass-licking con-artist with a pretty face.' He loosened his tie as if he were only just beginning. 'And I'd be interested to know how many of his so-called "followers", apart from all those half-brained rock stars, were women.'

'You know, Vic, anyone would think that you were jealous.' And she stood up and moved to the window.

'Balls! I'm just stating a few belated facts.'

'With your usual charm.'

'Someone had to say it.' He leaned arrogantly back in his chair. 'And how do we handle the Melissa Barton-Carr angle – that our breathtakingly lovely socialite just happened to be staying in her father's chateau in the depths of a French forest with our "Golden God" and decided to go joy-riding as well?'

'Her father has conveniently taken care of that aspect of things, Vic – you already know that,' she said evenly, but there was a warning note in her voice. She did not want to be reminded of the ease with which Matthias seduced others. It came too close, hurting, and would probably go on hurting long afterwards.

'Good old Sir Richard – Billy the Kid of Fleet Street – nicely wrapping his beautiful brainless daughter in tinsel. Christ, when I think of how many people he's managed to trample practically to extinction on his way to the glorious top and still managed to come up smelling of roses, even got bloody knighted . . . !'

'We were supposed to be talking about the fate of the campaign.'

'I loved the lines in the *Mail* today: "Tycoon's daughter tried to persuade star to turn back . . . sacrificed herself for the sake of an ideal. . . ." What fucking garbage; everyone knows she was getting laid!'

'Sometimes, Vic, you should learn to keep your mouth

under control,' she said icily. 'And don't you think it's just a little foolish to look a gift horse in the mouth – it can only help the campaign.'

He snorted contemptuously in response.

'If that's going to be your attitude maybe I should speak to Pete Morgan.'

He stared at her for a long moment.

'No,' he said slowly as his anger finally dissipated, 'that won't be necessary. It was my campaign to begin with, if you remember, and I'll see it through to the bitter end.' He stood up. 'And, after all, isn't it the adman's motto to "keep the client happy", even, apparently, when the client happens to have dropped dead.'

'Very witty, Vic,' she responded sarcastically.

'Oh, you ain't seen nothin' yet. . . .'

He smiled thinly and walked away from her. She watched him leave with a feeling of unease, her eyes resting on the closed door after he had gone. A barely touched cup of coffee was on her desk and she sat down to drink the lukewarm liquid with a sense of relief. Vic was getting worse, and there was something too smug about him now. Maybe he thought he'd still out-manoeuvre her, still be sitting in her seat at Samuels before too long. . . . But she cast the thought aside; he had irritated her enough and she knew that part of that irritation lay in the fact that she believed half of what he said about Matthias was true. She hadn't wanted to believe it, but as the knowledge of his death began to sink in she found herself wondering at the ease with which he could become all things to all people, wondering how he could promise so much to her when he could give so little. He had meant what he said at the time, like so many others, but he couldn't really come up with the goods, and she smiled wryly, sadly, and wondered ultimately and with a trace of pity whether his death had actually saved him. Her thoughts swept back to the tape of his concert at Wembley five years before; Matthias had ruled then, his whole being all-knowing, rapturous, omnipotent and they had loved him, loved that wild, crooked, wanton face just as she had. For a while.

She looked down at his file lying open on her desk and the brilliant photograph which looked back at her, and slowly closed it. Her gaze was dragged reluctantly to the other photograph on her desk and she was stung once more by confusion and pain as she looked into the big handsome face with the infectious grin watching her from a silver frame. Livia would know everything, remember everything, of course, as if she kept a score-card in her head. Francesca caught a sharp, wary breath. But she wasn't ready for Livia, not yet.

Christmas was beginning to weigh heavily. Sian glanced at the list of directors, account supervisors and those in key positions, and ticked them off against the number of hampers she had ordered from Harrods. All the secretaries and PAs were to receive a bottle of Joy as a gesture of goodwill from Francesca and anyone left over a bottle of Dom Perignon. There were still the final details of the Christmas lunch to tie up and she sighed inwardly with exasperation as she remembered how Zoë had booked it for the 20th and how she had had frantically to ring back the Ritz and change the day. The signing of the merger was set for the 20th and the Christmas lunch had been assigned to the 18th as Zoë had been told at least half-a-dozen times. Sian looked up as the door to Vic's office opened and Zoë walked out. She seemed happier these days and there had been no talk of the abortion. It was almost as if it had never happened – because she had closed her mind off to it, shutting it out so that it couldn't interfere with her life, so she thought. But Sian wondered about Zoë's relationship with Vic, if there still was one, wondered if she would ever tell him. Not Zoë, Sian decided, and in any event she had said as much. Maybe it was the wisest thing to do if she wanted to keep her job; somehow Sian knew instinctively that Vic would not tolerate having that sort of emotional burden around his neck, would certainly choose to lock it out of his daily existence. Out of sight, out of mind. Immediately her thoughts turned to Adam. He had suggested that they meet on a weekly basis, and as soon as it was practical he would see Petie, but for a second time he had cancelled and now she had agreed to meet him in the Mayfair Hotel in two days' time. They would have a drink, maybe two, and she wondered warily what he would suggest then. Once before he had booked a room at the Mayfair and they had stayed overnight, and she had luxuriated in the small extravagances he had showered upon her because she had been in love with him. This time she could not stay overnight, which would probably mean that they would book out of their room late that evening and he would put her in a cab, and she would travel home alone, like an exile. She did not like the picture she had conjured up, but it had taken shape in her mind involuntarily and there was nothing she could do about it. Maybe she was tired. Glancing at her watch, she pressed any more thoughts down to think of later; it was time she was leaving.

'Are you off now?' Zoë asked, as Sian began to tidy her desk.

'Just about – and you?'

'Oh, I'm not hanging around tonight,' she replied quickly. 'Vic has a meeting with Pete Morgan now, so once I've finished this list I'm compiling, I'll be following you.'

'Well, don't stay too late . . . ,' Sian said finally.

December had brought a soft insipid rain, but now the weather was turning cold and the rain poured down in icy sheets. Sian watched the pavements turn to silver from the safety of Samuels' marble steps and then turned back inside; she had left her umbrella behind.

The sixth floor was half in shadow and everyone seemed to have gone home. Geoff had not been in all the afternoon and Francesca had for once left early. Sian's gaze fell on Zoë's desk which was now cleared and silent, and then crossed the room to her own. As she reached down for her umbrella which lay under her desk and against the wall her eyes caught a glimpse of a pale light from under Vic's door. Frowning in puzzlement she stood up and listened for a moment: there was definitely someone in Vic's office. She was tempted just to leave and forget it, but sighing wearily she moved over to the door, knocked quickly, and walked into the room.

Later she wondered if she would ever forget Vic's stunned face as he looked back at her. It had only taken an instant to absorb what was happening, but somehow the time seemed to last much longer, like a scene in a film set in lurid slow motion. His shirt hung out and his trousers were draped incongruously about his knees. She could not see Zoë's face because she was bent over in front of him and her hair was falling across her head in a tangle of blonde curls, hiding her features, as Vic moved against the stark white flesh of her buttocks.

Vic waited until Sian had closed the door softly behind her before continuing. Her entrance had startled him for a moment, but it wasn't really important and Zoë had hardly noticed, only beginning to mumble something as if she may have heard, but in response he had merely leaned over and pushed her head down, before she could see the door slowly closing and realize what had happened. He hadn't finished and didn't intend to stop now as he switched to the thing which mattered to him most, his gaze returning automatically to the plump roundness of Zoë's bottom, and any more thoughts of Sian, Samuels or the new horizon of GKP slipping effortlessly away in the wake of his climax.

Zoë smoothed down her skirt and turned to look at Vic who was busy erasing any remnants of their sex with a handkerchief.

'I thought I heard something . . . ?'

'Did you?' Vic replied vaguely.

'Yes.'

'Oh, it was nothing,' he said smoothly, pulling his underpants up and fastening his trousers.

'Nothing?' she asked quietly.

And he looked into her pretty, predictable face and was suddenly struck anew by the fact that she bored him.

'It was only Sian.'

'Sian?' Zoë felt a thickness gather in her throat.

'Yes, Sian,' he replied with a shrug. 'She must have seen the light and wondered who was in here – she soon found out.' He grinned then, but Zoë could only look mutely back at him as he slipped his arms into his jacket, pushing the soiled handkerchief deep down into one of the pockets.

Philippe leaned his head back against the cushion-soft seat and closed his eyes. It was a week before the signing of the merger and Ed had insisted that the few minor changes he wanted made be personally instigated in London and before the 20th, but almost at the last minute he had suddenly declined the trip saying that he wasn't up to it and that Philippe would go in his place. He had had no choice, but he had been more than angry as Ed had theatrically brought his hand up to his brow as if at any moment he might keel over. It was all bull, and if he thought that by pushing him into the trip he and Francesca might get together somehow he was really living on cloud nine, but of course, Ed had denied anything of the kind. Philippe turned impatiently to the window as the plane fled along the runway and lifted gently into the air. In any event, he told himself, she was not his style, they were worlds apart. Ed just wouldn't see it, but he'd better see it and get off his back. But then Ed was getting old, too old, and he wouldn't see that either. He was getting forgetful, too, and several times recently had lost the thread of a conversation altogether. The clients didn't seem to mind, in fact they seemed to enjoy it as if Ed was putting on a performance just for them. 'Good old Ed, docsn't know when to quit . . . the sort of guy who made America what it is today. . . .' Ed would quit only when he dropped because the word 'retire' just wasn't in his vocabulary. Philippe drew a breath; Ed would be hanging around his neck, suffocating him, as long as he could still see straight – Ed's own willpower would see to that. After all, Dunmar-Rock was all he had if you didn't count Peanuts. And himself, of course . . . 'his own flesh and blood'. A soft, cynical smile began to tip the edges of his mouth as their previous argument came back to him in all its bitter detail. Ed was a fool – and there was no fool like an old fool.

They had hardly spoken a word all day. Zoë had studiously avoided any conversation and Sian had not forced her. Vic had walked in with an almost jovial air, disappeared for a meeting and then taken a long lunch. He hadn't returned. It was coming up to 5.30, but there was still a short report to re-draft on the merger and the following day's meeting with Philippe Sanchez. Sian shrugged inwardly; it didn't matter that she'd be working late, it would kill time until she left to meet Adam. Her eyes lifted to Zoë who was already starting to clear her desk; obviously she was leaving early and Sian sighed softly with relief. But she couldn't watch her leave, there would be too many echoes from yesterday. Instead she got up and made her way to the kitchen, a coffee wasn't a bad idea anyway. Even as she began spooning some granules into a cup she heard Zoë's footsteps as they moved towards the lift and there was her brief, barely audible, goodnight.

Sian brought the coffee back to her desk and sat down heavily. She turned to the window, brooding, and watched as the persistent rain made silver tracks down the glass. For a moment she tried to picture Adam in his office, behind the sleek white desk, the same pictures hanging on the walls, the same fig tree standing in the corner of the room. Several times they had made love in his office because there had been nowhere else, no time, at least that was what she had told herself. But she had been in love with him, hadn't she? She remembered too well how even the mention of his name, the sound of his voice had made her stomach lurch and how she had woven pretty, potent dreams of her future life with him. But that had been well over a year ago and now she was letting it all start again, just as if there had not been that painful, wretched time in-between when Adam had so conveniently made his exit from her life. He wanted it all, of course, and she supposed that she was still prepared to give it to him. Maybe she wasn't so different from Zoë, after all, she thought with bitter sadness.

It was clear that Samuels was still very much alive as she made her way through the reception area. People still waited in the deep soft seats and telephones still rang as if the day was just beginning. A Christmas tree stood elegantly on one side of the gleaming double doors – perfectly shaped, tall, studded with red, green and silver ribbons. Sian caught the heady scent of pine as she passed and suddenly became aware that it was the first time the run-up to Christmas had even begun to touch her. She smiled to herself as she thought of Petie and the presents she had accumulated for him so far; he was too young, of course, but it didn't matter and he would love it all anyway. He was a surprisingly good child, she realized all at once, quick to smile, easy to love. With an unreasonable, stinging sense of guilt she felt that she didn't deserve such goodness, not when so often she had secretly wished for that other life which was past, lost, utterly out of reach. The screeching sound of wheels made her look up as the big black shape of a cab began turning into the rainswept street. Sian pulled her coat tightly around her and ran forwards. It was a fifteen-minute drive to the Mayfair and she would probably be late, but Adam would be there, waiting, because he would be so sure that she would come.

The cab was forced to drop her a few yards beyond the hotel, and as she struggled in the half-light to find change for the accustomed tip she had a sudden urge to get back into the safe confines of the vehicle, but instead found herself waiting for the driver to take the money from her open hand and then watching the cab move inevitably away. Her gaze turned warily to the entrance of the hotel and she began walking mechanically towards it. The rain was making her hair wet, and she could feel it slide down her face and inside the thin collar of the blouse she had chosen with such care. She thought of Zoë then, and Vic, and the slick, smug smile he had given her that morning. The light from the hotel doorway slanted amber across the pavement as she stepped over it and her feet began to take her down the sloping street towards Berkeley Square and the tube station. If she was lucky Petie might still be awake by the time she got home.

'I'll have to discuss this point in particular with Ed, but I don't think he'll have any objections.'

Francesca nodded in response and then added, 'I take it the clients who grumbled about the merger have quietened down now?'

'All of them – except for Klein, but we've been busy buttering him up over the past few weeks and now he's beginning to respond to Ed's generosity. He's just a greedy bastard, that's all,' Philippe said, with a touch of impatience.

'PRS is your biggest, or should I say, *our* biggest client,' she said carefully.

'Don't worry, Klein may be difficult, but he's not stupid; even he can see the benefits of the UK merger and the expansion of the international network. He knows that PRS are uniquely placed to take advantage of our planned globalization strategy.'

'Has he actually said so?'

Philippe smiled.

'He has implied that we're likely to receive the go-ahead on two $20 million global campaigns in the new year.' He had been waiting for the right moment to spill the beans. He watched her carefully controlled face and then let his eyes move to her hands, saw how the fingers tightened with anticipation around the pen she was holding.

'What sort of products?'

'Curiously they're both launches. The first is a hair product which claims to halt hair loss one hundred per cent, but doesn't unfortunately show promise of promoting new growth as yet – even so, it will practically sell on its own. It's called 21 at the moment. The second is a twenty-four-hour female contraceptive pessary which is supposed to be 99.9 per cent effective against pregnancy – and AIDS – , but they haven't come up with a name yet; we might have to do that.'

'Sounds good – if it really works.'

'Klein says that it has passed every test so far and that it's only a question of another few months.'

'But are we really prepared to launch these products globally?'

It was Geoff's voice reining-in her galloping thoughts. She had almost forgotten he was there.

'I'm already working on it,' Philippe replied evenly, turning towards him. 'It looks like we'll be aiming at a sixty- and a thirty-second commercial for use in thirty-two countries in eighteen different languages.'

'Christ!' Geoff exclaimed.

'That includes our associates, of course. . . ,' she interjected. It could work, Francesca thought with growing excitement, as figures and percentages soared into her mind, with a lot of judicious planning and a little luck.

'They're our main weak point – certainly creatively, but almost all of the creative work will come out of the New York shop, so we won't need to concern ourselves too much with that problem for the time being, but what we will have to concern ourselves with is a foothold in Hong Kong, Singapore and maybe Thailand. I'd like to include Japan, but as you know it's practically impossible to set up an associate agreement let alone *own* an agency there because of their intransigence. But 21 should go down well there, even through a distributor, as I've heard that Japanese men are very vain, particularly about hair loss – apparently some are even prepared to fly first class to China in search of hair elixirs.' He smiled dryly and then continued, 'Leaving 21 and its possibilities aside, I also think that a tour of the network might be in order, say, for the beginning of February?' He looked directly into her face. 'It would be a good idea if you could make it.'

'I can make it,' she said, looking back at him and then slowly returning her gaze to the paper held in her hand. 'And do you agree with our proposal for a PR strategy?'

'I would have waited a little longer . . . ,' he said, as a half-smile settled on his lips, 'but you've obviously covered every eventuality.'

'I think so,' she replied, feeling vaguely irritated.

'Prime PR is eighth in the UK PR tables – it's a good move,' Geoff added. He had hardly been able to contain his glee when Francesca finally decided on Derek Richie's operation rather than Gilmore's, although it hardly mattered now. Gilmore had dug his heels in over being wholly owned just as she had predicted, whereas Richie had opted for the forty-nine per cent. Prime came more expensive, but it was still a good buy and the bonus was that Gilmore was now out of the Samuels' picture.

'Oh, I agree; it was just the timing I had doubts about,' Philippe said easily.

'There's no need,' Francesca responded, pressing down her irritation with an effort. 'Have you had any more thoughts on a US acquisition?'

'Of course. Perhaps when you come over for the signing next week we can discuss it further.'

'Still Creamer Dickson or Regis McKenna?'

He nodded.

'Have you had time to digest the report on management consultancy?' she said abruptly, unsettled by his calmness.

'You really want to branch out in a big way, don't you?' he said with a trace of humour.

'There's no reason to stop us – we're still behind our immediate competitors in almost every field. I want to change that and, after all, management consultancy grew by over twenty per cent last year. We'd be foolish not to consider it.' The dream she had nurtured for so long, that of a 'mega-agency' handling the richest accounts and in the top three global rankings, maybe even number one in the world, seemed much more than just a possibility now.

'I already have,' he said quietly. 'I've lined up a meeting with Deloitte Haskins & Sells among others for January.'

'Good,' she said at last and found herself staring back at him for a long moment, feeling mildly foolish. 'I'm glad we're thinking along the same lines.'

'So am I,' he said impassively and slowly began gathering his papers together as if he had decided that their meeting was now over.

It had been Philippe's idea that the three of them have dinner that evening to clear up any further loose ends before he returned to the States the following day. The evening went smoothly and it was only towards the end that Geoff pleaded a headache and therefore an early return home. Francesca's eyes followed him as he left and she wondered if that was all there was to it. A month before he had seemed a different man, but now his joviality seemed forced and he was too eager to work late or to take on extra responsibilities. Whatever it was, it was personal and it was highly unlikely that Geoff would confide in her.

'He's good,' Philippe remarked.

'Yes, he is.'

'And Brunning?'

She looked at Philippe warily. 'Different.'

'You know that whatever the press release may have said sooner or later there have to be some major management changes?'

'I know.'

'I'd like Geoff to figure in the US reshuffle somewhere.'

'Maybe I need him here.'

'Maybe he'd like to make up his own mind.'

'And maybe *you're* moving just a little too fast this time.'

He grinned suddenly as if he'd been found out and she was reminded of Ed's words that 'Philippe had the Midas touch'; it wasn't so difficult to believe now.

'Shall I take you home?'

'Thanks.'

The house looked small and dark as the car drew up outside and she closed her eyes for a brief moment as the spectres of Michael, Livia, Matthias – and papa – slid unbidden into her mind.

'Would you like to come in for a coffee?' The words slipped out before she had time to think about them and she could see the surprise in his face.

'Why not?' he replied easily. His eyes glanced quickly over her in the half-light of the car and he thought that she could almost have been in mourning – the burgundy dress had turned black and the grey smudges beneath her eyes made them rise, large and too luminous, out of the pale flesh of her cheeks. She was unhappy and he hadn't even seen it; throughout the afternoon and evening he'd been too interested in trying to score points.

'I like it . . . ,' Philippe said, as she brought in a tray of coffee. It would be difficult not to like the house, he thought with a trace of envy, and although it was perhaps a little modest in size for his taste it was nevertheless superbly decorated. There were several beautiful Italian antiques which had been cleverly blended with pieces of classic modern furniture, and above all it was light and somehow harmonious. Finally his eye settled on several framed photographs.

'Your family?'

'Yes.' And she supposed that they still were.

'Is this your mother?' He moved across the room and picked up a picture of a slender blonde woman dressed in pale cream. A carefully posed photograph, he thought with a touch of amusement, like a statue carved in ivory. Not like Francesca at all.

For a long moment she stood there with the tray still caught in her hands, watching him.

'No . . . no, it isn't,' she said unsteadily.

'Oh. . . .' He gave her a searching, curious look and slowly placed the picture back on the table. 'I'm sorry, I didn't mean to pry.' And he was struck by the certainty that he had somehow opened a Pandora's box.

'You're not prying – you're simply asking a normal, human question,' she said in a remote voice. 'Black or white?' And she turned her face away from him.

'Black . . . thanks.'

'I have a strange disjointed family, Philippe, and I discovered very recently that it is even stranger than I had thought.' She sat down and he moved to a seat opposite her.

There was a brief odd little silence.

'We all have skeletons in cupboards that we would rather keep closed.'

'But mine is a rather special cupboard with rather special

skeletons. . . .' She tried to laugh, but felt only the sad imitation of a smile begin to make her mouth tremble. Oh, God – she was going to make a fool of herself!

'I told you all about mine,' he said gently, sensing her panic. 'And Ed has a cure for skeletons, ghosts, lurking bad memories. . . .'

'Does he?' she asked, forcing the smile to stay on her lips.

'Well, as far as he is concerned you have a choice – you can forget them, swear at them, or buy them off.' It was a feeble attempt at defeating her misery, but he was relieved to see that the tears that were obviously hovering so close had not yet fallen. 'He called me a "schmuck" and "an ungrateful bastard" not so long ago.'

'Why?' she said as curiosity pressed down her wretchedness.

'Because I probably am. . . .' And as he looked at her lovely unhappy face he thought that Ed hadn't been far wrong. 'And because, maybe, I have developed the art of keeping skeletons in cupboards.' He looked down into his coffee cup, motionless, held there by embarrassment as he searched desperately for something to say.

'It was too bad about Matthias and the campaign,' he said at last and then added quickly, 'although I understand from Geoff you're coming to some sort of an agreeable arrangement with his agent.'

Her eyes seemed to look back at him too sharply, almost as if they reproved him.

'Yes . . . it was *too bad* . . . ,' she repeated softly, and was unable to resist the contempt which crept into her voice. 'In fact I have to be present at a memorial service for him tomorrow morning. I knew him quite well.'

'I'm sorry.'

'It doesn't matter.'

But he knew it did.

'Would you like another coffee?'

'No, thanks.' He drank what remained and placed the cup and saucer back on the tray. 'Maybe I ought to leave. I think it's been a long day for both of us.' He stood up.

'You're probably right – I didn't realize quite how tired I was.' It was a lame way of explaining away the chink he had seen in her armour and how close she had come to spilling out her chaotic feelings.

'But you'll be okay?' he asked a little awkwardly.

'Of course,' she said quickly, carelessly. 'As I said, I'm just tired. Now, let me show you out.'

She stood a moment at the door as he walked down the path, unmoved by the cold that was starting to take hold and the icy mist that was beginning to ghost up from the sodden ground. He was nice, she realized, and surprisingly kind beneath that cool calm exterior. No doubt after her little performance he probably thought she was a caricature of the typical career woman – emotional, neurotic and lonely. She sighed heavily and with a touch of defiance as she closed the door; it hardly mattered anyway.

Philippe drove the car back in the direction of the King's Road. Wearily he loosened his tie and drew in a breath as he recalled her curious reaction to the question about her 'mother', and then he had managed to follow it up with what had clearly been another taboo subject, Matthias. She had obviously known him more than 'quite well' from her reaction. He felt a mocking blade of jealousy pierce him as he remembered the pictures he had seen of the ex-rock star in New York and more recently in the duplicate file they had on the campaign in his office. He was a very good-looking guy, and he used to make good songs, but Philippe had remained unconvinced by his new 'Mr Clean' image. Sooner or later he would have peaked and then faded irrevocably out of sight. But the prestige of the campaign had been good for Samuels and that was all that counted. Perhaps Francesca had counted on more. He smiled humourlessly as he guided the car into the luxurious expanse of Park Lane; at one point during their ill-fated conversation he had been teased by the thought of comforting her, moving over beside her and somehow taking her into his arms. That would have been what his mother would have suggested: 'A woman needs a man's arms around her when she cries.' But what an ass-hole he would have made of himself.

# 9

Francesca felt Vic move restlessly from one foot to the
other as he stood next to her. The church was crowded
with 'mourners' and the attendees read like a list from
*Who's Who*. Her eyes swept quickly over the rows of
people and apart from the expected mass representation
from the record business and pop world there was also the
tall, bony, unmistakable figure of Sir Richard, a repre-
sentative from the government, a younger member of the
royal family and even the Archbishop of Canterbury.
Matthias would have loved this, she thought with cynical
amusement, – and those who didn't really care and who
had come for the easy publicity would love it too; there
were several TV cameras and a score of the press outside.
But her eyes stopped and settled on the fragile form of
Lucas Chant who stood immobile, head bent and somehow apart from the rest of the congregation. He will be
lost now, unless he allows himself to become engulfed
with work on the campaign and the setting-up of the new
foundation. And Matthias' words came back to her like an
echo, 'a lost, lonely waif . . . and I found him.' But Lucas
would be on his own now, she thought uneasily, and it
was more than possible that the shadowy past of 'Kevin
Crowley' would come back in all its unwelcome glory to
haunt him with the shallow release that drugs might give
him. He was weak and had no reserves of strength to back
him up except those that Matthias had given him; maybe,
just maybe, that might be enough. He looked up then and
turned towards her as if he had felt her eyes. There was a
small sad smile on his face. If she prayed for anyone that
day, it would be for him.

'Apart from Vic, everyone can make it to the Christmas
lunch,' Sian said.

'Why can't he make it?' Francesca said with annoyance.

'He says he has an appointment that can't be changed.'

'What appointment?'

'He didn't say. . . .'

'Or he wouldn't tell you. . . .'

Sian gave her a knowing smile in response; Vic had practically told her to mind her own business.

'Well, we'll just have to try and manage without his subtle charms, won't we?' Francesca replied dryly.

Their conversation was interrupted by a tap at the door and Zoë's blonde head appeared around it as it opened.

'Sorry to bother you, Francesca, but there's a policeman waiting here to see you.'

'A policeman?' Francesca repeated and glanced quickly at Sian.

'You'd better show him in . . . I'll get back to you later, Sian. Thanks.'

He was probably not much more than twenty-one, she thought, as he entered the room, cap under one arm, but it only took him a few practised moments to tell her that Michael was in hospital after trying to take his own life.

'How?'

'I think it was an overdose, Miss.'

She closed her eyes for a long moment as a vision of their last meeting came back to her with painful clarity. It would probably have been obvious to anyone but her that he was capable of doing such a thing and she had hardly given it a thought.

'I'd better get to the hospital.'

'He's not in any danger now, Miss, and we can drive you there if you like.'

'That won't be necessary, thanks, I'll take my own car.' She moved quickly across the room to get her coat and thought suddenly of Livia. 'Has anyone else been informed?'

'A Mrs Montague-Howe – his mother, I understand.'

'Yes, that's right.' Livia had dropped the name Gaetini as soon as her husband had died and reverted to her maiden name. Michael used it on occasion too, when it suited him.

She walked out of her office followed closely by the young constable.

'I don't know how long I'm going to be away, Sian,' she said, pausing briefly at the younger girl's desk, 'but if anyone asks simply tell them it's urgent and personal. I'll explain later.' She was hardly aware of making her way down through Samuels to the car-park. Inevitably her thoughts drew her wretchedly to the past. She had told Michael to get out because he was too selfish to see her own misery, so intent was he on making Livia see that he could be independent of her. Francesca caught a sharp, guilty breath – he was her only real link with the past, no matter how tenuous, and in her despair she had forgotten how weak he was, how hollow his dreams were – and because of it she had nearly destroyed him.

He seemed to be asleep as she approached the side of the bed, but as she drew a chair up he opened his eyes and she looked back at the empty pale face and was reminded unhappily of Lucas Chant.

'I am a fool, aren't I?' he said softly.

She made no answer, but moved her hand up so that it covered his.

'I tried to do everything too late . . . and it's funny, Fran, but I knew it all the time.'

'You should have come in with me, like I wanted from the very beginning,' she said at last.

'It wouldn't have worked; we're too different, you and I.' He looked away from her in embarrassment, remembering their last conversation. 'In any case, I wouldn't have been much help. I'm not really very good at business – as you've seen.'

'You haven't had the right sort of experience, that's all,' she said lamely.

'No, no – I have no gift, no aptitude – not like you, or father. . . .'

It was her turn to look away as he shifted his gaze back to her face.

'I'm sorry about what I said . . . ,' he whispered.

'It doesn't matter now.'

275

'Yes it does.'

'It hasn't really sunk in. . . .'

'You must ask mother, get it right. . . .' He sighed then and there was a sob in his voice. 'I get things wrong,' he said flatly, but with bitter self-knowledge. Like the share deal. He had taken the tip totally to heart, believed in Nigel's confident, easy smile. Because he wanted to, and because he wanted to show Francesca that he could be clever, too, without mother. But it hadn't worked and the shares had gone down and stayed down. Nigel had finally said that 'things were not what they were a year ago'. Where had he been a year ago? Oh, he could have sold, of course, but at a loss, and he couldn't have faced Francesca with that. And there would be no going back to Nigel now, no more 'certain killings' on a stock exchange that was unlikely to give them. And the so-called overdose . . . he should have known that he'd never have the guts to go through with it. Three different types of pills – tranquillizers, pain-killers and sleeping-pills – all neatly laid out on the locker in his hotel bedroom, and he had taken them all slowly and surely; and almost immediately the panic had set in, and then the dizziness, and then the nausea. Somewhere in the waking nightmare there had been the all-embracing figure of his mother standing unnaturally still, and then she had gone and her going seemed to wrap icy fingers around his heart. In his terror he had called room service first and then the porter's lodge before getting through to reception. Even then that wasn't enough. He had finally stumbled to the door of his hotel room and lain prostrate across the threshold to be sure that someone would find him. And they had. He had got that much right.

'Not always.' Francesca's voice snapped him reluctantly back to the present.

'Most of the time.' He looked desolately up at the white empty world of the ceiling, catching at the same time the edge of the blanket and twisting it in an agony of anguish between his fingers. 'Mother knows I do – I suppose that's why she's so over-protective.'

'Oh, Michael . . . ,' she said gently and in exasperation, 'she's eaten you alive. . . .' She looked into the pale cameo of his face and wondered how she had thought him golden like Matthias. Flawless. Her eyes suddenly pricked and stung. Where had it all gone?

'I'll go back now, of course,' he said, ignoring her remark. 'But at least I can comfort myself with the knowledge that I know that I tried to go it alone, even if it didn't work.'

She caught a breath and her eyes slid away from him to the window. And it seemed that they sat there a long while, wrapped in their own silence as the afternoon drew to a close and what colour there was left in the sky faded to white, to grey, to purple as evening unfolded.

'It's happening already . . . ,' Nick said sharply.

'What do you mean?'

'If you remember, Caroline, we were supposed to be going to Camden Market on Saturday afternoon.'

'I hadn't forgotten; and we can still go, I just promised my mother that I would help her choose a coat, that's all.' She watched him with a growing feeling of discomfort. 'We can arrange to meet somewhere.'

His eyes travelled deliberately over her as she stood in the doorway of his office and he wondered with irritation how it was possible that someone could be so naive.

'As easy as that,' he said abruptly.

'I don't see why not.' She was frowning now, not wanting to hear what he would say next.

'And you'll be late. . . .'

'I won't be late, Nick.'

'She'll see to that.'

'I think you're being unfair. She's hardly mentioned you since you met and there have been no lectures, or rows. . . .'

'Doesn't that seem just a little strange?'

She sighed heavily. 'I thought perhaps she might finally be letting me live my own life.'

'Oh, Caroline, don't be such an innocent!'

'Anything's possible, . . . as you keep telling me,' she said reproachfully.

'Not with your mother.'

'She couldn't have been nicer than she's been recently. . . .'

'It's called "creeping". . . .'

'Oh, Nick, don't.' She didn't want to hear any more, didn't want to think that her mother would be so devious.

'Twice over the past ten days you've had to change the time or the day we'd arranged to go out because your mother had some beautiful excuse for you to be elsewhere.'

'It's Christmas, Nick, and I've already told you that she belongs to several committees, that this is a particularly busy time of the year for her.'

'I know you have, but I wonder if dear old Guy were around whether she'd be so keen to drag you away.'

'She's not a monster. . . .'

He stared at her for a long moment.

'Have you thought any more about Boxing Day?'

'I haven't had much chance.' She lowered her gaze as her thoughts switched to the 'post–Christmas' dinner he wanted to cook for them both and how her mother had already pre-empted him by arranging a cocktail party the same night.

'I see,' he said, drawing a breath. 'All it takes is a one-syllable answer – yes or no.'

'There's something else that night,' she replied helplessly.

'Something else?'

'A cocktail party.' She swallowed slowly. 'But I'd like you to come. . . .' It wasn't true. It would be a disaster, just like the meeting with her mother.

'Whose cocktail party?'

She cleared her throat knowing that whatever she said would be wrong.

'My parents'.'

'You mean your mother's.'

'You're very welcome . . . ,' she said defensively, but he knew she was lying.

'Balls, Caroline,' he said softly, and somehow it was worse, that softness, than if he had screamed at her.

'It won't last long,' she pleaded.

'You're still trying to play two games at the same time, aren't you?' He shook his head gently.

'I'm not trying to play anything.' She looked hopelessly down at her hands. 'I just want it all to come out right somehow.'

'Your mother, me, and no doubt Guy, are in here somewhere, all grinning happily because Caroline has managed to spread herself around – albeit rather thinly.' He examined her sharply. 'You can't do it, Caroline.'

She made no answer and then slowly lifted her eyes back to his face.

'Guy isn't in this anywhere.'

'Maybe not with you, but he's hanging in there somewhere. I'm what your mother would call "a passing phase" or "a nine days' wonder", and because she's pretty sure that we won't last you can bet your life that Guy will be the first to know.'

'You can't be certain of that.' But it made such easy unpleasant sense.

'Oh, Christ, Caroline! I'd love to say "where have you been all your life?" – except that I know.'

She hated it when he spoke to her as if she were a child.

'So you won't come to the cocktail party?' she said at last.

'Do me a favour . . . let's forget Boxing Day altogether, shall we?' he replied harshly, all patience gone.

'Is tonight still on?'

He wanted to say 'no' outright, but lacked the courage because he still wanted her, still needed to see that soft wounded expression weave itself across her face – I suppose so,' he said sullenly. 'But I'll be late – I have to finish re-vamping this script for the Matthias campaign.'

'How late?'

His eyes glinted, warning her, as he placed his pen slowly back on his desk.

'Forget it.'

'Nick, I just want to know how late. . . .'

'I said forget it.'

'I don't want to forget it.'

'Well, I don't want to spend what will be left of my evening with you watching the clock. Okay?!'

'That's not fair.'

'Haven't you heard yet, that Life just isn't fair.'

Her eyes reproached him again and reluctantly he felt himself grow hard just by looking at her. He closed his eyes in exasperation and turned away.

'I don't suppose you've given any thought to the other question I asked you, either?'

'I wanted to get Christmas over with first,' she said lamely. That answer would be wrong too, but at the moment she couldn't contemplate telling her parents – her mother – that they wanted to live together.

'Perhaps we should forget that as well.' He didn't mean it, didn't mean any of it, but she would drive him crazy.

'Why are you being like this?'

'Because I'm fed-up, that's why.' And angry, and hurt, and just a little humiliated.

The brittle silence which followed seem to go on and on until her unsteady voice broke the quiet.

'I'd better get back.'

'I suppose you had.' He didn't look at her and when, finally, he did lift his eyes to the doorway she had gone.


'Are you interested?' Vic lolled back in his chair, pencil twirling between his hands as he waited for Aidan's reaction.

'It sounds good,' Aidan said slowly. He had been a little surprised by Vic's call; they had not been in contact since their lacklustre meeting some weeks before. Vic had not been over-impressed by his thinly disguised attempt at getting back at Francesca.

'It *is* good.'

'I've been at Gaetini & Kemp a long time.'

'Oh, come on, Aidan – give me a break! I hope you're not going to give me all that garbage about loyalty, commitment, fair play, etcetera, etcetera.'

'That's not what I meant.'

Vic's eyes flicked sharply over him and he began to smile.

'You mean that makes you more marketable, that you want more money?'

Aidan brought his hands together so that the fingers touched and nodded slowly.

'A boy after my own heart,' Vic replied cynically.

'I am executive creator director, Vic, hardly something to be overlooked.'

'And I'm sure you wouldn't let me do that.'

'I just want to make sure that I've covered everything as thoroughly as possible. After all, I'm not going to make a big change just for my health – I have to be sure I'm doing the right thing,' he said defensively.

'Oh, you'll be doing the right thing, Aidan, make no mistake about that. Gower's very interested in having you and, okay, you won't be *sole* executive creator director any longer – but I think joint creative director isn't bad considering that GKP is ten positions higher in the agency rankings than our beloved chairwoman's little hot-shop. You're taking a big step in the career stakes.'

'*If* I decide to take that step.' Vic's sure smugness that he would take the new role irritated him.

'Let's stop assing around, Aidan, we both know you're going to take the job. You'd be a fool not to.'

'I'd like the round hundred grand. . . .' The proposal had been hovering timidly behind his lips ever since he had sat down. He was already getting seventy-five thousand at Gaetini's, with a company BMW thrown in, naturally. But GKP was another ball-game altogether.

'I see,' Vic said smoothly. 'What you might call "a Geoff Seymour". . . .'

'Seymour's record salary for a copywriter was made over five years ago, Vic; it's history,' Aidan said aggrievedly. 'I don't think a hundred grand is exactly going over the top now.'

'Gower will expect results.'

'I'll give them to him.'

'Then you'll no doubt want him to know what sort of car you intend to choose. . . .'

Aidan smiled dryly.

'A Porsche.'

'You do disappoint me – I thought you'd at least aspire to a Ferrari like our glorious leader.'

'Give me time.'

'So I can tell Gower that you accept the position of joint creative director. . . .'

Aidan nodded.

'. . . provided, of course, that he agrees to your terms?' And Stu would, naturally. They had both anticipated Aidan's greed and also his arrogance about his abilities; offering him eighty-five was just a blind – a hundred grand was the least Stu had expected to pay. Even so, it was still a good price to pay and, once it got into the press, GKP's profile would go up even more as far as the advertising world was concerned. After all, an agency that was prepared to pay high prices for its creative people must therefore have very high creative standards. Vic smiled inwardly, he would 'leak' Aidan's move from Francesca's beloved GK before his own so that by the time he left Samuels in early January it would look as if he and Aidan were just the tip of a large unhappy iceberg. Henry wouldn't like that at all.

'Let's have another drink to seal the deal,' Vic said, and reached for the bottle on his desk. 'By the way, Aidan, didn't you do the creative work on Miami Citrus?' He poured a further large scotch into each of their glasses.

'I think you know I did.'

Vic grinned, but somehow it just didn't reach his eyes.

'And you got to know Sally Wyatt, the marketing director, pretty well, I hear?'

'Did I?' Aidan responded sarcastically.

'Let's stop kidding around,' Vic said impatiently, 'I just want to know whether you can persuade her to change agencies, i.e. go with you to GKP.'

'So that's it,' Aidan said slowly.

'Yeah . . . that's it,' Vic retorted. 'Well, can you?'

'Possibly.'

'What does possibly mean?'

'I haven't called her recently.' And he hadn't intended to. Sally was what could be called a 'nice girl', a smart nice girl and she had convinced herself that she was in love with him on the basis of a few dinners and a few not-so-hot tumbles between the sheets, which wasn't so smart. He couldn't stand all that emotional stuff. Naturally, he had backed off.

'Well – start calling.'

'I'll do my best, Vic,' he said, with a trace of reluctance.

'Do I detect a lack of enthusiasm here?'

'I said I'll do my best. . . .'

'Well, just remember when you're "doing your best", that there could be a very large bonus in this for you if you can swing it. With your obvious charms and the fact that you masterminded, if I may say so, the *brilliant* artwork for the ads, it shouldn't prove too difficult.' He pushed his chair back and slowly stood up which meant that the meeting was over. 'Remember, Aidan, Miami Citrus is worth over a million.'

'I know that, Vic.'

'In that case it won't be very hard for you to start figuring out percentages will it?'

'How much would there be in it for me?'

'I think we'll discuss that some more when you finish doing your best with Miss Wyatt, don't you?' He moved around his desk towards Aidan.

'Okay, okay . . . ,' Aidan said wearily.

'Great,' Vic replied and gave him a patronizing pat on the shoulder. 'I'll call you when I've finalized things with Gower.' He opened the door and guided Aidan out. Zoë's desk was empty and he frowned; he had specifically told her to stay there until the meeting was over, but the sour look on his face was quickly replaced by a thin easy smile as Francesca came out of Geoff's office. He walked over to her.

'Aidan's just on his way out. . . .'

'I can see that, Vic.' She glanced briefly at Aidan, examining him sharply.

'Just wanted to know how things were going at Gaetini & Kemp, particularly creatively,' he said with exaggerated innocence.

'You could have saved Aidan the trip and simply asked me.'

'Oh, I wouldn't do that, Francesca – and waste your valuable time?'

'Your sudden show of consideration is almost bringing tears to my eyes, Vic.' A small derisive smile settled on her mouth. 'Now, if you gentlemen will excuse me. . . .'

Aidan watched her move away from them, silently torn between antipathy and longing. She was a bitch and he had lost her a long time ago, but he still wanted her. Maybe when he was making love to Sally Wyatt he could pretend it was Francesca. The thought almost made him want to laugh out loud.

'See you, Aidan,' Vic's words of dismissal cut abruptly into his thoughts.

'Oh, yes, sure,' he replied vaguely and made his way to the lift.

Vic followed Aidan's retreating back, his mind returning automatically to Miami Citrus. Samuels had lost the account well before Francesca's arrival as chairman; when she was at Gaetini & Kemp, she had orchestrated the pitch and won the client over against all the odds. Now it would go to Gower & Kid-Porter if Aidan fulfilled his part of the bargain. Gower & Kid-Porter. Stu had almost promised Gower & Kid-Porter-*Brunning*. Vic swallowed deep in his throat; it was something he had always dreamed of, like having your name up in lights. Henry could keep his bloody chairmanship, keep the bloody merger, and Chairman bloody Gaetini could keep her grandiose global visions for those who weren't too bored to listen – and he would simply sneak out under their noses taking some of the family silver with him. Because he had what he wanted and the beauty of it was that it hadn't cost him at all.

The traffic was bad and as Francesca sat behind yet another set of red lights she reached for the unopened packet of cigarettes which always sat in the glove compartment. Her mind swept briefly back to the office and the uncomfortable confrontation with Vic. He and Aidan together made quite an unpleasant combination and for some reason he wanted to make it deliberately obvious in his usual unsubtle way that there was something going on. She took a long drag on the newly lit cigarette and blew out a slow cloud of smoke. But Vic, and Aidan come to that, would have to wait; there were too many other things going on to allow them to waste her time. She drove the car with the mass of other vehicles flowing past Hyde Park Corner and on into Park Lane. Livia was staying at the Dorchester until she left the day after tomorrow, with Michael. Surprisingly she had not tried to avoid a meeting and when Francesca had phoned her she thought she could even detect a curious trace of lightheartedness in Livia's voice. Of course, she had got her son back and it didn't seem to matter how or what the circumstances. And naturally they would now spend Christmas together, just as Livia no doubt had hoped. She stepped out of the car and gave the keys to the waiting doorman and made her way through the revolving doors into the spacious foyer. Livia had a suite overlooking Hyde Park near the top of the building and as the lift took her higher and higher she tried to picture the woman she hadn't seen for over ten years. There had been no official severing of ties, no irreconcilable arguments, only a slow insidious breach which at first Michael had filled and then inevitably failed to do so as the years passed. She had been left alone. A mocking smile touched her lips as she thought of the hundreds of days through hundreds of nights when she had lain in the darkness wondering what she had done to deserve such an exile. It had never occurred to her that it could all be so simple. The lift doors opened and she stepped through them, quickly taking note of the hotel room numbers. Livia was not far away now. There had been no nervousness up until this moment. In fact she had surprised herself by the calmness which had settled upon her since she had decided to come. But as she drew ever closer to their meeting she felt the old confusion, the old fear, which was usually so carefully submerged, rise to the surface like a fragile bubble, and she was that child again, standing apart, looking on, wishing somehow that she could be different, or that Michael would go away for a long time so that in his absence her mother would suddenly give the love she gave so lavishly to him to her instead.

There was a large bowl of salmon-pink roses in the corridor close to Livia's door and Francesca was suddenly reminded of Michael and the flowers that rested beside him in his hospital room. It was because of him that she was here; otherwise she could have gone on in painful ignorance of the apparent reason for Livia's implacable attitude towards her. She knocked on the door, two soft but steady knocks, and waited. It opened slowly and Livia stood framed in the doorway.

'Francesca. . . .'

'Hello, Livia. . . .' She had never called her Livia before.

'Come in.'

It was astonishing how little she had changed, how much the same she was even to the skilfully styled head of white-blonde hair which she remembered so well, and Livia still wore Chanel, safe, immaculate Chanel as the beautifully tailored navy dress testified. But she seemed somehow curiously smaller, Francesca thought, as she followed her into the lavish gilded suite, almost as if the passing of the years had compressed her into a less awesome mould. Yet there was still the same severe grace, still the same pink-white skin and cool fragile beauty that had been her father's undoing. Livia turned back to her as she reached the centre of the room and beckoned her to sit down.

'You've turned into quite a beauty, Francesca – and with some style.' There was a tray sitting on the table between them. 'Would you like tea?'

This was not what she had expected, not how she had imagined this interview would begin – as if they had only just met, as if they were almost total strangers. And for a moment she found herself just staring up into the face which looked so impassively back at her. And there *were* lines: fine threads reaching out from the corners of Livia's china-blue eyes, fine threads like small stitches pinching the pink painted lips, and there were tell-tale smudges, like thumb-prints, brushed beneath her eyes. Like discovering cracks in a marble statue.

'Thank you, tea would be fine.' She watched the long pale hands as they relaxed into the ritual of making tea, her gaze inevitably pulled to the magnificent ruby and diamond ring which had always seemed like a landmark on Livia's left hand. 'How is Michael?'

'Better – thank you.' She smiled carefully and leaned across, white china cup and silver spoon held between her fingers. 'He is, of course, returning to Menton with me the day after tomorrow . . . from what I can gather from him he has had quite enough of his adventure.'

'Taking an overdose is hardly an "adventure",' she replied softly. 'He's very unhappy.'

'It was an accident. He assures me that there was no question of him wishing to take his own life.' There was suddenly that old edge of hostility in her voice. 'He's never been able to manage well on his own; it was obvious from the very beginning that this whole escapade would end in disaster.'

'He's not a child. . . .'

'Some people never grow up, Francesca,' she retorted. 'He's like his father in that respect. . . .'

The words were dropped effortlessly into the air and then seemed to stay there as they both stared at each other.

'Michael told me.'

'Yes, I know.'

'Is it true?'

'Is what true, exactly?'

Francesca caught a sharp breath, hating the moment, hating Livia.

'That neither you nor father were my real parents.' Somehow her practised words sounded farcical, like something out of a Dickens' novel. She almost expected Livia to laugh.

'Michael should not have mentioned this to you; after all it happened so long ago it can hardly matter.'

'It matters to me, Livia – it matters very much to *me*.'

The china-blue eyes opened a little wider as if in surprise, as if they could not imagine why it should matter at all.

'If you insist.' There was an odd little silence as she took a long sip of tea. 'I am not your mother – I would have thought that that would have been obvious to you years ago.'

'Really,' Francesca replied flatly.

'Your father wanted you . . . ,' she continued, looking away from her, '. . . I never believed him when he said that you were his.'

'Why not?' There was a tight knot gathering in her throat as she watched Livia's vague, abstracted expression.

'I never believed him on principle – he was such a child – and the girl, or should I say girls, he got himself involved with were all after his money, all trying to find some claim on him.' She snorted softly in contempt. 'What better way of staking a claim than by professing to be having a man's child?'

'So you don't know.'

'I knew your father.'

'I don't think you knew him at all.'

'I think I am better qualified to answer that than you.'

'Why?'

Livia's eyes swept her face abruptly.

'This conversation is not likely to lead anywhere.'

'You married him for his money.'

'That is a very crude way of putting it.'

'But it's nevertheless true.'

'We had a contract.'

'He loved you.'

'Carlo was a very emotional man.'

'You knew that when you married him.'

'Of course,' she said smoothly. 'As he knew when he married me that I was his opposite in that respect. And he thought that I would change, or that he could change me.'

She shook her head gently as if in disbelief. 'People don't change.'

'But you had his child.' She couldn't imagine Livia making love, having sex, being pregnant.

'That was part of the contract . . . a son within the first five years.'

'How fortunate you were that Michael was your first child,' she said with a trace of bitterness.

'Yes, I was. Pregnancy and all that it entails was not something that I looked upon with relish.' She turned her face to the window, remembering. There could never have been any more children for her, whatever the contract may have said; almost from the day the pregnancy was confirmed she had been ill, and once the sickness and tiredness had subsided there was the slow gross change in her body through the hot Italian summer, until she thought she would explode and that relief of any kind would be a blessing. But the birth had been the worst part of all – pain which went on and on and on, tearing her in half, and when finally they had handed her the small crushed bloody thing to fondle she had turned away with exhaustion, disgust and indifference, and they had looked at one another with shock in their big round muddied eyes as if she were some kind of monster. Yet Michael had inexorably won her over; she had even been persuaded to suckle him at her tender swollen breasts, and that had been the beginning, that sudden primitive surge of mother love of which she had never thought herself capable.

'Father wanted more children. . . .' And he was her father, wasn't he?

'That wasn't possible.'

There was no need to ask why.

'Then you can't be surprised that he would look elsewhere – for affection at least.'

'You mean sex.'

'No, not necessarily.'

'Most men don't know the difference.'

'But you forget that I can remember how affectionate he was.'

'It was a long time ago.'

'You weren't interested in him at all, were you?'

Livia seemed to pause, reflecting.

'No . . . no, I suppose I wasn't.'

'And I was brought in to keep him happy, whether I was his real daughter or not.' She had wondered about this all along, ever since Michael's strange unhappy revelation; it seemed the only logical conclusion.

'I didn't want you at first, naturally,' she responded without emotion, as if she were talking about the gift of an unwanted pet. 'But Carlo was surprisingly insistent and there was, of course, the possibility of a scandal if the girl – your mother – decided to open her mouth, which did seem likely at the time.'

'Who was she?'

'Who? Your mother?' Livia reached for the pot of tea. 'I've no idea . . . Carlo never told me and I never asked; there didn't seem much point.'

'It didn't occur to anyone that I might like to know one day – that I mind find out?'

'As I said, Francesca, it was all a long time ago and perhaps as things stand it is better you don't now start resurrecting the past and trying to find out who your mother is.'

'What's that supposed to mean?' As if she couldn't guess.

'Your father was not always exactly selective in his choice of mistresses.'

'How do you know if you profess to have taken so little interest?' She felt the beginnings of anger.

'It doesn't take much imagination to visualize the sort of woman who would accept, shall we say, his favours. . . .'

'Because you couldn't?' she retorted sharply.

'That really is no concern of yours.'

'After all,' Francesca added sarcastically, 'you did keep your part of the contract.' At least on paper.

'Yes, that's right.'

'And Michael.'

'I don't think there is any reason to pursue this further.'

She placed her cup and saucer quietly back on the tray. 'I'm afraid I must ask you to leave now as I have to go to the hospital very shortly.' Even Livia had her limits.

Francesca looked at her for a long moment, suddenly aware of a slow desolate seeping of disappointment. This was all there was, this woman who had somehow taken up so much of the pain in her life, who had seemed to hold the key to those strange insidious feelings of confusion which had haunted her for too long.

'Why didn't you divorce?' she said finally.

Livia stood up, studiously smoothing down her skirt.

'He didn't want that.' She smiled carelessly. 'He liked the illusion of the family, the big immutable institution of the Italian family . . . he liked having a blonde English wife with old, even aristocratic, family connections who had borne him a blond bouncing son. As for myself, I was quite happy as long as he left me alone, and he did once he realized that I would leave him if he presumed too much.'

'And he loved you. . . .'

'Yes, I suppose he did.'

There was nothing more to say and she followed Livia mechanically across the room to the door, but she found herself recalling the long weighted silences of her child-hood when her parents had not spoken, or the moments when her father seemed unable to stand his carefully ordered existence any longer and his voice had suddenly erupted like a volcano, echoing through the marbled halls and passageways of her childhood, careless of servants, careless of children. She cringed inwardly as she remembered the other times, the times he had cried: raw, pathetic sobs of misery, muted and distorted by the walls which divided them. When a man cried it seemed so much worse than a woman, more shocking, uglier as if the release of his despair must mean that it was greater, deeper somehow. And these outbursts had been followed by the ever-increasing intervals of his absences until, sometimes, she thought he would not come back. But he always had.

'Poor father,' she said softly as the door was opened.

'Perhaps,' Livia responded.

And the nothingness in her voice made Francesca wince as she walked away.

'I've arranged to have you discharged tomorrow. We'll be in Menton in time for dinner.' Livia sat close by the bed, her long fingers stroking his smooth wrist. 'That's what you want, isn't it, darling?'

Michael nodded dumbly. It was easier like this and he was tired of fighting.

'We could go to the casino at the weekend if you feel strong enough, and I thought we might go to Florence too – there's a wonderful collection of marbles at Bellini's. . . .'

Michael nodded again and her fingers closed tightly around his hand.

'We'll forget this ever happened – won't we?'

It was a plea. He turned to her in surprise and saw tears hovering like drops of silver.

'You won't leave me again, my darling, will you. . . . ?'

He swallowed slowly in an effort to push his misery down, but her eyes dragged up his loneliness and all at once he was moving towards her so that her arms would hold him, comfort him, love him. He sighed inwardly, inevitably. It would always be like this.

In their own inimitable way and under Francesca's instructions, the Ritz had made Christmas discreetly cheerful. The circular table with its centrepiece of silvered evergreen designated for the Samuels' guests not only sported hand-made Christmas crackers, but individually wrapped gifts also sat at each place-setting.

'It looks fantastic!' Zoë said excitedly, as she approached the table.

'It certainly does,' Sian replied with satisfaction and thought of the hectic taxi ride she had made through a choked Piccadilly only an hour before to ensure that the presents had been delivered safely from Harrods and everything was as it should be.

'But Francesca's going to be late . . . ,' Zoë said, with a trace of annoyance.

'Only a few minutes – she had to take that call from the States and then she and Geoff are going to be driven straight here by one of the company drivers.'

'But the traffic's so bad . . . ,' she persisted.

'Look, Zoë – we can stay here the whole afternoon if we want, there's no need to panic.'

Zoë nodded reluctantly in response and thought of Vic. He was also having lunch somewhere in the West End and said he wouldn't be back too late . . . and then he had given her a conspiratorial wink which told her what to expect on his return. Things had been much better lately, even allowing for Sian's unfortunate discovery, and she didn't want the status quo messed up by getting back to the office too late. With a sigh she glanced at the table-settings and saw that she had been placed between Geoff and Pete Morgan. They were okay, she thought with indifference, but what did it really matter; Vic wasn't around anyway.

Sian watched Zoë move to the chair where she would be sitting. Somehow they had managed to get their relationship back on a reasonable footing, even if it was a little strained at times. There had never been any mention of the incident in Vic's office and she supposed there was hardly likely to be now. But maybe their sordid little affair had done her a favour, maybe it had made her see Adam in a different, less favourable, light. He had been infuriated when she hadn't turned up at the Mayfair, had called her several times to find out 'whether she had grown up yet' and she had been relieved to find herself feeling vaguely amused by his outrage. But then, last night, he had telephoned again to say 'that he understood why she had done it' and there had been only conciliation and satin-smoothness in his voice, promising that he would make things different, that Petie would somehow play a more prominent role in his life. She realized that things had curiously turned into a sort of game, that Adam was finding playing 'cat and mouse' more stimulating than her new role as the caring compliant mother who had been his ex-mistress. She drew a sharp weary breath – Adam had probably never been stood up before.

'Hi. . . .'

She turned around abruptly and found herself staring into Geoff's familiar face.

'Hi, Geoff.'

'Looks like you've done a really superior job here,' he said easily, surveying the table.

'Most of it was Francesca's idea . . . I just obeyed orders.'

'I think you're being your usual modest self.'

She smiled and the old unease was forgotten. For the past two weeks they had conveniently avoided each other, both embarrassed by what had passed between them and which now seemed to have been so unnecessary.

'Are you going away for Christmas?' she asked.

'Well, as you know, I have to be in New York for the signing and will probably do a bit of shopping there, but then I'll come home. I'm not going to be doing anything exotic, although some friends have asked me to join them for skiing in Verbier; I could be tempted by that.' It was a lie, most of his friends had families who claimed them and a single man was a difficult prospect to fit in over Christmas. Of course, at one point he had thought that perhaps he and Sian . . . but that had been neatly knocked on the head. And Joanne would be in Nassau, he remembered, with a trace of painful envy. Finally, there was his mother, of course, he thought guiltily, and she would be expecting him, and as much as he loved the old girl, it was hardly the most exciting prospect of the year. But he pressed the thought down as Francesca walked towards him followed by two faithful old hands from Gaetini & Kemp. Behind them came Pete Morgan and Nick Keogh who had been asked to the lunch because of their work on the Matthias campaign. Technically she was breaking tradition by having anyone outside Samuels' top hierarchy, but maybe it was a good thing. Even if Henry and Vic had managed to make it, the lunch would still have needed a necessary injection of new life to make it go with any sort of a swing.

'I think we'd better start getting ourselves organized,' he said, as Sian stepped back to make way for the new arrivals.

'I think you're right,' she replied, and moved forward to guide the guests to their seats.

Geoff watched her for a moment, touched by regret; she looked good today – womanly, earthy somehow – and there was also an unusual air of self-assurance about her. He sighed inwardly. That, he supposed, came from breathing the same air as someone as nauseatingly smooth as Adam Gilmore.

Francesca's eyes swept briefly around the table; the lunch was going well. She had been disappointed that Henry, once again, had turned down yet another company invitation. It seemed strange that a man who had built up a small empire like Samuels would seek to avoid the very people who had helped him to do so. But that was Henry and he was probably too old to change, and at least he had agreed to be present at the signing of the merger. There was Vic also – but Vic wasn't so much of a loss. Even as a picture of his face slid reluctantly into her mind she recognized the familiar outline of his back half-hidden behind another table of Christmas revellers. He was standing in the reception area outside the restaurant. She felt her mouth tighten at his incredible audacity and then her eyes were moving with wary suspicion to the person he was talking to. Stuart Gower, chairman of Gower & Kid-Porter. It could be no one else; the thick red-gold side-burns were legendary in the business, as was the big jowly crimson face. Vic was leaving Samuels. Francesca brought a glass of wine to her lips and wondered at the same time why the thought had not struck her before. Only that could account for his smugness of late, for the gaps in his diary where no appointment had been made and yet he had been absent and unavailable. There was Aidan too, of course, although he might have nothing to do with Vic's proposed plans – if that was what they were. But the more the idea took shape in her mind the more it seemed logical; Vic had clearly been unhappy from the very beginning, after all she was occupying the place he had wanted; she was chairman and likely to stay chairman; and a woman, which naturally could only add insult to injury as far as he was concerned; he was also no longer Henry's confidant, no longer in the limelight – and that would not suit Vic at all. If she had stopped to think about him properly at any time since her arrival the fact that he might leave would have occurred to her as a distinct possibility. And naturally he would have had plenty of offers because of his experience and position; because of his network of connections; because of his big bad mouth; and because, most of all, he could leave and take with him a part of the Samuels' billings. What is more, he would have realized as would his potential employer, at this delicate stage of the merger and its probable repercussions, no matter how small, that it could nevertheless still unsettle or even upset clients so that they might be persuaded to change agencies and go with him. She took another sip of wine and began mentally calculating what accounts Vic would probably go for. It was still only a hunch, but her gut reaction told her that it was much more than that.

Vic shook Gower's hand as they met in the foyer and then turned his head to one side so that he could just glimpse the Samuels' table on the other side of the room. It was quite possible, of course, that at least one of the party had seen him, but ironically he hadn't planned it this way; it was a little too obvious, even for him, he thought dryly. Meeting at the Ritz for a drink before they went on to lunch had been Stu's idea and it was only at the last minute that he had recalled Zoë telling him that the Christmas lunch was also going to be held there. It had been too late to change the arrangement and, in any event, he didn't want Stu thinking that he was bothered by the presence of the Samuels hierarchy. He could explain his way out of it later should there be any questions. Vic loosened his tie as he followed Stu past the opening to the restaurant, but he found his gaze inevitably pulled back to the table on the far side of the room, and Francesca. She was watching him as he looked back at her and he thought with an uncomfortable feeling of surprise that she had probably known that he was there all the time. She would, the bitch, he thought uneasily and lifted his hand up in an awkward wave. But he shrugged inwardly; why the hell should it matter now even if she did make a good guess at what he was up to? She was flying to the States tomorrow and he had already laid the ground-work well and truly for his departure. By the time Christmas and New Year had woven drunkenly to their usual close and the business world had begun to wake up again Chairman Gaetini would find that she was just a little too late.

'Did you ever meet him?' Sian asked Nick as she began taking apart the cracker they had just pulled together.

'No, but I wanted to.' And he thought with regret of the life-size cardboard image of Matthias which still stood in his office. It was the nearest he had ever got.

'So did I. Francesca was going to arrange a launch party once the campaign was completed and ready to run. . . . He would have been there, of course.'

'Maybe we would have been disappointed.'

'Maybe,' she said quietly and found herself recalling Francesca's ashen shocked face on the news of his death. 'But there must have been something special about him, something that made you want to sit up and take notice – I mean, apart from his very weird and wonderful past and obvious good looks.'

'Yes, I suppose so,' Nick replied thoughtfully, 'but there's no way we're ever going to find out now, is there? Not even if his glorious plans for a new type of global movement would actually have ever come off. I couldn't help thinking that the States would have been a better place for him and his ideas. . . . The Yanks love someone with his sort of profile, who will lead the way to a cleaner better world and the road to righteousness. . . .' He grinned.

'Provided they don't have a past,' she added wryly.

'Everyone has a past – but he could have got away with his wild years because he had, apparently, renounced all the drugs, all the parties, etcetera, etcetera. He never tried to hide what he had been.'

'I don't know – I could never see him as any sort of saviour or whatever; I think I would always have associated him with those so-called wild years.'

'You forget that the Americans are not so cynical as we Brits. And the funny thing is that Matthias didn't actually give himself any of those "holier than thou" labels, the press and the public really did it all.'

'But he never denied it.'

'Because he knew it would probably help him to get where he wanted to go. . . .'

She shook her head slowly.

'Which doesn't make him very different from your average advertising man. . . .'

'Maybe not – but he wasn't trying to sell soap or champagne or sun-tan lotion – he was selling the idea of a better world, for whatever reason.'

'I know, I know . . . but I just couldn't see him that way.'

'To be quite frank, neither could I.' And he grinned again, his gaze sweeping quickly around the table as he did so, still a little surprised to be sitting there. 'Are you doing anything special for Christmas?'

'Only if a typical family Christmas can be called special – but I'm still looking forward to it.' And she surprised herself by realizing that she was. 'And you?'

'Oh, about the same.' He thought of Caroline then and the dinner he had planned which had been so irrevocably cancelled. 'I had hoped to spend some of it with my girlfriend, but somehow I don't think that's going to happen.'

'Oh . . . ' she said lamely, noting the passing unhappiness in his eyes. 'But isn't there still time enough for her to change her mind?'

'I don't think so – at least not where her parents, or should I say her mother, are concerned.'

'I see.'

'Her father's okay, I think . . . but her mother's a real pain in the ass.'

'What are you going to do?'

'I think the question is – what is Caroline, my girlfriend, going to do?'

'I suppose the only answer to that is that she's going to have to choose.'

Nick shook his head gently and refilled her glass of wine.

'Exactly – I was afraid you'd say that.'

They were back in the wood-panelled boardroom and once again Francesca found herself gazing at the charming examples of American folk art which Ed had chosen with such care. She liked this room, she realized all at once, and it seemed a good omen that the merger document should be signed here. She shifted her gaze to Henry who sat at the head of the table with Ed; he had the aura of a large well-fed cat, contrasting sorely with Ed's slight craggy frame. Slowly he stood up, his hand smoothing back the rich mane of white hair.

'I'm not going to make a long speech . . . ,' his eyes swept the upturned faces around the table, '. . . most of you know that's not my style.' He seemed very serious, for Henry, but there was a gleam of humour in his eyes. 'I started in this business over twenty years ago and the only thing that mattered to me then was creating great advertising, and during the seventies my dream began to take real shape because I was lucky enough to witness Samuels' growth from a one-client agency to an eighty-client hot-shop during a period of exceptional expansion. But I was fortunate in getting together a terrific team of people who knew instinctively what I wanted and where I wanted Samuels to go. Naturally with their invaluable talent it wasn't long before Samuels became a name to be reckoned with in the UK agency rankings. Yet times change.

Creating great advertising in a moderately sized shop can become a two-edged sword if you're only looked upon as juicy bait and likely to be swallowed up sooner or later by one of the mega-agency networks. I didn't want that for Samuels. I was forced to realize that there was a great big beautiful world outside the UK and that Samuels had something unique to offer – if the right sort of formula could be found – and by formula, I mean an international partner in every sense of the word. Because I also realized that we couldn't do it on our own. It was this realization that led to the first exploratory meetings with Dunmar-Rock and ultimately to this gathering today. In merging with our US cousins we are joining two very different, but very healthy, very talented agencies which can only learn and grow with each other.' He paused for a moment and brought his gaze to rest on Francesca. 'But there is one person here who really made the whole deal possible and who gave me the final push in the right direction.' He smiled then. 'Ladies and gentlemen, I give you Francesca Gaetini. . . .'

She rose from her chair and was surprised to feel a few wild butterflies playing havoc in her stomach. She swallowed slowly and the words she had so carefully prepared seemed to fade and die on her lips, but then her eyes fell on Geoff's familiar open face and on the one directly opposite her – Ed puffing on the usual fat cigar, a satisfied smile just perceptible on his mouth as he gazed expectantly at her.

'Thank you, Henry.' Francesca looked down for a moment at the single sheet of paper held in her hands. 'I've waited a long time for this meeting and all that the signing of the merger document will mean for our two companies in the coming years.' She paused deliberately. 'Samuel-Rock will have forty-five offices in thirty-two countries and a total group billing in the region of nearly $2 thousand million. We've even managed to retain the number one slot in the UK agency rankings and jumped to fifth place in New York in the latest *Advertising Age* tables – not bad for a beginning.' She paused again. 'But it *is* only a beginning – we don't come close to the global giants, the monoliths, the mega-agencies like Saatchi's or Omnicom. That will take time and there is still some of that elusive commodity left, despite what the so-called experts may say to the contrary. But we're going to have to work, and work hard, and we have all the essential ingredients at our finger-tips – we have the right people, the right resources, the right expertise, the right philosophy and above all outstanding creative talent to make the right kind of magic our clients want.' She glanced at Henry and Ed and then, finally, Philippe. 'We must think *big*, gentlemen, we must think *globally*, because, although the world may be getting smaller, the advertising stakes are getting larger and I want to ensure that Samuel-Rock gets a nice juicy slice of that mouth-watering global cake out there. . . .' She let the piece of paper rest on the table as her eyes swept the room. 'Finally, I just want to say how glad I am that we're all sitting around this table – how glad I am that Ed Rock and Philippe Sanchez decided in their infinite wisdom to join with us in this exciting new venture.' Her mouth pulled into a broad smile and with that Ed jumped up and thumped the table with enthusiasm. . . .

'And, by God!' he said, grinning, 'there's so much business out there – it's beautiful!'

It was a superb dinner, in a superb restaurant – the Four Seasons in the Seagram building. Francesca had forgotten how perfect it was. She sighed softly with satisfaction as she reached for the exquisite glass of cognac at her finger-tips. It had been a good day, somehow much better than she had imagined; even Henry had enjoyed it although he had naturally managed to back out of the celebratory dinner and flown back to London. Typical Henry. But it was still an outstanding success, no one could dispute that, and also a relief that all the research, negotiations and talk over the past few months were over. She leaned back in her chair; not even Livia and her soulless, acid tongue could spoil this moment of triumph for her.

'What are you doing for Christmas, Frankie. . . ?' Ed

said as he broke in on her thoughts. 'You don't mind if I call you Frankie?'

'No, I don't mind at all,' she said with some amusement. 'As for Christmas – well, I haven't really decided.' In fact there was nothing to decide; she had almost forgotten that it *was* Christmas and now it came back to her in all its unwelcome nostalgia because there would only be her empty flat. 'How about you?' she asked, turning to him.

'I'm too old to ski, too old to chase some broad round the Christmas tree – even if there was one to chase – there'll only be Peanuts and me this year.'

'What about Philippe?'

'What about Philippe?' he repeated sourly. 'He's entertaining his goddamn spick step-brothers and their kids, that's what Philippe's up to – and I definitely don't fit in to that picture even if I wanted to.'

'I'm sorry.' And her eyes shifted curiously to Philippe.

'I don't suppose. . . .' Uncharacteristically his words trailed off and she thought she saw the ghost of a blush seep into his face.

'What, Ed?'

'Well . . . unless you've really got any plans laid . . . you could always spend the "big day" with me and Peanuts in Berkshire County . . . it's beautiful now, really beautiful . . . covered with a thick blanket of virgin snow. . . .'

'You should have been a copy-writer, Ed,' she said, stifling a laugh. But it was a wonderful idea and what a relief it would be to leave London and all the unhappy chaos of recent events behind her.

'Okay, okay, Frankie,' he said, 'Will you come or not?' He hadn't been keeping a check on her for the past two months for nothing. He knew all about her family, or lack of it, and all about her brief unhappy affair with that crazy rock star or whoever he had been trying to set himself up to be. People like him, Ed mused silently, only knew how to walk through life on a tight-rope; usually they didn't live long enough to find out that it just doesn't work that way.

'I'll come, Ed.'

He grinned, widely, and his face cracked into a thousand satisfied lines as his gaze slid easily to Philippe who sat across from him. It might not be such a bad Christmas after all.

So, she was back in New England, a white transformed New England, in the same pretty chintz room she had occupied before. She could hear Ed downstairs, hear him pottering about in the kitchen as he prepared breakfast, as the rich smell of percolating coffee drifted up through the wooden floors. She turned away from the window and her eyes were automatically pulled to the modest pile of presents lying on the bed. There had been just one day for her to do any shopping and she had jumped in a cab with Geoff to Bloomingdales and eventually ended up at Tiffany's. Francesca picked up a small cylindrical parcel, a silver cigar-case for Ed. She had also bought a box of the most expensive havana cigars she could find to go with it. A be-ribboned scarlet stocking was filled with doggy goodies for Peanuts and, finally, there was even a little something for Philippe – a black cashmere scarf because she remembered he looked good in black, and because Ed had said that he might find time over the holiday to come down, but he doubted it. Well, at least she was prepared. Slowly she walked around the large brass bed and stopped before the mirror. For the past three nights she had slept better than she had done in months and it showed. Even in blue jeans and the big casual white sweater she had bought for herself she knew she looked good, younger, fresher, as if she had somehow managed to lose the past somewhere between New York and Berkshire County. It didn't seem to matter so much that Michael was with Livia, that she was excluded, that she would have been alone if it weren't for Ed, because she realized that this was where she wanted to be – there was no confusion, no painful reminders here. Not even of Matthias.

Ed was wearing an apron with 'I love New York' blazoned across it as he handed her an enormous cup of coffee.

'Like it?' he asked. 'It's an early Christmas present from Peanuts . . . I just couldn't wait until tomorrow to put it on.'

'That's cheating.'

'I always cheat – didn't you know?'

There was no answer to that so she sat down, quietly happy just to watch him as he finished laying the breakfast table.

'You didn't want to spend Christmas with your family . . . ?' he asked casually. It was a question he had been longing to put to her, but he had wanted to wait until the right moment, if there was one.

'I think you know that my father's dead. . . .' She paused, carefully trying to choose her words.

'You don't have to say any more if you don't want to.'

'I don't mind so much now. Just recently, a few things have been cleared up which have explained a lot to me.' A vivid picture of Livia's cool arrogant face slid into her mind. Somehow it didn't matter any longer. After all, wasn't she freed from all that laming heaviness Livia had burdened her with ever since she could remember? 'It's rather a long story. . . .'

'We've got plenty of time.'

And she told him, every word, every slice of memory which rose painfully to the surface and was then finally blown away.

'You know . . . when I was little I even used to pray that my hair might turn the colour of Livia's and Michael's, that pure-white-blondeness, because I thought that might make it easier for her to love me.' And she was suddenly moved by an enormous sense of pity for that child, that black-haired lost child, who had lain in the darkness of her room, so lonely, night after night.

'But you've got beautiful hair!'

'Thanks, Ed. . . .' And she smiled with an effort because he was almost angry.

'Anyhow, your mother – sorry, Livia – sounds as if she has a few hang-ups herself,' Ed said finally and quickly began refilling her cup with some more coffee. Her eyes were beginning to glisten ominously.

'I've never really thought about that aspect of things.'
She had blocked it out.

'Perhaps you should. . . .' He stroked his chin thoughtfully and then began to light up the inevitable havana
cigar. 'Seems to me Freud would have had a ball with
Livia. In fact I know the name of a very good therapist in
New York; maybe I should send her his number. . . .' He
tried to keep his tone humorous, although if she was going
to cry she would cry. He knew that much about women,
and he was here after all. There was something worse
about crying alone. 'Maybe your brother too; he sounds as
if your mother has very successfully castrated him – if you
know what I mean.'

'She wouldn't be amused,' Francesca remarked.

'Is she ever amused . . . I mean, does she ever laugh?'

'You know, Ed – I don't think I can remember her
laughing.' And she couldn't; Livia had smiled and the
smiling had usually been very careful, very sweet.

'Jeee-sus! What a woman . . . not even a sense of
humour!' He shook his head in disbelief. 'Your father
must have wondered what he had got himself into.' Poor
bastard.

'If he *was* my father . . . ,' she said quietly. 'And, in any
case, he loved her.'

'He loved you too, didn't he?'

She looked at Ed for a long moment.

'Yes, he did.'

'Well, then what are you complaining about?' he said,
with a trace of impatience. 'I feel pretty sure he was your
father – and, even if he wasn't, *you* and not the iceberg
queen, Livia, seemed to be the centre of his universe. Am I
right?'

'I suppose so.'

'*He . . . loved . . . you*,' he said slowly, emphasizing
every word as if she were a child and might not understand. 'That's rare, *love*, the real thing, I'm talking about –
not all that schmaltz they talk about in the movies and
those trashy novels.' He turned away from her as silent
tears began to roll slowly down her cheeks and she stared

305

past him unseeing to the window, her heart tight and swollen, as if it were aching for all the love that might have been. From somewhere far away she felt Ed's thin fingers pressing comfortingly into her shoulder and his voice breaking gently through the memories. 'You were lucky, kiddo, whether you realize it yet or not. And the fact that he was or wasn't your father doesn't come into it.' He blew out a long cloud of smoke. 'You got the goods, Frankie, forget about the packaging.' He got up and went over to the stove, and came back bearing two plates of egg and ham. 'Come on, now, wipe those beautiful eyes and let's eat . . . it's Christmas Eve, remember? And we're supposed to be full of joy, you know, happy and all that mush.' He sat down again and gave her a searching look. 'You haven't forgotten about the tree? Like I said, it's got to be up and running before nightfall.'

'I haven't forgotten about the tree, Ed,' she said, looking back at him. And she would make sure that it was the best tree ever.


'There's more snow on the way . . . ,' Ed said, as he lifted his eyes to the leaden sky. 'I can smell it.'

They had taken a long walk during the afternoon and as they neared the house once more he looked quickly at his watch. He frowned and looked back at the sky. 'It'll be going into dusk any moment.'

'Does that matter?' she asked.

'Oh, no, no – not at all. I just didn't realize it was so late.' He plunged his gloved hands deeper into the pockets of his sheepskin. 'I think my fingers are going to fall off. . . .'

'I'll make some coffee as soon as we get in.'

'It's going to take more than coffee to thaw me out – I'll go for a large scotch.'

'Without ice?' she said lightly, as a smile began to lift the edges of her mouth.

'Definitely without ice. . . .'

'I think I hear a car,' Francesca said, stopping at the bottom of the steps to the house. And suddenly Peanuts dived past them barking wildly.

'You hear a car . . . ,' Ed responded, smiling with a trace of satisfaction, as the large patch of white on his dog's haunches disappeared around the side of the house.

Philippe stood in the light from the porch as several children spilled out of the car behind him, followed by an older man, his step-brother, Bernardo. He looked up as the main house door opened and Ed walked out still totally muffled in his old sheepskin. Francesca stood behind him, framed in the doorway, and for a long moment Philippe found his gaze resting on her before he was pulled to one side by Bernardo as Ed came down the steps. Ed had told him at the last minute that she *might* be coming and by then it had been too late to change his plans. For the past four years he had demanded that Philippe spend Christmas with him, despite the fact that it meant bringing Bernardo and his three children along. He was the eldest of his step-brothers and the only one to stay close to him, and he was also a father without a wife, Elena having run off with a meter-man too many years ago to count now. Ed began shaking Bernardo's hand and ruffling the children's hair as Francesca slowly made her way down the steps towards them. Philippe cringed inwardly. He had not wanted her to see him in this sort of light – not with Bernardo, much as he cared about him; not shy truck-driving Bernardo, with his baggy ill-fitting suit and flabby paunch.

'Hi, Philippe . . . I think this is a surprise . . . or is it?' She could see his embarrassment and longed to tell him that it didn't matter, but Philippe wasn't that easy.

'Ask Ed – he's been planning this for weeks,' he said sourly, and with an effort forced a smile on his face as he shook her hand. Soft hand.

'You might like to introduce the girl, Philippe, god-dammit!' He had chosen to ignore Philippe's remark and began turning the confused children towards her. 'They're all girls – Victoria, Rosa and Maria.'

'I have no sons,' Bernardo remarked sorrowfully, as he took Francesca's hand, stumbling over an enthusiastic Peanuts in the process.

'Some people are never satisfied,' Ed said as he began ushering the children into the house. 'We're going to get more snow, kids, lots of it!'

'He's really enjoying himself,' Francesca said, grinning.

'Ed usually does,' Philippe replied dryly.

'He is a good man,' Bernardo said promptly and then lowered his eyes as he saw the look of sharp surprise in his young step-brother's face at the unexpected compliment.

The Christmas tree had already been unveiled by the time they reached the living room and it was easy to see why Ed had been so insistent that it be ready before nightfall, before the children arrived. Of course, he had known all the time. She smiled as she watched him help Bernardo remove the children's coats and at the look of approval on his face as the three girls stood shyly staring up at the mammoth tree.

'Okay, okay,' Ed said suddenly, clapping his hands. 'Dive for it, girls . . . and don't knock the tree over; Frankie took most of the afternoon to put it up.'

'Did you?' Philippe asked, turning to her.

'I enjoyed it,' she said, looking back at him with a trace of defiance and then her eyes returned to the girls burrowing around the tree. 'What's happening?'

'Ed always lets them have a "Christmas Eve present" – but they have to find it.'

'He thinks of everything.'

But Philippe made no answer, somehow he was beginning to feel just a little out of his depth. And as he looked at Ed crouching down towards the youngest child, helping her tear a carefully wrapped parcel apart, he thought that anyone walking in on the scene would take Ed for their grandfather, which was just what he wanted. It didn't seem to matter to him that it was all a load of bull, all wishful thinking. Philippe closed his eyes for a brief moment in an effort to push down the meanest thought of all still tucked away in the blackest part of his heart – that Ed was doing all this for him, like all the other times; that this 'repeat performance' was yet another of his bribes to win him over.

The snow did come, falling all through the night, just as Ed had predicted, and even as Francesca dressed she heard the shrieks of delight from the excited children, followed by the thumps of small feet as they ran down the broad wooden staircase. She looked to the window and watched as the whiteness fell in gentle wavering sheets. A designer Christmas day, she thought with some amusement. But then her eyes returned to the presents now stacked on the pine dressing-table; there were not enough. She had nothing for the girls or Bernardo. Yet she had picked up several boxes of fruit soaps and exotic bath oils along Fifth Avenue; they would do – they would have to. Bernardo could have the extra large pair of white woollen socks she had bought for herself to combat the snow; maybe he wouldn't notice the neat little monogram carefully stitched in white silk on one side.

The living room floor was already covered with a forest of paper by the time she made her way downstairs. She stood a little awkwardly in the doorway as Ed and Bernardo made a poor effort at clearing up the mess whilst the girls tore at the parcels that were still waiting to be opened, but the smallest girl, Maria, turned away from the turmoil as if it were all suddenly too much and made her way over to Philippe. She climbed into his peaceful lap and they both sat observing the chaos unaware that they were being watched.

'I wish I had a camera . . . ,' Francesca said and moved over to him. 'Happy Christmas.'

Philippe felt a flush of crimson rush into his face as he looked up at her. And he wondered if she had any idea what she did to him when she walked into a room.

'Happy Christmas.'

Then there was a chorus of 'Happy Christmas' as Ed, Bernardo and the girls realized she was there.

'Hey, this is for you,' Ed threw a long narrow box half-way across the room to her. It was quite light and she shook it gently before proceeding to open the black and gold wrapping. It was a beautiful box and the lid slid off as if it had just been oiled to reveal a swathe of white tissue paper. The silk shone through even before the last piece of tissue was removed and she lifted out a stunning piece of lingerie in black silk and lace.

'Ed. . . .' She drew a sharp breath in pleasure and embarrassment.

'For the girl who has everything – hope you like it – Phil thought you'd go for the black. . . .' He winked and she saw him shoot a warning glance at Philippe. Obviously Philippe had had nothing to do with the gift.

Francesca placed the exquisite garment back in its box and fetched her own presents from the hallway. Ed adored his cigar case, although it did turn out that he already had one, and she thought secretly that he adored Peanuts' stocking even more; Bernardo loved his socks and the girls smelt their soaps dutifully before returning to the mammoth doll they had each been given, by Ed of course. For some unaccountable reason she had saved Philippe's gift until last and he took it from her with a touch of awkwardness, carefully untying the deep blue ribbon and paper as she waited expectantly beside him. And all at once she realized that Ed was watching them, examining them almost too sharply, and she was glad that her hair hung loose so that it would hide the redness that suddenly made her neck and cheeks glow.

'It's beautiful . . . ,' Philippe said slowly as he draped the scarf across his arm.

'I didn't really know what to get you; I didn't even know whether you'd be here. . . .'

'No, really . . . it's beautiful.' And he was touched by guilt because it had been the same for him and yet he had left the buying to Ed, stubbornly refusing to acknowledge her.

'Okay – brunch now, and then a walk – and I'm not doing all the cooking myself!' Ed's words broke in and Philippe felt a soft tingling of relief as the familiar voice snapped the moment.

It was, she thought, a wonderful unexpected day, perhaps one of the best she had ever had. Francesca looked over her glass at Ed's nodding head and at Bernardo's red one; they would soon both be asleep, like the children who had gone to bed only an hour before, totally exhausted and totally satiated. Finally she looked at Philippe who had stood up to gather the plates together.

'Perhaps we should help them up to bed. . . .'

'You know Ed wouldn't like that.'

'Maybe I could take Peanuts for "his nightly"?'

'That's a better idea . . . ,' he remarked and smiled. 'I'll come with you. We can leave all this for the morning.' And as if the dog had only been waiting for this moment, he appeared from behind the door and Francesca began to laugh.

'Nothing changes,' Philippe added dryly and reached for their coats.

The sky had frozen and the darkness lay soft and thick with the snow. It was incredibly quiet and Francesca stood quite still with Philippe beside her, watching the big wobbling form of Peanuts weave in and out of the paralyzed undergrowth.

'It feels so right here, somehow,' she said quietly and thought that her words sounded inadequate, as if they weren't sufficient to describe how she really felt.

'I know what you mean,' he replied and lapsed once more into silence and the sudden closeness that seemed to have sprung up between them.

'It was very good of Ed to invite me.' And she turned slowly to look up into his face.

'He's not so bad.' And he supposed he wasn't, or maybe it was her, because when she was so close all thoughts of Ed seemed to turn to nothing and he was lost.

'You should try giving him a break sometimes,' she said softly.

'Maybe I should make that my New Year's resolution.'

'Maybe you should.'

He looked back at her but her face was nearly invisible in the semi-darkness because there was no moon, but he could smell her sweet woman-smell. There was a sound from somewhere inside the house and he didn't want to hear it because he didn't want to break the cord which now seemed to tie them so tentatively together.

'That's Ed,' she said.

He sighed inwardly.

'And that's Peanuts,' he added as the dog came up to wait patiently beside them. 'We'd better get back inside.'

'I'm going to have to leave tomorrow morning,' Francesca said, as Ed piled an unwanted waffle oozing with syrup on her plate. There would definitely have to be a diet when she got back.

'Why, for Chrissakes!' Ed demanded. 'It's New Year's Eve in a couple of days.' His head ached from too much port the night before and the glare from the snow made his eyes wince whenever he looked out of the window.

'There are a few things I have to do.'

'You mean work?' he asked impatiently. 'But no one's going to be working between now and next week unless they're crazy.'

'I am. I have to clear something up – or at least try to.' She had had almost no time to call the clients she thought might be involved in any 'poaching' Vic might try to do if he was thinking of leaving. Most of them would be away, of course, but she needed to do some groundwork on each of them, speak to Geoff and even Henry at the very least. Francesca realized only too well that she hadn't been at Samuels long enough to build up any sort of relationship with the clients and that's where Vic's strength lay. New England was too far away for telephone calls and a nagging feeling told her she should be in London.

'You really think it's that important?' Ed persisted.

'Wild horses wouldn't drag me away from here, Ed, if it wasn't important.' And this was not the time to discuss what Vic might be up to. Ed and Philippe could know all in good time if it was necessary.

That seemed to satisfy him for a moment before he spoke again.

'It's my birthday on the 16th.'

'Oh, I didn't know. . . .'

312

'I want a party for my seventy-third – right here – will you come?' It was another demand.

'I think you know I'll come.'

'Okay – then I give you permission to go back to London tomorrow.'

'Thanks, Ed,' she said with a trace of sarcasm and caught Philippe's gaze as he lifted his eyes to heaven. Even Bernardo laughed.

But much later when she had gone to her room there was no enthusiasm in putting the few things she had brought with her into a suitcase; she had always hated packing and she supposed that that would never change. It had been a strange, beautiful Christmas somehow and it would hit her hard to leave this house again – Ed, Peanuts, even Bernardo and the girls. And there was Philippe, of course, elusive Philippe who always seemed a step away. She smiled wryly as she placed the box containing black silk and lace into her suitcase; *that* had been all Ed's doing, of course, – never, never Philippe. She brought the lid of the suitcase down with a heavy sigh and realized that there was something missing; there was no bulge, no small mountain where her walking boots had been, they were still standing in the kitchen wrapped in polythene waiting to be packed.

The house was almost in darkness as she made her way down the stairs, except for the light from the fire which still seemed to burn with surprising life from what she could see beneath the door. Frowning softly she opened the door and immediately saw the reflection of Philippe's long legs caricatured on the wall as he stretched out in a chair.

'Oh, I'm sorry,' she said quickly.

'It's okay – I was just about to go up anyway.' He stood up and secured the guard around the fire. 'I thought you'd be asleep.'

'I've been packing and then I suddenly realized I'd left my boots down here.'

'You could leave them here, you know, as you plan to come back for Ed's birthday. I don't suppose you'll be

313

needing them much in the blizzards that will be sweeping London.'

She could see a small smile on his face. Mocking. And she was stung by the similarity with Matthias.

'Are you okay?' Even in the fading firelight he could see that her face had drained of colour.

'I'm fine – really.' And as he walked over to her she was relieved to see the similarity die, that it was only Philippe – tall, dark, elusive Philippe.

He watched her for a long moment as she looked back at him and he was reminded of all the times, all the nights he had wanted her, and it was only now, in this shadowy darkness when she suddenly seemed so vulnerable, that he was able to summon any courage to reach out and touch. He found himself taking her rich hair between his fingers and then letting them slide slowly down to her face which he tilted so that it was lifted towards him. He was surprised that she said nothing, that she made no move-ment to turn away from him, that she remained so still. It was all so easy then – her open mouth, her round luminous eyes, the lovely neck and the feeling of her body as it pressed against him, filling all the vacant hollows and the long length of his loneliness.

# 10

The Christmas tree was too perfect, Caroline decided, as her mother began lighting the candles sitting on each branch. There were no 'silly' things – no little snowmen, no Santa Claus, no strips of silver foil to break up its carefully designed, untouchable image. Mother was an incredible snob, of course, but it hadn't really bothered her until now. Her attention was diverted abruptly by the slamming of a car door in the drive and she knew that the first of the guests were arriving for her parents' cocktail party. She stepped out into the hallway and made her way to the kitchen where trays of drinks were just being prepared. Caroline leaned across the scores of canapés and picked up a gin and tonic and wondered briefly whether it would help keep her sanity over the next two hours. Immediately and with a sinking heart her thoughts turned to Nick; she hadn't seen him since their unfortunate conversation in his office. Once or twice she had tried to phone him, but he was never there and she lacked the courage to go and see him in person because she had no new answers to give him. And he had not called her. She took a long sip of the gin and tonic and made her way back into the living room, or 'blue room', as her mother preferred to call it. Several people were already standing by the fire-place and making the usual appropriate noises about the house, the garden, the tree. Almost as soon as she stepped into the room her mother's ever-busy eye noticed her and she was dragged across the room to be introduced.

'You know Mr and Mrs Allenby, of course, Caroline. . . .'

She nodded in response: nice, boring old George, her father's one-time partner who still refused to give in to retirement.

'And Mr and Mrs Goldman.' The Goldmans had made money out of shoes and were filthy rich, apparently, which was probably why they were invited, Caroline mused, particularly as privately her mother always referred to David Goldman as 'that Jewish cobbler person'.

The doorbell went again and she moved away to answer it, to escape, but saw her father pass the door from the direction of the kitchen to do what she had intended; she knew instinctively that he had been having a quick drink without his wife's knowledge. Several male voices seemed to fill the space in the hall and then the tall figure of her brother, Robert, came walking into the room followed closely by two 'army chums'. He was home on leave, but seemed to spend most of the time out of the house. Caroline had always liked her brother, yet sometimes she realized that she hardly knew him at all; they had spent most of their childhood in boarding schools miles apart and after disappointing 'A' level results Robert had gone straight into the guards instead of Oxford as his parents had wanted for him. But he seemed happy enough and his friends were just about bearable, Caroline decided – if only they weren't such drips. She felt a sudden vice-like grip on her elbow and found herself looking into her mother's tightly restrained face.

'You should be circulating, Caroline . . . not standing in the middle of the room with an empty glass in your hand,' she hissed. 'Here's Group Captain O'Hare – now try and be nice to him.'

One of the hired help came past with a tray of glasses and Caroline reached over for another gin and tonic as her mother moved towards the door; she was beginning to understand why her father drank so much. Group Captain O'Hare had large doughy fingers, as she had found out to her cost when she had been seated next to him at a formal dinner party. First he had moved his chair just a little too close to hers, then came the coarse rubbing of his thigh up against her own, followed quickly by his sweaty palm on her knee and she had been in a nightmare of what she should do. Eventually she had got up and left the room, feigning a headache because she hadn't the nerve to plunge a fork into his greedy fingers as had been suggested under such circumstances in one of the women's magazines. But he had been more than slightly drunk and she knew that in some people's eyes that would excuse him. But she couldn't and wouldn't. Naturally her mother would have said that she was imagining things, that Rollie O'Hare was a man of 'the old school', which would, of course, put him on a par with the Archangel Gabriel, as Nick had remarked when she had told him about the incident.

'Caroline . . . my dear,' he said, grinning through thick saliva-covered lips, the rim of his handle-bar moustache already coated with a thin layer of alcohol. Like a caricature out of one of her brother's old Biggles books.

She looked up at him with barely concealed distaste, but he remained totally unmoved and she wondered at how easy it seemed to be for him to push the memory of their last meeting so conveniently away. Maybe he didn't remember, and even if he did, perhaps it was of such little significance to him that he would be surprised if she should recollect it at all. They stood together for a few minutes exchanging achingly tedious pleasantries until boredom obviously overcame him and he moved away. There was another vice-like grip on her elbow and she sighed inwardly expecting to be confronted again by her mother for having 'failed' in her duties. But it was Guy.

'Hi . . . ,' he said awkwardly.

For a moment she was so stunned that she could only look back at him. There had been no mention of Guy coming to the party. Her mother had intimated that it was a strictly 'family and friends' affair and at the time Caroline had been so busy thinking about Nick that she had not thought that her mother might include Guy under the 'friends' category. Somehow it had not occurred to her at all. But it should have.

'How are things?' he asked with forced brightness, staring into her blank, unwelcoming face.

'Fine, thank you,' she said at last.

They stood in an uncomfortable silence until he spoke again.

'Charlotte's having a New Year's Eve party. . . .'

'Yes, I know.'

'I thought we might go together. . . . '

She swallowed slowly and thought of Nick.

'Why did you think we might go together?' she asked quietly.

'Well – your mother – she said. . . .' His voice trailed off weakly as he saw the darkness begin to gather in her eyes.

'What did she say, Guy?'

'I must have misunderstood.'

'I'm sure you didn't.' Her eyes flicked sharply over his face. 'I'd be interested to know – really.' There was a small thin smile touching her mouth and he mistook it for encouragement.

'She said that things weren't working out between you and this . . . new chap.'

'Was this before you received the invitation from her or after . . . ?'

'Oh, before . . . ,' he said innocently. 'She's been very kind, keeping in touch with me ever since . . . ,' he swallowed deeply, 'well, you know. . . .' he finished awkwardly.

Caroline looked across the room at her mother who appeared to be in deep conversation with Richmond's locally celebrated poet, her forehead creased in appropriately meaningful lines.

'I wonder if you would excuse me, please, Guy.' Without waiting for him to reply she walked away, across the room and out into the comparative freedom of the hallway where she called a cab.

It didn't take long to pack; two suitcases and a large shoulder-bag would do, at least for the time being. But her luggage was much heavier than she expected as she dragged it impatiently to the top of the stairs, and it was only with real effort that she was able to keep the noise it made on the polished wooden stair to a minimum. On reaching the bottom she pushed all three pieces into the large porch and began smoothing down her skirt, and it was only then that she realized her father was standing watching her from the doorway of the kitchen. In an instant his eyes travelled from her white face to the suitcases standing mutely at her side. He walked slowly towards her.

'You're going then . . . ?' he said gently.

'Mummy's made it so difficult . . . ,' she said sadly and felt a prickling sensation in her eyes which could only herald tears.

'I know, I know.' He felt a tightness in his throat, like a knot, as he looked into the tear-bright eyes, the reddening nose and face of his daughter.

'It's not fair on Nick. . . .' And her lip began to tremble.

'Of course it's not,' he said helplessly and gathered her against his chest.

And she was embraced and comforted by the smell of wool, pipe tobacco, whisky, which were all her father. But the sound of a car in the driveway made her look up.

'Your cab, I think,' he said softly, releasing her.

She nodded and turned to her cases, but he moved quickly past her and picked them up and was already walking through the door before she followed him.

'You're not to feel you have to stay away, do you understand?' he said firmly and then saw the doubt in her eyes. 'Your mother doesn't have the last word on everything. This is your home.'

'Thank you so much, daddy.' And she felt the tears start again, but pressed them down because she couldn't stand seeing that sadness in his face.

'There's no need for thanks. . . .' He pushed a strand of damp hair from her cheek. 'And if things don't work out . . . as I said, this is your home,' he finished lamely as he helped her into the waiting car.

'I know, Daddy . . . but I don't think you need worry.' A picture of Nick's face slid into her mind and she realized how much she wanted him. He had known better than she did that it would have to be her decision in the end, her choice. And she wondered with a surge of curious surprise why it had taken her so long.

*

'This is highly confidential, Zoë,' Vic said. 'After tomorrow it really won't matter much any more, but I thought the least I could do was to let you know now.' In any event, he needed her. There was a document and letters to be typed up concerning his move to Gower & Kid-Porter and there was no way that he could avoid her finding out. 'So I thought we'd start our day with a bang – I'm leaving Samuels, Zoë – it's all wrapped up.'

She stared back at him for a long moment as if she did not understand.

'Leaving Samuels . . . ,' she said with disbelief, '. . . for good?'

'For good and all!' he said grinning broadly.

'But when?' she asked anxiously. 'And where?'

'As soon as possible . . . the day after tomorrow probably.' He leaned smugly back in his chair. 'I'm going to be made Deputy Chairman of Gower & Kid-Porter.' He had naturally spoken to Henry who had been strangely and irritatingly calm about the whole thing, but then Henry practically lived in an ivory tower these days. He was out of touch with what was really happening, way out of touch. There was, of course, no question of serving notice even though it was written into his contract. Even Henry realized that it was hardly wise, if it wasn't too late already, of course, to have a high profile guy like himself hanging around like bait to entice Samuels' clients into another hot-shop. Vic smiled to himself; *and* he was getting a good pay-off to offset those three months, just as he had expected, which would more than cover the cost of that villa he had wanted for so long in Marbella – and, of course, there was still the sale of his shares in the company – it would all turn out rather nicely. He was snapped out of his thoughts by an abrupt sniff from Zoë. Vic blinked and then sighed heavily; fat tears were pouring down Zoë's cheeks.

'Christ, Zoë . . . this is business . . . part of growing up,' he said impatiently; hating the tears, hating it when women cried.

'I can't come with you, can I?' She looked back at him pleadingly through a haze of tears.

'Not this time, love. . . .' He shook his head in mock sorrow. 'Believe me, I tried to persuade Stu Gower to bring you in as part of the package, but apparently it's not company policy – and naturally he couldn't start a precedent. You understand that, don't you?'

She nodded slowly, staring at the white piece of sodden tissue which she was twisting and turning between her trembling fingers.

'We can still see each other, of course . . . ,' he said at last. At first he had thought of cutting her out of his life altogether, but then he realized that in all probability she would be made Geoff's secretary as he was still trying to make up his mind from the scores of girls he had already seen. After all, surely it was better the devil you know. . . . Geoff never was any good with women, he thought meanly, whether in bed or out of it, from what he could gather. Vic laughed soundlessly. He had even decided to suggest Zoë to Geoff himself before he left – 'to help the poor kid out' – and she would therefore be in a prime position to know exactly what was going on at Samuels: what companies their smart-ass chairwoman intended to stoop and conquer, what pitches were lined up, what new business contacts dear old Geoff had in mind.

'Can we?'

'Of course, love. You didn't think I was just going to walk out of here without even looking back, did you?' He gave her what he hoped was a consoling smile. 'After all, we've had quite a lot of fun together over the past two years, haven't we . . . ?'

She nodded again.

'And don't you worry about your job, or anything like that. I'm going to talk to Geoff and see if we can't slot you in as his secretary, or PA, or whatever you want to call it. I don't see why there should be any problem.'

Vic stood up and was relieved to see that her face was already brightening. He held out his hand and she took it with pathetic eagerness, accepting the brief embrace which followed like a prize.

'It'll all be okay, love – don't you worry about a thing,' he said finally and opened the door, his hand unable to resist a last patronizing grope at her bottom as she walked away from him.

Sian looked at the pile of files and correspondence on her desk with resignation. Francesca had been particularly cheerful, which was an improvement on her strange mood before Christmas, but she was allowing her an extra couple of hours at lunchtime to indulge in the January sales and that more than made up for the work she would have to do on her return.

'Coffee?'

Sian shifted her gaze to Zoë's pretty, healthy face and smiled.

'I'd love one – thanks.' But she frowned as Zoë walked across the office to the kitchen; her eyes were red-rimmed as if she had been crying.

A steaming cup of coffee was brought promptly back to her and as Zoë settled herself back behind her desk she looked up and caught Sian's searching look.

'What's the matter?'

'I just thought that it looks as if you've been crying. . . .'

Zoë gave an unhappy sigh and bowed her head as she half-heartedly stirred her coffee.

'You mustn't say anything to anyone,' she said at last.

'About what?'

She sighed again.

'Vic's leaving.'

'Leaving?!'

'Ssssh . . . Sian . . . it's highly confidential.'

And she wondered with wry amusement if Zoë really knew what the word confidential meant.

'But why is he leaving?'

'He's had a better offer,' she replied sadly.

'And you're not going with him?'

'No – I can't, apparently.' Her eyes slid away from Sian's face. 'But he tried to get me included in his package,' she added defensively, 'but Stu Gower said it wasn't company policy.'

'Gower & Kid-Porter?'

'Yes.'

'When does he leave?'

'He says as soon as possible – probably tomorrow, or the day after,' she finished limply.

'What are you going to do?'

'He thinks that he can slot me in as Geoff's new secretary.'

'Oh, I see – but does Geoff know?'

'He's going to speak to him.'

They stared at each other for a long awkward moment.

'We're still going to keep seeing each other, of course. . . .'

Sian forced a smile and found the vivid, unwelcome image slipping into her consciousness of Vic and Zoë when she had walked in on them in his office.

'Well, I hope it works out for you,' she said lamely.

'Vic thinks it will,' Zoë said sharply, as if she had just read Sian's mind.

The telephone rang and with relief Sian turned away from Zoë's pinched bright face to answer it. At first she thought it was a wrong number, but then her mother's broken voice began to make terrible sense as she told her what had happened. The voice seemed to go on and on, and Sian found herself pressing the receiver against her ear as if she could not hear clearly enough, found herself taking down the address of the hospital and the name of the doctor as if by some miracle all her limbs were still functioning as they should and all was well with the world. She put the receiver down.

'What's up?'

It was Geoff; he had been standing in front of her over the last few moments and she had not even noticed.

'Petie's had an accident.'

'Bad?' he asked gently.

'I think so.' The words sounded as if they came from another place, another mouth.

'Do you need a lift to the hospital?'

'I thought I'd get a cab,' she said expressionlessly.

'I'll take you.' He ripped the piece of paper from her jotter with the address of the hospital and then looked briefly across at Zoë who was sitting watching them with her mouth half-open. 'You'll tell Francesca, Zoë?' She nodded dumbly.

It was almost too warm in Geoff's car despite the cold outside and Sian felt perspiration pouring down her back and between her breasts as she sat rigidly next to him.

'What happened?' he asked at last, unable to stand her silence any longer.

She closed her eyes for a moment as if she were trying to gather her thoughts and then blinked them open.

'He was in his pushchair on the pavement outside the house. My mother only left him there for a few seconds; she'd left her key in the lock. Just as she was coming back down the path a motor-bike skidded out of control and came off the road straight into Petie. . . .' Her hand came up to her mouth and she thought her heart would suffocate from the pain. Not right or left of Petie, but dead centre, almost as if it had been planned by some malignant deity. 'He has multiple lacerations, broken ribs, head injuries . . . I don't think too much was left out, Geoff . . . ,' she added bitterly and a tight choking sob which had been waiting too long in her throat broke free from her mouth.

'Okay, okay – now let's get to the hospital,' he said helplessly and fished a handkerchief from his pocket in a futile gesture at comforting her.

For long dreadful minutes she didn't speak, but as they neared the hospital she lifted her face and stared mourn-fully through the window.

'Sometimes . . . sometimes, Geoff, I've wished that things had been different, that maybe it would have been better if I'd made other choices, other decisions. . . .' How often had she wished that she were free? Free of Petie in the most secret part of her heart.

He glanced at her quickly, and was shocked by the grief, the emptiness, the desolation he saw in her face.

'Sometimes I've wished myself back, a year, two years ago – before it all happened, before Petie. . . .' She couldn't say it even now.

'Stop it, Sian,' he said suddenly. 'I know what you're trying to say and it doesn't mean, or signify, anything.'

She shook her head almost in anger as if she didn't want to believe him.

'Do you think you're the only one who looks back and longs for the past, as if just being there would make everything right again? And do you really think that if you were able to go back that it would change anything? You'd still be the same person, Sian, and you'd still make the same decision.'

She shook her head again and tears for the past, the present and the future cascaded down her cheeks.

'You love Petie, don't you?'

He was everything to her, and she hadn't realized it until now. She nodded hopelessly.

'Nothing else matters then, does it? Stop being so bloody hard on yourself – you're human like the rest of us.'

She made no answer and he sighed inwardly and with trepidation as the gates of the hospital came into view. A surge of despair made him grip the wheel of the car even tighter and he wondered bitterly who would bother to give bets on the winner of a collision between a motor-bike and a little boy.


'So you agree with Henry?' Vic asked with a small smile. She was sitting opposite him and he supposed that she looked particularly good today – if you liked that sort of thing. He noticed with some irritation that she was wearing a deep blue raw silk shirt almost identical to the one his wife had recently purchased. On Francesca it looked like a designer classic which it probably was; on Sue it looked like something from Marks & Spencer. But then everything Sue wore looked as if it came from Marks & Spencer.

'As far as I'm concerned, Vic, the sooner you leave the better.'

'Well, that's what I call straight talking. . . .'

'So long as we understand one another.'

'I think we've always done that, Francesca,' he said sarcastically.

She made no answer and bent her head over the piece of paper on her desk. Vic moved forward slightly as she began to write some figures down, but his eye was immediately caught by the dark cleft of her breasts as she leaned over. A pity she was born with a brain, he mused, as he endeavoured to press down the beginnings of an erection.

'You've already been in touch with Richard Best about your shares?'

'Naturally.'

'And naturally, you've already finalized everything with Henry about your pay-off figure. . . .'

'I think you know that.'

'Just checking, Vic – you know how thorough I like to be.' She looked back at him and smiled thinly.

Oh, he knew all right, but there was such a thing as trying to be too clever and she would find out about that soon enough.

'Henry also said I could keep the Mercedes until the end of the week, but that won't be necessary – Stu Gower is going to drop a Ferrari off for me sometime this afternoon.' A red one, just like yours.

'How generous . . . let's hope you make his generosity worthwhile, Vic.'

'Oh, I'm sure I shall, Francesca,' he replied with a barely concealed sneer. 'Over the past few months –,' since you arrived, '– I've seen changes in the company that have been just a little too hard to swallow. Samuels used to have a unique character of its own, a sort of family atmosphere, and now it seems that it's going to get too big and lose all of that. It's trying to ape the mega-agencies, the big bureaucracies that are beginning to forget what advertising is all about. I don't like that.'

'Change can be difficult for some people. . . .'

His mouth twisted into a sullen frown.

'Not change for the sake of change.'

'And being number one in the UK agency rankings isn't a positive sort of change, Vic?'

'I didn't mean that.'

'And do you really think that Samuels can stay moderately sized – like "a family", as you so quaintly put it – *and* very creative without one of the multinational mega-agencies coming along with one of their usual tempting offers and buying it up?'

'That's pure speculation.'

'No. Competing is what this is all about, Vic, not speculation. And sooner or later the smaller, moderately sized shops won't be able to compete and will become prime takeover targets because they won't be able to cope with the demands of global marketing.'

'Bullshit,' he said, his hostility out in the open now. 'There are plenty of people in ad-land who still remain unconvinced by this global–vision crap!'

'I'm not interested in them, Vic – they're time-wasters – instead of looking forwards, they look backwards, or don't look at all.'

'Maybe they believe in looking before they leap.'

'Maybe they're just scared to take a risk.'

'You're taking a big risk with Samuels. . . .'

'You're wrong there, Vic, – because I'm going to make sure that *big* is going to be *very beautiful* as far as Samuels is concerned.'

'I hope you're right.'

'Do you?' Who the hell was he trying to kid?

Their gazes locked for taut, uncomfortable seconds until he stood up.

'By the way, I've asked Geoff if he'd be willing to take Zoë on – I'd hate to think of her having to look for another job because I can't take her with me.'

Francesca raised her eyebrows as she looked back at him.

'I'm sure she's touched by your concern – but the final decision will naturally lie with Geoff.'

'Of course.' He began walking towards the door.

'And I trust you've managed to say a nice goodbye to our clients with your usual charm. . . .'

He turned and looked back at her.

'Naturally – I've known most of them for a long time.'
What was she getting at?

'Paul O'Neil at de Vico's is a nice guy. Geoff and I had a meeting with him on Monday morning. . . .'

'Should that be of interest to me?' Oh, but it was.

'I just thought you might like to know, for old times' sake as it were, that we're getting rid of Julian Baring and that Paul is, of course, in total agreement.'

'Paul . . . ,' Vic winced inwardly and felt his face redden as all his carefully hoarded pleasure began to evaporate. He had been banking on O'Neil changing agencies; once he had gone into the catastrophe the merger was likely to be and the conflicts that could possibly ensue he had all but agreed when Vic had spoken to him last.

'Really,' he said coolly.

'Surely you must have been aware that Baring has been enjoying too much of the little white line . . . ?' She watched his face carefully. 'He's even been given his marching orders from that horoscope programme he does for Thames before the "shit hits the fan", if you'll excuse the expression.'

'I'd heard a vague sort of rumour,' he lied.

'And I thought it was one of your pet campaigns, Vic?' she said dryly.

He made no answer.

'Anyway, I'm sure you'll sleep better at night knowing that the revised campaign will be in more capable hands.'

'What do you mean?'

'Julian's going, as I've just said, and we're already in the process of re-casting.' She moved around to the side of her desk and sat on the edge, folding her arms. 'Paul's very pleased with the idea I've already drafted, as a matter of fact.'

You bitch.

'How does a trio like Harold Wilson, James Callaghan and Edward Heath strike you . . . ?'

'What is it – a political rally?' he said sarcastically.

'Very witty, Vic . . . but naturally nothing of the kind.

They're simply the sort of people Paul would like to see drinking his sherry . . . and his port, for that matter.'

'I'm sure your "idea" will make his company a bundle . . . ,' he said aggrievedly.

'I'm sure it will, Vic – he's going to be signing a nice, neat, re-vamped contract to prove it.'

He swallowed slowly. She had gone behind his back, knowing somehow that he was leaving, knowing what he was likely to do. Stu had been counting on de Vico and the £4 million worth of billings; he had practically promised it to him.

He stood staring at her for a long moment, pressing down the filthy oath that waited hovering behind his lips.

'Well, if that's it, I'll be going,' he finished lamely and forced a tight smile to settle on his unhappy mouth.

'That's it, Vic.'

She watched him walk across the room, waiting for some last bitter word or gesture, but he only left the door of her office swinging sullenly open as he passed through the empty mouth of the doorway.

Vic didn't know just how unlucky he was. If she had waited any longer Paul O'Neil and de Vico's would have gone over to Gower & Kid-Porter. But he hadn't covered his tracks well enough and she supposed that he didn't think that he had had to. The argument he had given O'Neil about the unpleasant effects of the merger and likely conflicts was a thin one, and she had destroyed each objection at the hastily arranged meeting on Monday. The clinch had been in telling him that his precious ad with Baring as the core element was too risky and that 'she had been surprised that Mr Brunning hadn't already mentioned it, as he was ultimately responsible. . . .' But naturally Vic hadn't mentioned it, because he was waiting until de Vico's had been taken under Gower's wing before letting O'Neil know. He had played his cards too close and now de Vico's MD clearly thought that he was only a self-seeking adman who hadn't covered his ass. Which, of course, he was.

She moved back behind her desk and looked down at

the piece of paper on which she had written some figures and names. Vic had managed to inflict some damage – three clients worth almost two million between them. It would all be in *Campaign* tomorrow, of course; he would have seen to that and consequently there would still be more questions asked which she would make sure to answer in next week's issue. And they would be the sort of answers Vic wouldn't like at all. There would be a photograph, too, and maybe she would frame it and send him a copy.

Francesca smiled wryly to herself – maybe she would send Paul O'Neil one too; it had been difficult not to miss the obvious admiration in his eyes when she had walked into his office. Naturally she had gone there prepared to pull out all the shots, so naturally she had dressed to kill. And it had worked so sweetly. No doubt the feminists wouldn't like it and the chauvinists would deny it, but it never failed. After all, wasn't advertising ultimately all about success, all about winning? And in this instance the means certainly justified the end result. Vic hadn't stood a chance. She shook her head gently and moved over to the window. But he was a survivor if nothing else and would think of something when it came to explaining away de Vico's to Gower. She smiled wryly to herself; it would be interesting to pitch against Vic in the future and she didn't doubt that he was thinking the same thing himself, except, of course, that he would be hell-bent on revenge and would have his 'little book of dirty tricks' on hand to ensure that he elbowed Samuels nicely out of the way. But revenge wasn't always necessarily sweet and if he got in her way too much with his mouth or his methods she would make sure that he wished he hadn't. Vic was a certain type of adman: glossy, brutal and brittle, a type with an eye on the main chance, the 'big buck', and be damned to anyone who stood in his way. Gower was welcome to him.

She leaned her head against the cool glass of the window suddenly feeling tired; Vic had a way of doing that to her, and with a sharp weary breath she looked out beyond the window. The sky was surprisingly clear for January, pale blue, and there was hardly a cloud. It was, she mused, the sort of day for a long, long country walk. In New England. Her mind somersaulted back to Christmas, to Ed and finally and inevitably to Philippe. He had surprised her with the way he had taken her into his arms, and that kiss which seemed to go on and on and on like a dizzying balm. But then he had released her, very slowly, very carefully, telling her at the same time that she should return to her room because it was so late and she had a lot of travelling to do the following day. She had been both perplexed and surprised at his mild insistence, and on the verge of refusing, of staying, but there was something in his voice that made her hesitate, and she had been unable to see the expression on his dark face because the light from the fire was fading too fast. So she had gone to bed and had lain in the darkness with an uncomfortable feeling of exasperation, and there had been little sleep. Francesca lifted her head up and followed the flight of a bird as it passed over London's sky-line. Elusive Philippe. A soft frown broke the set of her face. Sometimes she wondered if he had kissed her at all.

The silence was broken only occasionally by the sound of hurrying feet passing outside in the corridor and the little pieces of conversation left floating in the air by muted voices. Geoff turned his gaze from the square pane of glass high up in the door back to the pile of tired magazines lying on the waiting room table.

'Would you like another coffee?'

'No, thanks. . . .' Sian sighed heavily and looked back at him. 'You don't have to stay – really.' But she didn't want him to go.

Geoff examined her pale face sharply. Her eyes seemed to have grown bigger over the past hour, round and over-bright, and it didn't take much to see the wide curve of her mouth trembling like a small child's.

'I know I don't have to stay – I *want* to.'

It had been he who had suggested that her mother

should go home. She was in mild shock herself and so he had put her in a cab clutching a small bottle of tranquillizers which she vowed she would never take, but Sian had telephoned her father and made him promise that he would make her take at least one. Petie was bad enough; she didn't want the collapse of her mother on her conscience too.

'Thanks,' she replied quietly and lapsed once more into unbearable silence.

'The doctor said he is a strong little boy, Sian . . . ,' he offered feebly.

'I know, Geoff.' She pushed back a lock of hair with unsteady fingers and then added suddenly, 'Do you have any children of your own?'

He shook his head.

'I wanted them, but my wife wasn't so keen. She kept putting it off until I stopped asking.'

'Doesn't she like children?'

'She never actually said so . . . I think she was simply more interested in her career.' And how.

'Where is she now?'

And who is she with. . . .

'Nassau – apparently on a modelling assignment.' But he hadn't believed her. Joanne was now in her early thirties, still looking a reasonable twenty-five if you didn't look too close, but her modelling years were definitely over.

'There's no chance of you getting back together?'

'No,' he replied sharply. 'A year ago I might have been fool enough to try, but not now.'

'I'm sorry.'

'There's no need to be sorry. I just wish that it had all happened a lot sooner. . . .' He had allowed himself to believe her too often, allowed the wasted years to slip insidiously by. 'It's amazing how easy it is to keep clinging on to a relationship that is dead or simply dying before your very eyes.' He gave a sad smile. 'And when you do finally realize you begin to wonder if you ever had a "real relationship" at all. . . .'

She made no answer because he was making her thoughts sweep inevitably back.

'I must tell Adam.'

He sighed inwardly, jealously.

'Do you want *me* to?'

Her face brightened immediately, and he hated the brightness.

'Would you?' Somehow she didn't want to speak to Adam herself; she was afraid of the tears, that she would make a fool of herself.

'Of course.'

She retrieved a small address book from her handbag and handed it to him.

'The number's under "A". . . .'

Not 'G' for Gilmore, not 'V' for Village, but 'A' for Adam. She must think me such a nice, foolish guy . . . wasting my time. Geoff walked slowly down the stark corridor to the telephone booths in the entrance foyer. The call went straight through to Gilmore's office and it was answered by the sweet drawl of his secretary. Geoff wondered meanly whether he was screwing her as well.

'Tell him that it's Geoff Buchanan from Samuels.' There was only a moment before Gilmore's sleek voice purred smoothly down the phone.

'Geoff – how are you?' He didn't wait for an answer. 'You're lucky to catch me; I'm just about to leave for the airport.'

'I'm calling on Sian's behalf, actually. . . .'

There was a pause then and he could almost see the confused expression on Gilmore's face.

'Oh, yes?'

'Her little boy,' – your little boy – 'has been in a nasty accident. Do you think you could come to the hospital?'

Another pause.

'That's going to be difficult, Geoff.'

'Can't you cancel your flight – postpone it, even – the boy's in the operating theatre now.'

'If only I had known sooner.'

'Nasty accidents aren't easy to arrange for people's convenience. . . .'

333

'I didn't mean to sound glib.'

'I think Sian needs your support.'

'This meeting's very important.' He didn't want to get involved; it was all coming too close for comfort. He should never have been stupid enough to resurrect their relationship, then maybe she would have left him alone.

'I'll call her tomorrow.'

'Tomorrow could be too late.'

'Look, Geoff – I have a family of my own to think about.'

'You mean you're not interested?'

'I didn't say that.'

'But that's what you meant.'

'I'll call her tomorrow.'

'You're a cheap bastard, Gilmore.' He supposed he shouldn't have said that. There was a sharp click and the phone went dead. He took a deep breath before slowly retracing his steps back to the waiting room. And she was still there, still sitting in the same immobile position as if her body had stopped functioning, but her eyes lifted hopefully to his face as he walked in.

'He's on his way to the airport – I just missed him.' It was only half a lie.

'But once he gets there we could page him, couldn't we?'

Geoff swallowed slowly; he hadn't thought of that.

'I think we'd probably be wasting our time; he's likely to be in too much of a hurry to notice.'

'But it's worth a try . . . I'll do it if you like.'

He looked back at her and said nothing.

'What's the matter?'

'I just don't think it's a good idea, that's all.'

There was an awkward silence as she stared into his face.

'You did speak to him, didn't you . . .?' Geoff was so easy to read.

'Yes, I spoke to him.'

'And he wouldn't come?'

'He really does have a flight to catch,' God, it sounded almost as if he were defending him, 'some kind of important meeting.'

She looked away from him.

'It was stupid of me to think that he would come.' She'd been stupid all along. Living a dream. They'd had a fling, that was all, and like Geoff had said, maybe there had never been 'a real relationship' at all. Just some good times, an affair with the boss. Adam was just a man, and there were thousands of men. But there was only one Petie, and his own father didn't give a damn.

'Would you like that coffee now?'

She nodded and then abruptly stood up as the door opened and Petie's doctor walked in.

'It's all right, Mrs Hart.' He smiled reassuringly at both of them.

She found herself almost wanting to laugh at the automatic title he gave her, except that her breath seemed to have stopped like a tight painful knot in her throat.

'Your son is a very lucky little boy,' he continued. 'A broken leg, a broken thigh, a cracked pelvis, bruised ribs and a cracked skull – but no fractures and very little internal bleeding.'

Her insides seemed to crumple to nothing and there was a blur where the doctor's face should have been.

'He's in some shock, of course, and he'll be in intensive care for several days, but children's bones knit very quickly and, as I said to you before, he's seems to be a very strong little boy.'

She started to cry.

'There's a bed available if you wish to stay the night . . . ,' he added gently.

She nodded.

'Coffee – or tea?' he said finally.

'I was just about to get one,' Geoff interjected.

'I'll arrange for something to be brought – I think you should stay with your wife.'

Geoff nodded dumbly as the younger man walked out and then he turned awkwardly to Sian.

'It's okay . . . he said Petie will be okay.' But if anything her sobbing intensified as a flood of suppressed grief and tension poured out. Geoff winced with pity; he couldn't bear it. For a moment he hesitated, afraid to touch her, but then his arms came up almost of their own accord and brought her into the safe harbour of his chest, crushing her against him. He began to stroke her hair, her cheek, her arm until the sobbing lessened and she was lulled like a baby in his arms.

'You don't have to cry any more,' he murmured softly.

'I know,' she said at last.


'How is she?' Francesca asked, as Geoff sank down into the softness of one of the armchairs in her office.

'Very shaken, naturally.' He looked back at her. 'Can I have a drink?'

'Of course,' she replied. 'I should have thought of it myself. A brandy?'

He nodded and then watched her as she poured two cognacs expertly into delicate glass bowls.

'And so it seems that her little boy is going to be all right?'

'He was very lucky, apparently . . . the motor-bike threw him, which was bad enough, but if it had pinned him to the wall he would have been crushed. . . .'

'God . . . ,' she said with a sharp intake of breath. 'If there's anything she might need, tell her she only has to ask.'

'I'll tell her.' He took a warming mouthful of brandy and drank it slowly, letting it filter through his tiredness. 'There's something else, Francesca. . . .'

'Something else?' She sat down opposite him.

'Miami Citrus. I was about to let you know when I heard about Sian, and you were already well into your meeting with Vic. Honeyfords have decided to withdraw the account from Gaetini's. Bill Miller, your new MD there, is practically blowing a gasket. . . .'

She made no answer for a moment, but cursed inwardly at her lack of foresight. It would have been Aidan, of course. He knew the people involved on the marketing side, he'd even accompanied her at the pitch and on the subsequent celebration lunch, and last, but by no means least, he had masterminded the artwork.

'And it's going to Gower & Kid-Porter,' she said finally.

'Yup . . . and Aidan O'Donnell's going with it.' He sighed and then continued, 'It's all in tomorrow's *Campaign*. I had a tip-off: there's even going to be a photograph of Vic and Aidan together, apparently – sounds very sweet.'

'Damn the bloody photograph. I should have anticipated this, Geoff – how blind can you be?' she said with exasperation. 'He and Vic have just been seeing too much of each other – Aidan's move wouldn't have surprised me, but I should have carried it one step further. . . .'

'You haven't got a crystal ball, Francesca, and you've had plenty of other things on your mind just recently.'

'That's no excuse.'

'In any event, if a client wants to go, they'll go, and that's all there is to it.'

'With a little persuasion. . . .'

'Vic's been sneaky, which shouldn't come as a surprise – but we've held on to the big one, de Vico, thanks to your quick thinking.'

She shook her head impatiently. Miami Citrus had been special. It had been the crowning glory in Gaetini's climb back up the tables in the year before she joined Samuels – she had taken it from right beneath their eyes.

'We'll replace it – our new business section has already notched up several new accounts and the quarterly figures look likely to be far more optimistic than our original forecasts.'

'That's not the point, Geoff. . . .'

He frowned slightly as she looked away from him. Poaching was part of the jungle of advertising, part of the merry-go-round. But Miami Citrus had been *her* baby, from *her* company, and she would not forgive Vic so easily for this.

'But I'll get it back,' she said softly. 'You just watch me.'

'I don't doubt that for a moment, Francesca.'

She shifted her gaze back to his face and he was relieved to see a small smile lifting the edges of her mouth, but it was the sort of smile that neither Vic or Aidan O'Donnell would like very much.

'I wanted to discuss Zoë, too,' Geoff said.

'Vic said you were considering taking her on.'

'It had crossed my mind, but I don't think so.'

'Why not?'

'One good reason is that she's not really what I'm looking for, and the other good reason is that she and Vic have rather more than just a secretary/boss relationship. . . .'

'Do they?' Francesca raised her eyebrows.

'It's been going on for some time and just before I came back from the hospital I asked Sian whether she knew anything about it.' He took another sip of brandy. 'She knew all right and what's more Zoë has already told Sian that they'll probably go on seeing one another after he's gone.'

'So you think she could be a sort of unsubtle plant . . . ?'

'I think so – I certainly wouldn't put it past Vic.'

No. It was just Vic's style.

'We'll pay her off.'

He made no answer.

'I don't want her around, Geoff.'

'She's just a kid.' He would be the one to tell her, of course, and then those big blue eyes would fill with tears. Shit.

'A very foolish kid.' She shook her head; she probably thought she was in love with him.

'Couldn't we slide her into another department – or even a subsidiary?'

'No, Geoff.'

He sighed heavily. Francesca was right, but maybe if Vic hadn't been so damn greedy and taken Miami Citrus she wouldn't have come down so heavily on Zoë.

'I'll make sure that we're generous to her.'

'Okay, okay,' he said at last and swallowed the rest of his brandy. 'Anyway, I'd better get back to the hospital – Sian's on her own.'

'That's very good of you.'

'Well. . . ,' he said awkwardly, '. . . it's the least I can do.'

338

His face reddened and Francesca smiled to herself with surprise. He was soft on Sian and she had never even noticed.

'As I said before, tell her if there's anything she needs she only has to give me a call.'

'Fine, fine . . . .' he said, standing up. 'I'll see you tomorrow morning.'

'You haven't forgotten that I'm flying to the States the day after tomorrow?'

He had and he sighed wearily.

'I'll be out of the office on Friday, I'm getting Concorde back on Monday morning – you can manage?'

'I'll manage.'

'I appreciate it, Geoff.'

He nodded and gave her a tired smile.

'Give Sian my love, won't you.'

He nodded again and his spirits slowly began to rise as he walked towards the door. I'd like to give her my love, if she'll let me, he thought with a trace of sadness. But he wasn't going to push so hard again this time and make a fool of himself. She was still getting over glib Gilmore and then, of course, there was Petie. Sian would need handling with kid gloves. But maybe it wouldn't be quite so difficult this time because some of the barriers had already fallen away and he thought he had seen something more than gratitude in her eyes as he had walked away from her. But he pressed down the seed of hope which had already begun to grow, pressed down the pretty dream that was beginning to take shape in his head, because this one he wasn't going to rush, this one he was going to handle very carefully, very delicately so that it wouldn't slip through his fingers and break like glass. He slung his coat over his arm and turned the desk-lamp off in his office. If he was lucky the traffic wouldn't be too heavy now, and he had promised her that he wouldn't be more than a couple of hours. And he always kept his promises.

Ed was standing on the porch steps with Peanuts, waiting to greet her as she stepped out of the car.

'Frankie – you look wonderful,' he said grinning.

'So do you. Happy birthday!'

'Keep your congratulations – I'm not seventy-three until Sunday!'

'I saw Philippe in New York before I came down. . . .' He had been warm but polite, and she felt more confused than ever.

'He works too hard, but he'll be here first thing tomorrow morning.' In fact Phil had refused to budge on coming down a day early and they had almost argued about it. Ed sighed inwardly and took Francesca's arm as they walked into the house.

'You've still got the tree up . . . !' she said with surprise as she walked into his living room.

'Didn't have the heart to take it down.' He waved his hand in a gesture of impatience. 'It still looks good, doesn't it? And I don't believe in all that stuff about bad luck if you don't take it down by the 6th. I've been doing it for years. You know my first wife, Bella-Donna, used to leave it up until Pentecost.'

'Bella-Donna?' Francesca started to laugh.

'Yeah . . . she was sheer poison!'

She shook her head as he blew out a huge cloud of smoke.

'I think I'd better take my things up. . . .'

'Okay – and in the meantime I'll make some good strong drinks because, believe me, we're going to need them. According to the latest forecast this little thaw we've had during the last few days is going to freeze overnight.' He brought the cigar back to his lips and then added, 'I thought we'd eat simple, but good tonight – Irish stew, and *with* dumplings, so you can forget about your figure.'

He watched her retreating back as she walked out of the room. Phil hadn't said a word about her since Christmas except with regard to business. Ed scowled with exasperation and looked down at the sluggish body of Peanuts who was sprawled across his feet. And he had been keeping a check on him as usual – he hadn't even been near another woman as far as he could tell. Anyone would think that the shmuck had turned gay . . . except that Phil wasn't that simple; he was a complex son of a bitch.

There was a freeze overnight. Francesca stared out beyond the window at the morning landscape which was becoming so familiar to her. A fringe of icicles hung above the glass and the garden was dappled with small circles of ice where puddles had frozen. But it was all still so white and she wondered if she would always think of this place as white and cold, yet ultimately warming. The sound of the car as it stopped in front of the house made her pause and for a moment she did not move, knowing that Philippe was just arriving. She took a deep breath and smoothed down the same white sweater she had worn at Christmas over the same blue jeans; it would remind her, if not him, that there had been some good times then. Maybe such things took second place with him, or third, or fourth, and that he was cold inside after all. But she didn't really believe that.

Ed had prepared a sumptuous brunch and she sat down gratefully as he began putting plates of ham, eggs and tomatoes in the middle of the table. Philippe followed him up with fresh bread and steaming mugs of coffee.

'I haven't forgotten the waffles . . . ,' Ed said, sitting beside her. 'And there's plenty of warm syrup to go with them.'

'You're making me feel sick, Ed,' Philippe remarked with a crooked smile.

'Well, all I can say is, that it doesn't take much to do that.' Ed shook his head.

'Okay, okay . . . ,' Phil responded. 'I asked for that.'

'And while I'm talking – you *are* staying until Monday morning, aren't you?' There was a warning note in Ed's voice.

'It's your birthday, isn't it?' Phil replied with a touch of sarcasm.

'Yeah, we all know it's my birthday – I just want to make sure that you're not going to leave half-way through.'

'Don't panic, Ed – I'm leaving Monday morning.'

'That's fine . . . all I wanted to know.'

'Who else is coming?'

'No one else. I decided we'd keep it small after all. I'm getting too old for all that razzmatazz.'

Philippe looked at him for a long moment. Ed turned away and smiled at Francesca.

'You two can take a nice long walk once we've eaten. I'll do the washing-up.'

'I'll do the washing-up, Ed,' Philippe said slowly.

'I said I was going to do that.'

'Not on your birthday.'

'It's not my birthday until tomorrow.'

'Same thing,' Philippe said too smoothly.

'He's right, Ed,' Francesca interjected. 'After all, it's only once a year.'

Caught. Ed stared sharply at Philippe, pressing an oath down. What goddamn game was he playing?

'But you will join us once you've finished drying your hands, won't you, Phil – after all, as you both keep reminding me, it is my birthday. . . .'

'Of course, Ed,' Phil said, with a tight smile. Why did the old bastard have to be so damned transparent? He wanted to work things out in his own way, in his own time, but Ed didn't give a horse's ass about that. Sometimes he wished that, just once, Ed would keep his big mouth shut, just once stop trying to run his life and leave him in peace.

'He's as stubborn as a mule,' Ed remarked sourly as they passed from the garden into the forest road.

'He's a grown man, Ed, and has a mind of his own.'

'That's what worries me.'

She started to laugh.

'What he needs is to settle down with a nice girl; that's all I want for him now, he's got everything else.'

'Maybe he doesn't want to settle down.'

'I don't care what he wants – he's never known what's good for him.'

'That's not really fair.'

342

'I know him a lot better than you, Frankie, and believe me I know what I'm talking about.'

'Perhaps he's simply waiting for the right girl to come along.'

'He wouldn't know the right girl if he fell over her. . . .'

'I think you're too hard on him.'

'Take you, for instance – any man would be a fool not to want you, and a bigger fool if he didn't want to make it legal.'

'Ed, please. . . .'

'I'm just stating facts, Frankie, –'

'I can be very intimidating at times,' she remarked and grinned.

'Bullshit! A woman with guts is just more of a challenge, that's all, – takes just a little more time and energy, but it's goddamn worth it in the end. . . .' And he chuckled with relish, but then added on a more serious note, '. . . sometimes I wonder if Phil didn't leave his guts out there on the highway some place.'

They lapsed into silence as the road narrowed into the path leading to the lake. It was very still and the heavy quiet lay soft and thick as if it had rendered every living thing soundless. She thought the woods seemed almost magical, too perfect, as if someone had just painted each tree, each twig, in black and white, and if she reached out and touched them the spell would be broken and the magic over.

'He likes you, you know that, don't you?' Ed's voice snapped her out of her reverie.

'Ed, please. . . .'

'Goddamnit! Why shouldn't I say it?!'

'Because you're treading on dangerous ground, that's why.' But she was glad he had said it all the same.

'I knew it from the very beginning . . . ,' he persisted.

'Ed . . . Ed . . . ,' she said helplessly.

'Don't Ed, Ed, me, Frankie – I know what I'm talking about.'

'Maybe he prefers blondes; my father always did.'

He stopped abruptly and looked into her face, noting the gleam of humour in her eyes.

'Don't get cute, Frankie – it doesn't suit you.'

She suppressed a laugh as they walked to the edge of the lake. It was frozen and covered with a thick, glittering layer of frost.

'Where's that damned dog?' Ed asked, looking around.

'He's behind us, Ed,' Francesca replied as Peanuts emerged from the shadow of some trees.

'This is about the only time you'll get him anywhere near that water – when it's not wet!' he chuckled. 'Scares him witless.'

Several birds circled the trees and then gradually flew lower and lower until they settled on the frozen water. They leaned forwards and pecked at the ice with their beaks, wings flapping, as if they could not understand why there was no swimming or fishing to be had. Peanuts watched them for several trembling seconds as they waddled temptingly about the frozen surface and then his legs took him forward at a bolt so that he skidded, half-running, but unable to keep his balance as he fell forward on to his stomach.

Ed heard the thump of the dog's paws on the ice, felt his stomach clench into a fist at the anticipated danger and closed his eyes for a painful instant as the scalpel-edge sound of ice breaking soared into his brain.

'Peanuts . . . you damned stupid mutt. . . .' He began to run, his breath rasping and dry, just as the black crack in the ice widened and splintered into a yawning hole which Peanuts slipped effortlessly into.

'Oh, God. . . .' Francesca followed Ed a few feet on to the ice and then stopped abruptly as she realized the danger they were placing themselves in. 'Ed – don't!'

'Get Phil, just get Phil – and bring a rope!'

She watched him for a moment as he gingerly approached the panicstricken dog before turning back to solid ground and the house. It seemed to take too long to reach the outskirts of the house and she was already breathless, but even as she moved quickly up the path Philippe was coming towards her.

'Where's Ed? What's up?'

'Get a rope or something – Peanuts has fallen through the ice. . . .' Maybe Ed too, maybe Ed too.

Philippe made no answer, but moved quickly to the outhouse from where he emerged carrying a long length of thick cording and some poles of wood.

'This will have to work – there's nothing else.'

They ran together and with each anguished step Francesca felt her mouth grow drier and drier. It was so cold now, and the water even colder.

Ed was lying across the ice, as close to Peanuts as he could get, his arm stretched out and hooked into the dog's collar. Even as they drew closer Francesca could see that Peanuts was no longer struggling, that his head was barely able to keep itself above the freezing water. Philippe took off his jacket and moved slowly towards Ed.

'Get back, Ed, I'll get him out.'

'I can't let go, Phil – he'll sink, goddamn him. . . .'

'Can you tie this cord around his neck?' He threw it forward.

Philippe watched Ed struggle with the cord. It was easy to see that his hands were stiff and blue from the cold, but somehow he managed to pull it through the collar. As his hold on the ancient piece of leather slackened, Peanuts' head began to slip under the water.

'Help me, Phil! He's going, he's going – I can't hold him!'

Philippe lay on his stomach and crawled forward, reaching for the cord which Ed was holding out to him.

'I've got it, I've got it, Ed – now slide backwards with me.'

'No, no, – I'll have to pull from here, otherwise we'll never get him out.'

Philippe cursed softly and began pulling as Ed plunged his hands once more into the water and around the dog's neck.

'Let me do it, Ed!' he hissed, as he saw how the old man's strength was waning. 'You'll never manage.'

'Okay, okay,' he said finally.

He anchored the cord around his waist as Ed moved

back to him and then gave the remaining slack cord to him as he moved past.

'Let Francesca help, for God's sake, Ed, and push two of those wooden poles over to me.'

He crawled forward with the two poles beside him, trying desperately not to let the cord slacken, but felt it slice through his fingers as he inched his way, his breath dying in his throat at the lolling lifeless head of Peanuts.

'Come on, boy, come on . . . ,' he said softly and gritted his teeth. With a heavy sigh he realized that it was impossible to pull the dog from the water; he was too heavy and the more so now as he was weighted down with water. Philippe closed his eyes and began to move backwards, sliding on the two poles which he had placed underneath his body and dragging Peanuts with him. The ice began to crack as the dog's body acted as a breaker and Philippe realized that he was in danger of falling through himself, if his arms weren't pulled out of their sockets first, but at least it seemed to be working. As they neared the edge of the lake the ice thickened and Peanuts' progress came to a sudden halt, but the water was shallow here and even if the ice did break under him as he was lifting the dog out he could wade to the shore. But it needed all three of them to take Peanuts out of the water and as Philippe watched Ed leaning over the dog's mute form he felt his heart shrink.

'He hates the water – the great galoot – and he's old and fat and dumb . . . ,' Ed said unsteadily as he pulled off his sheepskin with trembling fingers to cover Peanuts.

'No, Ed,' Francesca said firmly as she took off her own. 'Do you want to catch pneumonia as well?'

'He's my dog and he'll have my goddamn coat!'

'Don't be a fool, Ed!' Phil said sharply as he laced the poles together and dragged Peanuts on to the make-shift stretcher. But Ed wouldn't listen and neither Francesca nor Philippe pressed the point as they saw his faded blue eyes begin to fill with tears. Peanuts wore all three sheepskins back to the house.

'Put him on the kitchen table.' Ed moved past them out

of the room and came back bearing several towels. 'We have to rub him down, get his circulation going. . . .'

Philippe looked at the silent body of Peanuts: cold, frozen, the pads of his paws torn and bleeding where he had cut them on the ice.

'Ed. . . .'

'Shut up, Phil.'

Philippe walked across the kitchen and picked up a small mirror hanging beside the sink. His eyes briefly met Francesca's as he moved back beside Peanuts. Wordlessly he placed it in front of the dog's mouth.

'You're in my way,' Ed said savagely.

'Let me do this, Ed,' he replied quietly.

'You bastard. . . .'

Even as they stood there looking back at each other a small, pale mist was beginning to gather on the glass.

'I don't believe it,' Philippe said open-mouthed.

'That about sums you up, Phil,' Ed retorted. 'Now get rubbing – we'll each of us take it in turns.' He stopped for a moment and massaged his arm as if he were cold. 'I'm going to call the vet.'

Francesca watched him carefully as he walked through the door to the telephone.

'He should lie down, Philippe – I think he's more shaken-up than he realizes.'

'I know – but try telling him that.' He shook his head with impatience. 'Why don't you pour some cognac and make Ed's a large one.'

She turned to go out of the room and came face to face with Ed standing in the doorway. He was too still and too white, and as he looked back at her his features contorted with pain and he began to slide slowly to the floor.

'Philippe!'

But he was already moving past her, already crouching down beside Ed.

'Call an ambulance – the number's printed on the phone, and give me one of those damned sheepskins.'

Ed stared back at the dark face as Philippe's hands tucked the coat tenderly around him, but abruptly he

closed his eyes and clutched at his chest as if he would fight
the agony that was shrieking through his body. Then he
lay very still, and there was only a dreadful silence and the
laboured sound of his breathing.

'I always knew that dog would be the death of me,' he
whispered suddenly.

'Shut up, Ed.'

'Why don't you ever listen to me. . . .'

'Don't talk, Ed – save it.'

'You're a stubborn son of a bitch.'

Philippe felt his mouth tighten as he looked down into
the ashen face, felt a thickness gather in his throat.

'She's a good girl . . . Frankie,' Ed persisted.

'Shut up, Ed,' Philippe repeated hopelessly.

'I always dreamed of having a kid like you . . . but it
never happened. . . .' His lips pulled into a small sad
smile. 'But you could have been, you see, you could have
been.' His eyes began to close, but then he was reaching
for Philippe's hand. 'I shoot blanks, Phil . . . I've been
shooting blanks for years . . . for ever.'

'It doesn't matter, Ed.' And as the fragile fingers closed
around his own he realized with a stab of anguish that it
didn't.

'You're a goddamn liar.'

'I mean it.'

'You're full of shit . . . you know that, kid?'

'Shut up, Ed.'

He looked back at Philippe for a long moment and then
his eyes closed very slowly, his body sagging gently as if a
great weight had been removed and he lay still.

She sat almost in darkness, leaning towards the fire and
gazing blankly into the blazing mountains of firewood
which seemed to die so quickly. Philippe had been gone
for over four hours. He had travelled in the ambulance
with Ed and left her to wait with Peanuts for the arrival of
the vet. Now the dog lay in the back of the room on a thick
pile of blankets, recovering from his ordeal; she could hear
his deep comforting breathing from where she sat and she

wondered sadly if he had any idea of what had occurred that afternoon. It had all happened so fast that even now it seemed only like a painful blur. The sound of a car's wheels crunching in the driveway startled her and she stood up, and then found herself unable to move from the spot because she was afraid to face Philippe. She heard his key turn in the lock and the sound of the main door as it closed behind him. Several long seconds passed before he opened the door and even then she just looked back at him, standing woodenly, waiting.

'He never regained consciousness, Francesca,' he said expressionlessly.

She made no answer. Not Ed. Not Ed.

'They said it was a miracle he had lived as long as he had.'

He looked away from her, his hand coming up to cover his face.

'Will you get me a drink.'

She poured brandy into two glasses and saw that her hands were shaking. When she turned back to him he had sunk down into the chair in which she had been sitting, his features set, too calm, and the rigidness of his control frightened her.

'He couldn't have known much about it . . . ,' she said gently, desperately, searching for something to say.

'He knew all right,' he said bitterly. 'Ed always knew – he was always goddamn right.'

'Stop it, Philippe – that won't help.'

He looked at her sharply and then his gaze slid back to the fire.

'Will you be leaving tomorrow?'

'Is that what you want?'

'I don't know what I want. . . .'

She drew in a breath and fought back her misery. Ed had been partly hers too, but now he was gone, just like everyone else she had loved. She was left empty again, lost, like all the other times.

'You have to think about the funeral arrangements,' she

said numbly, as a wave of unbearable loneliness and sorrow rose up to suffocate her heart.

'I don't have to think about anything.'

She swallowed hard, hating him suddenly for ignoring her pain, hating him for releasing the tears too heavy to hold back which began to cascade down her cheeks. For Ed, herself, even Philippe.

'Well, don't then,' her voice trembled. 'Don't think about anything.' She stood up and put her drink angrily down on the table. But as she went to move past him his arm shot out and gripped her wrist.

'Don't go.'

She choked back a sigh as her tears dragged up a sob and she forced herself to look at him.

'What do you *want*, Philippe?'

He pulled her down to her knees so that she was looking up at him and he swallowed painfully, deep in his throat, as his eyes swept over her, drawn by her grief, by the lovely wounded tear-stained face. Very slowly his hands slid over her shoulders, trailing down the length of her arms to rest on her waist. He stopped abruptly then, his eyes fixing themselves upon her, on each sweetly damp feature, and his gaze beat her down so that she was forced to look away. But he tilted her chin back and wordlessly brought the soft white sweater up and over her head so that her breasts were naked. For long scalding seconds he could only look at her, but then the silence was broken by his heavy anguished sigh as he lifted her towards him. The scent of her flesh made him dizzy and he closed his eyes, raking her neck, her breasts, her belly with his teeth, bringing his hungry open mouth against her skin again and again. And somewhere, somehow, far away he was vaguely aware that she whimpered, that the wetness of her tears stung his face, that her skin jerked beneath his touch, that her hands had come up to bury themselves in his hair, but then he was pushing her backwards, down, down, so that he covered her. Almost savagely he pulled the bluc jeans away so that there was nothing left and pinned her arms back as if he were afraid she would, even now, slip away from him. But she made no sound as he bent over her, made no sound as he plunged into her, her face neither changing nor moving – only looking back at him with deep liquid black eyes as he moved above her, as he drove harder, faster, obliterating all the barriers, all the pain, until the terrible grief buried for too long rose up and up into his throat and he opened his mouth with a raw, heart-wrenching cry.

The fire had folded down upon itself and now there were only dying embers and the warmth of her to keep the cold, searing dread which hovered just out of sight from creeping up on him. Ed was gone and there was nothing to mark his going except a great aching wound. And he had never known. Never known it would be like this.

'You won't go . . . ? he asked.

'Oh, Philippe . . . ,' she said, with gentle exasperation. 'I'm not going anywhere – not now.'

His eyes began to prick and burn in the darkness and he turned to her in curiously peaceful sorrow, crushing her against him, too hard, so that she gasped. Of course, Ed had known all the time.

For those who have enjoyed this book, may we recommend the following coming shortly from **Rowan**.

## THE WIND IN THE EAST
*Pamela Pope*

There are two things Joshua Kerrick wanted in the world: one was money to buy a fleet of drifters; the other was Poppy Ludlow. But Poppy and Joshua are natural rivals. This vivid historical drama traces their passionate story among an East Anglian community struggling to make its living from the sea.

## FRIENDS AND OTHER ENEMIES
*Diana Stainforth*

Set in the sixties and seventies, the rich, fast-moving story of a girl called Ryder Harding who loses *everything*—family, lover, money and friends. But Ryder is a woman of true grit and through sheer guts and determination she claws her way back and turns misfortune into gold.

## THE FLIGHT OF FLAMINGO
*Elizabeth Darrell*

A strong family saga unfolds against the backdrop of marine aviation in its heady, pioneering days before the Second World War. When Leone Kirkland inherits her autocratic father's aviation business, she also inherits his murky past, and Kit Anson, his ace test pilot. Leone needs Kit and she could love him—but he has every reason to hate her.